PRAISE FOR

Maya Banks

"A must-read author . . . her [stories] are always full of emotional situations, lovable characters and kick-butt story lines."

—*Romance Junkies*

"Heated . . . romantic suspense . . . Intense, transfixing."

—*Midwest Book Review*

"Grabbed me from page one and refused to let go until I read the last word . . . When a book still affects me hours after reading it, I can't help but Joyfully Recommend it!"   —*Joyfully Reviewed*

"An excellent read that I simply did not put down . . . A fantastic adventure . . . covers all the emotional range."

—*The Road to Romance*

"Searingly sexy and highly believable."   —*RT Book Reviews*

PRAISE FOR

Lauren Dane

"Delicious eroticism."

—Anya Bast, *New York Times* bestselling author

"Scorching hot [and] suspenseful."   —*Fallen Angel Reviews*

"[It] just might fry your circuits."   —*The Best Reviews*

"Sexy, pulse-pounding adventure . . . that'll leave you weak in the knees."   —Jaci Burton, *New York Times* bestselling author

Cherished

MAYA BANKS

LAUREN DANE

HEAT | NEW YORK

THE BERKLEY PUBLISHING GROUP
Published by the Penguin Group
Penguin Group (USA) Inc.
375 Hudson Street, New York, New York 10014, USA

Penguin Group (Canada), 90 Eglinton Avenue East, Suite 700, Toronto, Ontario M4P 2Y3, Canada
(a division of Pearson Penguin Canada Inc.) • Penguin Books Ltd., 80 Strand, London WC2R 0RL,
England • Penguin Group Ireland, 25 St. Stephen's Green, Dublin 2, Ireland (a division of Penguin
Books Ltd.) • Penguin Group (Australia), 250 Camberwell Road, Camberwell, Victoria 3124, Australia
(a division of Pearson Australia Group Pty. Ltd.) • Penguin Books India Pvt. Ltd., 11 Community
Centre, Panchsheel Park, New Delhi—110 017, India • Penguin Group (NZ), 67 Apollo Drive,
Rosedale, Auckland 0632, New Zealand (a division of Pearson New Zealand Ltd.) • Penguin Books
(South Africa) (Pty.) Ltd., 24 Sturdee Avenue, Rosebank, Johannesburg 2196, South Africa

Penguin Books Ltd., Registered Offices: 80 Strand, London WC2R 0RL, England

This book is an original publication of The Berkley Publishing Group.

This is a work of fiction. Names, characters, places, and incidents either are the product of the authors'
imaginations or are used fictitiously, and any resemblance to actual persons, living or dead, business
establishments, events, or locales is entirely coincidental. The publisher does not have any control over
and does not assume any responsibility for author or third-party websites or their content.

PUBLISHING HISTORY
Heat trade paperback edition / August 2012

Library of Congress Cataloging-in-Publication Data

Banks, Maya.
Cherished / Maya Banks, Lauren Dane. — Heat trade paperback ed.
p.   cm.
ISBN 978-0-425-24753-2
I. Dane, Lauren.   II. Title.
PS3602.A643C48 2012
813'.6—dc23
2012011792

PRINTED IN THE UNITED STATES OF AMERICA

10   9   8   7   6   5   4   3   2   1

CONTENTS

Exiled
MAYA BANKS

Sway
LAUREN DANE

Exiled

MAYA BANKS

Huge thank-you to Cindy Hwang
for her patience with this story and for going the extra mile
to make it much better. And for listening to my endless whining!

And thank you to Lauren Dane
for agreeing to do this anthology with me.

Prologue

Prince Alexander Carrera stared at the photo of the beautiful, smiling girl and his heart was seized by panic. Time was not on his side. Not his friend. Indeed, it was his worst enemy.

Just four years earlier, he'd met Talia Montforte, or rather she'd been thrust into his life, a whirlwind from which he'd never really recovered. But she'd only been a girl of eighteen and he could not have her, no matter how much he was enchanted by her. She was too young, too innocent. His attraction was inappropriate. He couldn't act then.

Now she was a young woman of twenty-two, and newly graduated from university in Paris. A young woman poised to start her life, a woman who had no idea how he felt about her or that he'd guided every aspect of her life for the last four years. That he'd waited patiently for the day he could claim her.

He turned when he heard his door open. Standing in the doorway were Sebastien, Garon and Nico, his closest friends. Men charged with his safety and security. The only people he trusted implicitly in a world where he could afford to trust no one.

His country was in turmoil. His future was uncertain.

But he knew one thing.

He could not lose Talia to another man. Another life. He could not stand by and watch her move away, never knowing that she held his very heart in her hands.

"It's time," he said in a low voice to the others.

He could see their gazes focused on the glossy photo in his hand. They knew of Talia. Knew what was to come, what his expectations of her were and what his expectations of them were.

"Send for her now," he ordered. "I cannot wait another day."

Garon frowned. "Now, Highness?"

Xander nodded. "Before it's too late. I will not lose her."

Chapter 1

There will be a time when I call for you, Talia. I'll expect you to come. Until then, you're needed here. Remain with your mother until she is strong and healthy again.

Talia Montforte shivered as the long-ago said words slid through her mind. Words she'd never forgotten, though there were times she'd wondered if the prince had truly meant them. She'd gotten her answer a mere week ago when the royal summons had arrived.

Now, as she stared out the window of the private jet, the island grew bigger as they closed in. She was nearly there, and Prince Alexander "Xander" Carrera waited somewhere on that island. For her.

Anxiety clutched at her stomach. She flipped her long, dark hair back over her shoulder and thought not for the first time that she should have pinned it up. But his instructions had been explicit. What to wear. How to fashion her hair. Everything to the letter had been dictated in the summons.

And God, had it been lengthy. Her cheeks still buzzed with

heat over the details. The questions. The medical exam. Her entire world had been upended the moment the messenger bearing the royal seal had appeared at her mother's home.

It was time, the message had said. There would be care provided for Talia's mother, but Talia was to come at once.

The last years had been turbulent years for her country. Xander's father had been assassinated. Talia had feared the worst for the royal family, but word had been leaked that they'd escaped safely.

The rebellion still raged and there was yet hope that the usurpers to the throne would be ousted so that the royal family could be welcomed back. The country waited. Talia had waited, never expecting that she would be summoned to him in exile.

It had been difficult to leave the life she'd resigned herself to. Only in the beginning had she had even a whisper of regret that things wouldn't turn out the way she'd planned. She'd wanted to attend university. Travel the world. Eventually come back to her country to contribute to the growing industry and economy of the small island nation off Spain's coast.

Instead her mother had been diagnosed with cancer and, faced with the inability to pay for the mounting costs, Talia had sworn off university and taken any odd job she was able to land. Until the day Prince Alexander—or Xander, as he insisted she address him—had arrived at her small cottage by the sea.

He'd swept in, issued orders for her mother to be transferred to a center in France that specialized in treating the form of cancer Talia's mother suffered. He'd then insisted that Talia attend university in Paris. He'd put her up in an apartment that was close in proximity to where her mother's care was being overseen and the school where she studied. He'd even given her a monthly allowance and made sure that all her living expenses had been paid.

And why?

She still didn't know why.

The only thing he'd ever said to her was that one day he'd summon her and she was to come at once. Of course she'd agreed. What person wouldn't? When faced with her mother's mortality and being able to ensure her mother's health and have her dream of attending university, the promise hadn't seemed too much to give.

Now she wasn't certain, because now she had no idea just what she'd traded in her bargain with the prince.

She shook her head as the plane touched down. Oh, she knew. Or at least now she had a very good idea. And it was no matter, because if faced with the same situation all over again, she'd do it without reservation.

Her pride. Her body. Her very soul. None of it was too precious a thing to sacrifice for her mother.

And, if she was completely honest, she was intrigued by the request.

The missive had been short and to the point. But what had come after had opened her eyes to exactly what it was the prince was expecting of her.

Mistress. Lover. Concubine. Whore?

No matter what word she put on it, nothing changed the stark reality of her presence on this island sanctuary.

She was a toy. A thing. She was for his amusement, his entertainment. His desire. His whim.

The plane rolled to a stop and as she looked out her window, all she saw was the sparkling waters of the Caribbean.

"You may remove your seat belt and come with me, Miss Montforte."

She unfastened herself with trembling fingers, then looked up to the staid-looking, gray-haired man who stood in the aisle waiting to assist her. She grabbed her handbag like it was a security blanket and slowly stood.

When she stepped onto the platform outside the plane, the bright wash of sunshine had her reaching for the sunglasses she'd stuffed in the pocket of her bag. For a moment she paused, soaking up her surroundings. The water sparkled in the distance and all around her was rugged landscape, mountainous toward the center and west and flatter to the east. The sky was as brilliant as the water itself, and not a single puff of white marred the perfect sheet of blue.

A hand touched her elbow and she started, jerking from her silent assessment of her temporary new home. Six months. For six months she'd agreed to live in this place. To be whatever the prince wanted her to be.

The man who'd escorted her out of the car and onto the plane in Paris was now assisting her down the steps toward a black Mercedes parked just a short distance away.

She smoothed the wrinkles from the silk skirt, a gift from Prince Alex—no, she must remember that he was to be addressed as Xander. He'd been very specific on that matter. He'd purchased her an entire new wardrobe, and baffling was the fact that he'd chosen the exact sizes she wore. Everything from underwear to shoes.

The lingerie was to die for. Sinfully sexy and yet ultrafeminine. Putting it on made her want to purr in delight and yet roar like a sultry seductress. She didn't even want to entertain what it all had cost. It would likely have paid for her mother's treatment twice over.

"His Highness awaits," the man said as he handed her into the backseat of the car.

In the front, another man wearing dark sunglasses glanced at her in the rearview mirror.

"Are you ready, miss?"

She nodded and then the door closed and the car immediately pulled away from the small jet.

They pulled onto a roughly paved stretch of road, but the farther they traveled it, the smoother it became. She glanced curiously around, wondering at the inhabitants. If there was a town. She hadn't been able to see anything on the flight in. It had all looked frighteningly barren of any sort of human activity, but it certainly didn't suffer from lack of vibrancy of nature.

Lush, green. Sparkling sands. Rugged mountains. She'd even seen a waterfall as the plane had made its descent.

The road meandered around a curve and then turned out onto a point on the eastern edge of the island. She leaned forward, spotting formidable gates that opened as if by magic as they approached.

They continued in and she gasped softly at the private paradise that existed beyond those imposing gates.

There weren't words to describe the grounds. Immaculately rendered. Flowers, so many that the burst of color was a shock to her eyes. Plants, foliage. Fruit trees. Palms. Flowering vines and bushes.

And nestled among it all was a palatial villa with a huge water feature in front of the sprawling entrance. She couldn't call it a fountain exactly. It wasn't one fountain, but a huge series of them, intricately designed. It looked like the villa's own private waterfall and oasis.

As the car pulled to a stop, she was gripped by sudden nerves that nearly paralyzed her. Finding solace that at least her eyes were hidden by the sunglasses she'd donned, she turned to see a tall man striding toward the car. He reached for the handle as the driver stepped out and opened her door.

"Miss Montforte," he said smoothly. "His Royal Highness bids you welcome to his home."

"So she came," Xander murmured as he stared down at Talia gracefully exiting the car he'd sent to pick her up at the airstrip.

"Did you doubt she would?" Garon asked dryly.

Xander's gaze never left Talia as Sebastien took her arm to escort her into the villa.

"Who knows the mind of a woman?" Xander said. "I've seen nothing to doubt that she would ever go back on her word, but when faced with my expectations, it's only logical to assume that any woman in her position would have second thoughts."

Garon's lips twitched in amusement. "Indeed."

"She's still a virgin," Xander said, unable to keep the satisfaction from his voice.

"That pleases you."

Xander lifted an imperious brow. "Of course it does. I may not be her only, but I'll damn well be the first."

"Some might argue that what you plan to subject her to is a bit much for an innocent."

Xander could no longer see Talia. Sebastien had escorted her into the front where she would await him in the sitting room. He twitched with impatience to go to her, but it wouldn't do for him to seem eager.

He wanted this to be on his terms. She would never know just how long he'd waited for this time to come. She was his now.

"You're a damn hypocrite," Xander said with no heat. "You're dying to fuck her every bit as much as I am."

Garon's lip lifted once more. The slight arch at the corner of his mouth was the closest he got most days to actually smiling.

"I don't have the taste for innocents that you seem to have."

"She won't be so damn innocent when I'm finished with her," Xavier murmured. "Besides, I don't have a proclivity for virgins. Just one virgin. Her. I find I'm very possessive when it comes to Talia."

Garon gave a snort. "And yet you'll share her with your most trusted men."

Xander shrugged. "It's who I am. It's what I do. I haven't heard you complain once."

Garon seemed to ponder the matter a moment and then his expression grew more serious. "No, I've not complained. But the woman in question has never been someone important to you. Talia obviously is. Think about what you do, Xander. Sex is sex. Kink is kink. I like a good time and a beautiful woman as well as the next man. But I would hate to lose trust or a friendship because emotions got involved."

"Then see that yours don't."

Garon shook his head just as Sebastien entered the library. He inclined his head in respect toward Xander. "Talia waits below as you requested."

"Tell me, Sebastien, do you find her beautiful?"

Sebastien lifted one eyebrow and then his eyes narrowed thoughtfully. "I'm uncertain of the point of your question, Your Highness. Of course she is a beautiful woman. Time has been more than kind to her. She's no longer a girl of eighteen but a lovely woman of twenty-two."

Garon stifled laughter at Sebastien's rather irreverent address. "Your Highness" only got brought out for sarcasm. Xander's security team were men who'd been with Xander for many years. Even before, they'd attended university together. Their friendship, trust and loyalty was unquestioning. Garon, Sebastien and Nico had been Xander's only friends during a time of unrest in his country and in return they were the only people Xander trusted implicitly.

"Some would argue that twenty-two is still very much a girl," Garon pointed out. "Virgin. Untouched. She seems very unworldly for a woman who's spent the last four years in one of the world's most sophisticated cities."

"Are you trying to insinuate that Xander is a dirty old man?" Sebastien drawled.

Xander chuckled and Garon did that half smile again.

"I think it's been well established that I'm a hopeless hedonist," Xander said. "The question is whether she'll be able to accept that."

Sebastien sobered and glanced between Garon and Xander. "Is that what this is then? A test?"

Put that way, it sounded cold and clinical. No, nothing about his feelings for Talia could be considered cold.

"Perhaps?" he said lightly, unwilling to let his friends see the depth of his uncertainty or his indecision. "Perhaps it is a test of myself as well to see if this . . . lifestyle . . . is what I need or if it's something I've merely wanted and enjoyed in the past."

"We'll endeavor not to fuck it up for you," Garon said dryly.

Xander lifted an eyebrow. "See that you don't. She is to be spoiled and pampered. Her every need and whim seen to. She is mine—ours—make no mistake about it. She will be molded and taught. She will submit without reservation. But in return she will be treated and respected as the princess I intend her to be."

"Fucking a beautiful woman," Sebastien said sardonically. "Such a chore. I think we should ask for raises."

Xander's gaze sharpened. "You won't be fucking her, Bastien. You're going to worship her and pleasure her as you've never pleasured another woman."

"I have no problem with that at all," Sebastien said in a lazy voice that was full of satisfaction—and anticipation.

Xander checked his watch. "We've kept her waiting long enough. Go find Nico. I want a few moments alone with her and then I'll expect all three of you to make an appearance."

Chapter 2

Talia sat dutifully on the couch in the huge sitting room she'd been shown into. After a few nervous starts, she realized that the prince wouldn't be making an immediate appearance and she turned so she could see out the floor-to-ceiling windows that overlooked the beach mere feet from the back terrace.

She hadn't been certain what to expect. Maybe a palace worthy of a sultan. Something ostentatious that screamed wealth and privilege.

The palace on Cristofino Island was straight from a fairy tale. Built in the 1600s, it had withstood conflict, wars and a major fire and still stood a proud monument to her country. Over the years it had been renovated, but special care had been taken to maintain the integrity of the original design.

Here on this island, while she could certainly see the expense in the surroundings, nothing was garishly opulent. The colors were warm and soothing. The furnishings were in soft leather, so comfortable that she'd sighed when she sank onto the couch. It had been too tempting not to run her fingers over the surface almost as if she were petting an animal.

As her gaze took in more of the outside, she realized that a large swimming pool was situated to the far right, jutting out toward the ocean. An infinity pool. It was raised a bit above the terrace itself and there was another patio and lounging area by the pool.

Simply put, this was paradise. And for the next six months it was hers to enjoy. In what capacity, she wasn't altogether sure, but this is where she'd live and she could certainly think of worse places for a man to indulge in his mistress.

Her cheeks heated again as the word popped into her mind. She'd been saying such words ever since she'd packed her belongings to come here. It was an attempt to walk into the situation with eyes wide open. No illusions. No misunderstandings.

The agreement involved sex.

Her virginity, her body, everything that made her the person she was would be surrendered to Xander.

Every time guilt or shame started to crowd into her mind, she was quick and fierce to battle it back. She hadn't sold herself cheaply. She wasn't certain what solace that would bring her, but no matter what, she'd enter this agreement with pride.

The one thing she would not surrender to the prince was her self-respect. He could strip her of everything, but her pride would remain and she'd never feel shame for choosing to honor an agreement struck in order to save her mother and secure her own future.

What was six months when compared to what it gained her?

"You look as though you are fiercely debating the meaning of life instead of enjoying your first hours in paradise."

Talia jerked around, her gaze honing in on the prince, who stood just inside the door. His pose was casual. Perhaps deceptively so. He wore simple linen slacks and a short-sleeved button-up white shirt that wasn't tucked in. It was bunched where his hands were shoved into his pockets and on his feet were leather flip-flops.

Somehow this wasn't what she'd envisioned at all.

And yet, as she'd acknowledged, perhaps the semblance of casualness was all wrong because she sensed power. A confidence that bordered on arrogance and the strength to easily bend her to his will.

She rose immediately, her breath rushing out in a shaky explosion. "Y-your Highness."

She dipped her head and curled her fingers into tight balls in front of her.

"The agreement is that you are to call me Xander," he said, though there was no reprimand in his voice. It came as a gentle reminder but the tone still sent a shiver up her spine.

"Xander," she whispered.

He took a step forward. "Please do sit back down. I'm sure you're fatigued from your journey. Would you like something to drink?"

"Water," she croaked out, only because it seemed rude to say nothing.

He raised his hand and snapped his fingers in the direction of an unseen person. Talia only heard footsteps as they moved away, but she'd never seen the person actually enter the room.

When Xander continued to stare expectantly at her, she lowered herself to the couch once more, though she perched on the edge, not nearly as comfortable as she'd been moments ago.

"Shall we pretend and have an awkward, stilted conversation about meaningless fluff or shall we get to the point of your presence here?" he asked bluntly.

She blinked but felt some of her nervousness abate. This she could deal with. No coy beating around the bush. No guessing what the hell she was supposed to do. Yes, she wanted to get to the point so she knew exactly where she stood and what his expectations of her were.

"I'd rather get to the point," she said softly.

His eyes gleamed, whether in amusement or approval she

wasn't certain. Time had been very good to him, though he'd certainly weathered several difficult years.

He'd always managed to take her breath away with one look. He was . . . beautiful. No, that was a terrible word. He was . . . addictive to look at. Not classically gorgeous like a playboy or someone polished to perfection. He wasn't suave and debonair but what he did have were strong features that screamed alpha male. A born leader. Someone who wore power like a second skin.

His skin was dusted with the sun, a gift from his Spanish-born mother. His eyes were the signature trait of the royal family. An odd shade of gold, amber and brown that made her think of leaves turning in the autumn.

His hair was dark but there were lighter glints, almost as if spending so much time in the sun had streaked it. He looked aloof, unconcerned with what others may think of him and he made her heart beat more rapidly just by walking into the room.

"I have no wish for you to experience any discomfort or unease," he said, breaking into her wayward thoughts. "On the contrary, I intend for the next six months to be extremely pleasurable for you."

She couldn't control the blush. It burst over her cheeks in a rush of heat. His lips lifted in a smile of acknowledgment.

"I believe the contract was rather detailed."

She shook her head and he frowned.

"What do you mean? You signed it. If you had questions, why didn't you ask them?"

She held up a hand, determined that sooner or later she'd find her damn tongue.

"Of course I agreed . . . Xander." She nearly choked on his name. It seemed disrespectful, and quite honestly, he intimidated her. He was a man who commanded respect and to address him so informally went against every instinct. "And the contract was clear on some matters. S-sex," she managed to stammer.

"Then what wasn't clear?"

She took a breath and leveled a stare at him. "What wasn't clear was why? And how . . ." She broke off and blushed again. "I don't mean how in regards to sex. I may be a virgin but I'm not an idiot. It's just that the contract was very . . . cold. It said in black and white that for the next six months I belonged to you. Okay, so what does that mean?"

He smiled then, white teeth flashing. His eyes glowed with all those warm, vibrant flecks of color and his look could only be described as possessive.

"I will of course describe in great detail what my expectations are."

They were interrupted by an older man, short in stature, hurrying in with a tray. He set it on the coffee table in front of Talia and then poured a cup of coffee to offer to Xander.

Xander frowned, refusing the cup. "You were instructed to see to her needs first. Always."

The older man's lips tightened as if he were chagrined at having committed the error.

"My apologies, Miss Montforte," he said.

His accent was British, though she certainly couldn't place the region. Her ear wasn't trained to pick up on the many variations of the English accent any more than she could pick out regional accents of the United States.

The man put the cup of coffee down and then poured a glass of ice water for her. On the tray was a variety of pastries, cheeses and fruits.

"Talia, this is Wickersham. He oversees the kitchen staff. He'll be seeing you later to find out your likes and dislikes, if you have any allergies or sensitivities to certain foods. Feel free to give him a list of your favorite dishes so that he can arrange to have meals to your liking."

She nodded numbly. This was so . . . bizarre. She was here

as . . . Well, she wasn't entirely certain. So far she was being led to believe she was some honored guest. A far cry from the whore she'd kept labeling herself as so she wouldn't forget the circumstances of her agreement.

She flinched inwardly. No, not a whore. She was owning her decision. Her choice. She could have walked way. Whatever happened, she was no whore. Having sex didn't make a woman cheap or tawdry. Making the best of a situation didn't make her a slut or any of the other words she'd said to herself in order to toughen her mind.

And who was to know anyway? Damn the world. She had what she wanted most. She had her mother, alive and well, recovering! And she had an education and four years in one of the most beautiful cities in the world. She'd seen and experienced things that she'd only dreamed about. Nothing would take those things away from her. It was time to pay the piper. That was all.

"Are you not hungry?" Xander asked.

She looked up, the glass cold in her hand. She was gripping it far too tightly. Wickersham had taken his leave and now there was only her and Xander and those damnable explanations.

"No," she said, proud of her poise. "I'd rather know what expectations you have of me."

"It's quite simple, Talia. You belong to me. I own you. Completely. While you are here you will obey me without question. I decide what you do, what you wear, when you sleep, when you wake."

Her eyes widened. "You want me to be . . . submissive."

"You *will* be submissive in all aspects and without reservation."

She swallowed nervously. "I—"

"Say what it is you're thinking, Talia," he said gently.

"It frightens me."

He nodded. "That's understandable. What about it frightens you? Is there a specific fear or is it that you fear having to obey me in general?"

"I don't know what you'll ask me to do," she whispered. "And . . . I don't like . . . pain. I mean and being tied up would scare me, I think."

He gave her a confused look before understanding dawned. Then he chuckled lightly. "Come here, Talia."

Her scrambled brain knew this was a command no matter how gently rendered it was and she hurried off the couch to where he sat diagonal to her in the overstuffed armchair.

"Sit," he directed, pulling her down onto his lap.

As soon as she settled onto his lap, his scent surrounded her, as did his warmth. It was heady. It made her nervous and eager all at the same time.

He touched her face, exploring for a moment the curve of her cheek and then he threaded his fingers into her hair.

His touch was electrifying. Each brush, each point of contact whether purposeful or incidental sent a cascade of chill bumps scurrying across her skin. She wanted to lean into his caress like a cat seeking more attention. She wanted to be stroked and petted. If she reacted so strongly now, what would it be like when they were naked? Skin to skin. His hands on her body.

Her senses surged to life and her nostrils flared, heat pooling low in her groin. There was no doubt she was excited. That she wanted him. Even not knowing fully what would be expected of her, she eagerly awaited the unknown.

He touched her lips, tapping, almost as if he knew she was preoccupied. Only when she turned to look fully at him did he speak.

"You assume because I demand your obedience and your submissiveness that I am asking you to enter into a BDSM relationship complete with whips, chains and God knows what else is running through your head right now. Am I right?"

She bit her lip, suddenly embarrassed. But what was she supposed to have thought? Then she slowly nodded.

He frowned, his lips twisting in distaste, as if the mere thought was reprehensible to him.

"I have no desire to hurt you. Quite the opposite. I want to bring you as much pleasure as you'll bring me. I have no intention of frightening you either. I have no need to restrain you if you're obedient. Tying you up would represent a lack of trust on my part. If I ask you to do something, I have every confidence that you'll do as you're told without me having to truss you up."

She sagged as relief lessened the tension in her shoulders. So far this wasn't going badly at all. Hell, it sounded too good to be true.

"Now that we've gotten that out of the way, let me tell you what you can expect. I am a highly sexual person. I like sex. I like kinky sex. I have no doubt some of my proclivities will shock you. You and I will be having sex frequently in all manner of ways. If I decide I want to have you in the middle of dinner, make no mistake, I'll bend you over the table and fuck you then and there."

Her cheeks were going to explode. An odd tightening sensation coiled in her midsection and spread to her nipples until they were hard and pointed. She had to refrain from fidgeting restlessly on his lap as the erotic words brushed over her ears.

"I'll have your mouth, your pussy and your ass," he continued in a quiet, firm voice. "There is no part of your body I won't avail myself of. You belong entirely to me. And as such, what I choose to do with your delectable body is also completely at my discretion."

She narrowed her eyes in confusion.

He smiled lazily, his eyes glowing as he looked toward the doorway. She glanced up, mortified that three men stood there. Had they heard any part of the conversation?

"And I'll choose to share you with them," he said, motioning toward the doorway. "Often."

Chapter 3

"You're scaring her," one of the men drawled as he ambled into the room.

There wasn't an undertone of deference and it didn't seem to bother Xander at all. Whoever these men were, they weren't the typical subordinates.

Talia eyed the three men as she went still in Xander's arms. He seemed to sense her unease because one hand tightened just above her knee while the other hand soothed up and down her arm as if to calm her nerves.

As if.

These were powerful men in their own right. Hell, maybe they were some type of royalty. Maybe the whole damn island was some posh refuge for exiled princes and the like.

Okay, she was starting to get hysterical even if she was exhibiting no outward signs. But inside her head, she was screaming *what the hell* and fast wondering just what she'd gotten herself into

This was beyond something as simple as being a mistress. Or whatever the hell word she wanted to call it. Maybe whore hadn't been far off the mark though she winced at the mere whisper of the word in her mind.

She was beginning to feel like a . . . thing. Something purchased, bartered, borrowed. Oh God. It was a revolting thought.

"You better say something damn quick, Xander," one of the other men said in a grim voice. "She's looking like she wants to jump out of the window."

"Perhaps I was a bit too blunt in the explanation of my expectations," Xander began.

"You think?" the first man said, shaking his head.

Xander sighed and then touched Talia's cheek so she would turn away from the men to look back at him. "Talia, these are my most trusted men. They act as my security team, but they are much more. They are friends. They are the only ones I trust implicitly. With my life and now yours."

He gestured to the first one, the one who'd said Xander was scaring her. "This is Garon."

Garon inclined his head in a nod even as his gaze burned steadily through her. He was . . . hard. He looked like a hard man. Not much give to him. Even Xander had made somewhat of an effort to make her feel at ease. Garon just kept looking at her with eyes that told her he'd have her soon enough.

"And next to him is Sebastien."

Sebastien had collected her from the car but she remembered little of her impression of him. She'd been too nervous about arriving and seeing Xander. Now as she studied him, she realized that he wasn't the sort of man she'd normally overlook. Tall, broad shouldered. Taller than Garon but leaner and not as stocky. Garon was . . . well, he resembled a boulder. Big and hard. An immovable force. Sebastien had dirty blond hair that was streaked as if he'd spent a lot of time in the sun. Garon's hair was dark and cut short. He looked like the type who never let it grow even a centimeter longer than the predetermined length. Sebastien . . . he looked a little more laid-back.

"And last is Nico, who hasn't yet decided to enter the room apparently," Xander said dryly.

Nico . . . He seemed quiet. He'd yet to say a single word. Garon and Sebastien had offered their dry opinions on the matter at hand. But Nico just stood back with those dark eyes and studied her intently like he was seeing right through her soul.

His hair was longer and jet-black. Sleek and shiny, hanging to his shoulders. He wasn't as tall as the others. He was probably just under six feet but somehow he seemed much bigger. His presence seemed to dominate the room.

"It is a pleasure to meet you, Talia," Nico said in a soft voice.

She wasn't sure what she was supposed to do and she sure as hell wasn't sure whether she was pleased to meet him or the others yet either, so she simply nodded and tried to hold it together until she could make better sense of it all.

"Sit, all of you," Xander commanded. "You're making her nervous standing over her. I want her to feel comfortable here."

Sebastien snorted. "After what I just overheard, you're going to have to do a hell of a lot more talking for her to feel comfortable."

Xander shot him a dark scowl but then directed an apologetic look at Talia. "You must forgive my bluntness. I'm not one for dancing around a topic. I thought it best that you know up front precisely what your stay here entails."

"I agree," she said faintly. "I do want to know. No surprises. Much better that way."

Xander touched her skin again, frowning. "You're cold."

Was she? She didn't feel cold. She felt incredibly over warm. In fact, she'd love to throw open the back doors to the patio and breathe in the sea air.

She shook her head to refute his assertion, but he didn't look convinced and in fact drew her farther into his embrace so their bodies were touching. She was flush against him. And that was supposed to help? Now she'd spontaneously combust and burn the whole darn villa down.

After a moment where he seemed to consider whether he should continue, he directed her gaze back to him.

"There are rules, and I hate to use such a cold, austere word. Perhaps we should again go back to expectations. You will find I like things a certain way. I have a regimen that I follow."

Garon chuckled and said irreverently, "You're an anal bastard, Z, just admit it."

Xander shot him a quelling look and then turned his attention back to Talia. "You may wonder why we aren't having this conversation in private."

She nodded before she could stop herself. She was very much wondering why she had to suffer this embarrassment. She'd never felt so uncomfortable and vulnerable in her life.

"Because they are in large part responsible for enforcing my expectations."

She peeked nervously at where they'd taken seats across from and catty-corner to where Xander sat in the armchair with her draped across his body. If what he was saying was what she thought he was saying . . . holy hell.

"It's really not complicated," Xander said calmly. "You'll take direction from me—and them as an extension of me. You'll never have to wonder whether you're performing to expectation because there will always be someone to guide you. You'll be apprised of some things from the start. The important things. The rest you'll learn as you go. I've already stated this isn't some sort of BDSM arrangement where we keep you tethered and crop you every time you step out of line."

At that, Nico frowned, his brows drawing together as if he found the very idea repugnant.

"And what are these things?" she asked, impatient to get to the point.

Xander drew in a breath. Good Lord, but he looked like he was readying himself to deliver a speech. Were there that many rules?

His hand slid up her leg, underneath her skirt and she froze as he rubbed lightly just over her hip where her panty line rested.

"Each morning you'll be awakened by one of my men. They'll bring what you'll be expected to wear, if anything for that day."

She frowned again. "What? I don't understand."

He didn't look pleased by her interruption.

"Perhaps the first thing we should get out of the way is that you are to be completely obedient to me, which means that you are to listen while I give you instructions, and you aren't to interrupt. When I am finished conveying my message, should you still not fully understand what it is I'm demanding of you, then you can ask for clarification."

She licked her lips nervously. She was already making a mess of this. This so wasn't something she could pull off. She may not be the type of woman who was ballsy and took her place in the world and damn anyone who tried to hold her back, but she *was* strong willed. She knew her own mind and she wasn't used to having to take orders from anyone. For too long, she had been the decision maker in her life and her mother's. It was she who told others what to do, what she wanted, how she wanted her mother cared for. And now she was expected to become a meek, biddable . . . mistress?

"I would love to know what you're thinking," Xander murmured. "Your eyes are so expressive."

"No, you don't," she muttered.

His eyebrows lifted and she heard Sebastien chuckle from across the room.

"Now if you'll allow me to get back to the things I was saying," he said. "In answer to your unspoken question, yes, there will be days I prefer you to wear nothing at all. You have a beautiful body, Talia. One I can't wait to avail myself of. Not only do I want to touch you, taste you . . . fuck you . . . I want to look at what is mine and appreciate your beauty."

She had no idea what to say to that whatsoever. She was too bombarded by the unnerving sensation of imagining his mouth on her skin. His hands. His cock deep inside her body. Her eyes closed until they were half lidded and a light shiver rolled over her shoulders.

Xander pressed his mouth to her bare shoulder. "That's right, Talia," he murmured against her skin. "Everything you're imagining and more. I promise you."

She was mesmerized by the husky tone of his voice. She was entranced by the experience of being in this man's arms while three men sat mere feet away, listening, participating, determining her fate.

It was surreal. A dream she was sure she would awaken from. It was such a far cry from what she'd been doing just weeks earlier before the royal summons had upended her carefully ordered life.

Fantasy? Fairy tale?

She hadn't yet decided. On the surface it seemed every girl's dream. Being whisked away by a handsome prince. Pampered, spoiled, catered to.

But there was so much more. It dipped into that murky gray area where she was no longer sure where she stood or if she would lose a part of herself in the process.

"I know enough about you to know you aren't a morning person, so I won't expect you to awaken early."

She cocked her head, narrowing her eyes. He only laughed. "There's much I know of you, Talia. Never doubt that."

Okay, so maybe they'd get into that later. She didn't want to distract him from the rules because it seemed more important she figure out her place, her role, here in this island paradise before she demanded to know just how careful an eye he'd kept on her in the last four years.

"You'll breakfast with one of the others, unless I decide otherwise. I'll join you for lunch and dinner. But you'll never eat alone, unless you wish it and then only if I grant you permission. If I'm unable to eat with you, one of them will attend you," he said, gesturing toward Garon, Sebastien and Nico.

She bit her lip again and glanced sideways toward the men who lounged casually as if this sort of thing was nothing new to them at all.

"Do I obey them as well?" she asked softly.

Xander eyed her seriously. "They attend me. They have strict instructions where you are concerned. They are to grant your wishes as long as they fall in line with what I would approve. If you have need of something, you only have to ask. They won't issue you orders that don't come from me, so if you're asking if you are to obey them, then yes, only because if they give you an instruction, it will have come from me. However, they are not your masters. I am. They aid me—and you."

She nodded her understanding, though she was doubtful. They all looked so . . . powerful. Not subordinate. Not even a little bit. She simply couldn't imagine them indulging her whims. They looked more like they'd give her an order to drop to her knees and suck their cocks.

Her face flamed with sudden heat. Her thoughts were completely out of control. Where in the world had that come from?

But then maybe it wasn't completely insane. Xander himself had said that they—all of them—would be having sex with her.

"There will be times when you are free to do as you wish, but I'll expect one of my men to accompany you. There are safety and security concerns so there is no need to be chafed or feel as though you are constantly on a figurative leash. There is the beach to explore, a pool to enjoy. I have a garden and there is a trail that leads to a waterfall, though I'd prefer you to be driven because it's quite a walk and it can be treacherous at times."

Again she nodded, some of her tension lessening. It didn't seem as though he was going to be completely unreasonable and keep her under lock and key twenty-four hours a day.

"But when I require your presence, you'll be with me. My expectations aren't hard and perhaps the easiest way to put this and shorten a lengthy explanation is to simply say that my expectations will change from day to day and you're to obey me without hesitation and make yourself available to me at all times. You'll find I'm not an unreasonable man. There is nothing that will please me more than to see you happy and satisfied. I expect in the beginning that we'll have a learning period where we become acquainted and at ease with one another. But I'm not a patient man. I've waited long enough to have you here and in my bed. I'm not going to wait any longer."

Her heart thudded harder. For a moment, she forgot the presence of the other men as she studied his implacable features. Waited long enough? What did he mean?

She licked her lips, wanting to ask just that, but then she saw Garon move from the corner of her eye and she bit back the question. It seemed too personal to bring up in front of others, and she didn't want to anger him by prying.

But it was a question that burned in the back of her mind, one that she knew she wanted the answer to. Because he acted as though he'd been interested in her as far back as . . . when her mother had become ill? Had it been longer? She could only remember ever being in his presence any extended period of time once before that day he'd arrived at her home—a day that had changed hers and her mother's life forever.

As one of her many jobs she'd taken on to help pay for her mother's medical care, she'd taken a position in the palace, assisting the gardener.

One afternoon, she'd been charged with taking fresh floral arrangements into the palace rooms. It was a chore usually done by the gardener's son, but he'd been away on an important errand

and so Talia had been given strict instructions on which rooms the flowers went into and the precise times when the chambers would be vacant.

The biggest rule for any of the palace workers was to be invisible at all times. They worked behind the scenes making sure all was perfect without ever gaining notice. To do so would risk immediate termination by the palace majordomo who oversaw all the palace employees.

Talia had been understandably nervous but also giddy with excitement to see into many of the rooms she'd only imagined. All her time was spent outdoors on the grounds or in the queen's private garden—a gift to her from her husband who knew of her love of flowers.

She'd just taken one of the arrangements into the king's suite of offices when the king himself, accompanied by his son and a group of foreign diplomats, had entered. She'd been so startled that she'd knocked over the enormous vase, spilling water and flowers all over the antique desk that had no doubt been in the royal family for generations.

She'd been so horrified that she'd immediately burst into tears. And even more horrified when Xander had rushed to help her clean up the mess. The king had whisked the group of men into one of the adjoining rooms, leaving Talia to clean up while Xander carefully picked up the pieces of the broken vase.

And then the palace majordomo had swept in, angry and apologetic to the prince, assuring him that Talia would be terminated at once.

What had happened next had shocked her so much that she hadn't been able to utter a single word.

Xander had actually scowled at the man and informed him that it was Xander himself who'd knocked over the vase and that Talia had rushed to help him clean the mess so that his father's meeting wouldn't be interrupted. He'd suggested that Talia be commended for her quick thinking and that under no circum-

stances would her position be terminated. The last had come out
sounding almost like a threat and the majordomo must have taken
it as one, because he'd paled and then immediately issued an apology to Talia for misunderstanding the situation.

As soon as the majordomo left to summon more help to make
sure the desk suffered no damage from the water and to get someone to finish clearing away the mess, Talia had stared openmouthed
at him.

"Why did you do that?" she whispered.

The prince stared back at her, warmth in his eyes. "It was a
mistake. Surely you didn't purposely dump flowers all over my
father's desk."

She shook her head vigorously. "N-no, of course not. I was told
no one would be here. I was just startled."

The prince smiled. "There you have it. No harm done. Now
perhaps you should make your escape before Philippe returns. I'll
make certain that he takes no action against you."

"Thank you," she said softly.

Then she had fled from the office, deeply shaken by her encoun-
ter with the prince. But she'd also fallen a little in love with him
that day. A fact made even more so the day he'd come to her house
to take charge of her mother's care and in effect, Talia's entire life.

Perhaps the seeds had been sown even then. Had he planned
even then for this day? For this eventuality? Had he decided she'd
be his so long ago?

His *what* was the main question, however. Lover? Mistress?
Whore?

And did it matter?

She owed him more than she could ever repay. Six months of
her life was nothing compared to all he'd given her.

But what worried her more than what she would be expected
to do while she was here was that when she left, she'd leave her
heart behind.

Chapter 4

"How long are you going to let her hide up in your room?" Sebastien drawled.

Xander turned from his view of the ocean, accepting the drink that Nico had poured. He sipped, savoring the flavor on his tongue before swallowing. Then he eyed his friend.

"Are you questioning my handling of her?"

"Oh, don't get all princely on me," Sebastien said in mock disgust. "You've been so impatient to get her here so it surprises me that you haven't gone and hauled her out. From the way you were looking at her when she arrived, I half expected you to have her between your knees sucking your cock before all the introductions were made."

Xander flinched at the crudeness but couldn't say a whole lot since Sebastien wasn't too far off the mark.

Garon frowned, though, and looked as though he would reprimand Sebastien for his lack of tact.

"Think about it from her perspective," Nico said, before either Xander or Garon responded. "Her entire life has been upended in short order. She's an innocent. God only knows what she was told by the representative you sent to fetch her. You told him to be quite blunt about what she was getting into. Now she's here and she's been told she's going to be having sex not only with the prince but three other men she's never met before in her life. She's young. Cut her some slack. She's probably terrified. Hell, Garon likely scared the wits out of her just by looking at her."

Garon's eyebrows drew together. "What the hell did I do?"

Sebastien snorted. "You're a big, mean-looking bastard. You don't have to do anything."

Xander smiled at Nico's defense of Talia and ignored the banter between Sebastien and Garon. Nico would be a great protector. She already had an ally in him. Which was good. Xander wanted only the best for her. He was glad that the loyalty Nico gave to him unwaveringly had already been transferred to Talia. Sebastien and Garon would follow suit. He was certain of it.

"Has Wickersham been up to inquire as to her eating preferences?" he asked Garon.

Garon nodded. "He came down half an hour ago."

"Good. She should have had time to settle in, collect her thoughts. Perhaps decided whether or not I'm the devil in disguise."

Sebastien snickered and Nico rolled his eyes.

"We've discussed this in great detail so I see no need to rehash it all over again," Xander said as he stared at the three men with whom he would share Talia's body. "I don't want her any more frightened than she already is. She is to be pampered and cared for. Even when you are indulging in her body and commanding her to pleasure you, you are to make sure she is receiving pleasure in equal measure."

"Good God," Sebastien muttered. "Enough with the sex lectures. You're starting to make me feel like some randy teenager about to make it for the first time with my dream woman."

"He's telling you that you better damn well respect her," Garon said gruffly. "You can be an irreverent asshole at times, Bastien. If she's on her knees in front of you, then count yourself fortunate and treat her like the treasure she is."

Xander smiled. Conquest number two and she'd only been here mere hours. He set his drink down and glanced up at the clock. "Perhaps I should go up and see about her. Dinner will be ready within the hour. I'll see all of you then."

He strode from the room, eagerness quickening his step as he mounted the staircase leading up to the second level. His suite encompassed a large portion of the upper story, but Garon, Sebastien and Nico all had rooms that boxed his in. They were his friends, yes, but foremost, they had devoted their lives to his protection.

The villa was heavily fortified, surrounded and monitored by military loyal to the royal family. But they remained an invisible force. He knew they were there, but they were rarely seen. Garon took reports from them and conveyed any concerns to Xander. Only he, Sebastien and Nico resided in Xander's inner sanctum. Only they shared in his hedonistic lifestyle. To the rest of the world, he was the model of propriety.

He paused at the heavy double wooden doors that led into his bedroom. He considered knocking, but then shook off the notion that he should somehow start his time with Talia by being . . . soft.

This was his room. It and she belonged to him.

He pushed open the doors and strode in, his gaze seeking her out. She wasn't in the sitting room that overlooked the expansive terrace he often ate his breakfast on. The view of the ocean was fantastic from there and he enjoyed the cooler morning air.

When he entered the bedroom, he glanced first in the direction of the huge bathroom but heard no sound that indicated she was there. As he moved farther inside, he found her standing to the right, staring out of the huge picture window to the ocean below.

Her suitcase was still unopened and perched by the bed—his

bed—and she was still wearing the clothing she'd arrived in. She looked deep in thought—she hadn't heard him come in. And her shoulders were tense as if she fretted over something. He frowned and cleared his throat.

She swiveled immediately, her eyes widening. In fright? Alarm? Or was it just uncertainty that made them seem too large for her face.

"It's been well over an hour, Talia. Why haven't you unpacked? Or changed? Dinner will be served soon."

The words came out more clipped than he intended. It wasn't his intention to reprimand her. He merely wanted to know why she'd done nothing since she'd gone up to the bedroom.

She swallowed nervously and then stared around the room as if she were lost. "I—I . . ." She trailed off and then directed her gaze downward, her shoulders drooping.

His frown deepening, he crossed the short distance between them and slid his hands up her arms to her shoulders, forcing her to meet his gaze.

"Is something the matter? Is the room not to your liking?"

She gave a halfhearted laugh. "Oh no, it's perfect. Everything's perfect. I can't imagine a more perfect place in the entire world. It's just that I wasn't sure . . . that is I'm just a little overwhelmed. This is obviously your room and given our previous conversation, I realize that I'm not likely to have a room of my own."

"This bothers you?"

"I'm not sure," she said honestly. "It's not that I'm being demanding. It just seemed so presumptive to just come into your private quarters and unpack my things. I began to worry. What if I put my things where you didn't want them? What if you intended me to only have a portion of the room? I don't know what your expectations are. Beyond . . . sex," she choked out. "You made yourself abundantly clear in that area. I feel like I'm in some sort of minefield and uncertain of where to step for fear of a bomb exploding in my face."

He sighed and pulled her toward the bed. He sank onto the edge and held her there in front of him as he stared up into her eyes. Eyes that carried a wealth of emotions, none of which he'd wanted her to feel.

"What I want is for you to make yourself at home. No, you will not have a room of your own. *This* is your room. What's mine is yours for the entirety of your stay. You belong to me and I keep what is mine close at all times. You'll sleep in my bed. You'll bathe in my bathroom. You'll dress in my bedroom. Your toothpaste and all your feminine accoutrements will be in my bathroom."

She slowly nodded her understanding but she nibbled nervously at her bottom lip, a gesture that he found endearing. She was a shy one. She certainly had her moments of spirit where she spoke her mind and stood up for herself, but she was adorably shy. He was looking forward to drawing her out of her shell.

The fact that he would be her first lover satisfied him on many levels. He very much wanted to draw those first sighs of pleasure. To be watching as she experienced what it was like to be possessed body and soul by a man.

He was as hard as a rock and throbbing painfully imagining the full seduction scene when he took what he'd considered his for many years.

He reached up to stroke her cheek and then gently prodded her lip until she set it free. Plump and swollen from her nervous habit, it was a temptation he couldn't resist.

He pulled her down until she was once more in his lap, her body soft against his. Cupping her face, he angled his mouth to brush across hers, tasting her for the first time.

It was heaven. So very sweet. For a moment she went completely still and then she softened against him, her lips melting over his.

She emitted a breathy sigh, allowing his tongue to slip inside her mouth.

She tasted of things he'd long forgotten. It had been a long while since he'd been so gentle and patient with a lover. But this was Talia. She was no woman to simply slake his lust with. She was no vessel to accommodate his sexual needs.

She deserved, and would get, the most tender of wooings. He would ease her into the role he'd envisioned for her. And he would be the one to take her virginity. That was for him alone.

He nipped at her lip and then slid his tongue deeper, tasting every inch of her mouth. Tentatively she brushed her tongue over his and he nearly groaned at the sweetness of the gesture.

She was so very beautiful. Perfection. All he wanted. Young. Innocent. Willing to please. Obedient to his every wish. His fantasies surrounding her had kept him up many a night and now that she was here, he could barely contain his impatience to mark her. To possess her and to live out every single one of those decadent fantasies that had lived so long in his head.

He was a depraved son of a bitch and she was an innocent virgin. The two seemed incongruous, but somehow he was going to make it work. He couldn't change who he was and he damn sure wasn't going to give her up.

She would adjust. She had to because he'd never let her go.

He drew away, though it took every bit of restraint he had not to roll her over onto the bed and take her now. Only knowing that she deserved better and that he was determined to give it to her kept him from acting on his urge.

"I'll have someone come up to unpack for you," he said in a voice he didn't recognize. Then he checked his watch. "You have half an hour to shower, if you so choose, and change for dinner."

Pink stained her cheeks. "And what should I wear?"

He smiled his approval. It hadn't been a test, but if it had been, she passed with flying colors. He would have allowed her to wear whatever she liked. He wanted her to be comfortable. But that she was already leaning in the direction he wanted her to go gratified him.

He touched her cheek again, fascinated by the softness of her skin. "You're very beautiful, Talia."

She flushed deeper but her eyes shone with delight at the compliment.

"You likely haven't checked the closets yet but they are full of clothing in your sizes. There is a particularly lovely sarong that is hanging next to a pink top that I think would look spectacular with your coloring."

She nodded and started to get off his lap, but he caught her hand and turned her back to look at him.

"Don't, however, wear any underthings. No bra. No panties."

Her eyes widened and her lips parted as a rush of air whispered past them.

He smoothed his thumb over her knuckles and then raised her hand to his lips.

"I won't expect you to plunge directly into my world. I'll ease you into it as much as possible. Soon, I'll expect you to wear nothing at all if I command it so it's better to begin getting used to any embarrassment or discomfort you feel now."

She slowly nodded her understanding, but her cheeks were still streaked with color.

"No one will know but you and I, Talia. And Garon, Sebastien and Nico, of course. But no one will be able to see. Except your breasts of course, but it's damn near a sin to restrain breasts as lovely as yours. I'll enjoy seeing what I can't yet touch and will enjoy the others looking upon your beauty as well.

"But it will give me even greater pleasure to know that underneath the sarong, you are bare and that if I so chose, it would be a simple matter of sweeping aside one delicate piece of material and you would be available for my immediate possession."

Her breathing changed, became more erratic and her pupils dilated.

"I, of course, would not do such a thing. Not tonight at least. You are a virgin still, and I don't want you to worry that your first sexual experience will be painful or rushed."

She swallowed and averted her gaze. He could feel her discomfort radiating in waves. He rose to stand in front of her. He gathered her carefully in his arms, tipping her chin upward so he could press a kiss to her lips.

"So shy. So modest. I want you to be comfortable around me, Talia. It is why I go to such great lengths to make this transition as easy as I can when I burn with impatience to have you."

"Thank you," she said softly.

One eyebrow arched. He hadn't expected her to thank him and he wasn't sure how he felt about it. She sounded sincere, not at all like she was mocking him. There was no hint of sarcasm.

As if realizing he hadn't been certain how to take it, she quickly took his hand, twining her fingers with his. It was the first overt gesture she'd made to touch him or to initiate contact with him, and he found it pleased him greatly.

"You must know how nervous I am. I'm terrified if you want the truth. But I appreciate how . . . gentle . . . you're being with me. It truly means a lot that you've done so much for me. Not just for me but my family. It's true you could do what you want with me. I'm here. Alone. There is no one to run to. I'm completely at your mercy and if you so chose, you could take me now. You could invite your friends in and force me to do whatever it is you want. But you've done none of those things and moreover, you seem to genuinely care about my feelings. About how comfortable I am."

He was horrified that such a thing had even crossed her mind. He wasn't even sure if he was capable of responding. The words were stuck in his throat, and he had to suck in air through his nose for several long seconds.

"Xander?" Her worried voice reached through the fog surrounding his mind. "Did I offend you? I'm sorry. I was just being truthful. I do appreciate your kindness and your generosity."

He put his finger over her lips before she could go any further. And then he shook his head. "I'm shamed that you would even consider for a moment that you had anything to fear from me. Nico was right. You *are* terrified. I should have done things differently. For this I apologize. It pains me that you would be frightened of being hurt and used in such a manner."

"I don't fear you," she said in a soft whisper. She squeezed his hand as if to emphasize her statement. "My fear isn't of you but of the unknown. Of failing you. Of not being what you want."

She fidgeted a moment, looked briefly away but then found his gaze once more. Her eyes were earnest like she very much wanted him to understand her thoughts.

"I was told in stark detail what to expect before I arrived here. But hearing it in abstract is one thing. I thought I had it settled in my mind but when I arrived and then suddenly here you are and these other men and it was all so overwhelming. I thought, oh God, this is real. And then I realized that maybe I would not be what you want. I have no experience. You know this. I don't know how to please one man much less four. I can't even imagine being naked in front of you."

His heart squeezed and he couldn't help the smile that curved his lips upward. He hugged her to him again, wanting nothing more than to allay her silly fears. Not please him? She pleased him just by being here.

When he pulled away, he trailed his fingers through her hair, smoothing it away from her cheeks and tucking it behind her ears.

"I like that you aren't experienced. If I'd wanted a woman with considerable knowledge, it would be very easy for me to have one. I don't want them. I want you. I will delight in teaching you everything you need to know about pleasing me and the others."

There was a hint of relief in her smile this time. Then she twisted his hand so she could look at his watch and then winced. "My half hour has dwindled to fifteen minutes. I must go now if I'm not to make you wait."

He caught her before she could slip away and simply held her a long moment before pressing a kiss to her forehead.

"Take your half hour, Talia. For this night, I find myself feeling very lenient with you. I will send Nico up to collect you in thirty minutes' time."

Chapter 5

When the knock sounded at her door, Talia turned nervously, still tying the ends of the sarong around her waist.

"Come in," she called, hoping she said it loudly enough.

The door opened and Nico appeared, his gaze seeking her out. Her hands began to shake and she glanced down to refocus on the task of securing the sarong.

Nico walked over and gently took the ends from her grasp. "Let me."

He tied a secure knot, leaving it loose enough to angle over her hips. When she thought he would have stepped back, he remained close and dropped one hand down the long slit that traveled the length of her leg from hip to ankle.

"Are you wearing anything underneath?"

Her eyes widened and for a moment she was too taken aback to say anything.

He slid his palm up the underside of her leg and over the bare curve of her behind. "I asked you a question."

Her brow furrowed. His hand was on her bare ass. He ought to damn well know she wasn't wearing underwear.

He continued to stare at her and his hand tightened against her skin.

"No," she finally whispered.

Nico nodded and then let his hand fall away, gently rearranging the sarong to cover her once more.

"Good girl," he murmured. "Xander will be pleased that you complied with his wishes."

There was a look in Nico's eyes that made her breath catch in her throat. She should have protested him touching her so intimately. But she'd been too mesmerized by that intense gaze. And Xander had made it very clear that she was to . . . submit . . . to his men as well as to Xander.

He guided her toward the door but paused as they stepped into the hallway leading to the stairs. "Are you nervous?"

She blinked, surprised that he'd ask and that he seemed to genuinely be concerned. Well, she wasn't going to lie.

"Extremely," she breathed out.

He took her arm, tucked it underneath his and gave her hand a warm, comforting squeeze. "Don't be. I know this is overwhelming for you, that this situation is . . . foreign. But know that Xander, myself and Bastien and Garon will never harm you."

There was no logical reason she should believe a complete stranger, but she found comfort in the quiet vow. There was no hint of deception in his eyes. Just earnest determination, as if he wanted nothing more than to reassure her.

No, it probably wasn't smart for her to believe anything at all, but she found she did. How she could trust this man, she had no answer for, but she found herself curling her fingers tighter around his arm as they descended the stairs. He'd suddenly become her anchor in a stormy sea of uncertainty.

"Are you afraid of me?" Nico asked.

There always seemed to be a surprise. It was a bad habit she had to break herself of. It seemed nothing was off limits and the normal boundaries of propriety were clearly not upheld here.

He stopped at the base of the staircase and glanced down at her, waiting for her response. He looked . . . well, he looked like he actually cared one way or another whether she was scared of him.

She blew out her breath. "You know what? I'm not. I probably should be. I should probably be a lot of things right now. I'm questioning my sanity. I'm questioning whether any of this is real, but oddly enough, no, I'm not scared of you."

He smiled then, and it was amazing the transformation. From the serious, almost somber countenance came a startling handsome light. His eyes warmed and he reached up to touch her cheek.

"I'm glad. I want you to promise me that if you ever feel threatened or afraid that you'll come to me."

She cocked her head to the side, enjoying the feel of those strong fingers on her skin. "I will," she promised quietly.

With seeming reluctance, he dropped his hand and then took hold of her arm once again. He led her through the spacious living room and into the formal dining room that overlooked the huge terrace that spanned the entire backside of the villa.

Xander was already seated. Garon stood to the side on a cell phone, his expression one of concentration. Sebastien was just taking his seat further down the table from Xander.

When they saw her, Xander rose, Garon simply shut his phone in midconversation and Sebastien stopped in midair, resuming his stance instead of continuing down into his chair.

"Come."

The one-word command from Xander sent a shiver down her back. It was delicious, though, and somehow being there beside Nico had infused her with confidence she badly needed. She glanced up at him, flashing a grateful smile before hurrying toward where Xander stood.

Xander's arm was outstretched and she instinctively stepped into the shelter of his body. He made a sound of approval as he curled his arm around her, pulling her in tighter. He kissed her forehead.

"You look beautiful. Did you carry out all of my instructions?"

She nodded and then verbalized the response, not knowing if a simple nod would be sufficient. "Yes."

"Show us."

That drew her up short. She glanced up at him, automatically seeking confirmation that he was serious. His lips tightened and she realized that she'd displeased him. But did he expect her to . . . ?

Apparently he did.

She started to argue, to tell him that Nico's hand had already been up her sarong and over her ass. He could certainly vouch for the fact that underneath the very thin, very sheer flowing material, she didn't have a stitch on. But she realized that any further delay would only make him more displeased than he already was.

Her hand shaking, she slowly reached down to pull aside the sarong.

"Turn so we can see," Xander directed.

She briefly closed her eyes and summoned all her courage for what she was about to do. She was naturally modest and didn't have one single exhibitionist tendency. Seeking the spotlight was not in character for her and the idea that she would be on display for these four men plus whoever else happened to wander through made her want to break out in hives.

"We're waiting, Talia," Xander said in a clipped tone.

She turned so her profile would be presented and then she carefully pulled the material up and over her hip until the curve of her behind was presented.

"More."

Using her other hand, she gathered the material that shielded the juncture of her legs and pulled it up and out of the way so that her entire lower half of her body was bared to their gaze.

She'd never felt so vulnerable in her life. Then she made the mistake of glancing up and making eye contact with Garon and then Sebastien. They were obviously aroused, their gazes burning over her skin. But there was blatant approval there and no disrespect. No tasteless remarks. No catcalls or whistles. Nothing at all except long, lingering looks filled with lust and a promise of the darkest kind of pleasure.

Her gaze cut to Nico, but he wasn't looking down. He was staring right back at her, his gaze fastened on her face, meeting her eyes, and in his depths she found support. Comfort.

Xander slid his hand over her behind and cupped her intimately before motioning for her to let go of the sarong.

"I'm pleased you followed my directive," he said. "In time, I'll cease to question and assume that you have obeyed me. But that trust must be earned. Right now we are still learning each other and it's understandable that you would have been reluctant to do as I asked. I'm very pleased that despite whatever discomfort you may have felt over fulfilling my wishes that you did so without question."

He leaned over and cupped her jaw, sweeping his mouth possessively over hers. "You please me very much, Talia."

She stared back at him, a little dazed by all that had occurred. And they hadn't even sat down to eat yet. She was still reeling from . . . well, pretty much everything. The entire day.

He pulled back the chair beside him and then eased her down, making sure she was comfortable. As soon as everyone settled into their chairs, fatigue and reaction hit her like a ton of bricks.

She stared down at the delicious-looking food and wondered if she had the energy to get through the meal.

"Talia."

She yanked her head up and stared down at Garon. Now *he* scared her. Not in an I-think-he's-going-to-kill-me way, but he was . . . huge. She had yet to see him smile or look anything but focused and somewhat fierce-looking. This was a man she'd never want to piss off in any way.

"Come here," he said.

She glanced hesitantly at Xander. Was he okay with this? Xander had said that orders would come through him, but he was sitting right next to her, so why would Garon have told her to come to him?

Still, she had no desire to anger Garon. Or Xander and since Xander returned her gaze very calmly, she assumed he meant for her to obey Garon.

God, but this whole thing was giving her a monster headache. Her nerves were shot and she hadn't even been here a full day yet.

She pushed back from her chair and unsteadily rose to her feet. Fatigue beat at her temples and her shoulders sagged as she walked the few steps to where Garon sat.

He reached for her hand and then sighed when she tensed. Then he simply pulled her onto his lap and tucked her legs between his so she sat sideways, leaning against the muscled wall of his chest and shoulder.

Just when she thought she couldn't be surprised by anything else, he forked a bite of the fish and held it to her lips.

"Eat," he said, still holding the fork to her mouth.

She parted her lips and he carefully fed her the bite.

One corner of his mouth tilted upward at her obvious befuddlement. It wasn't as if she could hide her complete what-the-hell look.

"You looked as though you were about to fall over," he said simply. "And I'm sure you're hungry. Lean against me. Make yourself comfortable while I feed you."

"But what about you?" she protested.

That lip twitched again and his eyes gleamed. "I don't think missing a meal is going to hurt me. Now stop talking and eat. The only way you're going to figure out that we aren't going to rape and murder you is for you to spend time with us and build trust."

She had nothing to say to that because it was the truth.

He not only forked bite after bite into her mouth but, at the same time, he rubbed her back with his free hand, stroking up and down in a soothing, comforting motion that had her sagging against him.

After a while he delved his fingers into her hair and then underneath it to massage her nape. It was sheer bliss.

For a man of his size and intimidation factor, he was surprisingly tender. His touch was gentle, even more so than Nico's had been.

When she peeked from the corner of her eye to the other occupants of the table, she realized what they were doing. The meeting earlier. Nico coming to get her for dinner. Garon feeding her. Xander's own familiarity with her. The kiss. The touches.

They were taming her much like they would a wild animal. They were getting her used to their touch, their demands. Acclimating her to the environment she'd been pulled into.

They didn't want her to fear them, and they were going to great lengths to build trust.

Some of the tension that had been building the entire day fled. She relaxed and let go of the jumble of questions crowding her mind. If she tried to look at the whole picture, it overwhelmed her. She had no clue how it could ever work. So instead she focused on just one thing. How it felt to sit in Garon's arms while he fed and pampered her.

That one was pretty easy to answer. He may be big and menacing, but he treated her like a precious piece of glass that may break if he breathed too hard on her.

His hand felt wonderful on her back and at her nape and the food was delicious, maybe even more so because of the intimacy of the act of him feeding her.

When she'd had enough, she sighed her contentment and leaned her head against his shoulder. He continued his conversation with the other men, almost as if she weren't there on his lap.

Wickersham brought in another plate and Garon ate a portion of fish while holding her against his body. She tried to focus on what was being said, but her mind was tired and it was hard to follow the conversation.

When she stifled a yawn, Garon only pulled her in closer to his body until her forehead rested against his neck. She closed her eyes, no longer able or willing to fight the urge to give in to her exhaustion.

She stirred against him just enough that she could snuggle farther into his warmth. She felt his lips brush across her forehead and she sighed at the pleasurable sensation of his kiss. Maybe . . . Maybe he wasn't so scary after all.

Chapter 6

Xander watched as Talia settled into sleep against Garon's burly frame. The big man held her as gently as he would the most fragile piece of fine art. He smiled to himself. Talia was responding well—far better than he'd anticipated.

The others were already devoted to her. It was evident in the way they looked at her. How they handled her and how gently they spoke.

Firm but gentle.

It had been his directive. He wanted Talia to know her boundaries. To know whom she belonged to and whom she obeyed. But he wanted to guide her with a gentle hand and tender touch.

The idea of causing her pain made him grit his teeth. He hated that she'd come all this way fully expecting him to demonstrate his mastery through pain and discipline or that he'd collar her or put even one mark on her beautiful skin with a whip or a flogger.

He was shaking his head before he could control the motion. Sebastien arched an eyebrow in his direction.

"Problem, Z?"

Xander's lips tightened. "I was just lamenting the fact that from the inception of our contract, she's assumed that she would be subjected to all manner of pain and discipline and God only knows what else."

Nico scowled. "I hope you've fully dissuaded her of that notion. Hell, we don't go around whipping women or punishing them for some supposed infraction."

Xander sighed. "There are those who think a submissive relationship automatically means bondage, spanking, absolute control. Hell, even slavery."

"Now you're just starting to piss me off," Garon growled.

Even as he spoke, he smoothed Talia's hair and shifted so he could hold her more securely. She never stirred and her eyelashes remained resting on her cheeks.

Sebastien shrugged. "People are into it. Whatever does it for them, I guess. Some women enjoy that sort of thing. Some men like it."

"Can you imagine, even for a moment, doing anything that would cause her pain or suffering?" Nico demanded. "Look at her, Bastien. She's curled up against Garon even though he probably scares her shitless. She trusts us, even if she doesn't fully grasp that. Can you imagine what would happen if we hit her?"

Nico sounded so appalled and horrified that Xander winced.

"Now wait just a damn minute," Sebastien snapped. "I was merely pointing out that some people were into that sort of thing and more power to them. If they like it, if it's consensual, then I don't have a problem with it. I did not say that I had any such intention toward Talia. Hell, it would be like kicking a puppy."

Xander smiled again.

"And what the hell are you so smug about?" Sebastien demanded, looking at Xander.

"Just that the three of you have already done precisely as I imagined you would upon meeting Talia. You're already protect-ive of her. She already has your loyalty."

Garon shot him a sharp glance. "Isn't that what you wanted?"

Xander nodded. "Indeed. But just because it's what I want doesn't mean that she would arouse that instinct within you. Tell me something, Garon. If I had told you nothing at all, would your reaction to Talia be any different? Or would you still be holding her as you are now, protecting her as she sleeps after being fed by your hand?"

Garon glanced down at Talia, his brow wrinkled in concen-tration. Then he looked back up at Xander, his lips set into a determined line. "No. Hell no, it wouldn't. Your damn orders don't have anything at all to do with what happens when I look at her."

Xander looked questioningly at Nico and Sebastien. Nico curled his lip in Xander's direction, a clear indication that he thought the answer should be obvious. Sebastien shrugged, but Xander saw the way his gaze tracked sideways to Talia, how he looked as though he wanted to be the one holding her.

"She needs rest," Xander said. "She's clearly exhausted and it's also obvious that this entire situation has put an enormous amount of stress on her. I want us to alleviate that stress as soon as possi-ble. I won't have her terrified of me when I make love to her the first time."

"I'll take her up," Garon said in a low voice.

"Leave her dressed. I'll take care of it," Xander said as Garon rose.

Garon nodded and walked slowly out of the dining room, Talia's long hair trailing over his arm as he carried her away.

Xander remained a moment, staring across the table at Nico and Sebastien.

"Tomorrow . . ." He toyed idly with his wineglass, swirled the small amount of liquid before setting it back on the table again. "Tomorrow her training will begin."

Sebastien cocked one eyebrow. "You don't think you're rushing things a bit? You seemed concerned about frightening her and now you want to throw her to the wolves the second day she's here?"

Nico frowned. "What part of her training are you referring to? Are we talking simple obedience or are we talking sex?"

"Both," Xander said bluntly. "I think as long as we continue to treat her gently and with patience but also with a firm hand, she'll respond quicker. We can't send mixed signals and go soft. If we strike the right balance, there'll be no need to worry that we'll frighten her."

"As long as part of this training is how to suck cock, I'm all for it," Sebastien said.

"Shut the fuck up," Nico snapped.

Sebastien threw him a dark look. "Don't get all choir boy on me now, Nico. You can't tell me that you aren't dying to get those exquisite lips wrapped around your cock. She has a mouth to die for."

Xander wouldn't chasten Sebastien for being Sebastien. It's who he was. Irreverent. Blunt. But he was solid and loyal to his bones. And he could hardly fault Sebastien for fantasizing about Talia's mouth when Xander had been tempted to put her between his knees ever since she'd arrived.

"Perhaps you can instruct her on the finer points," Xander drawled.

"Hell yeah," Sebastien breathed out.

Xander rose from his seat. "I'm going up. I'll see you both at breakfast. I intend for us to spend the entire day with Talia. The more time she spends in our presence, the faster she'll be at ease with us."

Nico nodded and Xander turned to stride away. He walked up

the stairs but never passed Garon. When he walked into his suite, there was still no sign of the other man.

The door to his bedroom was slightly ajar and Xander pushed in, his gaze taking in the scene before him.

Garon was carefully tucking Talia into Xander's bed. She was still fully clothed, or rather still wrapped in the sarong and the spaghetti-strap top.

Talia murmured something in her sleep and Garon smoothed a hand through her hair, murmuring something back. Evidently it soothed whatever worry she may have had because she snuggled deeper into the pillow and settled. Her soft even breathing filled the room.

Garon stared down at her a moment longer and then backed off the bed. When he turned, he came face-to-face with Xander. Garon dipped his head in acknowledgment.

"She's all yours, Highness."

"I'll see you at breakfast," Xander said, repeating the good night he'd given the others.

When Garon was gone, Xander undressed, stripping down to nothing. There was still Talia's clothing to deal with. As long as she slept in his bed, she'd never have the barrier of clothing between them.

If he knew anything about himself and the three men he trusted so implicitly, in a matter of days, Talia would never wear a damn thing twenty-four hours a day.

They'd want her naked so they'd have unfettered access to her body and when they weren't making love to her, they'd want to look at her and know she was theirs. Their woman. Their possession.

Xander smiled as he turned her carefully over and she murmured a sleepy protest. He untied the sarong and left it for the time being. He then slid the straps of her top down her bare arms and simply peeled the shirt down over her hips until it tangled with the material of the sarong.

He rolled her forward onto her side and pulled the clothing away, tossing it onto the floor. Then he rolled her back so he could look down at her soft curves and the beauty of her skin.

She was magnificent.

It pained him not to touch her. He wanted to explore her body. Give her the pleasure he knew he could provide. But she was tired. She wasn't even aware of his presence and it seemed wrong—a violation—to do anything more than ensure her comfort so she could sleep well this night.

With a resigned sigh, he crawled into bed and picked up the remote to douse the lights. Maybe he was getting soft, the very thing he'd just warned the others about.

He'd told them they had to be firm but gentle. Let her know right away what their expectations were and what the boundaries were.

With any other woman, at any other time in his life, he would have taken without guilt. He would even now be sliding his fingers through the dark curls between her legs and savoring the essence of her femininity.

And yet here he was, holding back because above all things, he wanted her trust. He wanted her faith. He wanted her to believe that he would take absolute care of her and that he would cherish her as he'd promised.

If that meant taking his time and exerting patience he had little to none of, then that's what he'd do.

He set the remote aside and then reached for her, pulling her flush against his body.

Tomorrow would be soon enough to introduce her to what he and his men expected of her.

Chapter 7

Talia awoke to sunlight streaming through the window, warming the bed and her skin. She pushed upward to her elbow, the sheet falling down her body to gather at her hip, so she could take in the breathtaking view of the ocean below.

The windows were cracked, allowing a breeze through. She could smell the salt in the air and hear the rush of waves as they lapped at the shore.

It was then she realized she was wearing nothing and that she was in Xander's bed. Her last memory was of falling asleep in Garon's arms the night before and yet she was here, nude.

She turned, half expecting to see Xander there, but the bed was empty though the pillow still had the indention of his head. She cocked her head, listening for any sound within the suite to signal she wasn't alone.

She glanced automatically to the grandfather clock across the room and breathed a sigh of relief. It wasn't terribly late. Though Xander hadn't given her any instructions on when she was to rise, she would have felt bad to have slept the morning away. It was only eight. If she hurried, she could be showered and dressed and downstairs in half an hour.

She shoved aside the sheets and threw her legs over the edge of the bed. She felt calmer today. Not as nervous and edgy as she had yesterday. But then she'd traveled a long distance and then had to deal with the overwhelming presence of not one man, but four.

She was halfway to the bathroom when the bedroom door opened. She froze, caught completely naked with nothing but her hands to cover her most vulnerable spots.

Sebastien stood there gazing at her, his expression unreadable. Then he leaned against the doorframe and crossed his arms over his chest.

His silence bothered her. It made her twitchy, like she'd done something wrong, only she couldn't imagine what. Of all the men, he seemed to be the most . . . infuriating? Maybe not infuriating since she didn't really know any of them that well yet. But he seemed more mocking. Or maybe he was amused by her. Regardless, none of the descriptors made her feet at ease with him.

"Is there something you wanted?" she asked calmly.

She wouldn't let him know how much he intimidated her. Not even Garon with his hulking size made her feel as insignificant as Sebastien.

He chuckled and pushed off the doorframe. "I believe Xander was explicit in that one of us would come to you in the mornings with what to wear."

She frowned. "Well, yes, he was, but there wasn't anyone here when I woke up. For that matter, I'm not even sure what time he wants me to be up or if he cares. But I at least thought I could take a shower while waiting for my wardrobe advisor."

He laughed again. "You don't like me much, do you, Talia?"

She cocked her head to the side and narrowed her eyes. "I haven't decided yet."

He gave her a slow grin. "That's fine. Because it'll be my cock you're sucking later. You don't have to like me for me to enjoy it."

She reared back, her mouth dropping open at his bluntness. Then she snapped her lips shut and glared at him. "Why are you purposely trying to bait me? Do you want me frightened of you?"

The others seemed to want just the opposite, but she hadn't yet figured Sebastien out.

"Frightened? No, that serves little purpose. I won't hurt you, Talia. I'm just not as soft as the others. While they aren't into putting marks on your pretty behind, I find I wouldn't mind having you over my knee one little bit."

"You wouldn't," she whispered.

"Don't knock it unless you've tried it," he drawled.

Her fingers curled into tight balls. "I don't like pain. I hate it."

"It's a moot point. I'd get my ass kicked if I tried to redden that delectable bottom of yours. Now, we've wasted enough time. Xander is waiting below for you to join us for breakfast. I'll wash you and then take you downstairs."

She stared at him like he'd lost his mind. "I can bathe myself. You're just supposed to lay out my clothes."

"I'm supposed to do whatever it is Xander tells me to do with you," Sebastien said, a bite to his words. "And your task is to obey without question. Now, if we're done arguing, let's step into the bathroom."

Numbly she followed him into the bathroom and watched as he turned the shower on, testing the temperature with his fingers before he turned back to her.

Then he began unbuttoning his shirt. When he reached the bottom, he left the shirt hanging and he unfastened his fly. She looked away as he started pulling his jeans down, her cheeks flaming.

"Talia, look at me."

The command in his voice gave her no choice but to obey. When she looked back he stood before her, completely naked. And did he have a beautiful body. Tanned. Completely tanned. So either his natural skin tone was dark or he tanned in the nude.

He was tall and lean but tightly muscled. There wasn't a spare ounce of flesh anywhere. Whipcord lean. He looked strong, every bit as strong as Garon must be but just . . . different. Different makeup. Different body structure.

He held out his hand and she reached for it, her gaze avoiding one portion of his anatomy. He drew her into the shower and under the spray.

She wasn't sure what to expect. If this was something sexual or clinical. She was pressed to his body. She could feel his penis at the small of her back, but he made no overt sexual gestures.

His hands were gentle as he soaped her body and he only lightly skimmed over her breasts and then between her legs, almost as if he truly didn't want to alarm her, which was a direct contradiction to his seeming indifference to her comfort.

When he was finished with her body, he applied shampoo to her hair and gently worked his fingers through the strands until he lathered the entire mass.

Then he turned her so the stream poured over her head. She closed her eyes and gave herself over to the pleasurable sensation. Who knew having someone take such intimate care of her could be nice?

If she expected to lollygag and enjoy the hot water for any longer than necessary, she was quickly corrected when the water shut off and Sebastien pulled her from the shower. A moment later, he enfolded her in a huge towel and briskly rubbed the moisture from her body. Next he set to work on her hair.

To her further surprise, he settled her onto the plush bench in front of the vanity, took one of the combs from the draw and began working the tangles from her hair.

This wasn't happening. Not in her world. It was bizarre and it unsettled her.

"Relax," he said brusquely. "You're wound tighter than a spring. I'm not going to bite you. Yet."

She found herself laughing and then glanced up at the mirror to see his look of amusement over her shoulder.

"See? I'm not so bad."

She just stared at him in bewilderment as he continued to comb out her hair.

"I can't wrap my brain around this," she said before she thought better of it.

He paused, cocked his head sideways and stared at her in question. "What do you mean?"

Her cheeks flushed and she swallowed nervously. "Nothing. Sometimes I speak before I think better of it."

He put down the comb and then turned her so she faced him. He framed her jaw with both hands and used his thumbs to brush over her cheekbones.

"I admit that I can be a complete asshole at times. I probably was a jerk to you earlier. I'm an irreverent bastard or so I've been told by Xander and the others on multiple occasions. But I'm not going to hurt you, Talia. You can say what's on your mind. Despite my cocky assertion that I'd like to turn you over my knee and spank your ass, I can assure you that I was looking at it from a sexual standpoint. Quite frankly the thought of having you over my knee and my hand on your ass makes me hot. But I'd never hurt you. And moreover, I respect honesty above all things. So if you have something to say, say it. I don't know what Xander allows, but when you're with me, you are always free to speak your mind."

She smiled tremulously and rubbed her cheek against his palm.

"I was merely going to say that I couldn't wrap my brain around someone who looks like such a badass doing a woman's hair for them. I mean no offense . . ."

Before she could continue and put her foot more solidly in her mouth, he chuckled and turned her back around. He rummaged in the drawer before pulling out a hair dryer. As he plugged it in, he said, "No offense taken. I'm comfortable enough in my sexuality to take any ribbing over taking care of a woman. I have three sisters. Younger sisters. My dad died when I was young and they were still babies. My mom had to work a lot to provide for us and so I did everything from braid their hair to picking out shoes and school clothes."

Her heart softened and she smiled. "I think that's awesome."

"There is no shame in taking care of the woman you're responsible for," he said. "In this case, Xander has placed the responsibility for your safety and your well-being and happiness in my hands and the hands of Nico and Garon as well as himself. Bathing you and taking care of your hair is a small thing if it brings you pleasure."

She closed her eyes as he stroked through her hair once more. "It does. Thank you."

He turned on the dryer and used a brush to pull her hair out so he could glide the blow-dryer down the strands. He was meticulous, covering each section until it hung past her shoulders, shiny and soft.

He'd made everything seem so normal that she'd forgotten she was sitting here completely nude while he dried her hair.

He shut off the dryer, leaned forward to put it back in the drawer and then stood behind her, putting his hands on her shoulders.

"Are you ready to go down now?"

She swiftly turned, his hands coming free of her shoulders as she looked up at him. "Naked?"

He lifted that brow, the one that made him look so arrogant and forbidding.

"But he said he would give me time," she fretted. "How can I go down there like this? It was bad enough last night when . . ." She swallowed her embarrassment and looked away.

He reached down and cupped one breast, using his thumb to brush over her nipple. The sensation was electric, startling her with its intensity.

"What is it you don't want us to see, Talia? Your breasts? I assure you they're perfect. Lush. High and firm. Nipples that make a man want to lick and suck."

Her skin was going to burn right off her cheeks.

"Stand up," he commanded.

Shakily she rose and bit back an exclamation of surprise when he lifted one of her legs so that her foot rested on the seat she'd just vacated. It opened her thighs and made her most intimate flesh accessible to him.

He slid his hand over her belly and down. She sucked in her breath as his fingers glided through the delicate folds and over her clit.

"Is it this you don't want us to see? Such a beautiful, delicate little pussy. Do you know what we'll see, what we'll imagine when we look at you? We'll be imagining how you taste. How good it will feel when we're pushing our dicks into that tight little passage."

She swayed and he caught her arm to steady her.

"Your modesty is endearing, but there's no place for it here. I think Xander had every intention of taking things slow, but the reality is he wants you. We want you. Xander isn't a patient man. He's not going to be satisfied until he's taken you and made you his."

"I'm sorry," she said huskily. "I'm not being the obedient mistress I promised to be."

He frowned and moved his hand from her quivering flesh. "Is that what you see yourself as? His mistress?"

Her lips turned down. "I'm not being derogatory or argumentative. I honestly don't know what I am. No one has told me. I don't know my place or who I am. It's . . . unsettling."

He tucked a finger under her chin and prodded upward until she was forced to meet his gaze. "Your place is here with him. With us. What you are is cherished."

Chapter 8

Xander was seated at the table with Garon and Nico awaiting Sebastien and Talia. He checked his watch and frowned. They should already be down.

He glanced up to see Garon and Nico also casting glances toward the doorway from time to time.

And then Sebastien appeared, Talia's hand curled tightly into his. She looked nervous and uncertain, but there was also a subtle difference in her demeanor this morning.

Either she'd calmed some of her fears with a good night's sleep or Sebastien had taken the matter in hand.

Garon hadn't wanted Sebastien to go after Talia so soon after her arrival. He'd reminded Xander that Sebastien was a hard-ass and a rebel at heart and that he tended to do things his way. But Xander knew two things. One, Sebastien was unwaveringly loyal to Xander and two, behind Sebastien's hard exterior was a man who adored women and would fiercely protect them against all harm.

Talia had already made conquests of Garon and Nico. Sending one of them served no purpose. He needed Sebastien to decide what Talia would mean to him, and from the looks of it, Sebastien had already decided.

Xander's gaze raked up and down her body, appreciative of such natural beauty. Perfection. Garon and Nico stared as well, their eyes gleaming.

She was . . . stunning. Soft in all the right places. Perfect breasts, high and firm. Nipples that were just the right size. Her hips were rounded and he'd already gotten a prime view, and feel, of her luscious ass.

Her hair hung to her waist in soft waves. Already he imagined it falling down around them both as she sat astride him, taking him into her body. Or spread out on the bed as he thrust into her from above.

He rose and extended his hand. "Good morning, Talia. You look beautiful."

The blush rose quickly, suffusing her cheeks with color. But she didn't hesitate. She offered Sebastien a smile and then slipped her hand from his to walk to Xander and take his.

He sat her beside him, ensuring there was a cushion on the chair so the wood wouldn't be cold on her bare skin. Unable to resist, he lifted her hand and kissed her knuckles, holding her hand to his mouth for several long seconds.

"I trust you slept well?"

She nodded. "I did. I was very tired. Thank you for allowing me to sleep in this morning."

"I think we've already covered the fact that I won't expect you to rise early. Until you are summoned, the mornings are yours to do as you will. If you choose to sleep, that is your choice."

He dished food onto her plate and he noticed that she waited, hands in her lap. He smiled and reached over to touch her cheek.

"This morning you'll feed yourself. You were very tired last night, which is why Garon chose to pamper you a bit. At times we'll want to indulge in our whims and feed you by hand. Today you are free to eat by yourself."

She reached for the fork and began to eat the portion of fruit. It was an exercise in frustration to watch her eat because every bite she took was a sensual experience. And she likely had no idea that she had four men ready to reach across the table, pull her onto it and bury themselves in her body.

At one point, juice spilled down her lip and she licked at it, running her tongue delicately over her bottom lip to wipe it away. Sebastien let out a groan.

"For God's sake, Xander. Let's get on with this morning's lesson already."

Xander shot him a look of reprimand. Talia looked up, confusion in her eyes.

"Eat," he said. "Pay Sebastien no mind."

He glared again at Sebastien and shook his head. Sebastien shrugged.

"Have some class," Nico muttered.

"But we all know I have none," Sebastien drawled. "I wasn't born with a silver spoon in my mouth like the rest of you. I can't be expected to live up to your lofty expectations."

"How about I just beat the shit out of you instead?" Garon proposed.

Sebastien laughed. "You can try."

Talia was staring at them like they'd both lost their minds. Xander sighed. He doubted they were making a good impression, but then he supposed Talia may as well see what she was in for.

His men bantered and bickered like brothers. In essence they were. All of them. They didn't share blood, but the bond was there. Unbreakable.

"After breakfast, we'll take a walk around the villa grounds and down to the beach if you like," Xander said to Talia.

Her eyes lit up. "I'd like that. It seems so beautiful. The water is so gorgeous it doesn't even seem real."

Sebastien looked disgruntled and Xander shot him a warning look. Xander was as impatient as Sebastien to move things forward, but he wanted Talia to relax and lose some of her nervousness with them before they introduced her to their hedonism.

When they finished eating, Xander motioned for Wickersham. A few moments later, he returned carrying a light, floral robe. Xander rose and held the robe open for Talia. She slowly stood and he helped her put it on.

"I don't want you too exposed to the sun," he explained. "There are comfortable beach shoes at the patio entrance."

She smiled and he stood there, unable to speak for several seconds. She was utterly stunning. Her smile lit up the entire room. Beautiful. Adorably shy. And she would be his.

He clenched his fingers into fists to stop the shaking.

"Don't forget you have an eleven o'clock update on the situation in Cristofino," Garon reminded.

"I'm unlikely to forget when my home occupies my every thought," Xander said icily.

He instantly regretted the shortness of his response. Garon was only doing his duty, but the inference that he would be too distracted by Talia's presence to focus on the turmoil back home was a prick to his pride.

To an outsider he might seem to be a spoiled, bored royal who had summoned an innocent woman to be his plaything while he was in exile. They might consider Talia a frivolity, a passing amusement. A mistress.

Talia was none of those. This wasn't the way he'd wanted things, but the situation in Cristofino hadn't shown any improvement and with Talia out of university, Xander knew he had to act fast or risk losing her.

Xander led Talia toward the door leading onto the terrace.

They stopped for her to slip on the flip-flops and for a moment he stared at the bright pink polish on her toes. For some reason, he loved it. On her it was perfect.

She wore no jewelry. It was a fact he'd noticed when she'd arrived. And it was a matter he definitely wanted to correct. There was nothing more he wanted to do than spoil her endlessly and lavish gifts on her. He wanted to drape her in diamonds and make love to her wearing nothing more than the jewelry he'd given her.

Shaking himself from his fantasies, he stepped onto the terrace. Talia inhaled deeply, closed her eyes and turned her face into the sun. The breeze from the water ruffled her hair and he was captured by how sensual she looked.

When she opened her eyes again, they simmered with pleasure. Warm and vibrant like the rest of her. She smiled at him, warming him to his toes.

"I can't imagine waking to this every day."

He smiled back. "And yet our home is an island every bit as beautiful."

Her expression saddened and the smile disappeared. "But I haven't been home in four years. And while I was there . . . I took it for granted, you know? When you live it, were born to it, sometimes you don't recognize the beauty until you've lost it."

"Very true," he said quietly.

He too had taken Cristofino for granted. Hadn't appreciated the beauty of his island home until it was lost to him. When—not if—he regained the throne, he would never make such a mistake again.

"Are things better there, Xander?" she asked anxiously.

They'd just gotten to the steps leading down into the lower garden with the pathway that led to the beach. He paused a moment, not wanting any distraction as they navigated the stone steps. Sometimes they were damp with the ocean mist and as a result could be slick.

He sighed, feeling heartsick and homesick all at the same time. "There is tenuous peace but the battle over government still rages. The majority want and are loyal to the royal family, but the minority is strong and are willing to use violence to achieve their purpose. The very last thing I want is bloodshed. It's why I agreed to this 'exile.' I effectively removed myself from the equation because the alternative is bloodshed for my people. After my father was killed, I knew the country was on the verge of full-scale war."

"What is to be done then?" she asked, her eyes sad.

"We wait. Quiet dissension. Rebel against the rebels themselves. Those who were unsatisfied with the rule of Cristofino are fast discovering that they have no clear plan of leadership nor are they qualified to govern a people who have no loyalty to them. It is my hope that through peaceable means, I can regain control—and my birthright."

"And if you don't?"

"I won't entertain any other option," he said quietly. "Though I am here, many that are still in leadership positions are loyal to me. They work within the system to gain support."

"That could take years," she said unhappily.

He nodded. "Yes, it could. But the end result would make the wait worth it. I don't want my country to be a bloodbath. If it comes down to taking by force or me standing down, I'll stand down because what I will have won will be contaminated by the lives lost and the blood shed."

She reached for his hand, squeezing it. "You are very noble, Xander. And wise. I too couldn't bear to see Cristofino turned into a battlefield where our people are pitted against each other in civil war. No one can possibly be hailed a victor in such circumstances."

Some of the ache in his heart lessened at the shining approval in her eyes. He twined his fingers tighter in hers and then guided her down the steps.

"Take care and stay close. I don't want you to slip," he cautioned.

She nestled closer to his side and he automatically put his arm around her, dropping her hand so he could hold her close. She fit like a dream. Soft, curvy. He could feel the lushness of her body through the thin layer of the robe she wore.

Yes, he wouldn't be able to wait any longer. All plans of a prolonged, staged seduction were out the window. There was no way he could continue to remain in her presence and not want to claim her.

She made an exclamation of wonder when they entered the floral garden. "Xander, it's beautiful! How do you not spend all your time here? I don't think I'd ever leave. And, oh look, a hammock!"

She started to pull away but then drew up short and went still. She looked at him with regret as if thinking she'd done something wrong.

He pulled her hand up to kiss the inside of her palm. "Never dim your enthusiasm around me, Talia. I'm not so rigid that you can't express your enjoyment without having permission."

She smiled, her eyes lighting up and then she dashed away, throwing herself into the hammock that stood in the corner. She was so exuberant that she nearly flipped right out of it. He made a lunge for her just as she righted herself.

Laughing, she stared up at him, arms thrown over her head, a dreamy look in her eyes as she swayed back and forth in the breeze.

"This is wonderful. I can't remember the last time I did something so lighthearted and . . . fun! I was always so busy with Mama and school."

Xander's heart twisted. He knew all too well how much time she'd devoted to her mother and to her studies. He knew she'd had next to no social life, which in turns delighted and saddened him. He wanted her to enjoy the things a woman of her age should enjoy, and yet the selfish part of himself loved the idea of being the one to provide those things for her. And he was savagely happy that she'd given herself to no one before now.

It wouldn't have mattered to him if she hadn't come to him a virgin. He would have wanted her still. But that she was still untouched gave him a measure of satisfaction that couldn't be described.

"I think I could stay here all day," she said wistfully.

He smiled and extended his hand to help her out. "I tell you what. Let's continue our little tour. We've yet to dig our toes into the sand. When we return for my call at eleven, I'll leave you out here in the hammock until I'm finished and summon you back inside."

She grasped his hand and let him pull her up. "That sounds amazing. Just lying here watching the sky and listening to the waves."

He took her hand again, liking touching her. He found he couldn't help himself. When she was close, he had to be touching some part of her.

"You can leave your shoes here if you like," he said when they reached the drop-off to the sand of the beach.

She shook off the flip-flops and then glanced up at him. "Not going to take off your sandals?"

"I hadn't thought to, no."

"Oh, come on. Lighten up," she teased. "Roll up your pants and we'll get our feet wet."

He couldn't have told her no for any reason. Not when she had finally relaxed and was creeping out of that shell of uncertainty. With an exaggerated, resigned sigh, he reached down to pull the sandals off and then rolled the ends of his trousers up to midcalf.

He reached for her hand again and stepped onto the beach. She made a sound of bliss and immediately dug her toes deeper into the powdery sand. He waited a moment and then tugged her toward the water's edge, several feet away.

The water slid inward, foaming over the sand before receding, leaving wet, packed-in sand. They moved closer and when the water rushed back at them, Talia let out a squeak and then danced back, dodging the water and leaving him to stand ankle deep.

He eyed her balefully. "Whatever happened to let's go put our feet in the water?"

She laughed and the sound sparkled like the sun dancing off the water. Then she rejoined him, this time remaining in place when the water once again rushed ashore.

She stared over the horizon, her expression one of supreme peace. Then she slowly rotated, taking in every detail of her surroundings.

Her hair whipped in the breeze, lifting off her shoulders and swirling like a mass of dark silk. The thin robe ruffled, baring parts of her skin depending on which way she turned.

He was treated to a tantalizing glimpse of her bottom and then the soft curls covering her pussy. And when she turned again, he could clearly see the outline of her breasts. The material molded to her nipples and it was all he could do not to drop to his knees, push aside the offending material and suck the velvety nub into his mouth.

Instead he simply pulled her into his arms and kissed her.

Her hair blew over them both. Each brush of the silken strands over his skin made him more eager to delve his fingers into the heavy mass and kiss every inch of her mouth, her face, her neck.

She made the sweetest sound of surrender, which only made him ache all the more fiercely. He considered himself a civilized man, despite his sexual proclivities, which might make him taboo to most people. But at the moment he was feeling decidedly uncivilized. More like a caveman set to haul his woman over his shoulder and into the cave to have raw, savage sex.

He feasted on her lips. Devoured them, tasted, licked, nibbled.

He slid his tongue over hers, savoring the feel of her in his arms and in his mouth.

There was no mistaking the erection threatening to burst from his pants. He only hoped to hell he didn't scare the devil out of her. There was no hiding it or disguising it. It pressed into her soft belly and he was dangerously close to spending himself in his underwear.

Instead of being wary, she drew away, her eyes half lidded as she stared up at him. She tentatively brushed her fingers down his body, closer and closer to his aching groin.

When she actually cupped the ridge of his erection, he let out a harsh groan that had her snatching her hand back.

He caught her hand and pressed it back. "God, no, don't take it back."

"I thought I'd done something wrong," she said huskily.

"You touching me is *never* wrong."

He let go of her hand and she left it there, carefully molded to the outline of his cock. He ran his fingers through the strands of her hair, futilely trying to keep it in check against the wind.

"I am controlled in every aspect of my life. My calm is legendary. And necessary when dealing with politics and the daily routine of serving my people. And yet with you I feel completely and utterly out of control. I'm not sure I like it."

To his surprise, she laughed. He'd worried that she'd be offended. Or that she would sulk or pout or take it as an insult. Instead her eyes danced with merriment.

He frowned, uncertain now of what was so hilarious.

"What's so funny?"

"You are," she said with an impish grin. "The uptight, staid prince is unbalanced by little ole me."

"Uptight? Staid? I'll show you uptight," he growled. "Or rather I'll show you something *tight*. Like how your sweet little pussy grips my dick when I'm pushing inside you."

She went silent, her breath hiccupping out in a forceful rush. For a moment he thought he'd gone too far. She'd been so playful and relaxed. He didn't want her to go back to being reserved and uneasy.

But then the corner of her mouth lifted and she cocked her head to one side. "Guess I'll have to wait and see this tightness you speak of."

"Feel," he murmured. "You'll feel it, and God help me, so will I."

She glanced down at his watch and then grimaced. "It's nearly time for your call."

Yes, it was. Time had gotten away and it had felt good to let go of all the worry and stress pressing down on him. Here, standing in the ocean, barefooted with pants legs rolled up, he felt a measure of freedom he hadn't felt in a long time.

His duty awaited him, but for just a few moments, he'd been able to be just another ordinary human being enjoying the company of a beautiful woman.

Chapter 9

A shadow loomed over Talia, momentarily blocking the sun. Her eyes, which had been half closed, flew open, and she saw Garon standing over her, a towel over one arm and holding a bottle of sunblock in his other hand.

"Xander wishes you to be better protected from the sun," Garon rumbled out in his deep voice.

"Uh, okay."

She reached for the bottle, but Garon instead extended his hand down to grip hers. She looked at him in confusion, but he tugged her gently upward until she rolled out of the hammock she'd been lazing in.

"There's a lounger just over there," Garon said. "If you'll disrobe, I'll lay out the towel so you can lie down on it while I apply your sunblock."

She couldn't help the flutter of nervousness that rose into her throat at the thought of once again being naked in front of him and whoever else happened to be watching.

The robe offered little-to-no coverage, but it still made her feel better to have something rather than be stark naked.

She took a deep breath, determined to get over the burst of panic that accompanied what would likely be a routine request from this point forward. Xander had told her as much already. Naked. He—they—wanted her naked at all times.

She let the robe slide over her shoulders and down her body to pool at her feet. She walked robotically toward the lounger, determined that she would get over this self-consciousness.

Garon moved around her and quickly arranged the plush towel and then motioned her down.

"Lie on your belly first so I can do your back. Then I'll have you turn over so I can do the rest."

Grateful that she could ease into the whole experience by shielding most of her nudity at least for a little while, she crawled onto the lounger and settled down, resting her cheek against the warm cushion.

For a moment she was tense, the anticipation wracking her already overwrought nerves. Then his hands came down over her shoulders and she went rigid.

"Relax," he murmured. "This is supposed to feel good."

The deep, husky timbre of his voice was a balm to her discomfort. She did as he commanded and let herself go limp. Her muscles ached but the moment his hands slid over her skin, she let out a sigh and sagged onto the lounger.

He worked with patience and great attention to detail. He left no spot uncovered as he massaged his way down her body.

When his hands closed over her behind, she let out a soft moan. Embarrassed to have let it slip, she clamped her lips shut and focused on enjoying the wicked sensations he invoked.

He lingered longer over the globes of her ass, massaging, caressing, sliding his palms up to the small of her back, spanning her waist and then working back down. She'd swear he was a professional at giving massages. She was out of her head with pleasure.

She was nearly unconscious when he lifted her into his arms and rolled her onto her back. Holy hell, but the man was strong. He very carefully put her down, making sure the towel was still in place. He even pushed back her hair, winding it around one hand before tucking it behind her neck.

If this was any indication of how the next six months was going to go, she was going to live a fantasy existence. She wasn't entirely certain about the sex aspect of it yet. She wasn't entirely ignorant of the practice. But the way they handled her told her that they would likely be generous and thoughtful lovers.

Waited on hand and foot by four gorgeous men. Pampered endlessly. Spoiled rotten. And this was supposed to be her repayment of a debt? If this was debt repayment, then she was going to have no compunction about incurring it regularly.

This time he started at her feet and damn if the man probably knew exactly what he was doing by making her wait for him to touch her more intimately.

The anticipation was killing her. Her insides began to quiver. Her breasts tingled, tightened, and her nipples were so hard that the slightest breeze brushing across the tips sent jolts of pleasure winging through her body.

Her groin ached and tightened unbearably. She was damp and her clit throbbed. And he hadn't even come near her pussy or her breasts yet. Maybe he wouldn't even touch them.

At this point, she might sob in frustration if he didn't.

Closer and closer his hands crept as he caressed his way up her legs. Both hands circled one leg, moving upward, parting her thighs. His knuckles barely brushed against her lips but it was enough to send a shiver rolling over her entire body.

Then he moved to the other leg and began lower, working his way higher until he reached the same spot.

To her utter chagrin, he moved up to her belly, smoothing more of the lotion over her upper pelvis and abdomen. He moved in a circular motion, sliding closer to her breasts with every stroke.

With one hand, palm flat on her belly, he moved up her midline, between her breasts to the hollow of her throat. She swallowed, her throat moving up and down underneath his fingers. He drew his hand away long enough to squeeze another small portion of the sunblock into his palm and then he carefully cupped the swell of her breast.

She inhaled sharply, her chest rising with the swift intake of breath. Slowly and methodically he worked in a circle around her nipple. Frustration rose sharp and unrelenting. She wanted . . .

She wanted him to do something. Something more. This was a slow, torturous tease. She wanted him to touch her. Images of his mouth sucking at her nipples flashed in her mind. She wanted that. Anything but this awful hunger that gnawed at her.

"Garon, please."

The softly spoken plea escaped despite her determination not to beg for what she wasn't even sure she could have.

His gaze met hers and she was drowning in those dark pools, mesmerized by the glowing intensity. He lowered his head and she held her breath until she was light-headed. Maybe this was why he hadn't touched her nipples. If he was going to put his mouth on them, he wouldn't have wanted to taste the sunblock.

Oh please, please, let him put his mouth on her. She burned with need. He'd stoked the embers into a raging fire. Every cell of her body screamed for release.

When his mouth hovered mere centimeters above her hardened nipple, he swept his tongue out and licked the point.

She nearly shot off the lounger. She gasped and bowed upward, shocked by the sheer force of her reaction. It was like being struck by lightning.

"Easy," he murmured, his voice gentle and soothing. "Relax."

How was she supposed to relax when every one of her muscles was tied into a rigid knot?

Lazily his tongue traced a circle around her nipple until it was puckered and painfully erect. And then finally, finally he put his mouth on her, sucking the bud between his lips.

She groaned and closed her eyes even as she arched into him, wanting more. Her pussy throbbed and her stomach clenched with desperate need.

He turned his attention to her other breast, giving it equal treatment. He was maddeningly patient and very exacting. She wanted it harder. Something more. Something to send her hurtling over the edge.

On his knees beside her lounger, his dark head to her breasts, he continued the delicious assault on her senses. But then a shadow fell over them, much like when Garon had come to her at the hammock.

She glanced up to see Xander standing at the foot of the lounger, his eyes smoldering with seductive heat.

How long had he been there? Had he been watching all along?

And then another thought alarmed her. Was this what she should be doing? Was it what Garon was supposed to be doing? He'd told her he was supposed to apply sunblock. Would Xander be angry at the liberties Garon had taken and that she'd enjoyed?

Garon didn't seem bothered at all by Xander's appearance. He never paused in his attentions and continued to suck gently at her breasts.

Her gaze locked with Xander's, but then he lowered himself to his knees and leaned forward on the lounger, his body covering her legs. She could no longer see his face but she could feel him. Warm and hard as he parted her thighs.

Oh God.

She jittered from head to toe when he traced a single finger down the seam of her folds and then down to her entrance where he dipped just inside, teasing and tracing the opening.

With a firm hand, he pushed her thighs even farther apart until her feet landed on the stone surface of the terrace. His fingers toyed with her, playing a moment before parting the folds.

The moment his tongue touched her, she shook uncontrollably. Every muscle contracted and she cried out in shock. In pleasure. In complete bewilderment of the overwhelming sensation of having two men using their mouths to pleasure her.

Xander's tongue slid sensuously around her clit and then over it. Traveled down her slit and to her opening. After teasing the entrance with erotic swipes of his tongue, he traveled back to her clit. He sucked gently, pulling the taut nub into his mouth while flicking his tongue lightly with repeated strokes.

She trembled, unable to control it. Her knees shook. Her fingers curled and flexed spasmodically.

Garon began sucking harder, alternating between her breasts. Then he added his fingers to the nipple not in his mouth and he pinched it carefully between two fingers, rolling the point and adding the edge she so desperately needed.

Xander slid his hands underneath her behind, cupping her ass, holding her to his mouth while he licked and sucked her into a frenzy.

A wave of heat flushed through her body. The sun danced on her skin, so hot she was sure she was sweating now. She was spinning out of control, no longer able to hold in the gasps and moans as her body tightened and clenched.

And then Xander slid his tongue inside her, sucking hard at her opening while Garon bit down on her nipple. It was like being rocket propelled. All the tension exploded from her body like a rubber band breaking at full stretch.

The recoil was breathtaking. Such exquisite, mind-numbing

pleasure rocked through her very core. She writhed helplessly, not able to remain still. Her body seemed to have a will of its own and she couldn't hold it all in.

She couldn't seem to catch her breath. She wasn't even aware of Xander lifting her until she realized she was in his arms and he was rocking her back and forth, murmuring to her in a soothing voice.

"Breathe now, Talia," he said.

He held her tightly, his heat surrounding her. His strength holding her up. Her body was hypersensitive. Each nerve ending was spasming to the point of pain. She shuddered, not even wanting to be touched. She couldn't bear it right now.

She clung to Xander, holding him tightly as she came down off the highest of highs. The concept of an orgasm wasn't foreign to her, but holy hell, until experienced, it simply couldn't be explained.

That had to have been the mother of all orgasms because if women felt like this every time, they'd never do anything but have sex twenty-four hours a day.

Xander chuckled. "I'd ask you if it was good, but I'd say your reaction is evidence enough that it was an enjoyable experience for you."

"Enjoyable experience?" she croaked. "An enjoyable experience is having afternoon tea with your mother. That was . . . I can't even describe it. It was amazing."

Garon laughed and she looked up, seeking him out. He was standing a short distance away, looking unruffled by it all. But when her gaze tracked lower, she could see that he wasn't at all unaffected by the experience. He was hard as stone, his erection clearly outlined against the denim of his jeans.

The more she slipped into the postorgasmic phase, the more shy she became. She was stark naked in the lap of the man who'd just gone down on her while another had sucked at her breasts like a man starved.

She buried her face in Xander's neck, willing the heat in her cheeks to go away.

Xander chuckled again and brushed a kiss across her hair. "So shy. Whatever are we going to do about you, Talia?"

She snuggled farther into his embrace, liking the intimacy of being held so closely. Her orgasm had been shattering, and she was left feeling vulnerable after being stripped so bare.

"Has she been fully covered with sunblock?" Xander asked Garon.

"Yes. Head to toe."

"Bring the beach umbrella over and set it up so we're shaded from the sun and then have Wickersham bring us drinks and a snack. I'll remain here with Talia while she rests for a while. I'll want her to recover before we go any further today."

Talia stirred drowsily against Xander as his words sank in. Further? Even as limber and sated as she currently felt, the knowledge that there would be more stirred her blood and fired some vivid fantasies about just what they'd have in store for her next.

Chapter 10

Talia drank sweet juice, snacked on fruit and cheese and dozed on and off in Xander's arms as the sun rose higher overhead. She was wonderfully content to remain in his arms as he fed her grapes and stroked her hair.

Through her haze, she remembered that it was a phone update on Cristofino that had called him away in the first place. Without moving her cheek from his shoulder, she murmured, "How did the update go?"

His hand continued to trail lazily up and down her arm and he remained silent a moment. Then he sighed. "There is still much arguing and bickering and there are daily protests in the capital and outside the palace gates. There is much unrest and it would seem that the dissatisfaction grows at an alarming rate with each passing day."

"I hate that," she said passionately. "I want to be able to go home. I want Mama to be able to go home. She's been away for so long. It's all she talks about. But I don't want her to see Cristofino like that. It would break her heart. She wept when she heard the news of your father's death."

Xander kissed her forehead. "I want my mother to be able to go home as well."

Talia lifted her head, pushing herself upward so she could look at him. His gaze was troubled, his lips set into a firm line.

"Where is she, Xander? Or can you say? You haven't spoken of her. There seems to be no news of her whereabouts. In Paris, the television stations reported that your mother and members of your family were able to escape but that you had remained behind. Is she safe now?"

"I can't discuss where she is now, only that she is safe and well cared for. We all wait, hoping that our people will not support the rebels' vision of government. If I return at the wrong moment, it could mean more violence. For now, it is better that I remain in exile. I won't risk my mother by having her return to an unstable country whose infrastructure is on the verge of collapse."

Talia lowered her head back down to rest on his shoulder. "I'm sorry, Xander. I know your uncle is responsible for much of this. It must pain you that he would betray your father as he did in his bid to seize power."

"I do not wish to discuss it," Xander said in a terse tone.

Talia went quiet, not wanting to further upset him. It had been stupid of her to ruin a perfect afternoon by asking him for details that she had no right to know.

After a while, Xander squeezed her to him. "I'm sorry, Talia. I shouldn't have snapped at you. What occurred in my country is still a fresh wound that will never heal until I've rectified the wrongs done to my family. I had no right to vent my ire on you."

She hugged him to her. "There is no need to apologize. I shouldn't have pried."

"Come, let's go inside. The sun is intense this time of day. Are you rested?"

A tingle of excitement slivered through her veins. What she thought he was asking was whether she was recovered enough to endure more. More what, she wasn't sure, but she was eager to find out.

"I'm perfectly rested," she said. "You spoil me so, Xander. All I've done since arriving is rest and enjoy the beauty around me."

He smiled and lowered his mouth to kiss her. "That is good. You are a woman meant to be spoiled."

He helped her to her feet and then got out of the lounger. They walked up the steps leading to the upper terrace. Outside the doors leading inside, they kicked off their shoes before Xander led her back into the villa.

The cooler air sent a shiver over her skin after her being in the sun for so long. It had been easy to forget that she was naked and had been for the majority of the day. How easily she was already becoming acclimated.

In the middle of the large sitting area was a large, plush-looking cushion.

"Go kneel on the pillow," Xander directed her.

Her first instinct was to hesitate, to question, but she was fast learning her role. She was also learning that she had no desire to disappoint Xander—or the others. They seemed so eager to please her and in return, Xander had asked only for complete obedience. She intended to give it to him.

She dropped his hand and walked to where the deep-red-colored cushion lay on the floor. It was thoughtful that if he'd expected her to kneel, that he'd provided a barrier to the stone tile of the floor.

She sank to her knees, settling onto the comfortable pillow.

"Up higher," Xander said from across the room. "Up on your

knees. Pull your hair back and then place your hands at your sides."

Gone was the tender, gentle tone of the man who spoke of spoiling her, replaced by the steel thread of command.

She complied, pushing up to her knees so that her bottom no longer rested on the backs of her legs. She pulled her hair over her shoulders, letting it fall down her back and then she placed her hands down at her sides.

"Very nice."

There was approval in Xander's voice that gave her satisfaction. She wanted to please him.

From the corner of her eye, she saw Xander take a seat in one of the comfortable leather armchairs a short distance away. She wasn't certain what exactly was in store for her, but she was hyped on nervous energy and intensely curious.

Her gaze jerked up when she heard footsteps. Garon entered the room. He glanced her way, his heated gaze traveling over her body, but he made no move toward her. Instead he went to sit in one of the chairs by Xander.

A moment later, Nico followed behind and he too gifted her with an appreciative look that curled her toes. But he, like Garon, found a seat to slouch in.

She managed to keep her frown to herself. Was she to be an ornament on display? She hated not knowing.

Several minutes passed. She grew fidgety and flexed her fingers. So okay, she probably wasn't good submissive material. It wasn't that she didn't have what it took to submit or to be obedient. She was just . . . impatient. And impetuous. She wasn't used to having to restrain herself or her responses. This all felt extremely alien to her.

Another set of footsteps sounded. She looked up and this time saw Sebastien standing across from her, his eyes gleaming as he took in her pose. Instead of going to sit as the others had, he walked toward her.

He stopped right in front of her and reached down to cup her jaw.

"I wonder if you have any idea how you look to me? To them? A beautiful woman, naked, kneeling in submission, awaiting our pleasure. I wonder if you realize how much power *you* have."

She raised an eyebrow at his choice of words. Power? She wouldn't have thought she had any. She'd signed away any power, any choice she had when she'd agreed to this whole arrangement. And yet somehow she thought he was talking about a different kind of power altogether. Feminine power.

He rubbed his thumb over her cheek, still holding her so that she was forced to look up at him. "Tell me, Talia, have you ever seen a man's cock?"

Her eyes narrowed. "You showered with me. Of course I have."

"Other than mine," he said softly.

"I've seen . . . pictures."

"So you've never held one. Never touched one. Never had one in your mouth."

She blushed and shook her head, not able to speak without squeaking in embarrassment.

He released her jaw and then reached for the zipper of his pants. The sound was loud in the silence, the rasp sending chills over her skin. He unbuttoned his jeans and pushed just enough that they were down around his hips.

"Well, my innocent little virgin. You're going to learn to suck cock," he said in a lazy tone. "When I've finished, you'll suck the cocks of every man in this room."

She watched in fascination as he reached into his underwear and pulled out his penis. It was already hard. Erect and long. Thick. Jutting upward toward his belly.

Yes, she'd seen it in the shower and yes, it had been somewhat erect. But not like this. Not so huge and powerful-looking. There was no way she was getting all of that in her mouth.

He fisted the base with one hand and reached for her jaw with his other.

"First and most important rule. No teeth. Tongue and lips only. Use suction but not too much. The idea is to tease and then—"

She rolled her eyes and slid her hand up his leg and gently pushed his hand from the base of his erection. Okay, so she was a virgin. It didn't make her an idiot. And no, she hadn't ever sucked cock as he'd so eloquently put it, but this wasn't rocket science. Instinct made up for a lot and she was certainly intelligent enough and had enough imagination that she could damn well rock his world without any condescending lectures on the proper way to give head.

He broke off with a strangled sound as she grasped his length in her hand and rolled her tongue over the head.

It was a heady sensation to have him in the palm of her hand. He was right. She did have power. She hadn't imagined it would be so sinfully satisfying.

He let out another gasp that sounded like a cross between a groan and an oath when she carefully sucked the tip into her mouth and glided down his erection, careful to keep her teeth from grazing the sensitive flesh.

She bowed her head, working down as far as she could take him and then rolled her tongue up the length as she retraced the path she'd just taken.

He was hard and hot against her palm. She tightened her hold, instinctively adding pressure. As she balanced the crown of his erection on her tongue, she rolled her hand upward. With her other hand, she reached to cup the heavy weight of his sac.

She pulled her head away, licking the very tip and over the slit before angling her head to look up at him. She smiled innocently. "Am I doing it right?"

His nostrils flared and he thrust his hand into her hair. He closed his fist, pulling it tight against her scalp. "Hell, yes, you little vixen. You've definitely got the tease part down. Where the hell did you learn to do that?"

The possessive growl and the hint of jealousy she heard in his voice amused her.

"I didn't learn anywhere," she said honestly. "I wanted to touch you. I was curious. I liked the way you felt in my hand and in my mouth. I just did what came natural."

"By all means continue doing what comes natural," Sebastien drawled. "I'm going to keep *my* mouth shut and let you do your thing."

Her fingers rubbed through the crisp hairs on his balls and at the base of his cock. She loved the contrast of rough and silky smooth.

She flicked her tongue out again to circle the head, inhaling his scent as she tasted him. His hand remained fisted in her hair. His grip didn't lessen, and when she took him deep, it grew tighter as he held her in place.

His hips surged forward, seeking more depth. At first she fought the invasion, the sensation of so much, so deep, unsettling to her. Her hands flew to his thighs and she tried to push back, but he held her firm.

"Let her go, Bastien."

Startled, Talia rocked back on her heels when Sebastien released his grip. His cock bobbed, hugely erect, almost angry-looking as he took a step back.

Nico had voiced the command and now from behind her, he framed her face in his hands, caressing and then delving into her hair, almost as if he were petting her.

"You get too carried away," Nico said in reprimand. "She is new to this. You can't treat her like someone used to rougher treatment."

Sebastien didn't look at all happy over Nico's interference. He reached down to grasp his cock and stroked back and forth before taking a step forward, closing the distance between them once more.

"Then you hold her and show her," Sebastien said silkily. "I want her mouth. I don't care how it's done."

Nico leaned down and pressed a kiss to the top of Talia's head. "Trust me. Leave your hands down. Let him direct the action. I'll be here, holding you and I won't let him go too far."

She had no idea what it said about her that she found the idea of Nico holding her head while Sebastien fucked her mouth . . . hot. Intensely erotic. Her entire body flushed with heat and her nipples hardened.

She relaxed in Nico's hands and allowed him to hold her in place while Sebastien fit his cock to her mouth.

"Open for me, Talia," Sebastien commanded. "Let me inside that gorgeous mouth of yours."

She sighed and breathed him in as he pushed forward. It was like the first time as he slid over her tongue. This time she forced none of the action. She was held immobile as Sebastien used her as a receptacle for his pleasure.

Nico's touch was gentle and reassuring and yet firm. He pushed forward, forcing her to meet Sebastien's thrusts, and yet he knew just when to pull back and ease her away before it became too much.

Soon, his hands left her cheeks and twisted in her hair, holding the mass in his hands as Sebastien worked deeper and harder into her mouth.

Her eyes cut over toward Xander. She wondered what he made of this. He wasn't participating. He hadn't uttered a single word. He seemed content to allow his men to dictate the scene.

When she saw the raw satisfaction on his face and the way he leaned back, taking in every detail, she realized that he liked watching. He was obviously turned on by watching the erotic scene unfold in front of him. It made sense, then, why he encouraged participation of the men closest to him and why he'd made it clear from the start that she would accommodate—and obey—them all.

"I'm going to come in your mouth, Talia," Sebastien said in a hoarse voice. "And I want you to swallow every drop."

Nico made a disapproving sound and then bent so his mouth was close to Talia's ear. "Relax and don't fight it. If it frightens you, just open your mouth and let it spill over your lips. Don't panic. I'll make him stop if it's too much."

She couldn't nod for Sebastien's forceful thrusts. Nico was there, his hands a comforting reminder. She closed her eyes and gave herself over to the experience of being between two completely different men.

For all of Sebastien's seeming hard-ass ways, his thrusts were measured. He didn't try to force himself too deep or too hard. He didn't gag her or try to stuff himself down her throat. But he was hard and he was in command. She never doubted that for a moment.

And then Sebastien's hands joined Nico's. Sebastien held her jaw while Nico's hands twisted in her hair and supported her neck.

Sebastien went tense. His legs rippled, the muscles bulging against the denim of his jeans. His arms went rigid and then he threw back his head, a sound of wild excitement rushing from his lips.

The first spurt caught her completely by surprise. It was warm and slightly salty. It hit the back of her throat and her first reaction was to reject it.

Sebastien continued thrusting, and his cock sliding through a mouth filled with cum made wet, sucking noises. She opened her mouth, gasping as more shot into her mouth.

Semen spilled over her lips and there was nothing she could do to call it back. It took all her concentration not to struggle and try to yank her head away. She was overwhelmed and consumed by the raw power of the experience.

His cock was slippery with his release and he continued to slide in and out, spilling more of the cum down her chin. All the while, Nico's hands gently caressed her neck and his fingers threaded through her hair. He murmured close to her ear but she couldn't hear over the roar of her own pulse.

Finally, Sebastien slowed and for a long moment he remained in her mouth, his fingers digging into her jaw. Then he loosened his hold and carefully withdrew.

His cock slid downward, hanging in a semierect state as he backed away. His gaze burned over her and she tensed, expecting censure.

He reached down with one finger and wiped off some of the semen from her lips and then slid his finger into her mouth.

She sucked it off and dutifully swallowed.

"Forget all I said about swallowing every drop," he said in a raspy voice. "My cum all over your mouth and chin, dripping onto the floor is the sexiest damn thing I've ever seen in my life."

He leaned farther down and kissed her forehead, his mouth gentle against her skin.

As he stepped back, Nico lifted her to her feet and then turned her. Garon handed him a washcloth and Nico carefully wiped away the remnants of Sebastien's release from her face. Then Nico pulled her into his arms, hugging her tightly against him.

She sighed and laid her head on his shoulder, liking the comfort of a quick snuggle.

He smoothed the hair behind her ear and then kissed the spot just above it before murmuring, "Go to Xander and rest a moment."

Chapter 11

Talia went to where Xander sat on the couch. Though he didn't
tell her what to do, she felt it would please him if she knelt before
him. In the very short time she'd been here, she'd formed the idea
that Xander was aroused and satisfied by visual representations.

Though he'd demanded her obedience and she'd signed a contract and then verbally agreed upon her arrival, until he saw it in
action, they were mere words and terms.

She stood in front of him for a mere second before she sank
gracefully to her knees between his.

Xander's eyes glowed and he reached to touch her cheek, her
chin, where just moments earlier the semen from another man had
smeared.

"Come to me," he said in a husky whisper. "Sit astride me. I
want to look and touch you."

She pushed upward and then moved forward, a little uncertain
as to what he wanted. But he reached out a hand, grasped hers
and guided her further between his legs. Then he wrapped his
hands around her waist and urged her to straddle his lap.

The position forced her thighs apart when her knees settled on either side of his legs. Her breasts were on eye level and her hair was wild and windblown over her shoulders.

"You're a beautiful woman. You please me greatly, Talia. As I knew you would."

Eagerness to assuage her curiosity overruled all good sense. She blurted out the question before she could think better of it.

"How could you know such a thing? Why am I here? I mean I know why, but why me in particular? You could have any woman, Xander. You must know that. There are women all over the world who would share your bed and participate in sex however you wanted it."

He didn't react to her barrage. He simply stared at her with those dark, sexy eyes. He slid one hand up her leg, around the curve of her hip and then up to cup her breast.

"Is it important? What is important is that you are here and you are mine. You've agreed to serve me, to pleasure me, in whatever capacity I wish. That is what is important to me, Talia."

Suitably chastened, she nodded.

"Tell me something. Are you still frightened of me? Of us?" He waved his hand to include Nico, Garon and Sebastien.

She frowned and nibbled at her lower lip and then slowly shook her head. "I was never frightened," she said softly. "Not in a physical sense. I mean, I didn't think you would abuse me in any way. I was nervous, not scared. There's a big difference. I guess you could say I was afraid of the unknown, of what your expectations would be, but I've never thought you were anything but an honorable man."

His eyes warmed as if he were pleased with her explanation.

"And tell me this. Does the idea of being with more than one man alarm you? Does it embarrass you? Or . . . does it excite you?"

She glanced over her shoulder, having no idea how seductively innocent she looked to the other men in the room. Garon swallowed, feeling a surge of protectiveness and lust—so strong his hands shook. Nico inhaled, captivated by the shyness in her eyes but also by the curiosity there. Sebastien felt a fist to the gut. He was impossibly sated but the memory of her mouth around him made his dick surge to life again.

He felt regret for the way he'd handled her. It was a defense mechanism, one he was well acquainted with. Rather than admit to any softness when it came to this woman, he acted the domineering bastard instead. It was all sex. All about his pleasure. Calculated. A bodily function, nothing more.

He knew it was bullshit, but Talia didn't. She likely thought he was the biggest asshole in the world and he suddenly wanted nothing more than the opportunity to make it up to her.

He stared at Xander over Talia's head, their gazes connecting. Sebastien grimaced, knowing it would convey more than words would and that Xander would understand. Xander knew him better than anyone, and he knew Sebastien was more guarded than most about allowing anyone to see him vulnerable.

Xander gave an almost imperceptible nod, letting Sebastien know he understood.

Talia found it hard to look Xander in the eye, but his hand cupped her chin, forcing her to do just that.

She sucked in her breath, bracing herself to be honest and truthful. She wasn't deceitful by nature. She hated lies and she felt compelled to be straightforward with Xander—with all of them. They'd been patient—somewhat—with her. And they'd treated her very, very well.

"I'm nervous about it," she admitted. "Not because I'm horrified. I'm curious too and maybe a little excited. You've all been . . . wonderful. It's been surreal, almost like some over-the-top fantasy you read about but never think to actually experience."

"That's understandable," he said with a nod. "You're a virgin and innocent of such things. I don't expect you to know exactly your feelings, but I want to know if you are truly frightened of anything we do."

She nodded, some of the tension knotting her shoulders seeping away.

He stroked a palm over her cheek and ran a finger over her lips that were still swollen from Sebastien's use of them.

"Tell me something, Talia, and I want you to think on it a moment before you respond."

Her brows furrowed and a flutter rose in her stomach at his odd tone.

"There is no question that I will be the one to take your virginity. You belong to me and this will be symbolic of that fact. But the question I put to you is whether you want them present and perhaps participating to a degree or would you prefer it to be you and I alone when I fully make love to you for the first time?"

Her eyes widened at the blunt question.

He touched his finger to her lips again to quiet any response.

"Let me finish."

She nodded.

"If they are there, they will be there to help you relax. They'll touch you. They'll caress you. They'll offer you comfort and support. But I and I alone will be the one who possesses your body."

She licked her lips and then pursed them thoughtfully. "What do you prefer, Xander? You like to watch. That much I've already realized. But do you like being watched?"

The corner of his mouth lifted. "Examining just how depraved I am?"

She shrugged. "You're the one who likes to watch your possession, in this case me, pleasuring other men. My virginity pleases you. I could tell it was important even before I arrived here. It was the first question I was asked when I was approached by your representative and then during my examination and testing at the physician you'd selected, he verified that my virginity was still intact. You have these conditions. You've set the rules. You want to be the first man I take into my body. So it's a logical question of whether you want other men present when you claim what it is you seem to value so much."

His hands slid over her breasts, toying with her nipples until she was ready to squirm off his lap. She was still buzzed, sort of on a high from the episode with Sebastien. It had left her hungry and aroused. On edge and unsatisfied.

"Yes, I'm aware of all that," he said smoothly, seemingly unperturbed by her turning the tables on him. "What I want to know is if you would find pleasure and reassurance in them being there. If you would enjoy their hands and mouths on you. Soon enough we'll all share your delectable body. I thought perhaps it would soothe any nervousness on your part if they were there from the beginning."

He'd effectively dodged any discussion on his preferences or proclivities, and she sensed they could go round and round all afternoon and never really get to the answers to any of the questions she posed.

She gave one more peek over her shoulder, glancing quickly at each of the men in turn, almost as if asking what *they* wanted. Maybe she was. But they all looked calmly back at her, as if telling her the choice was hers and hers alone and that they would abide by her wishes.

Again, she felt that sensation of power. Of holding perceived power over these men. It didn't at all jibe with how she'd thought this whole experience would be like, but she felt less vulnerable now that she realized she wasn't completely without power or control.

In Garon and Nico, she saw the promise of support. She also saw a sensual light that told her they wanted to be present even if they weren't going to be making love to her. But they would be, right? Xander had said they'd touch and caress. They just wouldn't penetrate her. And there was so much more to lovemaking than just the actual penetration.

Then she glanced back at Sebastien, not at all sure what she would see in his eyes. She caught her breath at the intensity of his gaze. He looked . . . grim and apologetic. As she stared at him, he slid a hand behind his neck and his shoulders heaved with the deep breath he took.

"There's something I want to say," Sebastien broke in.

He glanced beyond Talia to Xander as if seeking permission.

Xander shifted and then lifted her so she sat across his lap instead of astride him. She could see the others more easily now instead of having to crane her neck looking over her shoulder.

Xander's hand slipped underneath her hair to her nape and he squeezed gently, rubbing and massaging.

"What is it you would like to say, Bastien?"

"I want to offer Talia an apology," he said gruffly.

Talia's eyes widened in surprise. She quickly shut her mouth when it gaped open.

"Say what's on your mind," Xander said calmly.

Sebastien rubbed a hand through his hair. "I was too rough and too impatient with you, Talia. The truth is, I wanted you desperately. Nico shouldn't have had to step in, but I'm glad he did. I shouldn't have used you the way I did. I—we—promised to treat you with the gentleness and respect you deserve. We made a pact to introduce you to sex with patience and reverence. I broke it and I wouldn't blame you if you wanted nothing more to do with me."

She stared at him in bewilderment. How could she explain that she'd craved that forceful dominance? Yes, she'd been intimidated at first. A little hesitant and overwhelmed. But the roughness had excited her. She was still on edge from the experience.

"I just want you to know, that if you want us—me—to be with you this first time, that I'll make sure you are pleasured beyond imagination. I'll make sure that you're cherished as we've sworn to do. And I'll do my best to ease any nerves or fear that you have of your first time being with a man."

Touched by the sincerity in his voice and seduced by the promise in the words, she glanced one more time at Garon and Nico and saw the same vow simmering in their gazes. Then she turned back to Xander, more confident in voicing her desires now.

"I want them there," she said in a low voice. "If . . . if I am to be with them, if you're going to share me with them, then I'd like for them to be there this first time."

Chapter 12

The sky was aglow with gold and pink when Talia stepped onto the terrace with Xander. The sun was gradually sinking over the horizon, leaving behind a splash of wondrous color that spread outward as far as the eye could see.

"It's beautiful," she said breathlessly.

Around the terrace, several torches had been lit and there was what looked like mosquito netting erected around the large area of the terrace.

"So the bugs won't be a bother," Xander said, noticing her observation.

Talia took the seat offered to her and Wickersham appeared at the table to pour wine. After he left and Xander took his own seat, Talia reached for her glass and studied him over the rim.

"How much of a staff do you employ?" she asked curiously.

His brows came together and he seemed puzzled by the question. "Are you concerned that they will see you or be privy to what we do?"

She frowned. She hadn't even considered that aspect and now that he'd brought it up, it did concern her.

"Well, no, I hadn't. At least until now. I was merely curious because I never see anyone. I know Wickersham is here. I know what he does and yet I rarely see him. Surely you have a staff to serve you and yet I only ever see you, Garon, Nico and Sebastien."

Xander smiled. "I employ a full staff, but I pay them to remain behind the scenes as much as possible. Particularly since you arrived. I didn't assign a maid to you simply because I planned for myself and my men to take care of all your needs."

"Oh, I wasn't complaining, I mean, I don't require a servant. I just found it so odd that the villa seems devoid of people I know must be lurking somewhere."

"They are paid to remain unseen but ready to handle any issue that arises."

She nodded and sipped at the wine. Wickersham returned, bearing dinner plates and the aroma wafted delicately through the air. She sniffed appreciatively and reached for her fork. The steak medallions looked perfectly cooked and smelled even more wonderful.

As soon as Wickersham retreated, Xander looked across the table at her. "If you're concerned that tonight won't be private, let me assure you that no one intrudes in my bedroom. I'll be taking you to my bed and there'll be no chance of anyone seeing or hearing what goes on when I make love to you."

"Thank you for letting me know," she said softly. There were enough things to be nervous about without adding a public deflowering to the mix.

But then she supposed it was sort of public since three other men would be present.

"Will Garon, Sebastien and Nico be joining us for dinner?" she asked.

Xander shook his head. "They await us in the bedroom. It's

my job to make sure you enjoy your dinner and that you are relaxed and at ease for what comes later."

"I hate to break this to you, but the fact that such a production has been made of this means I'm just going to be even more nervous," she admitted.

He put both his fork and knife down, frowning as he stared across the table at her.

"Production?"

She sighed. "I feel like a virgin sacrifice, like I'm going to be led to the altar for the ceremonial deflowering. It feels . . . well, it doesn't feel natural. A girl has expectations about the first time. Sometimes they're unrealistic, but we still imagine how it's going to be."

"And how did you picture this first time?"

She chewed absently on a bite of the tender, delicious meat and then sighed as she set her fork down as well. "Maybe not so clinical? It doesn't really matter, because there's no possible way for my first time to go anything like I'd imagined because at no time did I ever think that I'd be on an island with four men who all expected to have sex with me. You have to admit, that's not something that happens every day."

If possible, he frowned even harder. "How did you imagine it?"

"I guess a little more . . . romantic. Maybe I just can't get over the idea that I've somehow sold myself—and maybe I have. I can't really explain to you how I feel because I can't even sort it out myself."

"You believe you sold yourself?"

She flinched away from the fury in his voice and then her eyes widened at the look of anger in his eyes. "Sugarcoating it doesn't change what I've done."

Xander shook his head. "I've done this all wrong. Forgive me, Talia. I never meant to make you feel . . . bought . . . or bartered. Or cheapened. None of those things."

He glanced at her plate, his mouth forming a grimace. "Please eat. We'll continue this conversation after you've finished. I don't want this to ruin the meal."

He seemed distressed by her evaluation of the situation, but how could he be? He set it up. A pure business arrangement complete with contract and terms.

She picked at her food, appetite mostly gone. Knowing what lay ahead and now Xander's peculiar reaction to her assessment of their "relationship" had done a number on her nerves.

He didn't want "this" to ruin the meal but what about the night? She was really starting to dread this whole ritual virginity thing. Sebastien may have been concerned with being too forceful but at least he hadn't drawn things out. He hadn't given her time to overthink every aspect of her presence here.

Now he was staring at her, as if waiting for her to finish the last bite. His own food had been left and he sat, tense, his expression pensive.

She sighed and pushed back her plate. "Is there something you want to say, Xander? I'm finished and I can't possibly eat with you staring at me anyway."

He rose abruptly and walked around to where she sat. He held his hand out. "Come with me, please. There are things I need to say."

It didn't come out as a crisp command. It lacked the authority and confidence that usually accompanied his requests. He sounded . . . uncertain and that unsettled her even more. What could he possibly have to say that would cause him such distress?

She stood, and he tucked her hand under his arm. He then steered her toward the steps down to the beach. He waited while she kicked off her sandals and then toed his own shoes off.

The sky had lightened to pink and blue pastels and in the distance one star shone, heralding the arrival of dusk. As they strolled down the stretch of beach, he kept them away from the water.

After a moment, he stopped and then let her hand fall down his arm until he grasped it and laced her fingers with his.

"Talia . . ." He sighed and brought her hand up between them so it rested against his chest. "I brought you here with a purpose. Perhaps, looking back, it was the wrong approach. It's difficult to explain really so I'll need to provide some back story."

"O-okay."

Her voice stuttered out in a whispery rush.

"I've been rather preoccupied with you since the first day I saw you in my office and you knocked over the vase. You were all of eighteen years old and I knew my attraction was inappropriate and yet I couldn't help myself."

Her eyes widened in shock and she stared back at him, mouth open at his admission. What he was saying was insane. Princes didn't become preoccupied with girls like her. Definitely not grubbily attired girls who'd been working in the garden.

"I inquired about you and when I learned of your mother's condition and that you'd foregone university to take odd jobs to pay for your mother's treatment, I knew I couldn't allow it to continue. Even if it meant sending you away for a period of time."

This was becoming more bizarre by the moment but it explained so much because her biggest question had always been why? She'd assumed that he was just a benevolent benefactor, that he'd wanted to do good. And he had. She certainly wouldn't take that away from him.

"With your mother making so much progress and you graduating from university, I knew that I could very well lose you . . . to another man."

He grimaced then and looked abashed.

"I would have done anything to get you to come to me and I used the promise I extracted from you when I saw you last to get you here. The contract was so you'd know what you were getting into. A way out I suppose. I wanted you to have no surprises. I'm not proud of the way I summoned you to the island but I don't regret having you here. You should also know that I had no intention of limiting this to a six-month period of time together. I didn't want to overwhelm you from the onset so I put a time frame, hoping you would think six months wouldn't be too high a price to pay for what I'd done for you."

"You certainly had that much right," she murmured. "That was precisely the way I looked at it. Six months of my life, my pride, my honor was nothing compared to the life of my mother and the education I was able to gain."

He flinched. "Is being here with me so abhorrent, Talia? Can you look beyond the way I got you here to why? Can you possibly understand and forgive my deception?"

She swallowed and met his gaze directly, butterflies fluttering madly in her stomach. "You said you had no intention of keeping to the six months, Xander. What did you mean by that?"

He cupped her chin, tilting her face upward. His lips hovered over hers, so close she could feel the brush of his breath across her lips.

"I meant that I have no intention of letting you go. Ever."

Chapter 13

Talia trembled in Xander's fingers. As his statement settled over her, she stared up at him, uncomprehending what she'd heard.

"And the others?" she blurted out. "Are they just part of the charade or is this the way you want things?"

His thumb smoothed over her cheek. His expression was serious, his eyes dark and searching. "They are part of who I am, Talia. I didn't lie or mislead you about that. Everything you were informed of prior to your signing the contract is true and indicative of what being with me will be like."

"Oh," she said softly.

"You agreed before. You asked for them to be present when I make love to you the first time. What's changed?"

She shook her head slowly. "Nothing. It's just . . . different now. It's hard to comprehend. You wanting me. I'm still not sure what it all means."

"I think what this all means is that I need to be asking you how you feel . . . about me."

He kissed her then. Warm and gentle. Almost tentative as if he worried she would pull away. She leaned into him, enjoying the hard strength of his body. The way he seemed to encompass her. He wrapped one arm around her and pulled her in even tighter while his other hand tangled in her hair.

"Xander."

He slowly drew his mouth away, though he still held her tightly.

"I'm ready for you to make love to me," she whispered.

All the nervousness of earlier, the feelings of awkwardness and the sensation of the entire episode being clinical and cold had evaporated once he'd given his earnest confession.

She was still a little dazzled and unable to articulate her feelings—how could she? What she knew was that she was ready to give herself unreservedly to this man on his terms.

He turned back toward the house, her hand gripped in his. Several times he slowed to adjust his stride to hers as they walked through the sand, but she could sense his impatience. Tension coiled in his body. She could feel the tightness of his muscles, how hard he gripped her hand.

When they reached the steps, he didn't bother with their shoes but simply whisked her onto the veranda and then inside the doors to the villa.

As soon as they reached the top of the stairs on the second floor, he swept her into his arms and carried her toward his suite. He nudged the door open with his shoulder and went straight toward the bedroom through the sitting area.

He paused just inside the door and turned Talia so she could see.

Garon stood by the window while Nico was sprawled in an armchair in the corner. Sebastien was on Xander's bed, leaned against the headboard with his feet propped at the end. They all turned their gaze on Talia and she shivered at the raw hunger in their eyes.

Excitement hurtled through her veins. She didn't fear this. It should terrify her by all rights. What she was doing just wasn't normal. It wasn't done.

It was erotic, forbidden and wickedly enticing.

Sebastien scrambled up and Xander strode to the bed where he placed her on the mattress. The simple sundress he'd had her wear for dinner suddenly didn't seem like much of a barrier when four hungry-looking men loomed over her.

She stared up as they circled the bed, standing, looking down at her with lust in their eyes. The feeling of helplessness was delicious. It sent a shiver of delight straight up her spine. Who knew that it would be such a huge turn-on to have sex with multiple men?

"Undress her," Xander said in a silky voice that sent a wave of goose bumps chasing over her skin.

Suddenly he was commander again. The authority. Gone was the earnest, almost vulnerable man who'd reluctantly admitted his feelings just moments earlier. In his place was a dominant, self-assured man who was incredibly aroused and ready to stake his claim.

For a moment, Xander was solidly in the background as the other three men descended on the bed. Sebastien was to her right, Garon on the left while Nico crawled up and hovered over her body.

Then Nico leaned down and swept her mouth into a tender kiss. His lips were firm, strong. His kiss was a reminder of all he'd promised.

As he drew away, his eyes flashed and he touched his hand to her cheek.

"We're here to make this very good for you. Whatever you want, whatever makes you feel good, you only have to say it and we'll make it happen."

She inhaled through her nose, her mind about to explode. This couldn't be happening. It was simply too mind-boggling to compute. This was a fantasy. A dream. It couldn't be real.

Garon slid his hand beneath her neck and lifted her upward while Sebastien slipped the straps of her sundress down her arms.

Nico pulled slowly at the bodice until it pushed over her breasts, freeing them from the slight restraint of the elastic binding.

Nico worked backward, taking the dress down her body as he moved closer to the end of the bed. At any other time she'd be cursing the fact that she had nothing on underneath the dress, but she was far too eager to experience this ultimate fantasy.

Garon's big hand glided over her belly and then up to cup one breast. She sucked in her breath when he lowered his head and traced a line around her taut nipple with his tongue.

On her other side, Sebastien stroked one hand over her hair before bending down to tease her nipple with his tongue as Garon was doing.

And then Nico kissed the flat of her belly, just over her navel.

She closed her eyes, reveling in the sinful decadence of having three men worship her with their mouths. Nico kissed a path down to her pelvis and then pressed his mouth to her mound, just above where her slit began and her clit already throbbed.

But he didn't touch her more intimately. Instead he carefully parted her legs and bent her knees so she was completely open and spread wide. Then he backed off the bed and walked around on Garon's side, but he went higher, climbing on the pillows next to her head.

He kissed her forehead and smoothed his hands through her hair while Garon and Sebastien continued to lavish attention on her breasts.

Xander stared at the erotic site of Talia being pleasured by the men he called friends. When Nico left her parted legs, Xander's gaze drank in the sight of her spread out. For him. His to claim and possess.

He had to remind himself that she was a virgin. She needed gentleness and patience from him. She didn't need him to be a raging sex fiend who fucked her into unconsciousness even if it was what he was dying to do.

He shrugged out of his clothing, his gaze still riveted to Garon and Sebastien as they sucked and toyed with her nipples. Their hands were splayed out across her body, possessive, a stark contract against her pale, fragile skin.

He wanted her like he wanted his next breath. He was afraid to touch her for fear of losing control. For a moment he stood transfixed by the sight before him, drinking in the sheer eroticism of hearing her soft sighs of pleasure.

As if sensing that Xander would stand back no longer, Garon and Sebastien pulled away and Talia lifted her head, her gaze meeting Xander's.

There was magic in that moment. It was like a fist to his gut. Trust. Shining in her eyes. Answering desire. But most importantly, trust. That he wouldn't hurt her. That he would bring her pleasure.

He put a knee onto the bed and pushed himself up and then crawled between her wide-spread knees. Planting his hands on either side of her body, he moved upward and then lowered himself down so that their mouths met in a heated rush.

Her breasts pressed into his chest. Her tongue met his, eager and impatient. Her legs closed around him, soft and silky against his skin.

She rubbed feverishly against him and made a purring sound deep in her throat that nearly sent him over the edge.

He closed his eyes and then slid his mouth down the side of her jaw to her ear where he licked and nibbled at the lobe. Just below it, he nipped and then sucked at the soft flesh.

She tightened immediately, her body convulsing against him. He smiled. He'd found a weakness. One of her sweet spots.

He grazed his teeth over the area again, and she moaned. He did his own amount of shivering when she slid her hands up his arms and then dug her fingers into his shoulders, holding on as he continued his relentless assault on her neck.

Methodically he worked his way down her body, tasting every

inch of her flesh on his way to her breasts. The plump swells were delectable. Firm but plush and so satiny to the touch.

Her nipples were hard and puckered, dark against the paleness of the flesh that had obviously never seen the sun. His Talia didn't sunbathe in the nude or self-tan as many women did. If the area of paler skin was any indicator, her bathing suits were extremely modest.

It made him a flaming hypocrite that he found satisfaction in the fact that other men hadn't been able to look upon her curves when he himself kept her naked at every opportunity and on display for him and the men he'd trusted to pleasure her.

He already knew he would be a possessive lover. Jealously guarding her from other men, or rather Garon, Sebastien and Nico would be charged with protecting her from all others.

All he had to do was look at her and he was seized by the insane urge to lock her in his bedroom and keep her naked and at his beck and call every moment of the day.

He sucked gently at her breasts, alternating between the two. He was hot and incredibly hard. His erection was painful, and it was difficult not to thrust himself into her body to seek relief.

Forcing himself to hold back and calm the roaring in his ears, the voice that told him to take her over and over, he instead continued to lick a path over her belly and lower to her sweet, feminine flesh.

He'd already seen the evidence of her virginity when he'd used his mouth on her before. He'd been careful then, not to breach the opening or cause her pain. But now he was ready to push inside her with a cock that was much bigger than the small opening made much smaller by the thin flap of flesh that signaled her innocence.

Sliding back until his knees were dug into the very edge of the bed, he nuzzled the velvety folds and then used his fingers to spread her farther apart so he could trace her sweetness with his tongue.

With the tip of his finger, he traced the nearly transparent flap of skin that covered part of her vaginal opening. He tested the strength, sliding his finger inside and pushing gently.

She immediately went tense and her head came up, her eyes flashing in alarm.

"It's okay, Talia," he soothed. "I'm going to be gentle, my love."

Sebastien moved close again and caressed her breast, his palm smoothing over her body in a comforting gesture. Garon also resumed his position and leaned down to suckle again as Xander continued his gentle exploration of her pussy.

He wanted her eager, aroused, nearly desperate for his possession. It was inevitable that he would cause her hurt. Her opening was small and he would have to break through the flesh to gain full entry into her body.

He lowered his mouth and licked sensuously over the sensitive flesh and working upward to tease her clit. She quivered beneath his mouth and he smiled, enjoying her reaction.

His men were doing their best to offer her comfort, support and pleasure. He wanted her to feel secure, never afraid. He wanted her full trust and he wanted her to know who owned her.

He sucked lightly at the tiny bundle of nerves until she writhed and moaned a desperate, needy sound.

"Xander, please," she whispered hoarsely.

He couldn't have denied her anything in that moment. He raised his head as Sebastien and Garon pulled away. Their gazes met and she was pleading with him with her eyes.

Carefully, Nico reached down, grasped her wrists and pulled her arms over her head. He threaded his fingers with hers, holding her hands in place.

Xander rose to his knees and positioned himself between her legs. He could barely stay upright. His erection was heavy and aching, so hard it was painful.

Sebastien took one of her hands from Nico and held it on the pillow next to her head. Garon cupped her breast possessively as Xander fit himself to her small opening.

With his thumb, he caressed her clit, rubbing it lightly in a circular motion as he began to push forward. She tensed again as he felt her began to stretch around him to accommodate his size.

Her forehead creased and uncertainty flashed in her eyes.

"Do it quickly, Xander," Sebastien muttered. "It'll be less painful that way."

Xander couldn't bear the thought of just plowing into her, but he also knew that Sebastien was right. Moving this slowly and stretching her until her flesh tore and opened for him was only going to prolong her discomfort. Better to have done with it.

He went still and she made a small sound of pain that sounded like a whimper. She was snug around him and he had yet to break through the flesh guarding her entrance.

"Hold on to them," he said in a strained voice. "I'm sorry, Talia. I do not want to hurt you more than necessary."

Before she could respond, he pushed through in one rapid motion. She cried out, but he felt the flesh give away and he was inside her snug passageway.

Tears glistened on her eyelashes and his chest caved in at the distress on her face.

He bent down, gathering her in his arms as he lowered his body to hers. It took all he had not to move within her but he was determined not to savage her with a mindless fucking when she was still adjusting to having a man inside her body.

He kissed away her tears. "Do you want me to stop?"

She shook her head and then raised her lips to his. "No, please. Just give me a moment."

He took what she offered so sweetly, sucking her tongue into his mouth and licking over it with his own. His body screamed at him to move, but his heart and mind told him to take care and to cherish the woman in his arms.

Breathless, melting kisses. The feel of her body against his. Her warmth surrounding him. The smell of her. The taste of her on his tongue.

His pulse echoed loudly in his ears, pounded at his temples. His jaw was tight as he pulled away from her swollen mouth. He stared down at her, drowning in her eyes, losing himself in her beauty and gentle spirit.

Very carefully, he pushed himself upward, gauging her reaction the entire way as he pushed the tiniest bit farther into her body.

Nico pressed his mouth to her forehead, taking up where Xander had left off and raining tender kisses over her face.

As Xander put more space between himself and Talia, Garon and Sebastien began to caress her belly, breasts and sliding up and down her midline, petting and soothing.

Talia gave a little sigh and seemed to relax. The tension that had been so readily evident in her face was starting to disappear and her eyes once more wore the glaze of passion and desire.

He slipped his hands underneath her bottom and cupped her buttocks and then carefully began to withdraw.

Her eyes went wide and then she closed them, breathing in deep when he inched his way forward once more.

She was a tight fist around his cock. Hot. Liquid silk. Grasping greedily as he moved within her.

He'd never felt anything so good, never felt pleasure so razor sharp and edgy.

She lifted her hips as if wanting more. When he complied, she bit her lip and wore a slight grimace. He swore under his breath and went still once more.

"No, don't stop," she said. "It's a little uncomfortable, but it doesn't hurt. Not like it did before."

"I don't want to hurt you more," he said hoarsely.

She smiled then, her eyes warming like twin flames. Sebastien and Garon were close to her now, caressing her skin and then lowering their mouths back to her breasts. Nico stroked her hair, his fingers tangling in the long strands. She gasped and arched upward when Garon and Sebastien started sucking in tandem.

She went wetter around his cock and his thrusts became easier, slick with her desire. He used her distraction and the pleasure she was receiving from Garon and Sebastien and began to move at a more rapid pace.

Placing his palm down on her belly, he slid his thumb down into her folds and over her clit. He rolled gently, gauging her reaction until he found just the right spot and the right amount of pressure to bring her pleasure.

Her breaths were ragged and she arched upward. Her hands seem to fly everywhere and then finally curled around the backs of Sebastien's and Garon's head, gripping tight as they continued to lavish attention on her breasts.

Her pussy spasmed around him and she let out a sharp cry as he increased the motion of his thumb over her clit. She was close, and thank God for it because he was nearly out of his mind with the need to find release.

As soon as she started contracting around him and went soft and damp, he thrust deep. He surged forward twice more, burying himself into the very heart of her. It was his breaking point.

Amidst her cries of passion, he let out a fierce groan as he began coming. God, it was nearly painful, but it was the most glorious of hurts. It was as if he'd been turned inside out.

He eased forward, wanting her in his arms. The others pulled back, leaving him and Talia wrapped in each other's arms. He cradled her close to his heart as he continued to twitch deep inside her.

This was ultimate satisfaction.

When everything else in his world had been upended, this was so very right. She was right.

He'd waited for what seemed an eternity to claim her, to have her here in his bed, but she was here now and he'd be damned if he'd let her go.

Chapter 14

"You're mine," Xander murmured when she stirred beside him.

The declaration sent a delicate shiver over her shoulders. Yes, she was his. In essence she was theirs. She felt as branded by the others as she did Xander even though he was the only one she'd taken into her body.

But they'd touched her. They'd tasted her. They'd surrounded her while Xander had claimed her.

In any other circumstance she would have thought the whole thing, well . . . creepy. But lying here in Xander's arms, remembering the way they'd all made her feel, "creepy" was the last word she'd use to describe the intense pleasure they'd given her.

They'd been caring. Gentle. It had all been . . . romantic. She felt silly even thinking the word and yet she couldn't imagine a more perfect experience for her first time. For the first time, she was glad that she hadn't given up her virginity before now.

Until now, it wasn't something she'd given a lot of thought to. She wasn't opposed to having sex, and more than likely had she had the opportunity, she would have done so. But between school and her mother, any intimate relationship with a man had been the furthest thing from her mind.

She sighed and burrowed her face into the hollow of Xander's neck. Inhaling deeply, she soaked in his scent. Rugged. Primal.

Unable to resist, she slipped her hand over his side and let her fingers drift down and then over his midsection, enjoying the lean, muscled flesh.

"If you keep that up, I'm going to take you again," he growled in a low voice.

She smiled against his neck. "That's not exactly a threat you know."

He let out a grunt. He sounded disgruntled. Then he nuzzled her ear. "It would be far too painful for you to accommodate me again so soon. As much as I'd love to slide into your body and spend the rest of the night there, we must wait."

She leaned up on her elbow, her hair falling in a curtain over her breasts. She glanced to where the others lounged and they met her gaze, almost as if anticipating she might have need of something. Such willingness to spoil her was going to have her in complete ruin. How on earth would she ever return to her normal life?

And did he have any such intention of allowing her to return after his surprising declaration? Did he intend to keep her as a mistress? Plaything? Pampered pet?

Shaking off those thoughts, she returned to her original intention.

"What I had in mind had nothing to do with you being inside me again. At least not there," she murmured.

Xander pushed himself upward, his eyes glittering in the low light.

She smiled, feeling suddenly naughty and mischievous. "Sebastien told me earlier that I would suck the cocks of every man present and yet . . . I didn't." She turned her lips down into a pout. "What a promise to break. And I was so anticipating it."

Xander glanced at the others. Sebastien viewed her with one raised brow. Garon and Nico looked like they'd been hit in the head.

Then Xander chuckled. "Just who's in charge here? Your promises of obedience are fast turning into promises of manipulation."

She turned, widening her eyes in innocence. "Well, if you don't want me to . . ."

"Not so damn fast, Xander," Garon rumbled out. "She does need practice after all."

"Definitely," Nico breathed. "And she can practice on me all she wants."

"Are you certain this is what you want, Talia?" Xander asked. "I wouldn't have you too overwhelmed."

She leaned down and kissed him, amazed that her self-consciousness had evaporated. She hadn't been sure she could act normally when surrounded by four men. But now she felt like a seductive temptress. She felt empowered and bold. She liked it.

"Maybe I want to be overwhelmed," she whispered against his lips.

Xander reached over to get one of the large, discarded pillows and tossed it toward Garon. Garon immediately rose and placed the cushion on the floor even as he was reaching for the fly of his pants.

Sebastien and Nico also rose and she stared appreciatively at the three as they took position around the cushion.

She wanted them . . . naked.

Knowing she was supposed to be the obedient one, she nibbled at her bottom lip and pondered whether they were desperate enough to have her mouth on their cocks that they'd do her bidding instead of the other way around.

Only one way to find out.

She scooted to the end of the bed on her knees and surveyed the three men gathered such a short distance away. Then she looked over her shoulder to Xander, sending him a seductive smile.

He pushed himself farther up, an amused smile on his face. "I think I may sit this one out and watch."

She pouted again. "You don't want me to pleasure you?"

His eyes darkened. "You will pleasure me by putting on quite the show and pleasuring them. When you are finished with them, then I'll have mine."

With a delicate shrug she turned back and regarded them lazily. "I'd really love it if you took off your clothes. You have such beautiful bodies. I want to touch and feel while I taste . . ."

"Hell," Sebastien muttered. "Xander, you've created a damn monster. She's become a seductive little minx and damn if she won't end up killing us all."

"There are worse ways to go," Garon drawled.

Nico said nothing at all. He merely started pulling his shirt over his head and she sucked in her breath at the beauty of his body.

Tan. Rugged. Muscled. He had a quiet confidence that radiated from him.

When he lifted his dark gaze back to her, there was no reluctance. Only desire. Then he started unfastening his pants and she found herself holding her breath as he pushed them down over his hips.

His cock sprang free and her gaze immediately widened. She immediately glanced to Garon, who was already naked, and then back to Nico.

He was huge. And he wasn't the largest man. Not that penis size had anything to do with it, really, but she hadn't expected him to be the most endowed of all of them. Somehow it didn't fit his quiet, tender image.

But holy cow, how was she supposed to fit all of that in her mouth?

Sebastien made a sound of disgust. "Put the damn monster away before she runs screaming from the room. I swear the women always look at you like that the first time."

Nico flashed a slow, cocky smile. "Jealous?"

Garon snorted with laughter.

Sebastien quickly pulled off his clothing and then stared back at Talia. "We're here, sweetheart. Come and get us."

As she started to the edge, Xander caressed the curve of her bottom and let his hand linger before she moved away. She turned, smiling back at him, and then turned her attention to the three men she was about to pleasure.

She honestly had no idea what she was doing, but she figured instinct made up for a lot. She hadn't really known with Sebastien, but she'd winged it fine. It wasn't as if there were *that* many ways to suck a man's cock.

Once in front of them, Nico reached out his hand for hers. She slid her palm over his, savoring the tantalizing glide of his flesh against hers. It raised the hairs on her arm and instilled an ache deep inside her belly.

Who would have ever imagined that she was such a sensual creature? It wasn't that she'd never thought about sex. What normal person didn't? She'd even imagined the act and how it would feel. But what she hadn't counted on was her boldness and how quickly she would adapt and feel comfortable with her sexuality.

Maybe tomorrow she'd be one big ball of embarrassment but tonight? Tonight was hers and she was going to indulge in every lusty whim, or at least this one.

She eased down to her knees, Nico still holding her hand. When she was settled, he let her fingers slide from his but he reached out to brush a knuckle over her cheek.

"You're beautiful, Talia. So beautiful and sensual. You granted us a privilege by including us tonight and I'll never forget that. I was honored, if not to be your first, to be one of the first."

Mesmerized by the husky flow of words, she took in a deep breath and then finally dragged her gaze from him to include Garon and Sebastien in her attention.

It was quite a sight. Three massive cocks on display right in her line of vision. Her hands trembled as she raised them. She had to remind herself that she was winging it and it would be okay.

Her palms closed around Garon's and Nico's erections and she rolled upward, keeping her grip firm. Then she lifted her chin, almost in challenge to Sebastien. He'd had no issue boldly taking charge before.

His hand came immediately to thrust through her hair, gripping the back of her head as he positioned his cock at her mouth. "Open."

The guttural command sent a heavy shudder through her body. Her breasts grew heavy and achy. Her nipples hardened painfully.

As soon as she parted her lips, he was inside. This time he didn't take quite the care he had during her introduction to oral sex. But she appreciated that because he was no longer treating her like a clueless virgin, never mind that before a few moments ago she *had* been a clueless virgin.

She continued to slide her hands up and down the taut erections as Sebastien worked his cock deep inside her mouth. She found if she angled upward, that she could more easily take him, and if she had a prayer of being able to fit Nico very deep, she was going to need all the advantage she could get.

Just thinking about it made her all sorts of shivery with delight.

Deciding to save him for last, she sucked her way down Sebastien's cock until the head was on the tip of her tongue. Then she let it fall and turned her head to Garon, eagerly anticipating this new experience.

She inhaled, wanting his scent, wanting to differentiate between his and Sebastien's. She gently stroked with her hand, simply soaking in every detail, her gaze roving up and down the hard lines of his body.

He was by far the largest of the four men. Built like a brick. Broad and muscled. He was the type one might expect to be clumsy or at least less graceful, but in truth, he moved with such ease, light on his feet, muscles rippling the whole time.

His legs were like tree trunks. Thick with muscles, the lines and ridges heavily pronounced. He was a man who took very good care of his body and obviously had a strict exercise regimen.

Flicking out her tongue, she teased the head, rubbing lightly over the slit. His breath hissed out, explosive in the quiet. He too thrust his hand in her hair, his big hand covering the top of her head. But his touch was gentle, in direct contrast to how fierce he looked.

She licked him again, tilting his cock upward so she could slide her tongue along the backside where the vein bulged and was plump.

His nostrils flared and his jaw twitched. His grip tightened in her hair and then he seemed to hold his breath . . . in anticipation?

She stared up at him from beneath her lashes, taking in every detail. Then, without looking down, she slowly sucked him into her mouth.

A garbled sound erupted from Garon's throat. What sounded like an expletive hit the air and he bounced up on his tiptoes as he strained to push deeper.

She took him as far as she could, swallowing rapidly to keep herself from gagging. He was so thick. Enormously so. He wasn't as long as the others, though he was certainly an impressive length, but he was most certainly thicker and she was already fantasizing about how he would feel inside her.

Each man was so different. She realized that each time would be a whole new experience for her. In essence, each first time with them would be like her first time all over again.

After a few moments of teasing him by taking him deep and then sliding him to the tip of her tongue, she slowly released him and turned to Nico, her eyes widening again as she got up close and personal to his straining erection.

He'd been stroking himself and even now he held himself in a firm grip at the base with his thumb and forefinger, the rest of his fingers curved around his balls.

It looked pretty damn hot.

She didn't reach for him. For some reason, she thought he would want her acquiescence. She made a symbolic showing of carefully sliding her hands behind her to the small of her back and then she leaned up on her knees, staring up at him, waiting.

He cupped her face in his hands, rubbing both thumbs over her cheekbones in gentle rhythm. He lowered one hand to her chin, using his thumb to carefully open her mouth. Then with the other, he grasped his cock once more and carefully guided it past her lips.

It was a tight fit. He felt more enormous than he looked. She stretched her lips around him and tried very hard to keep her teeth from grazing him, but she didn't see how it was going to be possible not to.

"It's all right, Talia," he soothed. "I'm quite used to it a bit rough."

"Comes with the territory," Sebastien grumbled.

"Relax and let me do the work," Nico said.

She inhaled through her nose and gave herself over to his command, his touch, his hold on her. With that she also handed him her trust. Faith not to hurt or overwhelm her.

The entire time he worked his cock farther into her mouth, he caressed her face with one hand. She closed her eyes at the pleasurable sensation of his touch, just loving his hands on her. She'd bet any amount of money that he made love like a dream.

She let out a dreamy sigh even before she realized she had.

"My God," Nico breathed out. "You have to stop that, Talia, or this will be over before it even begins."

Her eyes flew open and she saw the lust shining in his eyes. His jaw was tight like Garon's had been, and she realized the very tight hold they had on their control.

He began to move, slowly at first until she relaxed enough for him to move more easily. He took long, measured thrusts followed by shorter ones to allow her to catch her breath. Every move he made seemed to be in consideration of her. She was a little in love with him already for just how sweet and understanding he'd been.

Finally he withdrew, his chest heaving. His hands shook as he pulled away and then Sebastien was there, taking over her mouth.

He slid deep and held himself there and then began a series of alternating deep and shallow thrusts. Nico and Garon moved closer in, their hands moving over their erections as she took Sebastien's down her throat.

Just as quickly, Sebastien pulled away and Garon turned her to face him. This time he wasn't as patient as he'd been before. Though he certainly wasn't rough.

He made several long, deep thrusts and then released her again.

For the next several minutes, she moved from man to man, or rather they took over and directed her movements. She was dazed by the sheer eroticism and had entered somewhat of a fuzzy state of heightened awareness.

She sighed and let out soft moans and every time she did, the men groaned and their movements became more forceful.

Back and forth, from man to man, hands on her face, in her hair, holding her, pushing against her. It all blended together until she was only aware of the cocks pushing in and out of her mouth.

"On your breasts," Nico rasped out. "Hold them up for me, Talia."

Nearly in a stupor, she cupped her breasts together, presenting them to him as he pulled out of her mouth and began jerking hard at his cock. A moment later, hot semen splashed onto her breasts and she gasped at the sensation.

He came in spurts, each one making her jump the tiniest bit. He gave one more pull, squeezing to the end of his cock and then he put his hand on top of her head and guided his still hard erection back into her mouth.

His taste was warm and salty as he pushed inward. He stroked for a few seconds and then withdrew, letting go of her head.

Sebastien stepped up, slid deep into her mouth and thrust hard for several seconds before he pulled out and directed his release onto her body. It hit her neck just below her chin and slid in a warm trail down her throat.

With a guttural sigh, he gave one last yank and then Garon stepped forward, his cock bumping impatiently against her chin.

"I want to come inside your mouth," Garon said even as he sank deep.

She nodded but there was no need. He was in control. If he wanted to come inside her, he would. It was as simple as that. If she'd had any reservations—and she had—about submitting to these men, they were gone in a heady swirl of lust and desire. And trust.

She trusted them to take care of her and to respect the gift that she'd given them.

Still holding her breasts to prevent anything from leaking onto the floor, she leaned into Garon, using her lips, her tongue, her mouth to give him as much pleasure as they were giving her.

"So good," he murmured. "So damn sweet. I've never felt anything so good in my life."

As soon as she put more suction, he went tense all over and then he cupped her cheek as if to reassure her.

"I'm coming, baby."

As soon as the warning came, hot cum filled her mouth, jetting to the back of her throat in forceful spurts. She swallowed rapidly but more spilled onto her tongue until finally she couldn't keep up and it gathered at the corners of her mouth and leaked out each time he withdrew to thrust again.

The wet sucking sound filled the room. She swallowed and swallowed again to clear her mouth until finally there was no more. His movements slowed and then he paused, holding himself still for a long moment.

"You're amazing."

The compliment rumbled out of his chest and he cupped her face with both hands before finally allowing his cock to slip free of her lips.

She automatically glanced down, curious about the sight of their release on her breasts and chest. There was a sticky sensation on her neck as she lowered her head. It was warm and wet on her body. Glistening in the low light.

"Clean her up and send her to me," Xander said in a low voice.

She jerked her head around, momentarily befuddled. She'd forgotten all about him. How could she not have? Nothing had existed for her but those three men pushing into her mouth.

Xander regarded her lazily from the bed but there was a fierce light in his eyes. Lust. Arousal. He'd obviously enjoyed watching her with his men. But then he'd already said as much. The unconventional arrangement centered around the fact that he liked and wanted to share his woman with these men.

What would have made him desire such a thing? Who could know and was there a distinguishable reason anyway? Some things just were. She liked grapes. Was there a deep explanation for why? No, she just did. Perhaps that was the way it was for Xander. He liked kink. Definitely enjoyed it. And he was in a position to get precisely what he wanted, so why not?

Nico helped her to her feet and held her a moment until he was sure she was steady. Sebastien returned from the bathroom with warm cloths, and he and Garon carefully wiped the traces from her body.

Then Nico pulled her into his arms, cuddling her close as he stroked her hair. "You were magnificent."

He kissed her forehead and then pulled away. Garon got her next, wrapping those big arms around her. When he was done, Sebastien swung her into his arms, surprising her with the motion, and then he carried her over to the bed where Xander lay.

After gently setting her down, he backed away and Talia's gaze drifted to where Xander was stroking his cock. It was rigid and straining upward, his balls drawn tight with each pull.

"I'm close," he grated out. "Get on your knees between my legs. I want you on top and I want you to swallow every drop."

She crawled over his legs and then settled between his thighs. As she bent over to take him into her mouth, a hand slid between her thighs from behind and softly stroked over her clit.

It was a shock to her already heavily aroused system. She nearly orgasmed on the spot and gave a quick gasp, halting her progress toward Xander's cock.

She glanced back to see Nico standing just behind her, his fingers gently exploring her pussy. He was careful not to touch the areas where she was sore, but his fingers on her clit felt so good.

"Here, Talia," Xander ordered. "Make me come so he can make you come."

Oh, that sounded wonderful.

She curled her hand around Xander's cock and did an upward pull before fitting her mouth to the tip. As soon as she opened her mouth to take him inside, Nico began rubbing her clit in a tight circular motion.

She closed her eyes, groaning as she sucked Xander inward.

"That's it," Xander breathed out. "Just like that. Use your

tongue. Sweet. Very sweet. Your pretty little mouth has gotten quite the workout tonight, hasn't it, Talia?"

She took him deep, wanting to elicit a reaction from him. She wanted this to be good, the best damn blow job he'd ever received.

He made a strangled noise as her lips came to rest against his pelvis.

"God, Talia."

It seemed to be all he could say.

She began to work up and down, eyes closed, moaning as Nico worked her toward a fast, impending orgasm. She was already so high, so worked up from her interlude with all three men that she didn't need much. She actually fought against it, not wanting it just yet. Not until Xander.

But she didn't have long to wait. Xander thrust upward with his hips as she moved down and immediately he began jetting into her mouth. She coughed and then swallowed and then her mind blanked. Everything seemed to go white as her release billowed over her, overwhelming her every thought and reaction.

She had no idea if she swallowed or not. She was helpless to control anything at all. The pleasure was sharp and unrelenting. So much bigger than it had been before.

When she came to awareness, she was facedown against Xander's pelvis and she needed to breathe badly. She rose upward with a gasp and realized the mess she'd made on him.

"I'm sorry," she began.

"Shhh, my darling," Xander said as he lifted himself upward.

He made a grab for the cloth tossed to him by Garon and he quickly wiped her face before cleaning himself up. Then he pulled her into his arms, hauling her over his body before leaning back on the bed.

She lay sprawled across him, limp, sated and thoroughly exhausted. Her eyes were already closing even as he murmured for her to sleep.

Chapter 15

Talia lay in the lounger by the pool, drifting into sleep as the sun rose higher overhead. Her sunglasses were perched on her nose and her eyelids were so heavy that she was losing the battle to keep them open.

The heat caressed her skin and she arched lazily before finally closing her eyes for good.

It had been a week since Xander had taken her virginity. In that time, he and the others had spoiled and pampered her endlessly.

It was an interesting contradiction. She was supposed to be their submissive and yet her every whim was catered to. Food, attention, tenderness was lavished on her. It was true they directed her movements. She was expected to obey. They'd foregone her wearing anything at all unless they went to the beach and then she donned a swimsuit so she wouldn't be chafed by the sand.

And yet she didn't feel . . . subjugated. Far from it. She felt privileged and cherished.

The problem was, they had yet to have sex with her.

Her imagination had done some serious stretching as she'd visualized all the different ways that they could make love to her. Some she was sure defied the laws of physics and others she wasn't sure were humanly possible, but now that she'd opened that door to the idea of multiple partners, it was a wide-open world.

Oh, they'd touched her. They'd pleasured her. She'd had more orgasms than a girl ought to be allowed to have. She spent most of her time in a sated stupor.

But no actual penetration.

Almost as if sensing her frustration and impatience, Xander had told her the night before that he wanted her to have time to heal before they were demanding of her body.

She wanted them to be demanding. She wanted to be demanded.

She wanted something, damn it!

She was well on her way into a coma when a noise roused her from her nap. She opened her eyes, thankful the shades were still in place. Garon loomed over her, a glass of lemonade in one hand and a tube of sunscreen in the other.

"Xander worries you aren't adequately protected from the sun."

Talia smiled. "He's sweet, but I lathered up a while ago."

Garon frowned. "When? You've been out here for several hours."

"Ah, hmm, well, I didn't realize it's been hours. Maybe he's right and I need more. I don't want to burn."

If she burned, they'd never touch her, and that was the last thing she wanted.

She started to reach for the tube, but Garon cast her a baleful stare.

"Are you thirsty?" he asked, holding the tube from her reach.

"Parched."

He frowned again as he handed her the ice-cold glass of lemonade. "You shouldn't lay out here in the sun without proper hydration. I don't know what Xander was thinking letting you come out alone when one of us isn't around to watch over you."

She smothered a laugh. He was too cute and growly and she didn't want to offend him because the thing was, he was very sincere. He took his duty as her watchdog very seriously. As did Nico. Sebastien, she'd learned, was all bluster and inside a total cream puff.

He liked to act all laid-back and like he didn't really care. He liked to pretend to be a hard-ass. But when it came down to it, he did every bit as much to fuss over her as the rest.

This was truly paradise. Completely removed from reality. She couldn't imagine any other woman possibly having such an existence. It was like something plucked from her deepest, buried fantasies and brought to life.

After being the caretaker for so long, she was finally the one being taken care of. It was . . . Well, she didn't have the words to describe how wonderful it felt. She couldn't really dwell on it without choking up.

She sipped at the lemonade and sighed in pleasure. Everything here was so simple. That in itself was a distinct joy.

"Your mother called for you," Garon said as he knelt by her lounger.

Talia sat up in the lounger and raised her shades with her free hand. "She did?"

Garon nodded. "Xander spoke with her himself. He assured her you were fine."

"Xander spoke to her?" Talia croaked out. "Did she realize . . . I mean did she know . . ."

"Who he was?" Garon asked with a smile.

Talia nodded numbly.

"I'm guessing you didn't tell her the whole truth about where you were going," Garon said gently.

Talia blew out her breath, her shoulders sagging. Garon took the glass from her before she tilted it over.

"No," she admitted. "I gave her the number Xander provided. The direct line to the villa. But what I told her was that I had been invited on holiday with . . . friends. She was so thrilled that I was getting out that I didn't have the heart to tell her all the details. She's always worried so much over me not having a life as she puts it. She frets endlessly that I'm not out there doing what young people do. She doesn't understand that I would do anything for her. Anything at all," Talia said fiercely.

Garon leaned forward to kiss her forehead. "What I think she knows is how special her daughter is and that she was happy that you were finally going to get to do something for yourself."

Talia nodded. "She was. She was so happy you would have thought it was her getting to go."

She turned her face up to Garon, anxiety curling in her stomach. "What did Xander say? How did she react? I don't want her to be . . ." She broke off, biting her lip.

"You don't want her to be what?" Garon asked quietly.

Talia sighed unhappily. "I don't want her to be ashamed of me."

Garon's brow furrowed and his lips formed a thin line. "Ashamed?"

Talia closed her eyes for a long moment. "This is nothing personal to you, Garon. Or the others. You've all been so wonderful to me. I feel like a pampered princess. I've never had a more wonderful time in my life. But the bald truth is, I signed a contract to be a glorified whore."

Garon's expression grew even darker, but she held up a hand to silence him.

"I know the word sounds awful, but let's be honest. I'm not saying that any of you treat me like some cheap, tawdry lay. God, far from it. I'm so lucky. I mean how stupid does a girl have to be to sign a contract like that and jet off to some remote island not having any idea what she's getting into? I'm damn lucky you all didn't turn out to be some monsters bent on making me a sex slave or selling me into slavery when you were done with me.

"But none of how wonderfully I'm treated changes the fact that I basically sold myself. For sex. I didn't want my mother to know that. To *ever* know it. She would die if she thought that I'd ever agreed to something like this out of gratitude for what had been done for her."

"And is that why you agreed to come here? Gratitude?"

"Of course. I knew nothing about any of you. My reasons may have changed or at least my feelings, once I arrived here, but when you were all just nameless, faceless entities and I received the summons from Xander, I felt like I owed him a debt I could never repay and if all he wanted from me was six months of my life, nothing was too much to give in repayment for my mother's life."

"And if he wants more than six months?"

Talia frowned, her brows bunched together in consternation. "Is that what he wants, Garon? I mean he told me he had no intention of ever letting me go, but you and I both know that's not likely. Were they abstract words? Said in the heat of the moment? I don't really know what he wants and I'm afraid to ask. I don't want to ruin this wonderful fantasy. I'm afraid to do or say anything to make it all go away. And so I haven't broached the subject since the night on the beach when he told me why he really brought me here."

"Lie back," he said in a gentle voice. "You're burning while we're sitting here talking."

She reclined again, knocking her shades down in frustration. Maybe she shouldn't have been so forthcoming with Garon. His loyalty was to Xander, and he'd likely tell Xander their entire conversation.

Garon's big hands descended on her body, rubbing the sunblock over her skin in slow, sensuous sweeps.

"It should be obvious to you that Xander has no desire for you to leave his side," he said. "And you said he said as much. He doesn't blithely say things he doesn't mean. He's very exacting and focused."

She reached up to push her glassed over the top of her head again. "Obvious? Garon, he's hinted that he has deeper feelings for me. I don't know if that's the right word for it. I'm not sure what his feelings are. Perhaps it's better to say that he's admitted to having a preoccupation for me for some time. Now what that means is anyone's guess. We have a contract. He says that was his way of getting me here. Okay, I'm here. What now? And what does he *mean* by saying he never wants to let me go?"

"Maybe he's waiting for you to decide what your feelings are for him."

She went silent as Garon continued the soothing massage with the sunblock cream. Xander had asked her what her feelings were the night on the beach and she'd neatly avoided the question. Instead she'd told him she was ready for him to make love to her, and maybe she'd thought that was statement enough.

Here she was frustrated because Xander wasn't very forthcoming when in fact he'd been far more up front than she had been. He'd put himself out there, admitting to . . . at least an attraction for her, and she'd given him nothing back.

"He probably thinks this is just a contract for me," she said quietly. "Something I have to do or something I feel obligated to do."

"Is it? I think it's a valid question."

She closed her eyes as he cupped her breasts and carefully smoothed the lotion over the plump mounds. Her nipples hardened immediately, begging for more attention.

"At first it was," she admitted quietly. "But then . . ."

"Then?" he prompted.

She frowned. "This is all very embarrassing."

He dropped one hand down between her thighs, sliding his fingers through her folds until he found her clit. He ran his finger over and then around the nub before withdrawing his hand. Damn tease.

But then he leaned down and pressed a kiss to her lips. It was startling. And unexpected. He was affectionate with her. They all were. But it always seemed to be in a group setting. Xander was always present. When he wasn't, the others took very good care of her, and they were at times, intimate, but this went beyond the task of pleasuring her. It was more . . . personal.

His tongue swept over her lips and then probed until she parted her lips to let him inside. He didn't maul her with his mouth, nor was he forceful. It was a gentle, sweet kiss that made her ache.

"You should know by now that nothing should embarrass you. At least not with us. I would hope you feel comfortable with me by now. You can say anything without fear of judgment, and I certainly won't make you feel shame for whatever it is you're thinking."

Talia ran a hand through a length of her hair and fiddled nervously with the ends. "I'm not sure I want Xander to hear this yet. I mean when he does, I'd prefer it to be from me."

"I don't report private conversations back to Xander. Not unless they are a potential threat to him."

She sighed again. "The thing is, I've always been a little half in love with him. Maybe even more. But I've always thought it was a crush that would go away with time and distance. I mean he did a lot for me and my mother. What if I'm confusing gratitude for love? But the more time I spend with him, the more bewildered I am because I just don't know what I'm supposed to do or feel. If he only intends to keep me for six months and then send me on my way, then what kind of an idiot would it make me to fall in love with him? With any of you?"

He lifted one eyebrow and surveyed her with that half smile

she had quickly come to associate with him. "Then you do feel something for us."

Her cheeks bloomed with heat. Trust her tongue to get away from her.

"That sounds stupid. I'm sorry. I don't know what the hell I feel. I wish I did. I know I should just relax, go with the flow, enjoy being surrounded by men who treat me like a goddess, but I over-think things. I always have. It's one of my faults."

Garon pressed his lips to hers again and he brought his hand up to touch her cheek. "Has it ever occurred to you that maybe we all have feelings for you as well?"

Chapter 16

Talia's head was spinning as Garon drew away, his gaze stroking over her face. "What?"

"Surely you can't be surprised by this. Or do you think we often have a woman here that we pamper and lavish attention on?"

She didn't respond because she really didn't want to put her foot in her mouth.

"You do, don't you?" Garon said, realization lighting in his eyes. He shook his head and sent her a look of exasperation.

"You can't blame me for thinking it," she defended. "I was sent a contract. I went through medical exams. I was 'briefed' on what to expect. It was all very clinical, as if it had been done a hundred times before. I honestly think or thought that I was the latest in a long line of diversions or at the very least the latest entertainment."

"Such an interesting conversation you two are having," Sebastien drawled.

Talia closed her eyes as mortification swept over her.

"Shut the hell up, Bastien," Garon said fiercely. "This isn't the time for your fucking sarcasm."

Sebastien strolled over, then pulled up one of the chairs to sit at the foot of Talia's lounger. "On the contrary, I have no intention of being sarcastic. Are you going to correct her assumption or shall I?" he said to Garon.

Talia frowned, unsure of whether this was all a big joke to Sebastien. She and Garon had been having a serious conversation. She had no desire to become the brunt of Sebastien's amusement.

"It depends on entirely on your presentation," Garon said sharply.

Sebastien curled his lip at Garon and then focused his attention on Talia. "Despite what you may think, you're the only woman Xander has brought to the villa. This is his . . . sanctuary. It's where he's spent most of his exile from Cristofino. I won't lie to you and say there've been no other women or that he's sat and pined endlessly for you. But none have captured his attention as you have."

He paused and drew in a breath. A shadow of uncertainty flashed over his face, surprising her. Sebastien was nothing if not cocksure.

When he found her gaze again, his eyes burned with intensity. Like he was sending her a clear message that he was dead serious.

"None have captured *my* attention as you have," he finally added.

"What are you trying to say?" she whispered.

"Perhaps it would be best if I were to speak for myself," Xander said from behind Talia.

She turned rapidly, nearly pulling a muscle in her neck. Xander stood there, hands shoved into his pockets, staring at her, Garon and Sebastien.

"Leave us," he said to the others.

Talia blew out her breath in frustration. Was she doomed to never be able to complete a conversation where she stood to gain information to help her make sense of this whole situation?

Garon and Sebastien stood. Garon ran his hand over her cheek before departing on Sebastien's heels. Xander walked around the lounger so Talia could better see him and then he glanced upward at the sun.

"I don't think you should remain out here any longer. I don't want you to get too much sun and grow ill. Why don't we go inside, have something to eat."

She shook her head mutinously. "Oh no. Not the ordeal of an awkward meal again. This is starting to make me crazy. If you want to speak for yourself, then do it now."

He cracked a slight smile. "Come, Talia. I'm not having this conversation with you out here in the midday sun. It's too intense. If you prefer, we'll go to my suite and Wickersham will bring us a light snack so you can eat while I talk. I won't make you wait."

She eyed him suspiciously.

"I give you my word," he said in amusement.

She sighed. "Okay, you win. We go inside. But if we're eating snacks, I want something full of sugar and calories."

He smiled indulgently and reached to help her out of the lounger. "I think that can be arranged."

Twenty minutes later, Talia was sitting cross-legged on Xander's bed with a tray of beautifully decorated confections in front of her. She ate one of the mini cupcakes and then licked the frosting from her thumb with relish.

There were chocolates too. And what looked to be a cake ball on a stick coated with white chocolate. It was beyond awesome.

But even as distracted as she was temporarily by the goodies Wickersham had provided, she wasn't going to let Xander off the hook this time. She wanted—needed—answers.

"Are you having any?" she asked, extending one of the long toothpick-looking sticks out to him.

He paced in front of the bed and shook his head.

"Why are you so tense, Xander? You've been kind of weird ever since the night you . . . made love to me."

He stopped and looked sideways at her. "Weird? In what way?"

She waved her hand in dismal. "Bad choice of words. Let's not get sidetracked here. I realize I'm supposed to be submissive. I know I signed a contract—a document you've basically said was a ruse. So am I to abide by it? How much of this whole thing is . . . fake?"

He scowled and stalked to the bed, sitting on the edge in front of her. "Not a damn thing here is fake. I did what I felt I had to do to get you here. And no, I don't want you to leave. I can't be any more explicit than that."

She lowered one of the chocolates back to the tray. "I need to know what's happening here, Xander. Garon and Sebastien have both hinted that they have feelings for me, that you have feelings for me. You told me that you were attracted to me all those years ago. You have to understand how very confused I am right now. Am I supposed to feel guilty over the fact that I have very real feelings for the men you have taking care of me? Men you've said yourself will be having sex with me?"

"I'm more interested in your feelings for me," Xander said quietly.

She swallowed hard and summoned her courage. "I think I'm in love with you."

He didn't look entirely thrilled with her statement.

"You think?"

She took another deep breath and prayed she didn't regret putting herself on the line like this.

"I'm pretty sure. If you heard my conversation with Garon, you already know the reasons I was uncertain. I've always been a little in love with you, but I worried it was youthful infatuation or that it would pass. But being here with you . . . It just feels right. It feels so perfect. Like it was meant to be."

She broke off, swallowing rapidly. She was getting carried away and sounding sillier by the minute. She lowered her head in embarrassment.

Xander reached out to cup her chin and he gently tilted it upward until she faced him again. "Meant to be is right, Talia. You were meant to be mine."

"But what does that mean?" she whispered. "I don't fit into your world, Xander."

He emitted a harsh laugh. "What world? My world is what I make it. My world is here while the battle rages on in my country. Things may never be resolved there. Whatever happens, I want you here. With me."

"And the others? How am I supposed to feel about them? I can't do what it is you want me to do and not have my emotions involved. I realize I'm new to sex, but it means something to me."

Xander smiled. "They are rather emotionally involved with you too, my love."

"And that doesn't bother you?"

She couldn't quite wrap her head around that one.

"I trust them implicitly. I trust them with my safety. I trust them with your safety. I know they would never betray me. Knowing they have feelings for you only solidifies my confidence that they'll never allow anything to happen to you."

"You must know that I have to return. I mean, to my mother. I can't just stay here forever."

"Of course not," he soothed. "I will, of course, take you to Paris to visit your mother. I had a long talk with her today on the phone. She sends you her love. I promised her I'd take good care of you."

"Thank you. That means a lot to me that you'd reassure her. I don't want her to worry over me."

Xander reached for the tray and then walked it out of the bedroom and into the sitting area. When he returned, there was a determined gleam in his eyes that sent butterflies tumbling through her chest.

"What I want is to make love to you, Talia. I've waited long enough. No others. No distractions. Just you. And me."

Even as he spoke, he put his hands on the bed and leaned toward her, forcing her back with his body. She landed with a soft thump and he hovered over her, hunger burning brightly in his gaze.

He put one hand between her legs and slowly circled her opening with one finger. His voice was full of tenderness as he spoke. "Are you still sore?"

She shook her head. "I'm fine, Xander. I want you to make love to me again. This last week has driven me crazy. I want you inside me."

He let out a groan. "And I want to be there. More than you can possibly know. This last week may have driven you crazy, but it's been hell for me. I would do nothing to hurt you, though. I wanted to make sure you could take me without discomfort the second time."

She reached up to pull him down to meet her lips. She couldn't and wouldn't summon any guilt over the fact that not a half hour ago, Garon had kissed her in a manner that was very different from their prior interactions. Xander had all but encouraged this . . . whatever it could be called . . . between her and the men he trusted. She was through stressing and letting the worry weigh down on her. From now on, she was going with the flow and just accepting.

Maybe this wasn't the most traditional arrangement in the world. But she was adored and pampered by men who genuinely seemed to care about her. They treated her with respect and not as the mistress or whore she'd been so prepared to label herself as.

They treated her like a woman they . . . loved.

"You have too many clothes on," she whispered when he pulled his mouth from hers.

He chuckled. "There you go with the bossiness again. I'm beginning to think we should amend that contract to submissiveness everywhere but in bed."

"You don't want someone who just lays here and takes it, do you?" she teased.

"Hell no," he muttered.

He got up on his knees to shed his shirt. Then he stepped off the bed long enough to get his pants off. She turned on her side, surveying his nudity with avid appreciation.

He lifted a brow at her close scrutiny. "Like what you see?"

"You're beautiful," she said simply.

"You're the beautiful one," he murmured as he pushed back onto the bed and over her.

He started at her forehead, kissing every inch of her face. He kissed her eyelids, her nose, each cheek and nibbled down both sides of her jaw in turn. From there, he covered her neck, alternating light nips and longer sucking motions she was sure would leave marks.

"I'm going to taste every inch of your body," he said. "Worship you like the goddess you said you've been treated as."

"Oh," she breathed. "No complaints here."

He laughed softly. "Somehow I didn't imagine there would be."

He paid extra attention to her breasts, patiently licking, kissing and sucking until she was nearly frenzied with anticipation.

It was evident he had every intention of drawing things out, and she wasn't sure she was going to survive it.

He closed his mouth over one nipple, sucked it gently between his teeth and then pulled upward until it was taut. Then he let it go and it puckered to unbearable hardness. He did the same to the other, giving it a little more bite that had her shuddering with delight.

"Xander," she gasped. "You're making me crazy. Please. I want you inside me now."

"Patience, my love," he said as he lazily rolled his tongue down her midsection to her belly button.

If he so much as touched any part of her below the waist with his mouth, she was going to come before he ever got inside her and she wanted him deep when she came apart.

"Xander, I'm close," she whispered urgently. "I want you inside me. I want to know how it feels. The other night was so intense. It was uncomfortable at first and I don't really remember much of the rest. Show me how good it can be. Please."

"Ah hell," he groaned. "How can I resist you?"

He slid his hand between them and through her damp folds before sliding one finger inside her. She tightened all over and already she could feel the impending build of her orgasm. She truly wasn't going to last very long.

"Stop me if this hurts," he said in a firm voice.

"I will." Over her dead body. There was no way she was stopping this train.

He rubbed his erection over her clit and then downward until he was rimming her opening. He tucked the head of his cock just inside her, stretching the entrance.

She held her breath, waiting, her entire body jittery with anticipation.

Then he pushed slowly inward. She let out a long sigh as she stretched to accommodate him. He felt enormous inside her. There was so much friction. It was . . . wonderful.

She stirred restlessly, the ache inside her only intensifying. She felt itchy, like her skin was alive. She wanted to wrap her legs around him and force him deep. Hard. Fast. She wanted him to lose that tightly held control.

It was as if he always held himself on a leash, never allowing himself to fully let go.

"More," she said, unable to articulate just exactly what she needed. But she knew she needed more. Definitely more. So that would have to do for now.

He seemed to understand because he withdrew and then thrust deep, with more force this time, though it was still evident he was holding himself in check.

"Xander, please. I'm not going to break. I'm not a virgin anymore. For God's sake, I've been waited on hand and foot. I've taken more hot baths than any human should ever take in a week's time. I'm completely and utterly healed from the first time. If you keep dragging this out, I swear to you I'm going to jump you, tie you down and have my wicked way with you."

He stared at her in astonishment for a moment and then burst out laughing. After a moment, he grew serious again, but there was still a gleam of amusement in his eyes.

"If you're sure."

"I'm sure, I'm sure! Just do it already. I need it harder. Faster. I'm dying over here."

With a growl that sounded eerily predatory, he hunched down over her, his body covering hers. He forced her legs farther apart with his thighs and then he began thrusting hard and fast. Rougher. Deeper. The slap of his hips against her thighs sounded loud in her ears.

Her entire body shook with the force of his possession.

The frenzy in which he took her lit fire to her senses. The orgasm that had quickly built fanned into a full-fledged inferno. Within seconds, she was pulled tighter than a rubber band at full stretch.

Closing her eyes, she gripped his shoulders, digging her fingers deep into his flesh.

"More," she whimpered.

"I'm giving you every goddamn thing I have," he rasped out. "Let go, Talia. Let go."

She needed just a little more . . . He thrust hard and then lowered his head to nip at the flesh just below her ear.

As soon as his teeth sank into her neck, she was hopelessly over the edge.

Her cry was sharp, almost desperate. She clutched at his shoulders and arched her hips to meet him, wanting more, wanting closer, wanting him as deep as possible.

Ecstasy, sharp and unrelenting, shot through her veins. Her pulse pounded at her temples. She could hear her heart beating, could feel it pounding against her chest.

Finally all the tension left her in one quick explosive force. It was like cutting a taut line and experiencing recoil. Euphoria quickly replaced her earlier desperation and she sank into the bed with a deep, contented sigh.

Xander followed her down, blanketing her with his strong, warm body. Their legs were tangled and he was still deep inside her. A part of her.

He pulled her head close until she was tucked underneath his chin. She cuddled up to him, content to have him remain there, covering her. She felt secure. Safe. Protected. It was a heavenly feeling.

She was so euphoric and in such a postcoital haze that she blinked sleepily, her earlier fatigue she'd experienced at the pool returning with a vengeance.

"Just a little nap," she murmured.

Xander smiled at how cute she was all cuddled up to him. She was warm and soft in his arms. All he could ever want.

After a long moment he stared down to find her sound asleep. He lowered his mouth to her forehead and pressed a kiss to her brow.

"I love you," he whispered. "I know I have a hard time saying it. I know I hide behind the others. But I love you, and one day I'll tell you when I'm no longer hiding behind anything or anyone."

Chapter 17

Talia was alone in the bed when she woke a mere hour later. She stretched languidly and then smiled. She felt like a very satisfied cat. Stroked, petted until she purred. And Xander had most definitely made her very content.

As she rolled, she found a blossom next to a propped-up note.

Meet me downstairs. Wear nothing. The others will be present.

The simply worded message sent a surge of excitement and quickly shook the comfortable lethargy that had settled over her.

She was to wear nothing, but it didn't mean she was simply going to roll out of bed and go down *looking* like she'd just rolled out of bed.

Hurrying to the bathroom, she swept her hair up into a bun so it wouldn't get wet and then took a quick shower. Afterward, she rubbed scented lotion over her body, applied a light spritzing of her favorite perfume and then did her face moisturizing and makeup prep.

She took her hair down, brushing it in waves down her shoulders. Though nothing had ever been said beyond that first instruction for the day she arrived, she knew they preferred her hair down. They rarely missed an opportunity to stroke it or run their fingers through it.

Pleasing them made her happy. She glowed under their praise and approval. And they did everything in their power to make sure she was happy and provided for.

For the first time in so very long, she was free of the worries and stress that had plagued her since her mother's diagnosis four years prior. All she had to worry about was following whatever directive was laid out to her and they'd been so undemanding when it came to her.

In a lot of ways it was freeing to be under the authority of someone else instead of being the primary decision maker in her life and the life of her mother.

She was . . . free.

Finished with university. Her mother was doing amazingly well. She was truly free to make her own decisions, live her own life.

A giddy thrill soared through her veins as she stared at her reflection in the mirror.

What had begun as what she viewed as a six-month period "delay" in starting her new life in order to repay a debt had in a lot of ways been the impetus for a new lease on life.

No matter what happened from this point forward, in the short time she'd been here, she felt renewed. Reinvigorated and optimistic about her future.

After applying the bare minimum of foundation, she did a quick brush of mascara to her lashes and then chose a shiny lip gloss she knew likely wouldn't remain on for long.

She smiled at that thought, remembering what the note had said. The others would be there. Maybe, finally they would stop treating her like she would break at the slightest touch.

Not wanting to keep them waiting, she did one last check of her hair and appearance and hurried toward the stairs. Midway down, she slowed and forced herself to be casual as she stepped into the sprawling living room.

Her pulse quickened because as soon as she entered the room, four sets of eyes immediately turned her way. All four men were in various stages of lounging. The television was on a sports channel that was giving updates on football scores, but the moment they realized she was there, someone hit the off button on the remote.

She walked boldly to the middle of the cluster of sofas and armchairs. She'd gotten over her self-consciousness when it came to being nude in front of these men.

"What do you wish me to do?" she asked in a quiet, sweet voice she knew pleased them.

Xander leaned forward in the armchair where he sat. He was adorned in khaki shorts and a simple polo shit. He was barefooted and looked completely comfortable. Sebastien was similarly dressed but he remained sprawled in his chair, drink in hand as he lazily surveyed Talia.

Garon and Nico were on the couch but both sat forward, eagerness lighting their eyes.

"Come to me," Xander said.

She walked to where he sat and he placed his hands on her legs just below her hips and then slid them upward and then around to cup her behind. He pulled her toward him until she was forced to straddle his lap.

His hands immediately went to cup her breasts. He palmed them, squeezed lightly just enough to force her nipples forward and then he put his mouth to one, sucking hard at the puckered point.

She loved it when he got all silent and commanding. She loved that, even though the others often participated in their erotic endeavors, Xander was always in control, even if it was simple as ceding control to the others. He was always there. Watching. And she found it incredibly arousing.

He pulled away, slid a hand behind her neck and hauled her down into a forceful, passionate kiss that took her breath away. He devoured her mouth as if he were starving for her, like he hadn't just made love to her an hour ago.

By the time he broke contact, she was sucking in mouthfuls of air, her chest burning from the prolonged ravaging of her mouth.

His hands stroked up and down her body as he stared into her eyes.

"Nico and Garon will prepare you for what's to come."

Her brow furrowed in confusion. He put a finger over her mouth. "They'll take care of you. That's all you need to know."

He kissed her again and then nodded in Nico's direction. And then Nico was behind her, touching her shoulder so she'd turn around. He held out a hand to her and she reached without hesitation.

He helped her from Xander's lap and led her to the couch where Garon sat.

"I want you to lie across Garon's lap, facedown, and relax."

The request made her nervous but she offered no hesitation because she didn't want them to think that she didn't trust them.

Garon helped her down, his big hands covering her body as he lowered her across his thick legs. He immediately began stroking her back and then rolled one hand over her behind, caressing the globes and squeezing gently.

Nico knelt beside the sofa and ran his hand lightly up the back of her leg to her behind and then traced a line up and down the cleft.

"I'm putting in a plug," he said in a soothing voice. "I'll go slow. I'll make sure there's plenty of lubricant and I'll be as gentle as possible. We want to give you a little time to adjust to having that opening stretched before we take you there."

She closed her eyes and clamped her jaw tight as shivers raced over her skin. It wasn't as if she hadn't anticipated such a thing. She just hadn't known when, and now that it was imminent, she was positively twitchy with excitement. Would it hurt? Would it be pleasurable? What would it feel like?

Then Nico leaned down and pressed a kiss to one cheek and then the other. Afterward he moved to the dimple just above the cleft of her behind and tongued it.

Lord but the man had such a sinful mouth.

When he pulled away, Garon reached down to part her thighs. For a moment, he slid his fingers through the folds of her pussy and fingered her clit, making her squirm in pleasure.

He withdrew after stroking her to a jittery mass and then he gently parted her cheeks to expose her anal opening.

Nico ran his fingers down the seam and around the puckered opening, warm gel spreading in their wake. He teased and caressed, adding more of the slick lubricant.

After a moment, he pressed one finger to the opening and gently pushed inward, stretching her to accommodate his finger. Her head came up, but Garon immediately stroked over her hair, soothing her with words and touch.

"Relax, Talia. He'll be gentle and he'll go slow."

Comforted by the quiet vow, she turned so her cheek rested against the couch and she sought Xander out.

He sat just across from her, his eyes glittering with arousal as he watched the scene play out in front of him. Then his gaze found hers, saw her watching him.

"You please me," he said in a low voice that carried over the silence.

Warmth traveled her entire body as she basked in the warm glow of his approval and the heavy desire reflected in his eyes.

Then she closed her eyes once more as Nico's finger slid past the resistance and inside her body. His mouth touched the small of her back even as he worked his finger in and out of the distended opening.

"Too much?" Nico asked.

"No," she whispered.

After a moment, he withdrew and then she felt the blunt probe of two fingers. She sucked in her breath as he began to stretch her once more, this time to accommodate two digits.

Her clit burned. She wanted to twitch and squirm at the odd heat that Nico was causing. She wanted—needed—clitoral stimulation.

He slid his fingers deeper, more lubricant was added. Then it felt like he parted his fingers, stretching her opening wider just as a new sensation was introduced.

The slightly rounded tip of what felt like rubber pushed its way inside, eased by the added lubricant. Slowly, he drew his fingers back, pushing the plug forward at the same time.

She flinched away when the burning sensation increased and she stretched even more than she had before.

"Shhh," Garon soothed. "Just a bit more and it'll be in. Take a deep breath and push back against it and you'll be there."

She did as he said, whimpered as the burn increased so much that she could no longer remain still. She squirmed and twisted and then suddenly the tension lessened and she was left with a sense of fullness that overwhelmed her.

Nico kissed each cheek of her behind as Garon rubbed and petted her back and shoulders. For several long moments, they continued their tender ministrations and then Sebastien walked over, slid his hands underneath her and lifted her from Garon's lap.

He sank into the armchair, cradling her in his arms. The fullness in her bottom increased as she changed positions and she let out a light whimper as she sought to situate herself to lessen the tension.

Sebastien eased his hand between her thighs, parting her folds and sliding his finger over her clit. She nearly bolted out of his arms. It was like an electric shock, magnified by the intensity of being stretched around the anal plug.

"I'll take the edge off, sweetheart," Sebastien murmured against her ear. "Relax while I make you come."

Relax? Relaxing was the very last thing she could do. She was wound tighter than a spring. Her senses were so heightened that she could barely breath.

She wrapped both arms around his neck and hung on tight as he continued to stroke her clitoris.

Then he moved his hand down so that his thumb replaced his finger over her clit and he eased one finger inside her pussy.

It was cataclysmic.

All the buildup came to a head in one enormous explosion that rocked her entire body head to toe.

She gasped but couldn't seem to draw a breath. The orgasm was sharp and edgy, nothing like anything she'd experienced to date.

Sebastien drew her in close, cradling her tightly against him as she shuddered through the last waves of her release. She clung to him, burying her face in his neck. He pressed a kiss to her temple and stroked his hand through her hair.

"Wickersham has prepared a fruit and cheese tray if you're hungry," Sebastien murmured. "We have wine and your favorite juices. We'll stop and eat for a while, but we want you to wear the plug to get used to it. Later . . . Later we'll take it out and replace it with something else entirely."

Chapter 18

Nico draped a quilt over Talia as she cuddled in Sebastien's lap just moments before Wickersham entered wheeling a cart full of fruit, cheese, breads and drinks.

It thoroughly warmed her that they were so mindful of her modesty. She'd certainly grown accustomed to being nude in their presence, but she was still painfully shy when it came to others in the villa being able to see her. Instead of pressing the issue and bending her to their will, they simply shielded her whenever it was necessary for someone other than themselves to be exposed. That kind of thoughtfulness endeared them all the more to her.

She's surrendered herself to them. She'd willingly given them her obedience. They could easily demand of her whatever they wished. But the knowledge that they didn't try to force on her things they knew made her uncomfortable made her . . . love them.

She knew it was crazy. All of it. She knew she was living some bizarre fantasy she couldn't quite make sense of, but then she didn't want to. If reality was what she'd lived for the last four years, she was more than willing to dive into the fantasy that was her current existence.

Garon went to the tray and prepared a plate of her favorites—how well they were acquainted with her tastes now. Then he turned, found her gaze and gave her that little half lift at the corner of his mouth that signaled a smile.

"Wine or juice?"

She was so buzzed from the whole day so far that she knew mixing alcohol in with her current rush would be a big mistake.

"Juice please."

He poured a glass full and then carried the plate and juice to where she sat and set the glass down on the end table within Sebastien's reach.

To her surprise, Sebastien took the plate, set it on her lap that was covered by the quilt and then he began to feed her bites of the fruit and cheese as tenderly as Garon had once done.

She already knew that Sebastien was a hard-ass shell with a soft center, but it surprised her that he was making such an overt gesture of tenderness and caring.

After a bit, he picked up the glass and held it to her lips so she could take several sips.

The entire time he fed her, the lower half of her body still hummed with arousal and was tingly from the intense orgasm she'd experienced.

If she moved even the tiniest bit, the plug stretched or moved just enough that the burn would start up all over again and blood rushed to her head. She stayed in a constant state of arousal and it was driving her insane.

She'd already started to imagine one of them thrusting into her from behind. Of driving deep, deeper than the plug rested. Of all the candidates, she knew it could only be Xander or Sebastien because there was no doubt she wouldn't be able to take Nico or

Garon. She was having serious doubts whether she could take them vaginally, much less in a much tighter area . . .

Sebastien held a strawberry to her mouth, waited as she bit into it and then when juice spilled onto her lip, he swooped in and sucked it off.

"Tell me something, Talia," he murmured a mere breath from her mouth. "Have you imagined taking more than one of us at a time? Having all of us working to pleasure you? Making love to all of us? Of having us inside you and then another and another until all you can feel is us and nothing else?"

She inhaled sharply and closed her eyes, vivid images splashing through her mind. Oh God, had she imagined. She'd thought of little else. Had anticipated when that time would come. Had they known? Had they purposely made her wait to heighten her anticipation?

"I'll take that as a yes," he said, a thread of satisfaction laced in his words.

She nodded. "I have."

"And did you like what you imagined? Do you want that to happen? It's important to us that you aren't frightened."

She immediately shook her head and turned to look at each man in turn before she finally turned back to Sebastien, her expression solemn.

"I'm not afraid. I trust you. All of you." She turned again so she could include the others in her view. "At first, I considered this"—she waved her hand around—"to be an agreement wherein I would hold up my end of the bargain. I approached it somewhat clinically. I told myself that six months wasn't too much to sacrifice for all that had been done for me and my mother."

Sebastien's arms tightened around her, but she maintained eye contact with the others. This was important. She wanted them to know. Perhaps it was even more important they know before they took that final step where they'd make love to her as a unit.

"But now, it's something I do without thought of gratitude or obligation. I do it because . . ." She sucked in her breath and took the plunge. "I care about all of you. I trust you. You've all been so absolutely wonderful. I feel like the luckiest woman in the world. There's nothing I want more than to please you. You have my submission, my obedience. You have my . . . heart."

Xander stood and somehow his presence seemed so much . . . larger . . . all of a sudden. His expression was fierce. Primal almost. He was beautiful to look at. Confident. Bold. So very alpha.

He strode to where she sat in Sebastien's lap and he tossed the quilt aside, baring her to their view. Then he leaned down hauled her into his arms and then kissed her with a savagery that she hadn't experienced before.

It was a mark of possession. It was a kiss that clearly told her she belonged to him. He was putting his stamp on her for all to see. And when he pulled away, there was a fierce light in his eyes that sent shivers quaking over her body.

"We're going to have you, Talia. And when we're through, you'll have no doubt as to who you belong to and who you belong with. You'll know above all else that you are owned body and soul."

"Then take me," she whispered. "For I am yours."

His jaw tightened and he walked swiftly toward the couch to where Garon still sat. He positioned her over Garon's lap, just as she'd been before. Garon immediately slid his palm over her bottom in a gentle caress while Xander stripped himself of his clothing.

She watched, her head turned to the side, admiring the sight of his naked body. When he'd tossed the remainder of his clothing to the side, he knelt beside her and smoothed his hand down her back and then over her buttocks.

He pressed a kiss to the small of her back and then murmured against her skin. "Garon will remove the plug and then he'll position you for me. I'm going to have your sweet little ass, Talia. And that's only the beginning."

Chapter 19

Garon placed one hand palm down over the small of her back and with the other, he gently pulled at the plug. It came out much easier than it had gone in, and the sensation as it slid out was edgy and breathtaking.

He rubbed over her ass, caressing the cheeks for several seconds as if to soothe away any discomfort, though there wasn't any, and then he lifted her, standing easily as he held her in his arms.

The couch had substantial depth and she easily fit facing the back so that her knees still remained on the cushion. He positioned her on her hands and knees and then gently pushed her head downward so that her ass was lifted higher into the air.

The vulnerability of such a position excited her. All four men could easily see her most intimate parts. She couldn't see them. Had no idea what they planned, and that only heightened her excitement.

Xander slid his hands over her waist and then to her behind, spreading her cheeks so that she was more exposed to him.

"Use your hand to touch yourself, Talia," he instructed. "Use your fingers on your clit. It will help when I penetrate you. But don't come. Not yet."

She reached up, pressed her hand to her belly and then slid it upward, over the apex of her legs and then delved her fingers into the folds to find her clit.

She sighed a little as she stroked herself, enjoying the pleasurable sensations as well as the anticipation of when he'd push inside her.

When the blunt head of his cock first pressed against her opening, she moaned and twisted restlessly, eager to have him deep within her.

He rubbed his cock up and down over her opening, aided by the slippery lubricant that Nico had used earlier. Evidently satisfied that he'd added enough to ease his penetration, he began to push against the tight resistance, forcing her to open under his relentless invasion.

She put more pressure on her clit and rubbed in a circular motion, finding just the right spot and the exact amount of pressure she needed. It made her want his entry even more. She was desperate for it.

He didn't just ram his dick into her ass, and for that she was grateful, even as much as she wanted him inside her. Instead he maintained steady pressure and kept pushing forward, opening her at a slow, steady pace until finally the head was inside.

"Ah, Talia, you're so tight," he groaned. "Like a fist gripping me."

Inch by delicious inch, he fed his cock into her ass until finally, finally she felt the weight of his balls against her pussy and knew he was all the way in.

She felt impossibly stretched. The burn was decadent. She felt she was indulging in the most forbidden pleasure and yet it was only just beginning. They'd made dark promises. Promises that had her desperate with want.

For a moment she had to stop stroking herself. She was too close. Knew that if she continued, if she touched herself even once more, that she'd catapult over the edge and into blissful orgasm. She didn't want it over with so soon, and he'd told her not to.

Then he withdrew, pulling slowly out, and the sensation nearly overwhelmed her. She panted softly, willing herself not to come even without the self-stimulation.

When he'd pulled out so that only the head remained inside her opening, he pushed forward again, a little harder this time and a little faster.

He continued the same pattern, gradually increasing speed and force until he was fucking her rhythmically and the slaps of his thighs meeting her ass could be heard throughout the room.

It was an entirely different feeling than when he'd fucked her vaginally. She couldn't even begin to compare the two.

And then she began to wonder how it would feel to have two cocks inside her. One in her ass, one in her pussy.

Her pulse beat thunderously, her pussy throbbed and her clit was swollen, begging for attention. Just one touch. One simple stroke and Talia would be off like a firecracker. But she purposely kept her hand still over her tender flesh, not wanting to end it.

Her fantasies were too delicious, her imaginings too vivid.

And then suddenly he withdrew, leaving her gasping at the instant void. Again she was lifted, only this time, it was Xander who picked her up. He turned, bearing her with him and then he sank onto the couch, his legs splayed.

Her back was to him and Sebastien stood before her, naked, hugely erect, his hand fisted around his cock.

Xander eased her backward and she realized his intention.

He positioned her over his cock and then put one hand on her shoulder to pull her down so that once again he pushed into her ass.

When he was balls deep in her ass, he leaned back and pushed his knees upward into the backs of her legs and then used his strength to spread her, leaving her bare and vulnerable to Sebastien.

Her ass was on the very edge of the couch. All Sebastien had to do was slide right between her thighs and he'd be right there at her opening.

She had no idea how this was going to work, how it could work, but she was nearly in nuclear meltdown at the image of Sebastien pushing into her while Xander was embedded so deeply into her body.

Sebastien slid his finger into her pussy and then he smiled. "Goddamn, but you're tight. I can't wait to get my dick inside you."

He removed his hand and then positioned his cock at her opening. She trembled from head to toe and realized she couldn't control the shaking no matter how hard she tried. Xander kissed her shoulder and stroked his hands up over her belly to her breasts.

Sebastien began pushing inward. It wasn't easy. He certainly didn't glide right in. After only an inch, he swore through his teeth and sweat broke out on his forehead. He looked like he was struggling not to come.

After taking a deep breath, he pushed more forcefully, this time gaining more depth.

She felt stuffed, completely filled, stretched to capacity but it was the most sinfully amazing sensation she'd ever experienced.

She started to fidget, but Sebastien was quick to stop her.

"Don't, honey," he croaked out. "Let me do the moving. I'm barely hanging on by a thread here. If you move, it's going to be all over."

She smiled and reached up to touch his face. It made her feel a little powerful to know she could make him want her this much, so much that he was having to work to maintain his control.

He pulled back and then thrust forward, much more forcefully this time. She gasped out just as he let out a harsh groan. Behind her, Xander's breath was explosive on her neck. All three of them felt the force—and result—of Sebastien's penetration.

He was deeply inside her now and she was completely filled. Xander was as far as he could go. Sebastien was pressed to her body, his pelvis mashed against hers. The three of them were tangled up, locked together by her.

"How does it feel?" Xander whispered in her ear. "Do you feel possessed, Talia? Do you understand that we own you? That you belong to us and that we are marking you as primitively as a man can mark a woman?"

She arched back, leaning into Xander's arms. His hands closed over her breasts, kneading the swells and then teasing her nipples.

"Come, Sebastien," Xander ordered. "She and I won't last much longer."

With a groan, Sebastien began thrusting into her, his body flexing and bowing. It was a beautiful sight, seeing this powerfully built man work to get inside her body.

She closed her eyes, reveling in the delight of being between these two men. She rested the back of her head on Xander's shoulders and let him hold her as Sebastien pushed forward with a roar and began to come inside her.

Sebastien leaned over her and captured her lips, kissing her with as much savagery as Xander had kissed her with just earlier. His hips jerked and pumped against her before he finally went still and remained locked within her for several long moments.

When he pulled out, there was a warm rush and she was surprised he made no move to clean her. They were always so meticulous in their care of her.

But then Garon moved forward and Xander whispered next to her ear, "Sebastien going first will make it easier for you to take Garon and Nico."

Her eyes widened and heat rushed through her body at the

erotic words. The imagery. The whole idea. Holy hell. Garon was
going to take her after Sebastien had basically provided a whole
lot of natural lubricant. It was kinky as hell, but none of the men
seemed bothered by it a bit.

Garon positioned himself but he leaned forward to kiss her as
the broad head of his cock rested at her opening. His mouth was
gentle on hers, sweet where Sebastien and Xander had been possessive and demanding.

"I won't hurt you, Talia," he murmured as he drew away.

She smiled back at him. "I know."

He pushed inside, stretching her with his enormous width. It
was true, he probably would have never gotten inside her on his
own. Not with Xander deep in her ass, making her vaginal opening a whole lot smaller.

But oh God, did it feel good to be so stretched around his beautiful cock. The friction was delicious. Every movement sent pleasure dancing through her veins.

Xander was wrapped so tightly around her. Her anchor. His
hands on her body. His cock deep inside her. His mouth against
her neck, her shoulder, pressed against her hair.

She didn't understand his connection to the other men. Why
he shared what he considered his with them. But she found that
the more time that went on, the less she cared. Some things just
were and she could hardly complain when she was the center, the
focus, of four sexy-as-sin men bent on fulfilling her every desire.

Garon found her gaze, seared her with the intensity of those
dark eyes. He pushed farther inside, infinitely patient, so patient
she found herself squirming, wanting him to let loose.

"Please," she whispered. "I know you won't hurt me, Garon.
I need it harder. I'm about to go out of my mind here."

Garon's breath came out in a harsh expulsion. He gripped her
thighs, held her tightly and then thrust forward, forcing himself
deeper into her body.

Oh God. She wasn't going to make it. How could she?

She began orgasming, wave upon wave rocking over her. She clenched around Garon. Through it all, Xander held her while Garon drove relentlessly into her. She cried out and gripped Garon's shoulders, dug her fingers into his flesh, needing something to hold on to as she came completely and utterly apart.

It was pain and pleasure all rolled into one. So intense that she couldn't bear it.

Garon thrust into her, the wet, sucking sounds reaching her ears, and it was then she realized that he too had started coming the moment she began contracting around him.

He leaned forward to rest his forehead on her shoulder and he shook against her as he remained embedded in her pussy.

She sagged against Xander, her body limp and hypersensitive to even the slightest movement. When Garon began to pull out, she groaned. He came free in a liquid rush and then stepped away from her only to be replaced by Nico.

She stared helplessly at Nico as he positioned himself at her entrance. Two men had come inside her. She'd just had the most awesome orgasm of her life. And Nico still had to fuck her.

She wasn't sure she'd survive this. If it was possible to die of pleasure, she was going to certainly do it.

Even wet from the releases of two men, she was snug around Nico as he pushed inward. He'd always been the most gentle with her. The most understanding. Always so sweet. But now he looked fiercely determined.

The possessive glint in his eyes made her shiver. She was staring at a man determined to mark her. Just like the others had.

His fingers dug into her hips and he held her in place as he thrust again, gaining more depth.

She was even more swollen now, not only from Xander being so deep inside her ass, but from her orgasm and Sebastien and Garon forcing their way through her tight passage.

Each movement from Nico elicited a ragged moan, and yet it wasn't painful. It was intense. It burned. It was beautiful. She'd never felt anything like it.

"Tilt her back just a bit more," Nico said to Xander. "I can't get all the way inside her at this angle."

The words quaked over her, eliciting another strong wave of desire and instant arousal. She wanted him there. Wanted him as deep as he could go. Already she felt the stirring of another climb to orgasm.

Her body tightened. Her nipples beaded. Her pussy clenched and she tingled from head to toe.

Xander leaned back, shifting forward so that he could recline further on the couch, which presented Talia more fully to Nico.

Nico stood over her, reached down with his thumbs and he spread her folds so that she was stretched even tighter around him. Then he thrust hard. Deep. Filling her fully, more full than she'd ever been.

She gasped, then cried out. She bucked upward and writhed against Xander. He held her tightly, murmuring to her but she couldn't hear over the roar of blood and the pulse beating loudly in her ears.

Nico was no longer the sweet, tender lover who'd taken such care with her on so many prior occasions. He was a man bent on claiming what he considered his.

His gaze bore into her, demanding response. He pushed into her, over and over, his control leashed, a powerful thing to witness.

"I want you to come, Talia. One more time. With me inside you. Come so I can fill you with my release, so that you'll have had us all deep inside you."

His command swept over like wildfire. Her pussy fluttered and went wild around him. Her belly clenched and she started to shake uncontrollably.

As soon as he began to jet his semen deep inside her, another orgasm tore through her body, so powerful that she lost awareness. The room dimmed around her and all she could process was the never-ending roll of ecstasy that billowed like a storm.

Then Nico pulled out. She found herself pitching forward, her knees digging into a pillow on the floor. Xander mounted her from behind, slid deep into her ass and began fucking her in earnest as cum slid down the insides of her thighs. Semen from three different men.

He rode her hard, without mercy, and she was still orgasming, her body coiling into a vicious knot as Xander continued to drive into her.

She rested her forehead on the floor, eyes closed as the haziness grew around her. She was dimly aware of Xander's roar of satisfaction. Of his pelvis flat against her ass, his balls resting against her pussy as he twitched and shot his release into her ass.

And then he pulled away. She could hear him stand. She turned her head so that her cheek rested on the floor and she could see them gathered around her, all watching as more semen slipped down the backs of her thighs.

Marked.

Possessed.

They'd taken her as they'd promised. Made her their belonging. Their cherished, pampered belonging.

She was exhausted and yet exhilarated. She wished she could see herself as they saw her right now. Wondered what she looked like with the remnants of their possession dripping down her body.

And then Sebastien stepped over her body, straddling her as he hunched down and pushed his cock into her ass.

Oh God.

She closed her eyes as he slid deep, pumping with quick, frenzied motions. He'd been finished long before the others had. He'd had the longest to wait while the others took their turns. Now he was hard and unbelievably aroused again and it was clear he had every intention of sating himself once more.

She lay there, existing in that delicious dream state while he hunched down over her and thrust in and out with deliberate, forceful thrusts. It was obvious he had no intention of drawing it out. Maybe he didn't want to overtire her. Within a dozen thrusts, he was already coming, his hands gripping her hips tight as he held himself deep.

And then he stepped away.

No longer able to hold herself up on her knees, she slowly rolled to her side, curling her legs up so she was in a comfortable ball.

"My poor darling," Xander murmured.

His voice was close and his breath brushed over her ear. She opened her eyes to see him crouched next to her. Then he slid his arms underneath her, lifting her into his arms.

"Come, my precious Talia. You and I will go have a nice long bath and then you'll rest."

She smiled dreamily and snuggled deeper into Xander's chest. She turned her face into his neck as he mounted the stairs leading to his bedroom.

She'd been used, much like a favorite toy, but it was the manner in which they'd taken her that had made all the difference.

She'd never felt so cherished or cared for in her life.

Chapter 20

After three months on the island, Talia had forgotten what it was like to live anywhere else. Her days were spent in luxury. Endless spoiling. Waited on hand and foot.

At times it was almost as if the men took turns commanding her, or that she would spend certain days with one and other days with another.

Xander was a constant presence but often he would stand back and watch. Silent. Dominant. He liked to see the other men dominate her. He liked to watch them fuck her, sometimes alone, sometimes in a twosome or even threesome and then afterward, he'd come in, when she'd been sated and satisfied by his men and then he'd fuck her with ruthless precision as if to remind her who she truly belonged to and that everything else that happened did so at his behest.

At night she slept alone, with Xander. He began every morning by rolling onto her, parting her thighs and driving deep. Other times he'd push her onto her belly and thrust into her ass. And then on occasion, he'd pull her head down to suck him off and relieve the morning erection.

Afterward he would leave the bedroom and then send one of the other men to prepare her for the day.

It was a routine she'd fallen comfortably into. She knew what was expected. Knew just how her days would begin and how they'd end.

They always began with Xander. They always ended with Xander.

What happened in between was anyone's guess and a source of constant excitement for Talia.

She stretched in the big bed she shared with Xander and idly wondered who would come for her today. Sometimes, they would fuck her before allowing her to rise. Other times she would go to her knees beside the bed before she was allowed to go downstairs and she'd have to suck their cocks.

And other times, she was pleasured beyond measure, given orgasm after orgasm until she was begging for mercy and had to be carried downstairs afterward because she lacked the strength to walk on her own.

As silly as it sounded, she was in love. With Xander. With Garon. And Sebastien. And Nico.

It was a complicated mess, but Xander would have her believe that the situation was the epitome of simplicity.

It wasn't something she could worry over, though, or she'd just drive herself crazy. So she went with it and found herself sliding deeper under their spell with each passing day.

Xander had told her he never had any intention of letting her go. She'd wait quietly for that six-month mark on the contract to expire and see what happened then.

"You're looking particularly satisfied this morning," Nico drawled from the door.

She rolled to her side, rose up on her elbow, making her hair fall across her breasts.

"Good morning," she said with a warm smile.

He returned her smile and strode into the bedroom to sit on the edge of the bed. His hand went automatically to caress her side and wander aimlessly down her hip and then back up to her breasts.

He liked to touch her, seemed to find great pleasure in it. He was more openly affectionate than the others, and by that she meant in a nonsexual way. They were all plenty adoring when it came to sex, but even casually, during the day Nico would often make affectionate gestures. She loved that about him.

"Today, you'll dress," he announced.

She raised both eyebrows in mock astonishment. "Dressed? What's this?"

He laughed. "Thought we'd go down to the beach. You'll need to be covered. You can wear your favorite sundress, a shawl and your big straw hat."

She sat up and stretched and then crawled to the edge to sit beside him for a moment.

"That sounds lovely. It looks to be a particularly gorgeous day today."

He nodded. "I'll go downstairs to wait for you. Take your time. I'll make sure Wickersham has your favorite breakfast prepared and then we'll go soak in the sun."

She watched as he got up and walked out of the bedroom and then she hugged her arms around herself, smiling in contentment. Evidently it was Nico's day to spend the majority of the day with her. Xander would join them for lunch in all likelihood. Most of his mornings were spent in updates and phone calls on the status of Cristofino. Toward the end of the day, they'd be joined by Garon and Sebastien and they'd delight in taking her in ways that made her head spin.

She pushed herself upward from the bed and went to take a quick shower. She left her hair wet after toweling most of the excess moisture from it because it would dry quickly in the sun.

After finishing in the bathroom, she found the sundress she

was to wear, grabbed the thin floral shawl that she'd drape over her shoulders and then reached up on the closet shelf for the wide, floppy straw hat that kept the sun off her face.

She hummed lightly as she headed downstairs. Often Wickersham would have breakfast out on the terrace for her since she'd developed an affinity for eating outdoors when the patio was still cool.

As she passed Xander's office-slash-library, she heard him speaking in raised tones.

"I will not bring Talia back to Cristofino with me under any circumstances. I won't have her associated with me."

Her mouth dropped open and hurt crowded in, squeezing the breath from her. She would have listened for more, but he dropped his voice, almost as if he realized how loudly he'd spoken and was now moderating his speech.

Who on earth could he have been talking to? Sebastien? Garon? Someone else entirely?

Numbly she walked toward the terrace doors, coldness settling into the pit of her stomach. As she'd suspected, Nico was already outside at the table where breakfast had been laid out. He'd fixed her plate and was pouring a glass of orange juice as she approached.

How the hell was she supposed to eat now? She honest to God feared that if she took one bite, she'd vomit it back up.

What could he have meant?

She nearly snorted over her own damn ignorance. What it meant was that she was his private little plaything and that it would never do for his relationship with her to become public.

He didn't want his "association" with her to be known.

It hurt and she had no defense against it. She couldn't tell herself that it was all right, that he was just a lying asshole and that she shouldn't care what he had said or what he thought.

Naïve or not, she'd believed him when he'd told her he cared about her, that he didn't want to let her go. She believed it when the others professed to have feelings for her. She wasn't going to waste time feeling shame for buying into something that had been so convincingly presented.

"Is something wrong, Talia?" Nico asked.

She glanced up to see concern etched on his face. She forced a smile and shook her head. Then she reached for her glass of juice, wondering how on earth she was supposed to be normal after hearing that little explosion from Xander's lips?

It was obvious he was angry about something, but there was nothing she could have done to upset him. She had no paranoia about that. She'd been accommodating, obedient and submissive at all times.

She nearly made a sound of disgust. She may as well be describing a lap dog. Dear God, she was starting to feel like such a fool for buying into this whole charade.

Knowing Nico was watching her closely, she made a show of picking at her food, shoving it around, choking down a few bites. Finally she had enough and just shoved it back, knowing she couldn't possibly stomach another forkful of the eggs and toast.

"Are you ready to hit the beach?" Nico asked. "There's a spot I'd love to show you, but it's a bit of a walk from here if you're up for it."

She licked her lips and swallowed, hating that she was about to lie to him. But then she felt lied to about pretty much everything at this point.

"I don't feel very well, Nico. I was fine earlier. Maybe it was what I ate."

His expression immediately became one of concern.

"Could I . . . Could I just go back upstairs and maybe lie down for a while?"

He was up and reaching for her hand before she even got the words out.

"Of course," he said, concern edging his voice. "I'll take you up and inform Xander at once."

Talia held up a hand. "No, please don't bother him. He usually doesn't join us until lunchtime. Perhaps I'll feel better by then." Liar. She wouldn't, but the last thing she wanted was Xander breathing down her neck until she wasn't so raw from what she'd overheard.

Nico looked torn but then he ushered her toward the door. "Is it your stomach? Your head? Tell me what's bothering you."

"Just my head," she said, sticking to the truth. Her entire head ached vilely and she wanted nothing more than to stick a pillow over it and close her eyes. Maybe then she'd wake up and none of this would have happened.

Even better, maybe she'd wake back in Paris and this whole three months would have been nothing more than a really erotic dream.

Chapter 21

Xander broke off his conversation with Garon and Sebastien when his office door swung open. He relaxed when he saw it was Nico, but then he tensed, realizing that Nico should be with Talia.

"Where's Talia?" he demanded.

A frown marred Nico's forehead. "She's not feeling well. I took her onto the terrace to eat breakfast. I knew you wouldn't want her where she would hear any of what's going on. She picked at her food. It didn't seem like she felt well. Afterward when I suggested a walk down the beach, which she's usually more than up for, she said she had a headache and asked if she could go up to bed."

Concern made his already shitty mood even worse. Talia wasn't a complainer. She hadn't had a single ailment, other than experiencing her monthly periods, and even then she'd seemed not to feel well only once.

"What's the situation, Xander?" Nico clipped out. "What the hell's going on back home?"

Xander sighed and dropped into the chair behind his desk. "It's a fucking mess."

"Not true exactly," Sebastien pointed out.

Xander shot Sebastien a look that told him he was fast approaching the line not to cross. Sebastien shrugged and turned to stare out the window.

Then Xander turned his attention back to Nico so he could fill Nico in on all that had occurred while he was busy with Talia.

"I received a phone call this morning from the newly appointed 'prime minister' of Cristofino."

Nico's expression darkened. "We have no prime minister. He is not recognized by our people."

Xander held up a hand. "Let me finish. All isn't well with the new regime. The people are indeed very unhappy with the direction that the insurgents are going. They want the royal family reinstalled. What was an effort to overthrow the monarchy with as little bloodshed as possible, apart from the assassination of my father," he added bitterly, "has now led to full-scale rioting and revolting in the streets of the capital. It's out of control and it's only going to get worse. The insurgents are basically waving the white flag."

"What the hell does that mean?" Nico demanded.

"What it means is that they're proposing a truce . . . and a compromise."

Nico sank into one of the armchairs. Garon was still standing, arms locked over his barrel chest while Sebastien stared angrily out the window. They were all loyal to Xander. To the royal family. They'd been loyal to Xander's father. They were loyal to their country. They hated that Xander had been forced out of the country and that he'd bided his time here, so many miles away while his country and people needed him.

"And what is this compromise?" Nico asked wearily.

"They'll reinstall the monarchy. My mother and sister will return to the palace. I'll be crowned king."

"That's not a compromise. That's capitulation," Nico said.

"Yes, well there's a catch," Xander said grimly. "They want to establish a congress of sorts who will govern alongside the king or act in an advisory capacity and reserve the right to have a vote of confidence if at any time they feel the king is not acting in the best interests of the country. The other thing? They want me there immediately to attend a full-scale media event announcing my return."

Nico stared back at him in shock. For a moment he didn't speak at all. He seemed to struggle with his reaction, almost as if he didn't want Xander to know his true feelings.

"Say what's on your mind, Nico," Xander said quietly. "You won't have said anything Garon and Bastien haven't already said, I'm sure."

"What about Talia?" Nico asked.

"I don't know," Xander said honestly.

It frustrated that the answer wasn't cut and dried. Not simple. He could rail against the fairness of having to choose between a woman who meant everything to him and the future of his country and fulfilling his destiny, but he'd always known that he would face tough decisions. He'd always known his life wasn't his own.

He didn't have the luxury of choice. Many choices had been made for him at birth. He didn't waste time lamenting it. It was his life.

He couldn't turn his back on this. It was what he'd waited for. The opportunity to return to his country. To have his mother and sister safely back behind palace walls. To lead his country as he'd been meant to do.

"I must return immediately," Xander said in a low voice. "I can't delay. Too much is at stake."

Garon's lips thinned. Sebastien turned from his place by the window, his mouth twisted into a frown.

"And Talia?" Nico said. "Where does she fit into all of this?"

"I can't—I *won't*—expose her to such a volatile situation. I won't have her associated with me in any way. If they knew I had any weaknesses at all, they would exploit them in a heartbeat. They'd drag Talia through the mud and have no mercy in doing so. She could even be in very real danger if it was determined she had any meaning to me. They'd use her to make me capitulate to any and all of their demands and they'd have no compunction in doing whatever was necessary to her to gain that capitulation. These are the men who ruthlessly murdered my father, their king. One young girl means nothing to them. I cannot risk her. I won't risk her. She may mean nothing to them, but she is everything to me."

There was silence in the room. Xander knew that his men had no more liking for the situation than he did. He could sense their frustration. It coiled and snapped like a living, breathing entity in the small confines of his office.

"She must return to Paris at once. Discreetly of course. None of you can accompany her. She must return the way she came. It's widely known that I am never without any of you. If one of you is seen in Paris or it's known you weren't with me in such an important time, it will open the door to investigation, and I won't risk Talia that way."

Garon let out a curse that was picked up by Sebastien and was explosive in the room.

"Goddamn it, Xander, she's going to think we used her," Garon snarled.

Xander wanted to put his fist through the wall. He sat there a long moment, trying to control the rage and helplessness that was boiling through his veins. He hated the helplessness.

Finally he spoke, but he knew his voice was tight and not his own. "I can't know what can be done until I return to Cristofino and assess the situation there. And in the meantime, I will *not* risk any harm coming to Talia, nor would I have her exposed to a media feeding frenzy. She deserves none of that."

"And what are you going to tell her, Xander?" Sebastien asked. "The truth?"

Xander expelled a long breath. "I can only tell her that I am terminating our agreement early and that she is free to return home to her mother."

Chapter 22

Talia lay on her stomach, pillow shoved under her chin as she stared out the big picture window to the splash of blue in the distant horizon. After having lain here for the last hour, she'd calmed down and lectured herself on overreacting.

She'd overheard two sentences with no context to draw from. She had no idea what Xander had been talking about and it was unfair—not to mention stupid—to fly off the handle when she had no idea what he'd really meant.

Now her mood was shattered and what should have been an otherwise beautiful day was in ruins because she'd gotten all emotional—and irrational.

It didn't help that she simply didn't know her place in this new world she'd been dumped into. Words were just words. And she'd heard them often. But what if she was a naïve twit who'd believe anything said to her as long as it was accompanied by sweet gestures and a gentle hand?

But the flip side of that was that perhaps she was reading way too much into an overheard snippet of conversation and as a result she was overreacting and being a cynical bitch.

She sucked in a deep breath and squared her shoulders—as much as she could lying sprawled across the bed, her chin dug into one of the plump pillows.

Enough was enough. She was not going to spend the day moping, nor would she allow this incident to make her second-guess every single aspect of her time here.

She'd simply ask Xander what he'd meant. She'd tell him what she'd heard and go from there. It was a simple enough solution, and it was what she should have done from the onset rather than spend an hour sulking in the bedroom.

Feeling marginally better about having a plan of action, she pushed upward from the pillow, shoved her hair that had fallen forward from her face and started to roll to her side so she could get up.

She froze when she saw Xander standing in the doorway of the bedroom, a grim expression on his face.

There was something off in his demeanor. Something that sent a curl of dread through her stomach and into her chest. Her optimism of just moments before evaporated, and her anxiety level shot through the roof.

"Nico said you were feeling unwell," he said, still not moving from his post at the door.

That wasn't like Xander. He rarely kept his distance from her. If they were in the same room, he was always touching her, or next to her. Often holding her or simply sitting beside her.

But he stood coolly aloof, surveying her with concern in his eyes and yet maintaining the distance between them.

"I'm all right now," she said softly, a lie. "I woke with a headache, but it's much better now."

He stood a long moment in silence. With each passing second

her dread mounted because this was so unlike Xander. Something was wrong. Terribly wrong and this time she wasn't going to scold herself for being paranoid.

"I'm releasing you from the contract you signed," he said in a quiet tone.

Her heart bottomed out and she stared at him, sure she hadn't heard correctly. A million questions buzzed through her mind but the only thing she could croak out was, "Why?"

"Things have changed. I must return to Cristofino. I've already made arrangements for you to be transported back to Paris—and your mother. I've let her know you'll be returning. She's looking forward to seeing you."

She pushed herself into a sitting position, stunned. So horribly stunned that she couldn't even manage a coherent thought, much less respond to the bombshell he'd just dumped on her.

She wanted to scream at him. She wanted to ask him what had changed. She wanted to ask him if it had all been a lie, but she didn't want to open herself to that kind of humiliation. She was humiliated enough.

She had pride. She may have foregone it to have ever entered into this devil's bargain, but it didn't mean she had none left. There was no way she was going to beg. She already felt like dying and she wasn't going to add to her misery by making an embarrassing scene.

It took everything she possessed to pull herself together and not to lose it right there in front of him. She'd never felt so used and degraded in her life. But he didn't have to know that. By God, she'd leave here with her head held high and he'd never, never know that he'd made her feel so worthless. She'd never give him that satisfaction.

"When do you want me to leave," she said calmly.

"The plane will arrive for you this afternoon."

She couldn't control the flinch no matter how much she didn't want him to see her pain. It would seem he couldn't wait to get her out of his life.

Temporary diversion. Plaything. Whore.

It would appear that all of those things were indeed true.

He was now poised to resume his life and she was supposed to resume hers. As if none of this had happened. As if she hadn't had her life completely changed by the months she'd spent here.

She slid from the bed, afraid her legs wouldn't hold her up. She put one hand down onto the mattress so she didn't go down as she faced him with what little pride she had in reserve.

"Will I be able to say good-bye to Garon, Sebastien and Nico?"

She tried to keep her questions and responses to the bare minimum of words because the last thing she wanted was to break down in front of him. He could be a cold bastard. Well, so could she.

He looked away for a moment. "I think it would be best if you just went. It will be easier that way."

Anger flashed, heating her veins. Heat crept up her neck and into her cheeks. "Easier for who, Xander? You? Them? Are you saying they have no wish to say good-bye? Are you all that eager to have me gone?"

For a moment, just a flash, she saw what looked like pain flicker in his eyes but it was gone before she could even imagine that's what it was.

"I'll send Wickersham for you when the car arrives to take you to the airport," he said just before he turned and walked quietly away.

Chapter 23

Talia didn't wait for the summons from Xander. She no longer had any desire to say good-bye. She packed the small bag she'd brought with her and left everything that Xander had provided for her behind.

None of it was hers, and she wanted no reminders of her shame. All she would leave with was her purse, her identification and the small amount of cash she'd arrived with three months before. She'd need the taxi fare once she reached Paris.

The gifts, the jewelry, the clothes, the underwear, she left it all on the bed and hanging in the closet. And she walked down the stairs in a worn pair of jeans and a T-shirt, the only two things in her entire wardrobe here that belonged to her.

Wickersham met her at the bottom of the stairs and informed her that the car had arrived. He would have walked her out but she waved him away. She needed no assistance in leaving. She'd get into that damn car herself and she'd never look back.

She was numb as they drove away. So cold that even the heat of the midday sun couldn't penetrate the icy shell that encased her.

She mechanically went through the motions of getting out of the car that bore her to the airstrip.

She barely remembered boarding the small jet or buckling herself into the seat. She closed the window shades, not wanting even a glimpse back at the island she was leaving. Nor did she want to think of *what* she was leaving behind.

Her heart. Her soul.

And she felt so incredibly stupid for allowing it to happen. For making herself so vulnerable and for believing in a fantasy. It was a hard lesson to learn but one she'd never forget.

She wanted to crawl into a hole somewhere and die, but she would never allow her mother to know of her heartbreak.

She dozed off and on during the flight to Paris, but mostly she stared at the closed window, reliving each and every moment of her time on the island.

Over and over she analyzed every word that had been said to her. Every touch. Every caress. Every thoughtful thing that had been done for her. The attention they lavished on her and how they'd spoiled her endlessly.

And the more she thought about it, the more befuddled she grew because it simply didn't add up. Her brain hurt from trying to make sense of it.

By the time she landed, she was a walking zombie. She knew she looked terrible and as much as she wanted to go straight to the assisted-living community where her mother currently resided, she didn't want her mother to see her this way.

Instead she directed the taxi to her small apartment in the Rive Gauche and when she stumbled inside the dark apartment that had been vacant for the last three months, only then did she allow the first tear to fall.

Chapter 24

Talia sat with her mother in the small living room of her mother's apartment that overlooked the gardens of the assisted-living facility. They were enjoying an afternoon cup of tea, a routine that her mom always adhered to and one Talia found great comfort in.

The fact that her mother was still alive to have tea with made her chest ache because she couldn't imagine the alternative. And it was a point she reminded herself of on a daily basis.

No matter what Xander had done, he'd saved her mother. In the end, no matter how heartbroken she was, how humiliated she'd been or the things that she'd done, none of it mattered in the face of her mom receiving lifesaving treatment.

"I'm so glad to have you home," Rose Montforte said, smiling over her cup of tea at Talia.

Talia smiled back, delighted to be able to genuinely smile. In the two weeks she'd been home, everything had felt so forced even though the joy she felt over seeing her mother again was certainly real.

"I feel as though you've changed so much, and I can't put my finger on how," she added with a slight frown.

Talia raised one eyebrow. "I was only gone for three months, Mama. How much could I have changed?"

She nearly choked on the question because the answer was pretty simple. She'd changed a lot. Maybe she'd grown up even. Or maybe she'd lost some of that youthful enchantment that came from feeling like you were untouchable. Perhaps everyone had to go through that at some point before they grew older and more jaded.

Rose tsked as she took another sip. "I don't know, but I see it."

Then her eyes widened and she hastily grabbed for the television remote and started clicking madly. The volume rose and Talia swiveled in her seat to look behind her to see what had grabbed her mother's attention so rapidly.

"Oh look, darling. There's Xander! Cristofino has been making the news so often lately. It looks as though things are going to work out. Why only a few days ago, the prince's mother and sister returned from Australia where they've been residing since the king's assassination. Such a sad state of affairs. It's high time we've gotten good news about our home. It makes me so homesick. Perhaps if things settle there, we can think about returning soon, yes?"

But Talia was riveted to the television and barely heard her mother's chattering behind her. She only had eyes for her dark-eyed prince, who suddenly seemed so much larger than life on the TV screen. So untouchable. Beyond her reach. Someone a girl like her should have never imagined being able to have.

The announcer's words hit her with the force of a car crash. She went numb from head to toe as she stared dumbly at the screen, listening as the reporter droned on about how it was expected that the coronation ceremony for Alexander would be forthcoming in a few days.

She had refused to watch anything pertaining to Cristofino since her return from the island. She loved her homeland and felt a deep devotion to it. It was of grave concern that so much turmoil had been visited on her home soil. But if the television was on and Cristofino was so much as hinted about, she rapidly shut it off or changed the channel because she couldn't bear to know what was going on with Xander.

She listened to the momentous announcement that the royal family would be restored, that Xander would be crowned king and assume the duties of the reigning monarch, just as his father before him had.

There was much celebration. The people of Cristofino gathered in the capital to dance in the streets. The royals had been welcomed home with jubilation and the insurgents had finally relinquished their military hold. Their reign of terror and intimidation was at its end.

Cristofino was free.

She should be as jubilant as her people were, but she felt dead on the inside.

All the words he'd whispered while making love to her. Worthless. All the times he'd told her he had no intention of letting her go. The attachments he'd allowed her to form with his men. And worse, she'd thought her feelings had been reciprocated.

A part of her understood. He'd made the right decision. How could he turn his back on his entire country for her? Just a girl. An ordinary girl. No one special. Certainly no one of nobility.

Xander would marry someone of his own ilk. Perhaps a princess of a neighboring country. There had been talk before the rebellion of an alliance with St. Francio and a marriage between Xander and Princess Charlotte. Perhaps now, with Xander as king, those talks would resume.

What a fool she'd been. She'd never felt so gullible and stupid in her life, and she made a vow right then and there as she watched

Xander address the people of Cristofino that she'd never allow anyone to make her feel this way again.

"Talia, are you all right, darling?"

Her mother's worried voice broke through some of the utter numbness that had settled over her. She turned, taking in her mom's expression of concern.

"I'm fine," she said calmly. Then she leaned forward, inching her way to the edge of her chair so she could reach over to grasp her mother's hands. "Let's go away, Mama. Wouldn't that be so much fun?"

Rose looked startled and then she set the cup down and grasped Talia's hand with both hers. "Go away? Where?"

"On holiday. Just you and me. We should celebrate. You're feeling so much better. The doctors have said that you're fully in remission. Your markers have looked good for the last year. And yet here we sit in this care facility when we could be out seeing the world."

A flicker of excitement lit up her mother's eyes. She grasped Talia's hand just a little tighter. "You think so? Oh, that does sound like a lovely idea. But could we really do it? It all sounds so intimidating."

Talia smiled. "I think it would be great fun. I've always thought it would be nice to visit Italy and Spain. We've been in France for four years now, and we've never even set foot out of the country and so much is right here and so close. A mere train ride away."

For a moment her mom stared at her with a complete look of befuddlement. Then more excitement danced in her eyes and she lifted Talia's hand, all but shaking it in her grasp.

"Let's do it. Oh, Talia, it would be such fun and I know how much you've wanted to travel. I've always felt so guilty because I know if it weren't for me, you would have already been out exploring the world."

Talia leaned forward, pulled her mom into her arms and hugged her fiercely. "Never say that, Mama. I wouldn't change a single thing. You're more important to me than anything else in the world. I would have done anything to keep you here with me for many years to come. And just think, now we can see the world together."

For a long moment, Talia held on tightly to her mom. She was so grateful to have her. Even though her mother had no idea what had transpired on the island or of Talia's current heartbreak, just being here with her mom and knowing she was going to be all right held Talia together.

She would make it. She would be all right. The Montforte women were a resilient bunch. Her mother was living proof. If her mom could kick cancer's ass and walk away the victor, then Talia could certainly survive a broken heart.

Chapter 25

"What the hell do you mean, you don't know where she is?" Xander demanded.

He stared at Garon, Sebastien and Nico, his pulse about to beat right out of his temples.

"She's gone," Garon said. "The utilities have been disconnected in her apartment, though when I had the manager let me in since it's in your name, it didn't appear as though she's moved out. Most noticeably, however, is that when I went to the facility where her mother has an apartment, I was told that Rose Montforte no longer resides there and that she has moved permanently. No forwarding address or information was given."

Xander swore. "Goddamn it, I sent you to bring her back. Here. To me. This is unacceptable. She's nowhere in Paris?"

Sebastien shook his head. "Not that we can find."

"What did you expect, Xander?" Nico asked, his lips twisted into a snarl. "You completely botched this entire thing. There are at least a hundred other ways you could have handled the situation and yet you let her walk away believing that we cared nothing about her."

"You shut the fuck up," Xander seethed. "I could not, would not, expose her to any danger. I couldn't bring her here. I didn't want her to remain on the island any longer, not when I was going to be thrust into the world spotlight again. Those bastards murdered my father. They would absolutely have used her against me. They could not know anything of her existence. It was the only way."

Nico bit out a curse and turned away, his posture stiff and unyielding. His anger and censure was no less than Garon's and Sebastien's. The last two months had been ones he never wanted to repeat. Talia weighed heavily on all their minds. And now she was gone.

"You find her," Xander said through clenched teeth. "I don't care how long it takes, how much it costs, you find her and you bring her home."

Talia finished sugaring her cup of hot tea and cupped it in both hands as she stared over the stunning view of the Italian coast. The water was so dark blue that it resembled a painting. The quaintness of the small cottage she and her mother were renting brought her comfort. It made her feel cozy and secure and after two months, she realized that she was finally feeling some measure of peace.

The nights were hard for her. Often she lay awake, remembering how it had been in Xander's arms. How it had been when all four men took turns pleasuring her. Even with her mother's warm companionship, Talia had never felt quite so alone.

She was glad now that she had saved and had spent sparingly the allowance that Xander had provided her while she was attending university. It allowed for her and her mother to travel extensively before Talia would have to decide where to settle and find a job. She knew now that she would never return to Cristofino.

And she had absolute zero guilt in using the money received from Xander to pay her and her mother's travel expenses. It was the very least he could do for how much he'd made her suffer.

A knock sounded on the door and she turned with a frown. Her mom had gone down to the market, insisting that she could go alone. Talia had worried about her being able to carry her purchases back by herself, but Rose had laughed and waved off Talia's concern.

She was healthy. She was whole. She felt better than she had in years. She was going to enjoy life and indulge in normal, everyday activities. Already she'd made friends with the elderly couple who lived in the neighboring cottage and she often spent mornings having tea in their neighbor's garden.

Talia hurried toward to the door, thinking that her mother likely had her arms full. She pulled open the door. "I knew you shouldn't have gone by yourself—"

She came to an abrupt halt, going completely still as she stared into the faces of Garon, Sebastien and Nico. Her stomach immediately knotted and her first impulse was to slam the door in their faces. Garon likely anticipated such a move because he immediately inserted his foot next to the frame so she'd be unable to do just that.

"What do you want?" she asked in a voice cold enough to freeze the Mediterranean.

"Let us in, Talia," Sebastien said in a quiet voice.

"No."

Garon raised an eyebrow in surprise.

"I don't have to obey you any longer," she bit out. "That contract is voided, remember? I'm no longer your submissive plaything for you to toss around whenever it pleases you."

Nico winced at the bitterness in her tone. Hell, she hadn't even realized she was still so bitter. She'd actually been feeling rather zen about the whole thing in the last few days, but now that they were here facing her, rage built like a volcano about to erupt.

And it pissed her off even more that whatever errand they were on, Xander was nowhere to be seen, but then he was likely newly married and on his bloody honeymoon.

She shuddered at the thought.

The one absolute she'd held to during their travels is no news, no television and no damn Internet. It had been freeing because what she didn't know couldn't very well hurt her.

"We've come to take you back home," Garon said.

She stared at him like he'd lost his mind. "This is my home. At least temporarily. At least until my mother and I decide where we'd like to travel to next."

"Your home is with us," Nico said quietly.

"Oh that's rich. Real bloody rich." And then a thought occurred to her and she looked at them in astonishment. "Xander has no idea you're here does he? He'd probably have a cow if he knew you were trying to get me back to Cristofino."

They all stared at her with perplexed expressions.

"Talia, Xander *sent* us," Sebastien said impatiently.

"Well, I'm not going anywhere," she clipped out. "Now if you'll excuse me, I have better things to do than to sign up for more humiliation."

"I know we hurt you," Garon said in a gruff voice. "And you have every right to be angry. But Talia, please, just listen to us. Come back to Cristofino with us so Xander can make this right."

"There aren't enough words in the dictionary for him to ever make it right," she said, sarcasm lacing every word.

"Talia, what's going on? Who are these men?"

The three men whirled around, enabling Talia to see her mother standing just inside the wooden gate holding two bags from the market.

Nico and Sebastien sprang into action, each reaching for one of the bags.

"We are representatives of His Royal Highness, Alexander Carrera of Cristofino," Nico said in a formal voice as he lifted the bag from her befuddled mother's arm.

"Well," Rose began, clearly at a loss as to what to say. "Why are you here and what do you want with Talia?"

"His Royal Highness wishes for you both to be presented at the palace as soon as it's possible to arrange the transportation," Sebastien said smoothly. "It is a matter of utmost importance. One of national security, one might even say."

Talia rolled her eyes and shook her head. What a load of crap.

Her mother's eyes widened and then she looked straight at Talia. "Well, we must go, of course. It all sounds quite important. We can't let His Highness down. Not after all he's done for our family. And for you, Talia."

Talia clenched her teeth so hard her jaw ached. "Mama, why don't you go in and fix these nice young men a cup of tea. I'm sure since they've traveled so far, they'd love refreshment."

If her mother noticed the sarcasm, she didn't remark, but then she seemed too frazzled by the idea that representatives of the royal family were on her doorstep.

"Oh, of course, wherever are my manners!" Rose exclaimed. "Do come in please. I'll have tea prepared immediately."

When the men would have followed Rose as she hurried past Talia into the cottage, Talia blocked their entryway and put her hand out.

"If you have respect for me whatsoever. If you have any modicum of human decency, you will not let my mother know the nature of our relationship or anything that occurred on the island while I was there."

Garon took her outstretched hand and pulled it to his chest, his expression pained. "We would never do anything to hurt you that way, Talia."

"You'll forgive me if I don't quite believe that," she said quietly. "I don't appreciate being manipulated in front of my mother. That was a dirty, underhanded trick and you damn well know it."

Sebastien crossed his arms over his chest and stared challengingly at her. "I'm prepared to do whatever it takes to get you back to Cristofino so Xander can clear up this whole mess. All's fair in love and war, and war, my love, has just been declared."

Chapter 26

"Why am I here, Nico?" Talia asked in a quiet voice as the limousine carrying her, her mother, Garon, Sebastien and Nico pulled through the palace gates.

It had been a whirlwind affair once they had her mother convinced of the necessity of her and Talia returning to Cristofino. She'd had herself and Talia packed in an hour flat and a private jet had been waiting for them at the airport to make the short flight to Cristofino.

The worst part was how cryptic the men had been. It infuriated her after the way she'd been tossed out of the villa that they were arrogant enough to think all they had to do was snap their fingers and she'd come like a well-trained dog.

Nico reached over and touched her cheek in a gentle caress. "Xander will explain everything."

She moved away from his hand, not wanting her mother to see the gesture.

"I'm sorry, Talia," he murmured in a low tone. "For everything. You can't imagine how much."

Tears burned her eyelids and she cursed that she could still feel anything even two months after her abrupt departure from their lives.

The car rolled to a stop and to Talia's utter astonishment, Xander's mother, the queen, came to greet Talia's mother when she stepped from the car. Talia watched agape as the queen kissed Rose on either cheek, tucked her arm underneath hers and promptly whisked her inside and away from Talia.

"What the hell just happened here?" she asked in bewilderment.

Garon's arm slid around her body and for just a brief moment, she savored his soothing warmth. She had no idea how much she missed and how much she craved their touch. Their hands on her body. Until now. It was a painful reminder of the cold, stark nights she'd spent alone ever since she'd left the island.

"Come with us," he said, his voice gentle. "You'll understand everything. I promise."

Still confused, she allowed him to lead her inside the palace, up the winding mahogany staircase to the second level. The level where most state matters were handled. Or the work zone as she'd learned it was called by palace insiders during her time here as the gardener's assistant.

When Garon led her into the very office where it all had begun, she nearly laughed at the irony. Here where she and Xander had first met. The meeting that had supposedly put them on a collision course culminating with her summons to the island villa.

She almost didn't see Xander, so off balance was she from the entire bizarre turn of events. He was standing to the far side, hands shoved into his pockets. He looked haggard, like he'd gone too many nights without sleep. Well, that made two of them.

He looked . . . relieved. And a little overwhelmed. He looked like it was taking all his restraint not to run over to her.

What the hell was going on here?

This felt like yet another bizarre chapter in a story that had begun months ago when she'd been sent that mysterious summons and her life had proceeded to change forever.

"Talia," Xander said, almost as if he were testing her name on his lips, or perhaps he was checking to make sure she was real.

Perplexed by his behavior, she couldn't quite summon the fury that had come so easily when Garon, Sebastien and Nico had shown up at her cottage in Italy.

"I'm here," she said. "You made it sound important, Xander. What's going on? You had them drag my mother along and we were on holiday."

He took a step forward. And then another. Before long he was right in front of her and she could see his hands shaking at his sides. She also realized that she and Xander were alone in the room. The others had disappeared and the door had been closed, affording them complete privacy.

"Important?" he echoed. "Bloody hell, yes, it was important. You're the most important thing in the world to me and I couldn't damn well find you! Do you have any idea how worried I've been?"

Her mouth popped open. "Of all the unmitigated nerve! You self-centered son of a bitch."

Before she could get truly involved in her diatribe, he grasped her shoulders and yanked her to him, closing his mouth over hers in a forceful kiss that left her gasping.

"Oh God, Talia," he said, his voice cracking under the strain of emotion. "I thought I'd lost you. I thought I wouldn't be able to find you. You have no idea the hell I've gone through not knowing where you were and if you were all right."

For a moment she was lost, and oh God, it felt so good to be back in his arms, his mouth on hers and all that dominant power rippling through his body.

Then reality smacked her hard and she jerked away, stumbling back to put distance between them.

"Are you crazy?" she croaked out. "My God, are you married? Because I'll tell you now, Xander, I will not be your mistress."

He looked as though she'd slapped him. "Why the hell would you think I'd be married?"

She shrugged. "I assumed once you became king, you'd find a nice princess to marry."

He bit out a curse and grasped the back of his neck in his palm. "Is that why you left Paris? Because you were upset by something you saw or heard on the news?"

She shoved her fingertips into the pockets of her jeans. Her mother had been horrified that she was wearing something so casual to meet the king, but Talia wasn't impressed, nor was she making special concessions for this man.

"I left Paris because it was time to get on with my life. I wanted to spend time with my mother and celebrate the fact that she's beaten a disease that takes so many lives."

Xander nodded. He lowered his hand from his nape, his expression more haunted than ever.

"There are things I need to explain to you, Talia. And then I have an apology to make. I hope when I'm done that you can find it in your heart to forgive me."

Forgiveness? He wanted absolution? Wouldn't a phone call have been sufficient?

He looked as though he wanted to touch her again, like it was a compulsion he couldn't control. Confusion weighed heavily on her because she understood none of this.

"The things I told you on the island. All of them were true. What I hesitated to say was that . . . I love you. Have loved you from that very first moment when I came upon you here in this office."

Hurt crowded in, squeezing the breath from her lungs. Her chest ached and tightened and tears stung her eyelids, drew up her nose until it burned and twitched.

"You have a very funny way of showing your love," she said shakily.

"You're right. I hide behind the others. I use them as a shield sometimes. It's wrong. It was unfair to you. You should have known how I felt about you. You should have never been left to question or to wonder."

She took a deep, steadying breath. "Xander, as much as I appreciate this speech, the fact is, you tossed me out of your villa like a used-up whore. No good-byes. No 'have a nice life.' Nothing. You couldn't get me off that island fast enough. I . . ."

She broke off and swallowed back the sob that threatened because damn it, she was not going to break down. She lifted her tearful gaze back to him. "I felt cheap. I felt used. I felt degraded. For the entire time I was there, I felt pampered and cherished. And all of that was gone in a matter of minutes the day you told me to leave."

This time he couldn't seem to control himself any longer. He pulled her into his arms and held her so tightly she could barely breathe. He buried his face in her hair, the sounds of his breaths harsh in the silence.

"I'm sorry. God, I'm sorry, my love. I never wanted you to feel that way. I handled it all wrong. I was so angry and resentful. I was in a no-win situation and all I could see was you slipping away. Of me being denied the one thing I wanted above all else. You."

She pried herself away. "I don't understand, Xander. What happened?"

"I had to return immediately to Cristofino, and I would give the rebels nothing with which they could hurt me. You, Talia. If they had known, if they had even guessed that I had any sort of feelings for you. If they knew of your existence, that you were with me. They would have used you against me, and it would have worked because I would have done anything at all for them not to have hurt you.

"I could not place myself in such a weak position. I could not return to my country a weak man. And you are my greatest weakness," he finished in a whisper.

She stared at him, unable to formulate a response. What was there to say? Her pulse was pounding painfully at her temples.

He ran a hand raggedly through his hair almost as if he did so in an effort not to touch her again.

"I didn't want you associated with me in any possible manner. Didn't want you traced back to me. I wanted it so that I didn't exist in your life and you didn't exist in mine. It was the hardest damn thing I've ever done in my life but I knew it was necessary because I couldn't live knowing something had happened to you. I've lost so much already. Cristofino has lost so much. I don't want to lose any more."

"Then why . . . Why am I here *now*?" she asked hoarsely.

He touched her face, cupped her jaw, ran his fingers through her hair, smoothed his fingertips over her brows. He seemed obsessed with touching her.

"Because I can't live without you," he whispered. "I won't give you up. I want you here. With me. Standing beside me. Always."

Her brows knitted together and she was honest to God starting to get the mother of all headaches. She closed her eyes, so confused she wanted to scream.

He brushed his mouth against her forehead and pulled her close into his embrace once more. Her body was cupped intimately to his. To anyone looking, there was no mistaking that they were lovers. Their embrace was too tender. Too knowing and familiar.

"Marry me, Talia. Be the princess I've always considered you. Be my princess. Be my queen."

Chapter 27

Talia went still in his arms, afraid to move or breathe. Then she shook her head, sure she hadn't heard correctly. Carefully, she pushed away and looked up at him, but his eyes were serious and grave.

"Xander, I'm nobody," she whispered. "I used to work for your groundskeeper. I can't marry you."

"As king I can damn well marry whoever I want," he said calmly. "And you aren't nobody. You're everything to me. That makes you the most important woman in all of Cristofino.

"I love you, Talia. I've loved you for a long time. I've botched and bungled my opportunity with you at every turn, but I want the chance to make it right. To make our relationship permanent. I know that the uncertainty you experienced on the island hurt you, but at the time I couldn't offer you anything more than the vague vow that I'd never let you go."

She touched her fingertips to her forehead as the ache intensified. "Xander, you know I have feelings for Garon, Sebastien and Nico. How could you want to marry me knowing this?"

He kissed her forehead, soothing away some of the tension. "That's the other point we have to discuss."

She frowned but he kissed away the frown until her lips relaxed.

"You've known from the beginning that I had, shall we say, different tastes and expectations. I trust Bastien, Garon and Nico with my life. Now I'm trusting them with yours. From this moment forward, they are assigned as your personal guard detail. Our wedding will be public, but our marriage will very much remain behind closed doors. And what goes on behind those closed doors is solely at our discretion. They don't want to lose you either. I thought they might kick my ass over the way I left things."

"Just what are you saying, Xander? You want to marry me, but you want things to continue as they were before?"

"That's exactly what I'm saying."

"Whoa," she breathed.

"You care for them. They care for you. I know that they'll guard you and protect you with their lives. In the privacy of our own home, we will continue to enjoy a lifestyle that we embraced on the island. You are my wife, but you will be pampered, adored and cherished above all others by the four of us."

She didn't have words. She was completely and utterly overwhelmed by all of it. She was torn from the very real anguish she'd gone through and the sudden surge of excitement—and wonder—of such a scenario.

"They . . . They're okay with this?" she whispered.

"The question is whether you're okay with it," he said gently. "It's a lot to take in and I wish that it could have all been handled differently. My plan was to get you to the island by whatever means necessary even if it meant coercion. It makes me a bastard, but I would have done anything to make you come to me. And then my intent was to seduce you with words and actions, make you fall in love with me—with the situation as it stood with Bastien and Garon and Nico—and then make my commitment known to you that no matter what happened with Cristofino, that you would always remain by my side."

"Oh," she murmured.

"And then I was blindsided by the sudden capitulation by the insurgents. I hadn't anticipated matters being resolved anytime soon—if ever. And I absolutely would not expose you to a potentially hostile environment. So I sent you away, but in my heart, I knew I would do anything to bring you home to me, even if meant relinquishing the throne and any part of Cristofino's future as ruler."

Tears brimmed in her eyes and spilled over onto her cheeks. She simply couldn't fathom all he was telling her.

"You love me that much?" she whispered in a choked voice.

"I love you more. More than you can possibly imagine."

"But why?"

He smiled. A tender, loving smile that melted her from the inside out. "From the very first day I saw you, I was enchanted. And the more I learned of you, of your unerring devotion to your mother, how you were so selfless and yet still had such a kind and gentle spirit, I knew that not only were you perfect for me, but you were perfect for Cristofino. I was so convinced of this fact that I only agreed to retake the throne if I was allowed to marry a very specific Cristofino girl. Thankfully, I was not forced to abdicate my throne before I ever regained it."

She stared at him in absolute wonder, unable to process all he was saying. These things didn't happen in real life. They were reserved for fairy tales. Stories told to little girls that inspired dreams of love and happily ever after.

And now it was happening to her. Dreams really did come true!

"Oh my God, Xander. I can't be a king's wife!"

He chuckled then and pulled her into his arms, holding her tightly in his embrace. "You will be the most perfect queen this country will ever have. I love you and so will our people."

"Oh, Xander, I love you too," she said against his neck. "So much. I was so devastated when I left the island. I left my heart and soul there and I never thought I would get it back."

He pulled away from her and stroked her cheek, wiping the tears away. "You will never know how sorry I am for the way I hurt you. I handled it badly, but more than anything I wanted to get back here so that I could settle the future. Our future. There was never a question of me coming for you, Talia. You were mine from the moment I saw you and that hasn't changed. Not even for a minute."

She smiled and nuzzled into his palm and then she shot him a more mischievous grin. "Now about this submissiveness . . ."

He laughed and it was a beautiful sound, almost as if it had been since the last time they were together that he'd found joy.

"In public, I want you to be the independent, fierce, kick-ass woman I know you to be. You will be a credit to our country and will be a role model for many young women. Behind closed doors, you'll offer me your submissiveness. Only me. Only I will receive that precious gift and no other."

"I think I can live with that," she said, her smile so big that her cheeks ached from the strain.

He took her hands in both of his, raising first one and then the other to his mouth. "As much as I want to keep you all to myself, the others are very anxious to see you and make amends for the hurt we've all caused you."

He rose from the couch, leaving her sitting there and he walked to the door, opened it and then moments later, Garon, Sebastien and Nico filed solemnly through the door.

Her heartbeat accelerated as she nervously found their gazes. She slid her palms along her pants legs and inched closer to the edge of the couch.

Then they surrounded her, making the first move. Garon went

to one knee in front of her while Nico and Sebastien crowded in beside her on the couch.

Sebastien pressed a kiss to her hair while Nico reached for one hand. Garon took the other and then they just kind of folded around her, hugging her to them, pressing in close so she was enveloped by their warmth—and their love.

"Is this what you want, Talia?" Sebastien asked against her ear. "Do you want us? All of us?"

She looked to each of them, giving them her full attention in turn. "I do want you. So very much. It's hard for me to believe, I mean I can barely take it all in. I thought . . ."

It was too painful for her to replay all that she'd thought and so she fell silent, emotion overcoming her as she stared into the faces of these men who cared so deeply for her. Who wanted nothing more than to care for her, protect her and place her needs and wants above their own.

Garon put his finger over her lips. "Forget whatever it is you thought and let us replace that sadness with new memories."

She lay her head on Nico's shoulder, simply absorbing the magic of the moment. Then she looked beyond to Xander, who stood there gazing at her with such love that for a moment she couldn't breathe.

This was really happening. It wasn't a fantasy. It wasn't a temporary break from reality. This was her reality. Her future.

And whatever obstacles they had to overcome, they'd do it together and they'd always have the undying loyalty of three men who'd devoted their lives to serving Xander and now her.

What more could she possibly ever ask for?

Sway

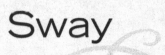

LAUREN DANE

This one is for my husband.
As they all tend to be. Because he's my everything.

Chapter 1

Levi found the studio easily enough. His brother hadn't lied. It wasn't far from his office, which was attached to his house on Bainbridge Island. He'd moved to the island five years ago, months after Kelsey had died.

The building smelled like every community center he'd ever been inside. He'd been in more than his fair share as he and his older brother had set up a mentoring program through the local school systems and they gave presentations at least once a month. Each door had a sign on it, but he didn't see anything about wedding basics, so he wandered into one of the classrooms to ask someone.

And then paused to watch as a couple dominated the center of the room. A ridiculously beautiful dark-haired woman was spinning, propelled by a long, lanky man as the rest of the people clapped along to the swing music.

It wasn't the male that interested him, though Levi was sure the man was talented. It was the nearly effortless timing of the woman as she went around the man, her legs and feet in perfect time with the music.

So quick and intricate, these moves.

Even he burst out with an exclamation when the man flipped her over his arm and she kicked her legs even as she was upside down.

A flash of some thigh as she hopped when she got to her feet and then she went in again as her partner actually flipped her up and over his shoulder.

They continued on for a few minutes more until they both took a bow and the male, apparently an instructor, began speaking to the people in the room again.

Perhaps he should take this class instead of the wedding dancing class his brother Mal's fiancée wanted him to take. Levi was only doing this for his brother. He could dance just fine. But it was a way of mollifying Gwen so they could keep her attention off the dancing up the aisle idea she kept pushing, and Levi would sooner die before he did that. He loved his baby brother, but that wasn't going to happen. Ever.

A bit more wandering and he finally found the room he thought was right.

"Excuse me."

The instructor turned to him and smiled. "Oh! An extra. Hold on one moment."

She rushed to the doorway before Levi could stop her.

"Daisy! Can you help? I've got one extra tonight."

He'd been about to interrupt to tell the instructor he wasn't interested in this class but was looking for another one. Until the aforementioned Daisy entered the room.

Long, dark hair had been captured into a high ponytail and it swayed as she walked. Big brown eyes. Not overly tall. Probably five and a half feet at most. Pretty, full lips glistened red. Her body, curvy and mouthwatering, was draped in a dress he could only describe as vintage. A full skirt and a tight bodice. Tattoos, though he couldn't see all of the half sleeve due to her dress.

It was the jitterbug woman he'd watched a little while before. She had a gorgeous smile as she looked from the instructor to Levi. But he kept going back to her eyes. After a perusal of the impressively high and full breasts of course; he wasn't a saint. She had beautiful eyes, but it was the intelligence in them that made him look twice and then again.

Suddenly it wasn't so bad that he needed a dance class. Not if she'd be his partner for a time or two. That way he could say he went to the blasted class and have an excuse to get his hands on her.

She took him in and smiled, holding her hand out. Bangle bracelets jingled and clicked with her movement. "I'm Daisy Huerta. Nice to meet you."

"Levi Warner."

The instructor clapped her hands to get everyone's attention. "Welcome everyone to introduction to dance. We'll cover several different styles of dance and rhythm over the next few weeks. Partner up and let's get started."

This was definitely not the class he'd signed up for. They'd discover this, he assumed, when they checked to see who'd paid.

Daisy stepped close, took his hand and he naturally pulled her close, his other hand at her waist.

"Leading already? All right then." When she quirked a smile, a dimple showed at the right corner of that full, lush mouth. "I love it when my partner is tall. Fits better."

Well now.

There was a lot of talking and people laughing self-consciously, but he didn't hear any of it. With his hand at her waist, there was nothing to do but slide into the dance as the music came on.

Rosemary Clooney took a deep breath and began to sing the opening of "Sway." And she bent to his will and began to move, sensuously, slowly, gracefully. Giving over to him easily as he led. That simple act of submission wasn't sexual. Not really. But it shattered all the reasons he'd been lining up to leave after that one dance. And tore at the walls he'd built around himself a long time ago.

His hand on her waist seemed to burn through the material of her dress as they moved.

He led every moment. Sure of himself. Propelling her just exactly where he wanted her to go. She relaxed and fell into the music. While others in the class worked slower, going step by step, Levi danced like he knew what he was about.

It was increasingly clear Levi wasn't a beginner of any type. It wasn't that she didn't like his hands on her, but he didn't need the class and it was only right she tell him. But she could wait until after the class. Just to be fair.

Until then she'd enjoy the hypnotic pleasure of being led by this man. She'd danced many times with many people, and it had never felt this forbidden and sexually charged. A shiver moved through her system, hardening her nipples, heating her skin. Totally inappropriate to get all het up over this one silly moment, but there it was so why not enjoy it?

"I saw you dancing. In the other room, I mean. How long have you been teaching dance classes?" His murmur nearly made her jump, she was so lost in the way he'd made her feel.

She licked her lips and didn't miss the way his pupils seemed to swallow the color in his eyes. Green, a pale green. Unusual. Especially with dark hair. His was nearly black, with salt and pepper throughout. It suited him. As did the scruff.

Really, he was a walking, talking dream of a man, and he smelled as good as he looked.

She managed to find her words again. "I fill in when they need me. My neighbor teaches Lindy Hop and swing dancing here. I help there most often."

"Is that what you were doing?"

"Depends on when you came in."

"At the end. Right before I found this room."

"Ah. We were jitterbugging at the end. A little bit of this and that. We did a fast Lindy Hop at the start of class."

"I'm sorry I missed it. You're quite good."

Charmed, she winked. "Not to toot my own horn or anything, but I'm pretty fabulous at it."

He grinned and the mischief showed in his eyes. Boy oh boy this man would be so much trouble for a woman. But it would be a good kind of trouble, she'd bet.

"You should show me."

"You want me to teach you how to Lindy Hop? By the way, you don't need this dance class." Damn, she'd planned to wait.

He laughed and all logical thought seemed to burst apart. He had a great laugh. Deep and sexy.

"Let me guess." She paused as they moved into a simple waltz, which he handled just as well. "You're getting married and your fiancée wants you to take classes. No, that can't be it."

One of his eyebrows rose. "Why not?"

"She'd be here with you. They always come. You know, to take the class together." And frankly, it'd be foolhardy to let anyone get near this one. And she also bet that if he had a woman, she came a lot in the other way as well.

And suddenly a rather vivid, totally filthy image of him over her, his perfect hair sex-messy, sweat gleaming, muscles working from the way he fucked her flashed through her head and she got very warm.

"It's my baby brother. He's getting married and she, his fiancée, wants all the men in the wedding party to take a class."

"You clearly know your way around a dance floor. At least for all the basics you'd need at a wedding. Shall I write you a note?"

His grin made all sorts of things tingle. "I'm not sure she'd accept it. But it would be amusing to present it to her. I like the way you think. My other brothers and cousins have all folded. I was the last holdout."

She bet Levi here didn't do anything he didn't want to. Dominant, this guy. *Mmmm.*

"The wedding dance class is down the hall. I think they gave it a snazzy name, but it's wedding dancing for dummies really."

"Do you teach that one?"

"No. They have a different kind of instructor in there." They told her specifically that they wanted more elegant-looking women doing the class. Fuck them. *Elegant.*

"Would you show me? How to Lindy Hop, I mean."

"Yes. But I think you're a more sensual dancer. Tango. Maybe rumba or cha-cha."

His mouth was beautiful when it canted up into a knowing smile. A cocky, arrogant smile and it shot straight to all her pinkest of parts. Just a few minutes with this man and it was totally clear he was exceptional. And out of her league. And a client of the studio. And probably too old for her, though she didn't care about that stuff really.

He pulled her a little closer but kept dancing. "I don't actually want you to, I just wanted to know if you would."

He kept catching her off guard. She liked it.

"Is that so? Why is that?"

He shrugged as they came to a halt while the instructor began to speak again.

"Do you like telling people what to do? Just to see how they react?"

He stopped, examining her carefully. His attention so very intense it was nearly physical. She tried not to gulp under such scrutiny but it was hard not to. She felt very much like Little Red Riding Hood having bumped into the Big Bad Wolf.

"I prefer it when their reaction is obedience."

A flush roared through her, hot and wild. A million things she wanted to say flitted through her brain but none of them seemed right. She was usually good at this stuff, the silly back and forth between herself and the students. But he was something altogether different.

He studied her a long time until he finally spoke again. "I'm going to go."

Her heart sank even as she struggled to keep her face relaxed.

"I don't need this class. But I showed up and I can honestly say so. Thank you for amusing me."

He stepped back and bowed as they took the first brief break. "I enjoyed meeting you, Levi." She waved to Tansi and left, heading back down the hall.

How strange her day had been. Flirted with by a rather intense older man who totally made her hot-for-teacher fantasies go wild. Not a bad way to leave work.

Chapter 2

She stood with her hands at her waist and looked the installation over. "I don't like the light. Switch it out for a different bulb."

This was her biggest piece yet. Hell, the biggest sale yet. Not a lot of money as things went, but enough to know she was making a living, even a small one, from her work. And that was important.

A mixed-media piece. Watercolor and paper. In three distinct parts, like a winged altar. It was going to hang in the large, open atrium of Cal Whaley's small office building.

Speaking of Cal, he wandered out, looking handsome and studious in his natty three-piece suit holding a sheaf of papers. He clearly hadn't been expecting her though, because when he looked up from the papers in his hands he started and then smiled when he saw her.

"Daisy!" He kissed her cheek. "What brings you . . . Oh, today is installation day." He noted the work. "I love this so much. Really brings some color and life into this space."

It did. With vivid blues and greens. Evocative of the water they were surrounded by, of the forest too. It had come to her on a hike they'd all taken nearly two years before. In the spring when everything had been clear and sharp. They'd been standing on an overlook, taking in Puget Sound and she'd been so glad to have had her camera to capture it. She'd spent another six months tinkering with the idea as she'd finished another project.

And the whole time Cal had been her biggest supporter, telling her he wanted her to do it already so he could buy it.

"It's not hard to look that great in this space." The windows soared to the third-floor landing, flooding the room with light, the art reflecting Eagle Harbor out in the distance.

"Now you need to finish the glass piece so I can buy it for that alcove over there."

She laughed, flattered and delighted.

"I've got to run. I have a client meeting in about twenty minutes. We need to have lunch soon." He bent and kissed her cheek.

"We do. Also, thank you, Calvin Whaley. For buying this piece."

He cocked his head. "I love it. I loved it before you had finished it. I laid claim to this over a year ago." He grinned. "So thank *you*."

It was those little moments that got her through the times when it seemed she'd never make it.

Turning back to the task at hand, she scrambled up the ladder with the level and the lightbulb she thought would work better.

Levi had loved this building for a few years. It was close to the ferry, but not too close. The view was incredible. He'd considered renting office space here before deciding to have a home office built. But one of the investigators he often worked with had space here they let him use when he had need of a conference room.

And now, three hours later he was hungry and sick to death of his clients, but they'd hammered out a deal both sides could live with and he could be done with this project.

"Will we see you at the luncheon next month?" Jessy Calhoun asked as she tucked a file folder into her bag.

He'd paused at the front doors to say good-bye to everyone.

"The fund-raiser?"

He sat on the board of several charities, including Created Families, which raised money and awareness for adoption and foster care. Jessy Calhoun, the woman who asked, also sat on the board. She and her husband Elton had adopted four kids and now that they were all in college, they were foster parents.

"I'll be there." He looked at the art going up in the lobby. "We should auction off something like this." The light caught it perfectly, creating a nearly seamless feedback between the water and the wall.

"I can find out who the artist is if you like." Jessy buttoned her coat.

"I can do it. I'll get back with you about it. See if we can't get him to donate something." Levi was remarkably good at getting people to donate things for auctions.

"All right then." She waved and was gone and he turned back, heading toward the spot where the people were installing the art.

And then one of the workers turned around and he realized it was Daisy. He hadn't forgotten her name. Hadn't forgotten the way she'd submitted to him as they'd danced. The warm, solid weight of her in his arms as they'd moved.

Today she wore a red bandanna in her hair, Rosie the Riveter style. With a jumpsuit to match and bright pink sneakers. She wore chunky black glasses and a tool belt.

She sent him a bland smile until she recognized him and it brightened. He felt it straight to his toes.

"Well, hello there, Levi. What brings you here today?"

"I had a meeting here in the building. I wanted to ask—"

"Levi?"

He turned to catch sight of opposing counsel standing on the stairs leading to the conference room.

He took Daisy's hands and squeezed. "I'm sorry. I have to deal with this."

He liked the disappointment on her face. "All right then. See you around." She stepped back and he had to force himself to move away from her and back up to work.

By the time he finished and came out, the art was up and she was gone. *Damn.*

The work was beautiful. Unexpected as he looked closer and saw the layers, the delicate paper against the bolder brushstrokes of the watercolors.

There was a small plaque that read: *#14. Ramona.*

He'd have to contact the owner of the building, Cal Whaley, to get the information. Too bad. He was hoping to get the info from the lovely Ms. Huerta instead. It was most likely a sign. If he believed in such things.

Daisy wasn't surprised to find Mary on her doorstep when she opened after the knock.

"I bring food." Mary Whaley, her closest friend, held up a cotton tote bag, the kind she always used to bring all manner of delicious treats to her friends' homes.

"Lucky me." She opened up and stood to the side to allow Mary to pass. Daisy followed her into the small kitchen. Once Mary put her things down Daisy gave her a hug.

"You busy?" Mary looked around as she put her jacket on the back of the chair.

"I am now that my friend has come and brought me dinner."

Mary's smile was fast as her eyes lit. "I'm trying a few new things. I need your opinion."

"Score." Daisy brought out plates and silverware. "These wedding-type gizmos or for the supper club?"

"I may have a catering gig."

"Yeah? Do tell!"

Daisy knew Mary had been trying to build her catering business for the last two years. The food truck biz was complicated. It was impossible to park the truck anywhere but private property in Seattle. She'd managed to work out some arrangements with property owners around town but Daisy knew what her friend really wanted was a full-time gig with far more certainty than the truck.

And, as Mary cooked better than anyone else Daisy had ever met, she wanted it for her too.

"Try the soup first. I'm going to get your broiler working to finish these other things."

"Is this a stand-up event?" She peered into the container of soup. The smoky scent of curry hit first.

"It is. But the soup will be in shot glasses. Easy to use."

She managed to find shot glasses. "I'm going to say up front a shot of that soup won't be enough."

Mary slid a tray of something into the oven.

Daisy drank the soup and it was better than she figured it would be. And that was already really good.

"This is criminally good. Can you use larger containers?"

"They have larger shot glasses that hold a triple shot. Or maybe an espresso cup. Hm. Going to think on it. I want it to get your senses ready for what's next."

Daisy toed off her shoes near the back door. "You gonna tell me the specifics of the gig or am I going to have to beat it out of you?"

"A friend of Adrian's needs a caterer for an industry thing."

Adrian was Adrian Brown, their best friend Gillian's fiancé, who also happened to be a huge deal rock star.

"So cool!"

"It could be, yes." Mary thrust a plate of something at Daisy, who quickly gobbled one up and groaned. "You like?"

"Honestly, I don't know why you always look so nervous. You're an amazing cook, silly. Now, tell me what this is."

"Figs with honey and cheese on homemade toasts. I worry they'll get soggy though."

Mary was an amazing cook. Clever, intuitive, she made art in her kitchen every single day and sometimes the only person who didn't get that was Mary herself.

Daisy arched a brow and put a hand on her hip as she looked toward her friend. "You'd have to imagine they'd sit around for very long. Which they won't. I'd push these things so hard. I'm assuming you'll need me to help staff this gig?"

"Would you?" Mary asked hopefully.

Daisy snorted. "Where else would I be? The money is good. The work is good but not overly hard. I get to sneak samples. That's all sorts of win/win. Plus I get to see you with everyone excited about your food like they should be. Just say when and it's on my schedule."

"Now Gillian just needs to choose a date for the wedding." Mary's corkscrew curls were currently being restrained by barrettes and some ponytail holders, but one had already won free at her temple.

"Don't you think that's what they're going to tell us all at Delicious next week?"

Delicious was the name of the supper club Mary had started many years before. At first, and mainly for the last several years, it had been for Mary's friends. They'd gather once a week, usually on Fridays, but recently it had shifted to Sundays to accommodate everyone's schedule.

More than just a woman who loved to cook who made dinner for her friends, Mary had turned Delicious into a hot secret everyone knew. And everyone wanted in. So much so that people paid a yearly fee for supplies and they'd be invited at random to a certain number of dinners or afternoon events.

Their friends, the core of Delicious, were always on the guest list. But for everyone else, it was an event to get their number called to attend a dinner.

"Yeah, probably. She's not one for coy, our Gillian. But this guy is good for her. He's been on her to set a date for the last two months. I can't imagine she's going to be able to hold out much longer. Especially now that the renovations on their new house are in full swing."

"Been a long time for her. I'm happy. Gillian deserves her happily ever after. And it'll be a great job for you too." She tipped her glass of cider in Mary's direction.

"He might want some big wedding with a crack catering staff instead of his new wife's friends."

Daisy snorted. "Yes, I'm sure. After one look at Adrian and his family you can totally tell they care about the thread count of the napkins and your china pattern."

A joke of course, as Adrian and his sister, also a rock star, had multiple tats and his brother ran a tattoo shop. Their friends were a wild assortment of awesome jobs, hair colors and wild backgrounds. Above all they were down-to-earth. They fit with Gillian's friends perfectly.

"I just want her to be happy."

"Of course you do. Jules will make the cake and you will make the food. That's Delicious."

It had been Daisy who gave the name Delicious not only to the weekly gatherings but also to her group of friends, the sexiest, funniest, most awesome women she knew. Women who were always there for each other. Whether it was to kick someone's ass to make them straighten up, or to defend and protect. They were part of her family. They were delicious in every way and it pleased her that it had stuck.

Daisy waved a hand at all the food. "This is awesome. More cumin in the meatballs maybe?"

"I was thinking the same thing. Maybe the sauce needs a tweak instead? What do you think of the cheese straws? Those I just made up a batch for because I know your grandma loves them and she promised me some jam if I made her some."

Daisy laughed. "She's greedy for your treats." She bit into one of the lighter-than-air straws. "So good. Oh what'd you add?"

"I used a new kind of cheese. It had black peppercorns in it. I'm going to premiere them at dinner. How was your day?"

"I finished a new piece. Want to see?"

Mary jumped up eagerly. "I can't believe you need to ask."

Other than her grandmother, Mary was always the first person she showed her new work to. Daisy knew she'd tell the truth.

They went through the small house to the studio out back. Daisy and her grandmother shared the space, a garage converted to a workspace for her grandmother and then when the time came, they added a kiln and space for Daisy's mixed media work as she'd begun to truly explore art professionally.

Suddenly nervous, she stopped Mary at the door. "Okay so this is something a little new for me."

Mary took her hands. "Hush you. Let me see it."

Daisy pushed the doors open and pointed. Mary took a few steps and halted, sucking in a breath as she took it in. "Wow. This is . . . wow."

Crimson and vivid green mosaic created the outline of a woman's body. Paper and pen and ink gave her more detail. Her arms arched above her head, wrists bound.

"Good wow?"

Mary turned. "Yes. Really good wow. Daze, this is crazy good. Hot. Gorgeous. I love it."

She grinned and hugged Mary tight. "Thank you. I don't know. It's not my usual thing but it . . . it just came out of me."

"When the others see this, there will be a fight to see who gets to buy it. I'd try to snag it now but then everyone would whine." Mary winked.

"I really do need to have more buyers than you guys. Not that I don't appreciate it and all."

Mary laughed. "Girl, you think we pity-buy your art? One of these days the stuff we snagged at a bargain will be worth enough to get our kids through college. We're smart. And lucky to have such a talented friend."

Pride warmed Daisy. She was lucky in her friends. "You're fabulous. I'm going to enter it for art walk."

"Oh! Such a great idea. If they turn you down, they're idiots."

Art walk had started as an informal thing some local artists had started five years before and now it was a regular event. Each quarter they had a themed one with specially chosen pieces on display in front windows all over town. Daisy had been dreaming about her work being in one of those windows ever since.

She'd grown up in her grandmother's shadow. Which was overwhelmingly a blessing. She'd had a great example to follow. Wonderful advice. A teacher, a critique partner at times. Her biggest cheerleader and also her harshest taskmaster.

But sometimes people seemed to believe she was only doing well because her grandmother opened doors for her. They took one look at Daisy, noted her age and wrote her off.

She wanted her successes to be something she made on her own. She appreciated her grandmother's help and advice a great deal. Never felt a need to apologize for it. But she craved independence in so many ways, having people take her seriously for her work was one of her ultimate goals.

Chapter 3

Levi wandered through the store. Dumb to go grocery shopping when he was hungry, he knew. But he'd been in one meeting or hearing after the next and his fridge was bare. He avoided the frozen aisle, saving it for last when he wouldn't fall on the jumbo boxes of popsicles like a starving man. Or maybe he would. At least he didn't have to cook popsicles.

The last week had left him a little ragged. Familial obligations right and left. A luncheon for his mother's pet project—a program to provide pro bono legal services for survivors of family violence. There had been many just a decade before, but continued cuts to social programs had devastated most and left the very few limping along on triage with long wait lists for women who didn't have the time to wait.

And then more wedding stuff for Mal. Dinners and fittings. Silly things he could have done on his own but for whatever reason Gwen made into one event after the next.

The thought of his brother kowtowing to the woman for the rest of his life made Levi tired. Malachi was smarter than this usually. She was a beautiful woman, but there were other beautiful women out there. She was shallow and petty. Their mother despised Gwen, which might be part of her appeal to Mal. All in all, dealing with any of the wedding stuff took a few stiff drinks and cotton in his ears to drown it all out.

Work of course. His uncle was nearing retirement. He had no kids of his own so the work was being split between Levi and his oldest brother Jonah. He'd been part of several different meetings with myriad clients to introduce himself and begin that handoff.

It was Friday night and he planned to make some soup and a sandwich and watch *Doctor Who* on the DVR while he polished off a few beers. And then he planned to sleep until at least ten the next morning.

A fine plan.

The produce section loomed to the left. Yes, apples and some bananas for smoothies. He grabbed them by rote.

Then he stopped dead in his tracks to admire.

A woman in formfitting yoga pants was bent at the waist, peering at something. She also had on a scoop-necked T-shirt and bent the way she was, her tits mounded up at the top of the shirt as he could also see the edge of her bra. It wasn't as if he was a pervert, but a woman with that much lush beauty on display wasn't something he'd feel bad looking at.

Her eyes were closed as she held a piece of fruit to her nose and breathed it in. Her nails were done a shiny red and then he realized who it was when she opened her eyes and her gaze locked on his as she straightened and stood.

"Hello, Levi." She put the fruit in a brown paper bag and tucked it into her basket.

"Daisy."

They stood close, just staring at the other. *Goddamn*, she was hot. In the dress she'd worn in the dance class the week before she'd been sexy and retro. But formfitting worked for her just as well.

"Like a bad penny."

He had to tear his attention from her breasts to figure out what she'd said. "What?"

"You keep turning up. Like a bad penny. Have you never heard the saying?" She cocked her head and he flushed at the long expanse of her neck, wanting to touch.

"How old are you?" He actually blurted this and then was horrified.

Her head tipped then, her hair falling back as she laughed.

"God, that was rude. I'm sorry. It's just . . ." He licked his lips. What the hell did he think he was doing?

"I'll answer your question. On one condition."

He stepped a little closer because he wanted to so badly. "And that is?"

"I'll only answer if you're attempting to ascertain my age because you're going to ask me to dinner or drinks."

He liked how bold she was. Liked the way she flirted.

"But not otherwise?"

Her smile brought out her dimples.

She shook her head slowly. "Otherwise it's not your business."

"All right. Point taken. How old are you?"

"Twenty-four."

Christ. Twenty-four? She was nearly twenty years younger than he was. He needed to turn around and walk away. And yet he continued to stand there. This couldn't go anywhere. She was too young. Too everything.

And damn if he didn't want a taste. Damn if he didn't want to see if that submission she showed while dancing with him could extend into other parts of her life.

"And so?" She blinked up at him with a challenge.

He was about to say no thanks, or still trying to talk himself into saying it when he said, "Can you cook? I can't except for sandwiches." He sighed. "What I mean is, I'm starving but I've eaten out for the last week except for a family dinner over the weekend. I'd like home cooking but the best I can offer you is soup and grilled cheese. If you cooked well, I'd prefer that."

She laughed again. "I'm not the best cook in the world. But lucky for you, my friend is one of those talented cooks and she brought me a huge amount of food just this morning. I can't tell you what any of it is. I just tucked it all into my fridge. But I can guarantee whatever it is you'll love."

"And you live in your own place?"

"No. Of course not. I live in a dorm with all my college pals. We play beer pong and have pillow fights in our underpants while giggling."

He'd been about to frown at her until she made the pillow fighting comment and then he went there in his head and had to fight off a hard-on at the thought.

She handed him a business card. "My house is here. Well, not the gallery part. I live in a small house on the same lot. Mine is the one with the blue shutters. You can meet me there in a bit. I need to take these figs to the same friend who brought me the food this morning. I'll be home in about thirty minutes."

"All right. I'll see you then."

She waved and he watched her head to the front to check out. At least he had time to run his own groceries home first.

Daisy knocked and went inside when she heard Mary call out. "Hey, I was at the market and I saw figs on sale." She held up the bag and Mary took them with a delighted sound before she kissed Daisy's cheek and hugged her.

"Awesome! I've been working for the last two days on a few new recipes with figs. Stay and be my tester." Mary drew her into the large kitchen where Mary's brother Cal and their friend Jules were already seated.

"Hey gorgeous!" Jules hopped up to come and hug Daisy.

"Hey you." She hugged Jules back and then moved to drop a kiss on Cal's cheek. "I can't stay. I have . . . I guess it's a date."

"You guess?" Jules's pretty features darkened.

"It's this guy I met in a class. Or it wasn't my class, I was subbing in the class and he was in it by mistake and he left and I left."

"Oh, hot guy in the suit. Yum." Mary put the figs on the counter.

"Yes, him. I just saw him at the grocery store. I'm going to make him dinner. Or actually serve him your food, which is better. I told him it wasn't my cooking all up front and everything." She added this when Jules's brow went up.

"Girl, I don't care about that. Who is this guy? You're letting a near stranger come to your house?"

"He's some uber professional hot dude. If I end up dead and stuffed in a freezer, tell 'em some pretty guy named Levi Warner saw me last."

"Don't make fun." Jules glowered and Daisy hugged her, loving how protective they all were.

"I'm not making fun of how you care about me. But he seems wary because of the age thing. It's dinner, not an engagement."

"He's legit." Cal sipped his beer. "Warner family is a big deal in some circles. They've got a law firm in Seattle. He's got a small office here as well."

"Is he throwing shade on you guys? I will totally kick him out if he is."

Cal laughed. "No, baby, but thank you. He does land use stuff. Not anywhere near what we do. He's even sent some of his local people to us when they needed representation on issues he doesn't do. But he's older than you are."

"He is."

Everyone made a deal about her age. Usually until they got to know her. It used to bother her more than it did by that point. At the beginning of Delicious, she was just eighteen years old. Gillian and Jules were already close friends. Mary and her brothers too because they lived right next door. Daisy had been the kid who ran errands for them. She'd made extra money in high school working for Jules's parents at their cafe so she knew them all. Liked them and wanted to be part of their circle. So she'd just done it. Showed up. And they'd let her in and they'd all grown close and now six years later she was one of them, twenty-four or not.

"Like how much older?"

Daisy shrugged. "He looks mid-thirties. But he's got one of those faces some men have. Could be up to fifty. Though I don't think so."

Cal interrupted. "He's got to be forty or so. He was ahead of me at UW. He and I both went to law school there. What's a forty-year-old man want with a twenty-four-year-old?"

Daisy indicated her body. "Dude. I mean, come on. Twenty-four-year-old boobs."

Cal blushed furiously as Mary and Jules laughed.

"Look, it's dinner. He's not a creep. I'd know. I can always tell. He's hot. We had chemistry. That's all we're talking about right now. And I need to run. He'll be at my house in ten minutes." She hugged and kissed everyone before heading out again and back home.

Truth was, she found herself deliciously intrigued by Levi Warner.

He was nothing like any man she'd been with before. Distinguished, she thought as she put her bags down in the kitchen and headed to her closet to find something to change into. He made her want to dress up to please his eye. Which was interesting in and of itself.

It was too late for a full new outfit and all that. But she could do better than yoga pants. She found some trousers and a shirt to wear over the tee she had on. A quick brush of teeth, some lipstick and a braid of her hair and she was ready by the time he knocked on the door.

She'd even had time to light some candles so the house smelled good when she opened her door to find him standing on her stoop with a huge bouquet of flowers and a bottle of wine.

"Come in." She took the flowers and led him to the kitchen, just a few steps away. "Thank you." She loved that he'd chosen a bunch of colorful wildflowers. They went perfectly with the vase she'd finished up a few months ago.

"I brought wine." He held up a bag. "And some beer too. I wasn't sure what you'd be serving."

"Put them here on the counter. Let me see what I've got. I just walked in. If you'd like, you can put some music on."

He wandered off, looking around and probably thinking she didn't notice it. The house was where her grandmother used to live and work after her grandfather had died. But she was in her late eighties now and lived in her parents' house. She and Daisy shared a workspace out back.

So the little house had become hers.

Little Dragon began to play through her speakers. She watched him pause to listen and then nod to himself as if he found it acceptable. This was a good sign.

She pulled out the containers Mary had left, peeking in and taking sniffs as she peeled the lids back.

"Mmm, pulled pork. Do you eat pork?"

He moved to her and she had no choice but to freeze in place. He was too much and not enough all at once and she didn't know how to process. So intense she wanted to run and rub herself all over him at the same time.

He was the most intense man she'd ever been attracted to. Though, attracted was a lightweight word for the way he simply assumed ownership of all her parts, leaving her mentally panting. And he hadn't even touched her yet!

He got even closer to look into the container she held. "I do."

Licking her lips, she stepped back to grab plates and put things into the microwave.

"Sit. I'll get you something to drink. We've got pulled pork, which will go awesome with the brioche she put in with it. Shrimp salad of some kind. Don't know what she calls it, but it'll be good. Other little puffy things and some crunchy bits and bobs."

"Beer please."

He watched through hooded eyes as she moved around the small space and served him. Watched as she tipped the glass when she poured the beer. Watched as she automatically dished him up a plate and handed it to him along with a linen napkin she casually put on his lap.

Watched and fell under her spell.

"I meant to ask you last week when I ran into you. Whose artwork is that?"

"Did you like it?" She nudged some chili sauce in his direction.

"I did. I take it you work for the gallery next door? I'd like to speak with the artist. See if he'd be willing to donate something to a charity auction I'm working on."

One of her brows rose. "I do work at the gallery next door, yes. It's only open a few hours a week. And I'm sure she'd be willing to donate something for a good cause. What's the cause?"

"Ah, sorry. I assumed and that was silly. I figured 'Ramona' was the name of the art, not the artist."

She laughed and paused to hum in delight after she popped something into her mouth. "You need to try that pickled thing there." She pointed. "Ramona is my first name."

He sucked in a breath. "It's yours then?"

She nodded. "It is, yes. What's the charity?"

He took her hand and kissed her knuckles before turning it, unfurling her fingers and kissing her palm. "You've got a lot of talent."

When he looked at her face again she was blushing. "Thank you. Oh!" She jumped up and headed to the fridge. "Tortillas. I knew I had something I was forgetting. Hang on, I'm going to warm them."

"Did your friend make those too?"

"No. My mom made them. Though she learned from my grandfather. He was the cook in the family."

"And what do they do? Your family, I mean."

"My father and sister run a dental practice. My mother teaches at a private elementary school. My grandmother is a painter."

"Ah, that must be where you got it then. Does the gallery sell other art or just your stuff?"

"The gallery is my grandmother's place. She and I work there a few days a week. My grandfather opened it when he got back from World War Two. We have some local artists we feature, as well as my work and my grandmother's. This is their land. My parents live in the big house. My grandmother now with them. This used to be her studio and living space." She waved a hand as she continued heating the tortillas.

He liked it. The house wasn't big. But it was vibrant and sensual. Her bed was in a far corner. Unmade. He loved the burst of rich color, the blankets and sheets a tangle of purple and orange. She had a huge collection of music and movies. Her electronics were all very good. He'd apparently been too busy looking at her butt in those pants to have noticed the art on the walls.

The space smelled good. Like her. Sexy. Spicy. Probably forbidden but he had no plans to get up and leave anytime soon. She wasn't a fluffy-headed young woman. Not at all from what he could see.

"And you? What do you do? Other than paint and give dance lessons?"

"I do lots of things."

"Is that so?" Goddamn, he hoped so.

She looked at him over her shoulder as she stood at the stove. Her mouth quirked up on one side. "Oh, that too. If you're lucky."

"Tell me about your art, then."

She returned to the table and he didn't try to resist the tortillas. Once he rolled it around the pork and took a bite he was glad. "Christ, that's good."

"I know. My mom is a really good cook. I could live on tortillas and butter. Mainly I work in mixed media. Paint, pen and ink, some photography. I've been working with paper a lot lately. Some sculpture and glass. Anyway, I'm always interested in helping when I can. What's this charity?"

"Foster family support. It's a private agency that works with public services. Parenting classes, legal support for those who formally adopt, therapeutic support if needed for the parents and other siblings."

She nodded and then topped his glass off, distracting him a little. "Sounds like a wonderful organization."

"It is, actually. We have an auction, it's coming up in two months. I'm one of the procurers."

She laughed. "I bet."

"What do you mean?"

She laughed some more and spooned up some pickled vegetables. "You're good at talking people into things, I wager. That's why they make you the procurement person."

"When you believe in the cause it's a lot easier."

"Tell me about yourself, Levi."

"Not much to tell."

"I have a confession," she said before swiping her tongue over her bottom lip and making it hard for him to breathe.

"That so?"

"You like saying that. I'm not surprised you're an attorney."

That surprised a laugh from him. "Do a lot of attorneys you know say that?"

"No. I don't know a lot anyway. Just Cal."

Cal?

"Cal Whaley?" The guy was handsome and Levi wondered just how she knew Cal.

She brightened at the mention of Cal's name and his suspicion grew.

"Yes, that's the one. He never says stuff like 'that so' either. But he's got this way of saying as little as possible while he's gathering all sorts of info from other people and they never even notice."

"How do you know Cal?"

She raised her brow again. "How do *you* know Cal? I mentioned you when I stopped by my friend's house earlier and he said he knew you. Also said you weren't a serial killer. He didn't think."

Torn between amusement and agitation he took her in. "Good to know he doesn't think I'm going to hack you up and put you in the freezer."

"Ew. I bet you never say things like that in front of your family."

She had this way of blurting things out that were startlingly true and intimate. But she didn't even know him.

"My family isn't prone to talking about serial killing." He shrugged.

"God, mine either. *Boring.* We talk about art and teeth. Oh and teaching. So you're a lawyer too and so I assume that's how you know Cal."

He nodded. "It's a small island. We do business from time to time. I use some space in his building when I have a large meeting and I'm not in Seattle. And you?" He was pretty sure Whaley was gay. But come to think of it, Levi had seen him with a woman a time or two and it was obvious it was a date.

"I've known the Whaleys most of my life. They only live just up the road a little. Ryan, that's Cal's brother, used to babysit me and my sister when we were kids. Mary, that's Cal's sister and one of my best friends, she's the one who made the food we're eating.

She takes pity on me and feeds me. That's her thing. She does it to everyone." Daisy smiled and it shot straight to his cock. "Would you like more food?"

"I think I'm full. For now anyway." He pushed back from the table. "You do the food since I don't know where anything is. And I'll clear the dishes." He stood.

"No." She placed a hand on his shoulder. "I'll take care of it. Go and sit. I'll be done in a minute or two."

First she put an apron on and god help him, his cock actually throbbed, it was so hard. So pretty and feminine, she put lids back on containers and bustled around, opening and closing the fridge and cabinets as she cleaned up. The couch he sat on was comfortable, set back in a bay window. A copy of Stephen King's *The Shining* lay open on the arm.

"All right then." She moved toward him. "Are you all right for beer? Would you like a top up or something else? I've got cider."

"I'm good." And he was. Utterly relaxed for the first time in a week. "Sit with me." He patted the couch and she dropped next to him, tucking her feet beneath her.

"What sort of law do you practice?"

"Land-use stuff mainly."

"Let's pretend I'm dumb and I don't know what 'land use' means." She fluttered her lashes and he found himself laughing again.

"Say you're a communications company and you need cell towers to provide your customers service. I help with permits and any sort of contract they might enter into to lease private and municipal property for that use. Sometimes I handle land reclamation issues. Say if a new company buys land and it's contaminated or being cleaned up. I help them get through the regulations and permitting process so they can get to work. It's not always fascinating, but I like making things happen."

"Making things happen takes a certain kind of talent." She took his hand and began to knead it before she turned and examined his palm.

"Are you going to read my lifeline?"

She leaned in and brushed a kiss over his lips. Just a breath of a touch and his entire body went hard. "No. I just like touching you."

He wasn't sure what to do with someone so straightforward.

"Right now you're thinking. What is it you're thinking, Levi?"

"I'm thinking you're very young."

She nodded. "I am."

"I'm trying to find a way around that."

"How about I explain to you that I'm twenty-four, not fifteen. And that I'm perfectly capable of making my own decisions and choices."

He took a deep breath and exhaled hard. "And I'm thinking I'm too old."

"Too old for what? Do you have trapeze fantasies or something? And how old are you? Sixty? Eighty-four?" Her mouth trembled as she held a smile back.

The pressure in his chest lessened.

"Eighty-*three*. Don't age me before I'm ready."

"You're not too old. I'm not too young."

She stayed where she was, his hand in both of hers. Those big brown eyes watching him carefully. Waiting for him. Christ. She had no idea what that did to him.

"I'm forty. I'm nearly twice your age."

"So what?"

"Yeah. So what?" He took his hand from hers and touched her chin, tipping it. "I want your mouth."

Her eyelids slid down a little and she took a deep breath. "Take it, then."

Chapter 4

She tasted like honey.

Odd and yet, not entirely unexpected.

Her lips were soft, opening on a sigh. He took her invitation and took the kiss deeper, his tongue sliding into her mouth.

His hand remained in hers, though he wanted to haul her close and take her to the couch. He hadn't wanted to get horizontal on a woman with this much intensity in a very long time.

The more he tasted, the more he wanted until need beat in his head like a pulse.

The depth and intensity of his desire shook him. Hit him so hard he had to fist the hand she wasn't holding to keep it from shaking.

He kissed like a master. Daisy knew she was in way over her head and all he'd done was kiss her. They weren't even touching except for lips and tongues and his hand in hers, but it was enough. Enough that it was a full-body caress when he groaned as she sucked his tongue.

So very controlled, this man. But it was there, just under the surface. Levi Warner was a very dominant male and she wondered if that extended to his sexuality.

Hoped so. It wasn't that she'd had many dominant lovers or anything. But he'd awakened something inside her. Curiosity, yes, but a sense of satisfaction in letting him lead. Something she'd never experienced before.

The weight of his focus on her was tangible. It made her a little drunk, needing more even as she barely managed to process what he gave her through a simple kiss.

It was enough to let him lead the kiss, enough to step back and wait for whatever he had in mind next.

Her body ached, her nipples throbbed and her pussy was wet and swollen. She shivered, imagining what he'd be like naked. In her bed. In his bed with her in it. Whatever, it didn't matter where, the naked part was important.

He was patient. So very patient as he continued to kiss her. A nip of her bottom lip that had her gasping for air. His beard stubble gave her just the right amount of friction. Nearly painful. Enough to make her imagine what it'd feel like against the skin of her inner thighs as he went down on her. And she bet he did it well. If his kissing was any indicator, he'd be a marvelous pussy eater.

With a sharp intake of breath he broke the kiss and stared at her. His pupils were huge again and it gave her yet another shiver of delight.

"I should go."

"You should?" She grabbed the front of his shirt without meaning to and released it quickly. If he left, she'd never speak to him again.

"Christ." He scrubbed a hand through his hair and she let the other one go. Whatever it was he was fighting with himself over, he had to deal with it. He was a big boy and she sure as hell wasn't his mother. Nor did she plan to beg him to stay.

She knew her worth as a woman. She'd been raised by not only a kick-ass mother, but her grandmother and sister were also strong, smart women. Whatever her concerns about her talent and art, she'd never beg a man for his attention.

He wanted her or he didn't. So she sat back a little and let him work through it.

"You're too young. I shouldn't even be thinking about sex."

She sighed. "You keep saying that. I'm far over the age of consent. Also, you're assuming a lot. I don't fuck on the first date."

Then he laughed and she felt better for it.

"You'd leave me with blue balls?" he teased.

"*I'm* too young? You give me that line and talk about my age? I'm sure I heard that one back in the day. Do you think I'll give you a pity hand job?" She grinned. He was adorable and damn, she might have broken her no fucking on the first date rule earlier, so it was probably good that they both stepped back for a moment. He made her feel . . . unfettered. And as lovely as it was, no man had ever made her want to jump so foolishly into something.

He grinned back. "Well, all right, it's been some time since I've used that line."

"What's next? Will you tell me you'll only put the tip in?"

He laughed and brought her to him, plopping her into his lap and squeezing her tight. And then he paused, as if he were surprised. But she liked it and wouldn't let him second-guess himself, so she gave him a squirm to remind him she was there, her ass against his cock, and his eyes lost focus a moment until they honed in on her mouth.

"When I put it in, it won't be just the tip."

She gulped. She knew it. It couldn't be avoided. 'Cause hell yeah.

"You're very sure of yourself."

"And you're very breathless when you say that."

"I'm not afraid of your age. I want to fuck you. I also want to eat four cupcakes at once but I restrain myself to two. I have self-control." She looked at him again. "*Sometimes*. Anyway, I like it when men are sure of themselves. Well, when they deserve to be."

"Is that so?" His eyes had darkened and his grip tightened. His cock was insistent against her trousers and she nearly came from how fucking hot it was.

"I don't know. Do you deserve to be?"

He slid his hand up her belly, between her breasts, to her throat where he collared her with his hand and she couldn't stop her sigh of longing. Or of the way she seemed to lose any rigidity in her spine and just melted into him. It was as if he'd flipped a switch inside her and she'd gone gooey.

Pleasure pulsed through her, slow and warm, leaving her lethargic.

He bent and kissed her again, his hand still at her throat. He cradled the back of her head with his arm and devastated her mouth. This kiss was more aggressive; his tongue slid against hers, teasing and taking, and when he nipped her bottom lip he laved the sting and made her moan.

"I think I do, yes." He placed her next to him on the couch. "But I don't fuck on the first date either."

She waited.

"What are you doing tomorrow night?"

The second date was a totally different set of rules.

"I'm actually busy. My friend is a caterer and I help her out."

His brow furrowed and she tried very hard not to laugh. It was probably the first time he'd heard no in ages.

"Sunday then?"

"I'm free for breakfast or lunch. I have plans in the evening."

"I'll be at a family thing on Sunday until six."

"Monday I'm free. After seven. You can take me to a movie."

"I don't want to waste time in a dark theater not looking at you. You're pretty amazing to look at." One of his brows slid up and she tried not to giggle and just barely made it. It would have blown the whole age reassurance thing if she had giggled. But he made her giddy, damn it.

"You say some good stuff, Levi."

"Monday night it is. How about sushi?"

"All right."

"I'll pick you up here at seven." He stood. "Give me a tour."

She allowed him to help her up. "You're imperious."

"I've been told that before."

He'd be worth it, she wagered. "Obviously this is the living and sleeping area." She waved a hand at her house. "Kitchen you've seen."

He wandered, looking at her pictures, her art. "What's behind that door?" He tipped his head to the left.

"Hm. I don't know if I should show you."

"The bathroom? Is it a mess?"

She opened the door. "It's my room."

He followed her inside and paused. "You sleep out there to keep all your clothes in here?"

"This is far more than a closet." She folded the throw she'd left on the little fainting couch she'd picked up at an estate sale the year before and took in the space she'd made her own in the years she'd lived in the little house.

Her clothes did indeed take up not just the small closet attached to the room, but two walls as well with pegs and shelves for all her various accessories. But bookshelves lined the third wall and a reading nook and vanity desk and mirror was on the last one.

He touched her clothes, a secret smile on his face.

"Tell me why."

"I can sleep out there just fine. But this is where I go when I need to be soothed, or to relax and read. I can sew in here. I get dressed and put on my makeup in here. Drink some wine, think about my next project."

"I like that. A room of your own, so to speak."

"Exactly. When I'm in here I don't answer the phone or the door. It's just alone time. I think you're the first man to have been in here who I wasn't related to."

"An honor indeed." He turned around the room and realized she'd revealed the inner heart of herself to him. This room was her intimate space. It smelled of her. Whatever perfume she wore bore a faint, but unmistakable mark on the air.

She had hats of all colors and sizes on hooks and in round, pretty hatboxes on shelves. Shoes of all kinds. Her makeup table, and how he loved to watch a woman get ready. A flash of memory of Kelsey lining her lips or dabbing perfume at her wrists came to him. A nice memory.

But this woman was altogether a different creature than Kelsey had been. Confident. Generous. Here.

He pulled out a red dress, examining it. Imagining how it would look on her. He wanted to see it against the warm tones of her skin. "You're a clotheshorse. I never would have guessed that about you."

"I love clothes. I always have. When I was a little girl, I went with my mom and grandmother a few times a year to estate sales and garage sales. We'd find clothes and bags, pieces of furniture. It's where I began to accrue pieces for my first mixed-media stuff."

"You'll wear this to sushi on Monday." He indicated the dress.

"Vintage. I bought that for twenty dollars at a garage sale. I had to replace the zipper. I hate putting in zippers." She took it from him, her fingers caressing the material. "One of my favorites."

He didn't disagree, only looked at her dress and drifted past the shoes in racks on one of the walls before hanging it on a hook near the bathroom door.

"Where do you work?"

"Studio. Come on then." She switched a nearby lamp off and started to lead him from the room, but he wasn't ready to go just yet so he snagged her as she passed, pulling her close.

"Thank you for showing me your room." He brushed a kiss over her lips.

"You're welcome. Now you know my secrets."

"I doubt that."

Her grin was cheeky as she led him from the room and out the back door.

It was a cold, clear night and the yard was quiet as she led him through it. In the distance he saw the bigger house, her parents' house, he figured. The lights burned against the windowpanes.

He could never live on the same property with his parents. He loved his family. But it was way easier to love them when he lived out here and they lived back in Seattle. The distance was a good thing. He wondered just how involved her parents were in her life.

"I share the space with my grandmother." Daisy flipped on the lights as they entered the studio space.

"This is beautiful." And it was. Soaring ceilings with windows would flood the space with light during the daytime. Just then he could see the stars high overhead.

"Thank you. My friend's brother is an architect. He did the plans and my friends and family did nearly all the building labor. We did have a plumber and electrician in because that was beyond our DIY skills."

He walked through the space, in awe. He hadn't told her this, but he was a huge art lover. He'd been raised to appreciate the fine arts by a mother who spent a lot of time and energy fund-raising for various art programs. He went to shows and gallery openings on a monthly basis. That Daisy was an artist as well as a scorching hot woman only made her harder to resist.

"This is all your stuff?"

"Down here, yes. My grandmother has a perch. That's what I call it. But she has a little loft up there." She pointed to a space with a comfortable chair, a couch and several easels. "She wants to be left alone when she works so she heads up there, puts head-phones on and does her thing. This is all my space down here."

Christ. To be her age and have so much talent.

"How long have you been doing this?"

"Those garage and estate sales I told you about? I was six when I bought this container of cards and letters. It was pretty. I liked the pictures and handwriting. That was the raw material for my first piece. I papier-mâchéd it into a series of little boxes. My mom still has them. It went from there."

"They were supportive then?" He paused to gape at a painting of a woman's upper body, her arms above her head as she arched. A shiver moved through him at the sight. And then craven greed to posses it. "This is . . . I want this."

"You do?" She sounded surprised and when he looked up he caught sight of her face. Wariness lived in her eyes. "Why?"

"It's stunning. I have a large, empty wall in my media room. This would be beautiful in it."

"I have plans for it."

"Like what?" He had enough money to outbid anyone who could possibly be his competition.

She looked him up and down. "Plans. I want to enter it into a contest of sorts. When that's over, if I win and get the placement that is, I'd be happy to discuss selling it to you. If you still want it."

He wanted it. Almost as much as he wanted her. This woman he'd so underestimated at every turn. He'd seen a beautiful woman, a young woman and he hadn't paid much attention to the rest of her.

But there was so much more to Daisy Huerta than he'd imag-ined at first. Anyone who could create something like this was someone he wanted to know.

"I want it. I'll want it in a week or a month." He got what he wanted. But he wouldn't say so. He'd show her.

Chapter 5

"So how was the date with a hot older dude?"

Daisy tied her apron better and looked back over her shoulder at Jules Lamprey, another one of her friends and fellow Delicious member. Jules was blonde. Stunning, with pretty blue eyes and a quick, charming smile. She was good people and Daisy adored her.

She and Jules were filling in on Mary's Saturday afternoon catering gig. She'd lost three servers she used often and needed the help so Jules and Daisy had stepped in, as had another one of their friends, Gillian.

"He asked me out for tonight but I had other plans. He then asked about Sunday, but that's Delicious . . . so." She shrugged.

"Invite him. So we can meet him." Mary popped a strawberry into Daisy's mouth. "What do you think?"

She struggled to chew the giant berry. "Is that balsamic? Yum."

"Yes. Adrian and Gillian brought it back from Italy for me." Mary beamed.

"Awesome. And no, not inviting him to Delicious. We have a

date for drinks and dinner on Monday night. Sushi." She didn't mention the dress thing he said, though it still flooded her with a sexual thrill every time she thought of it. Of the way he'd just told her what to wear. Of the way she got off on it.

"Why? Are you ashamed of us?" Gillian winked.

Gillian had been the first of their group to get engaged. They'd watched her fall in love with Adrian Brown, the father of her son and all-around Super Hottie McHot Pants rockstar over the last six months. Gillian was a very private person and it had been hard for her to open her life to Adrian. It had been her friends who'd continued to push her, knowing they needed each other. Knowing Gillian deserved to be loved.

So of course she got a kick out of needling Daisy right then.

"It's only a second date. You guys are special. He doesn't get any of you unless I know he'll be around awhile. Otherwise it's a waste. You're all too wonderful to waste. And I don't want my lovely dinner to be wrecked with date angst. Plus, as you're finally going to tell us when you've decided to stop living in sin with your baby daddy, I want to have all my attention for celebrating."

Gillian laughed, delighted. "Are we that obvious?"

"When you came back from Italy you had a new ring. Obviously he proposed all official like. And you both say nothing for a month as we pester you about it. When you say you have an announcement we just assume. Unless you're knocked up. Which would also be awesome."

Gillian blushed. "I'm not pregnant. We'd like to be at some point. But he's got a lot of stuff to deal with right now. He'll start recording his new record soon, the new house is being renovated. Though for heaven's sake my house is just fine." She shook her head but affection was all over her features.

"Just know we expect to meet him at some point. How else can we know if he's worthy of you?" Jules kissed her cheek and grabbed a tray. "Ladies, shall we show this engagement party just how awesome Luxe Catering is?"

"Hell yes."

Busy, she'd said.

Sunday brunch with his family could not be as entertaining as spending time with Daisy would have been.

Unbidden, a smile came to his lips as he thought of her. Of the way she'd lured him back to her little house and had proceeded to get her ass kicked at cards while she made them margaritas and ferried snacks in as they'd played.

She didn't expect anything from him. He didn't expect anything from her. They just got to know each other a little and played cards while listening to music.

It had been a long time since he'd woken up on a weekend so totally happy and relaxed.

"I hear you brought in a trip for two to Mexico, a winery weekend and some art for the auction lunch next week." His mother sipped her club soda. He'd arrived twenty minutes before but all his brothers still hadn't arrived, leaving him to fend for himself with Liesl Warner. He'd get even for that later.

"Yes, yes, I did. Rebecca and Howie Slaughter donated the house and plane fare. A local Bainbridge artist donated a rather arresting ceramic piece."

Daisy had let him choose between several pieces and he'd been unable to look away from the fragile red rose wrapped in barbed wire. It was a small piece. The contrast between the nearly see-through ceramic rose petals and the barbed wire was startling. A piece like that could sit on a shelf or a table and would catch your eye when you least expected it.

Truth be told, he had plans for that piece in his own house. He had the perfect place for it, a shelf in his bedroom. Low and near his armoire, the light would hit it in the mornings. And it would go wonderfully with the painting he would buy from her.

"Nice job. You know your brother and . . . Gwen will be here shortly. Did you attend that class you promised to?" Liesl probably tried to keep the derision from her voice at the mention of Mal's fiancée's name, but it rang through anyway.

In the background, his father laughed and pretended to cough.

"I went to a dance class. My instructor even offered to write me a note." He paused to smile at that. "I *am* capable of dancing at a wedding. This topic has now been exhausted. As has my patience. Two years of this. He's the one sleeping with her, so why do I have to do all this nonsense?"

His mother blushed and he saw the smile she wrestled back into a frown. "Levi Warner, you will watch your language."

"Ah and there's my family." Eli walked in, pausing to kiss their mother's cheek before nodding at their father.

"Darling, you should have been here thirty minutes ago." Liesl gave her third youngest a raised brow. Levi flipped his brother off behind her back.

"Traffic."

"Funny how you all live in different directions and yet you're all late."

Luckily, before she could get too wound up, Toby and Jonah showed up with roses and a pastry box from their mother's favorite bakery on the Eastside.

"When do we eat?" It was only that Toby was Toby that he was able to get away with such things. And he did it knowing Mal was going to be in big trouble for being the last late person.

Their father shot him a look and Toby only laughed.

"It's a wonder I made it through all five of you."

"That's because you're exemplary, dear." James raised his glass in his wife's direction and they all joined him.

That's when Mal stormed in.

"You're late."

"Gwen wants me to sign a prenup."

Liesl laughed but it was sharp enough to draw blood. Levi sighed and caught Jonah's eye. As the two oldest they should really corral their mother. But they'd let her wind down a little before they stepped in.

Liesl shook her head. "Why are you arguing with that? We've been telling you to have her sign a prenuptial agreement for months now."

"I don't want to go into this marriage planning to fail. I won't do it." Mal's mouth hardened and the brothers gave each other a quick look and stepped in.

"You are worth a great deal of money, Mal. If you two divorce, you would stand to lose half of it. It's not planning to fail." Levi shrugged and walked past, looking back over his shoulder as he did. "It pains me to say this, but I agree with Gwen here."

"I'm not worried. She'd never do that to me."

Their mother set her glass down and Jonah hurried to intervene. "Malachi Warner, stop fucking around and do what you need to do."

"Jonah!" Their mother put her hands on her hips and glared at him.

"Mom, I'm sorry but this is basic man stuff. Sometimes you need to say the F word." He turned back to Mal. "Anyway, nut up and sign this thing. Be an adult. You have responsibilities to your family and your future. You have to stop this philosophical bullshit about how you're planning to fail. Fuck you, Mal. Did you think it would be easy to do this? Being a grown-up is hard."

Levi watched Mal slowly buckle against Jonah's stone-cold, big-brother scolding.

"Do you have it? The contract?" Jonah circled back and Levi took over.

"At the very least, let us look at the thing. No harm in that, right? Where is she? Why don't you call her and tell her you're here at dinner and you'll see her later. That way she won't worry and you can cool off before you see her again."

"You guys are dicks. Sometimes it's okay not to look at life like a business arrangement." Mal grumbled it, but he moved to pull the contract from his bag and hand it to Jonah.

"Apologize to your mother for being a butthead." Toby handed Mal a glass as he passed by on his way toward the dining room.

Mal took their mother's arm and escorted her. "I'm sorry I lost my temper. And I'm sorry you had to hear Jonah say that filthy word so many times."

Levi kept his head down as he stuck back with Jonah to read over the contract.

"Why do you think she pushed it?" He didn't trust this sudden burst of concern from Gwen.

"It has occurred to me that perhaps the contract might be far more favorable than a standard prenup or even a generous divorce settlement. I don't trust her. It's all those big white teeth. She's a chipper fascist. Nothing worse."

Levi snorted and watched his father keep an eye on Mal. James Warner was no idiot; he was thinking the very same thing he and Jonah were.

"These percentages and timelines," Jonah paged through, "seem off. But I don't know what the standard is. Not my area. I know a few family lawyers in the building. Maybe one of them could take a look." He kept his voice down as Mal excused himself to call Gwen.

Levi had a better idea. "Better yet, I know a guy on Bainbridge. Cal Whaley. I can see if he or one of his people can take a look tomorrow. If it's standard, they'll see it right away. If not, they'll need more time and we'll know. And he's not here in town. Mother will calm down if that's the case."

Jonah handed the contract over and Levi popped out to tuck

them into his case and leave a message with his assistant to get with Cal that next day if possible.

His mother sent him a look when he returned and sat across from her. "It'll be fine," he murmured.

Liesl knew her sons weren't perfect. Loved them all in her own fierce way. But she had expectations of them. Their standing in the community was important to her, something she considered a great accomplishment. They were expected to work hard, use their status and money appropriately, to give back through charity work and to avoid any sort of scandal.

She was protective and ruthless when it came to her family. An admirable, if annoying at times, quality in a woman.

As much as Levi disliked Gwen, he hoped like hell that feeling in his gut that she was up to something was wrong.

He came home and stood in his bedroom looking out over the water for a long time.

Ten years ago he'd had a wife. A wife and a house big enough to start a family in. And then two years after that he'd had an empty house and a train wreck of a life to clean up. So he'd sold the house and come out here to Bainbridge. Though so close to Seattle, he could walk down the street and no one would look at him and think about what had happened. He could fucking live without the history of his life weighing him down so much he could barely move.

Bainbridge had been a good choice. One he hadn't regretted since the first night he'd stood there and looked out, knowing it was his view, knowing it was his house, knowing his future had a clean slate instead of the debris of a fucked-up, shitty wife who drove drunk up the off-ramp and hit someone else head-on, killing her instantly along with the baby she'd been carrying.

He shoved away from his place and headed to the shower. He didn't miss Kelsey. Not anymore. It didn't hurt to think about all the what-might-have-beens, because all he could do was be thankful she hadn't killed anyone else that night.

So he'd dated and fucked around. Plenty of beautiful women in the world. Most of them made him happy in bed. Some amused him out of it. But he didn't have to open up and let any of them in. He didn't have to give them anything he couldn't bear to part with. And it had been good.

But Daisy Huerta was something else. Something different and vibrant. He wanted her in a way he hadn't wanted the others. With the others he could be casually rough. Never to harm, but he could hold wrists and fuck hard and they were all right with it.

Daisy though . . . he wanted more.

Stripping off, he got the water started and stepped in, groaning at how good it felt.

He wanted to do all sorts of things to and with Daisy. He soaped up and gave over to the inevitable, grasping his cock in a soapy fist and thrusting.

Her lips, plump and red, that tongue . . . he wanted to fuck her mouth, watch his cock disappear between her lips and come out, wet and shiny with her spit. He wanted to order her to take him deeper, suck him harder. Wanted to pull out and come all over her beautiful tits.

His balls crawled up close to his body. The vision in his head driving him toward climax faster and harder than usual. She'd look fucking spectacular on her knees before him. He wanted to dress her up in the finest lingerie, wanted to shower her with pretty things, things she'd wear or use and think of him. He wanted to be on her mind the way she was on his.

Wanted to sink his cock deep into her cunt and see the changes on her face as he did. Wanted to watch her tits jiggle as he thrust deep, wanted to feel the slick, wet heat of her around his cock, wanted that juice to drip down his balls.

He arched into his fist when he tweaked his left nipple, thinking about what hers would look like. Wondering how her pussy would taste. He knew the sweet seduction of her mouth, that taste and heat of her there. Would she be as delicious when he took that first lick? Would her clit harden against his tongue as she begged for more?

He sped, needing to come, needing to be in her.

What would her skin look like as he fucked her? Glistening with sweat, the marks from the flogger on her ass like pink kisses. That brought a grunt from his lips. He rarely used toys or tools. But with her? With her how could he resist?

She wouldn't be a plaything like the others. He couldn't hold back with her like he did the others. She called out to be dominated. To be cherished and cosseted, pleasured and spoiled.

She wasn't to be played with because with a woman like her it wouldn't be a game.

It was a risk. A woman who was nothing like all the others. A woman like her was indelible, the kind a man didn't forget. Ever. He came in a hot rush as thoughts of what she'd be like propped up in this shower stall, his cock deep inside her, ran riot in his head.

And even as he finally found sleep an hour later, it was with her face in his mind's eye.

Daisy sat at the large table with all her very favorite people in the world. Jules to her left. Cal and Ryan, Gillian, Adrian and their son Miles. The family of her heart. Mary busily moved around the room, making sure all the other diners were happy, but she came back to the table frequently to check in with them and visit a moment.

Gillian leaned close to speak. "You're grinning in that way you do right before something like a new dress shows up in my front hallway. What are you up to?"

"I was just marveling at how lucky I was to have you all in my life."

Surprised pleasure flashed over Gillian's face. "That's lovely. I'm glad to have you right back."

Mary came back to the table. "I've got a few minutes before dessert." She sat and Jules handed her a glass.

"While you're here, we wanted to talk to you all." Adrian spoke and Gillian straightened, taking his hand.

"Finally." Jules snorted.

Gillian raised a brow in her friend's direction, but then spoke to the group. "We've set a date for the wedding. The second weekend in July. After the holiday. Mary, would you be our caterer? Jules, will you handle all the desserts? Daisy, would you design our rings?"

"Wow, you two are like an entire economy unto yourselves." Mary grinned. "I wouldn't be offended if you wanted to look at other caterers. I'm assuming this will be a big wedding and I've only done small-to-medium ones before."

"Oi you. Not only will you be expected to cater our wedding, but we have *two* events we need you for as it happens. The wedding itself will be small. Just immediate friends and family. We're having it at the new house."

Adrian looked to Gillian and then his son, smiling. Daisy liked him a lot. She had her doubts at first. But he'd proven himself to be a damned good father and the kind of man Gillian needed. "And then something larger. A reception my manager wants to throw. Industry people and that sort of thing. They wanted us in Los Angeles but I said no. We'll do it here in Seattle. There's a planner who'll be contacting you with all the details but that one will be in early August."

While Daisy was sure her friends would be amazing as caterers and pastry chefs, she wasn't too sure about ring design.

"Are you sure you want me? I know some great jewelry designers."

"None of them know me. Know us. You know not just me and Adrian, but Miles. You're special and perfect because I love you and you're family." Gillian smiled and Daisy fought back tears.

"I can get you some ideas by the end of the month."

"All right." Adrian squeezed her hand and looked to the group again. "You're as much my family now as my brother and sister are. This will be a big family affair. It means a lot to Gillian and me that you're all such an important part of our lives and so naturally our wedding too."

"And I know you will be busy supervising all the food and stuff at the wedding, but you're all under orders to have enough non-Delicious staff so that you can enjoy the reception with us. Got me?" Gillian gave them all a look and everyone nodded.

Daisy raised her glass. "To Gillian, Adrian and Miles."

"To love." Gillian toasted back before first kissing her son's cheek and then Adrian's lips. Daisy wanted that, she realized. Wanted that connection with someone. Wanted a kid and a husband and a happy ever after.

Chapter 6

Levi pulled into the driveway and caught sight of her immediately. The dress, the red dress he'd chosen, was vivid against winter's gray. She stood on the stoop of the gallery speaking animatedly to an older woman she looked a whole lot like.

He froze a moment. This was like meeting the parents. And he hadn't done that for many, many years.

He made himself walk from his car up to the steps. He was a grown-ass man and he could meet someone's grandma without proposing marriage.

Daisy turned and caught sight of him. Her smile drew him closer.

"Take a coat. It's a pretty dress, but you need a coat or you'll get a cold." The little old woman looked him up and down. "He's wearing a coat. See?"

Daisy nodded sagely. "You're right. Levi Warner, this is my grandmother, Delores Huerta. Grandma, this is Levi."

He took her hand and shook. She appeared fragile, but her grip told him otherwise.

"It's a pleasure to meet you, Mrs. Huerta."

She smiled at him, a twinkle of mischief in her eyes, and he liked her immensely right then.

"Make her put on a coat." She kissed Daisy's cheek and headed around the gallery, waving. "Have fun."

"I need a coat." Daisy laughed and he followed her into her house where she grabbed a white coat and gloves which made her look like a glamorous starlet from the 1940s.

He helped her into the coat and escorted her out to his car. She waited for him to open her door, which he really liked.

"You look beautiful in that dress," he murmured as they drove. It pleased him beyond measure that she'd worn it.

"Thank you. You look pretty beautiful yourself."

At the restaurant, she held his arm and let him do the door opening and the chair pulling out. He knew she didn't need it, but he wanted to and she allowed it because of that. The pleasure of that knowledge warmed him.

She mixed his wasabi and soy carefully, looking up to catch his eye to be sure it was the mixture he preferred. He watched her hungrily and wondered what she'd look like totally naked. When his beer arrived, she poured it for him.

He hadn't been waited on like this. Ever. Not in this personal way she did. Sure, he'd had waiters pour his beer and serve his food, but this was Daisy, taking care of Levi, and it got to him. Got to him like so many other things about Daisy Huerta and he couldn't seem to stop thinking of her. And how she was different.

Which was stupid. Because she *was* different, different enough that she was totally off the menu when it came to anything long lasting. It wasn't like he could bring her home to his parents. A twenty-four-year-old artist with tattoos and all that in-your-face, lush beauty. His mother would be unfailingly polite to her and when she saw him next she'd cut him to shreds with his responsibility and his future and how wholly unsuitable a girl like Daisy was for a man like him.

He shouldn't be there with her at all. But he was. And he had no plans at all to change that.

"How was your weekend?" His fingers brushed hers as he took the glass and then sipped.

"Lovely, thank you. Worked and hung out with my friends Saturday. Yesterday my friend announced her wedding date at long last over dinner. Yours?"

He sighed and she laughed.

"That bad?"

"Family drama." He shrugged. "Not as fun as being with friends and hearing wedding dates."

He was very stingy with his life, she noted. It annoyed her.

"The rest of your family lives in Seattle?"

"Mainly. One of my brothers is in Kirkland, another is in Redmond. The rest live in Seattle. What about you?"

"My entire family lives on Bainbridge. I'm spoiled to have them all so close. Why did you decide to be a lawyer?"

"Why did you decide to be an artist?"

"Do you always answer questions with questions?" She paused when the first plates began to arrive. She grinned when she noticed they'd given her an extra plate of yellowtail nigiri. Her favorite. She winked at the server in thanks. He blushed.

"Do you know that guy?"

"I worked here for two years. On weekends usually. They know my favorites." She shrugged.

"You know a lot of people."

She laughed and popped one of the nigiri into her mouth, pausing to enjoy it. "I do. I imagine you do as well." Only she doubted they were servers at restaurants and dance instructors. "I promise to answer any of your questions totally honestly, if you answer some of mine. Really it's quid pro quo."

A half smile touched his lips and, *man*, she wanted to see him naked.

"Why did you decide to be an artist?"

"I grew up not really knowing it was so unusual to be an artist. My grandmother has been a painter for as long as I can remember. I watched her do it. Make it work. Have a career in art. So I never had those oh-it-can't-happen moments. They had lean years of course. But she kept on. So when I started making papier-mâché she got excited about it and they—she and my grandfather—displayed my little boxes in the gallery. And they sold." She laughed at the memory. "Anyway, I like to create. I'm an artist because I like making things."

He sipped his beer before speaking. "I decided to be a lawyer because my father is one. I saw him argue a case. I must have been eleven or so. I remember seeing him in a totally different light after that. He was so self-assured and clever. I wanted to be that. Wanted to change things with my brain and words. Two of my brothers are architects, but I hate math. Don't tell my mother that." He smiled and she relaxed. His demeanor warmed as he opened up to her. "After that day I made a plan and I stuck to it."

She bet. The man sitting across from her wasn't one who let life happen *to* him in any way. "Of course you did. I like that. You're very ambitious. And this is your family business? The law firm?"

He nodded. "Me, my father, my older brother and my uncle and a few cousins."

"It's sort of fun working in the family shop."

He laughed. "Yes, I suppose we both are, aren't we?"

What she really wanted to know is how he was forty and unmarried. But she didn't want to ask right then. He'd probably think she was looking for a marriage proposal, though she just wanted to know him a little better.

So they ate and chatted about silly stuff until they were finished and it got suddenly a lot more serious at the car.

"Would you like to come over? Have a drink?"

She took a deep breath and nodded.

It wasn't as if he'd never brought a woman back to his place, but this one, well, this one made him a little nervous.

She fit against his side perfectly as he walked with her up the stairs from the garage into the house and then she paused, sucking in a breath.

"This is breathtaking," she murmured and broke away, wandering toward the wall of windows he so loved to stand and stare out.

She looked remarkably right there, the night silhouetted around her curves like a lover. The heels she wore were very high. Her back arched, showcasing her ass and legs that were surprisingly long for such a petite woman.

"You do realize your body is ridiculously beautiful, don't you?" He took her coat and noted the pleasure on her face at the compliment.

He stepped away and hung her things before he turned music on, needing the buffer because with her it always felt so raw.

"I could play coy and pretend I don't." She shrugged a shoulder and turned to face him and then walking to where he stood, mesmerized by her. She slid her hands up his chest. "I'm not very good at coy though." She tiptoed up to kiss his neck, just at the place below his ear. "I know what I want. I know who I am."

"Good." He hated coy. Hated women who danced around what they wanted.

His arm encircled her waist as he caught her hand in his on the other side and they began to sway. She leaned in, her cheek against his chest and melted against his body.

Here in the dark, in the private of his home, the lush sensuality of her body sharpened his hunger.

It was slow between them, not quite careful.

He buried his face at her neck, breathing her in, the softness of her hair against his cheek.

"It's been some time since I slow danced. I'd forgotten how delicious it was," he murmured as he kissed her jaw, over her closed eyes, her nose and then to her glorious mouth.

Desire beat at him. Urgent. Greedy. And he let it take over with a tug on her bottom lip between his teeth until she made a sound, low and deep. That response arced through him like electricity.

He gripped her upper arms firmly and it made her mindless. Shivers broke over her and her knees went rubbery.

She swallowed hard as his lips slid down her throat, licking and nipping the skin until she nearly shouted at him to do more.

"Are you with me?" He pulled away from her body enough to look into her face.

She nodded because words had escaped her.

"Thank God." He bumped her, walking her backward until she hit a wall. He pressed his weight against her to hold her in place.

The way he handled her made her mindless to anything but him. His hands at her upper arms, his body against hers to keep her where he wanted. Whatever he did, it was so raw and delicious.

Before she'd even registered it, her dress was slipping from her shoulders and he'd bent his head to kiss over her collarbone. Her hands on his shoulders held him to her, but she also felt the fine tension there.

"Don't hold back," she whispered.

"I'm not sure I could even if I tried."

"Oh now, that's not true." She licked her lips and watched the dress pool at her waist as his hands went to her bra, peeling the cups back with a groan.

He pinched her nipples, tugging and twisting the bar in each until her hips jutted forward all on their own. She was pretty sure she'd never been wetter or more ready for sex. Ever.

She may have said something; she sort of went away for a moment as he palmed her breasts and squeezed. Not hard enough to hurt, but hard enough to bring that edge of pain. Hard enough to remind her he was there and he wanted her.

The edge of his teeth slid over her shoulder and she stuttered a breath and it seemed as if a warm weight settled over her system. It was so good, so right, all sorts of chemicals flying through her, rendering her slightly stoned.

Could it be so very easy for him to push her into sub space? The temptation to explore that with her was so overwhelming he had to close his eyes against it.

He'd told her he wasn't sure he could hold back. But he could. And he had been for a long time. But he hadn't exaggerated how much of a temptation she was.

"I want to see you in the light."

Her gaze cleared and she nodded as he led her up the stairs and toward his bedroom. Her dress was still on halfway, exposing breasts that made him want to fall to his knees and praise.

Both nipples pierced. He exhaled at that memory.

"I'd like you to take your clothes off and sit on the bed, please."

He'd been about to soften that once he got past his surprise that he'd said it. But she shivered and he realized she was totally on board with it. And then he couldn't fight it anymore.

He leaned against the doorjamb and watched as she reached behind her body and unhooked her bra.

"When they're covered by a bra and a dress they're amazing. When they're free they're magnificent." And holy shit they were. High and full, a metal bar in each nipple. His mouth watered to taste.

She smiled, not shy at all. And then she unzipped the rest of the dress and stepped from it.

Stockings.

Garter belt.

High heels.

Teeny panties.

The last time he'd seen a twenty-four-year-old naked, he'd been twenty-six or so. The experience was not overrated.

"On second thought," he said as he pushed to stand and stalked toward her, "leave the stockings and heels on. Those panties . . . well, I'll take care of them."

"Should I sit?" Her usual saucy demeanor had softened, gone obedient.

Again he had to close his eyes a moment to get himself straight. It had been a very, very long time since he'd opened this part of himself to anyone else. "Yes." He opened his eyes and settled his gaze on her. On the lush curves she sported.

She sat, as he'd told her to, and he got to his knees, spreading her thighs wide. Her skin was as soft as he'd imagined it to be. Her scent teased as he leaned in close, breathing over her cunt through her panties. The material was whisper thin; he could see the darkness of her labia, knew just beyond was a slick, hot world he planned to explore for as long as possible.

She whimpered, her fingers digging into the bedspread and when he pressed a kiss against her pussy she jumped a moment and then squirmed. Turning his head, he breathed a kiss over her inner thigh and then slid the panties down and off. She'd worn them over the belt like a smart girl.

"Are you going to get naked? Because I'd really, really like to see that."

He kissed her thigh one last time and then spread her pussy open to his mouth. He took a long lick and sucked her clit between his lips, tickling the underside with the tip of his tongue.

"Yes."

He drew circles around her gate with a fingertip, sliding it down to her asshole here and there, enough to keep her whimpering and gasping. Enough that he was glad he was still in his clothing because all he wanted was to get inside her cunt and fuck her.

But that could wait. He needed her orgasm first. Wanted her

to know who gave it to her, who she was there with. Then he could think straight and fuck her the way she deserved. He hoped.

"Your cunt tastes salty sweet." He swirled his tongue through all that soft, wet flesh as she trembled.

He opened his eyes and found her looking down her body at him, her lids half mast, her eyes glossy, lips parted. There was no hesitation there, nothing but pleasure.

He continued to flick his tongue over her clit as he turned his wrist and slid two fingers deep.

Tight. Hot.

He knew he found the right place when she jumped and then rained honey all over his hand. He stroked that sweet spot and ate her cunt like it was meant to be eaten.

She must have let go of the bed because her fingers slid through his hair and then she tugged, pulling him closer, rocking her hips. Taking what she wanted. His cock throbbed angrily, approving mightily.

He hummed and she made another sound, a weeping sort of moan, and then she came, her back arched, pressing her pussy into his face as she pulled his hair and goddamn, he loved it.

Slightly dazed from climax, her inner muscles still jumping, Daisy watched him stand, his lips shiny from her pussy.

And then he flicked open a button on his shirt and snagged her attention again.

"Why don't you undress me." Not a question. Not a request.

But it didn't need to be. She stood on slightly shaky legs and slid her palms up the fine cotton of the shirt until she got to the collar and began to unbutton.

His chest was broad. Hairy but not in a disgusting way. Threaded with gray here and there, which only made him a million times hotter.

She dragged her nails down that gorgeous, hard chest, over his nipples and rejoiced in his snarl of pleasure when she did.

Unable to resist, she leaned forward to take a taste, spreading the shirt open wide to lick over his left nipple and then his right. Left it seemed, got more of a response so she went back to flick her tongue over it and scrape her teeth against it as she pulled back.

He watched her, his expression inscrutable. She caught her lip between her teeth and walked behind him to remove the shirt and fold it carefully before placing it on the back of a nearby chair. His back was nearly as impressive as his front and called to her hands and lips as she paused to kiss and caress, sliding her palms around to his waist where she unbuckled his belt and pants, teasing with little touches of her fingertips and nails.

He turned suddenly, hauling her close for a kiss.

With his hands on her, when he was so sure and hard and in charge, everything inside her seemed to swell up, close to exploding. It was so very much. She'd never felt this way with anyone.

The kiss tasted of her, she thought as he pulled back. His pupils seemed to swallow his eye color, his expression was intense as his gaze slid to her breasts.

"I love that you're pierced."

She was sure glad of it.

"Can I take your pants off?" She didn't quite know why she asked, only that it felt like she should. So she did.

Then he slid a hand into her hair, freeing the last of it from all the pins she'd had holding it up. It fell around her shoulders and then he pulled her close again. By the hair. It sent a freight train of sensation straight to her nipples, which brushed against his chest, the slightly wiry hair abrading them just right.

"Yes. And then I want you on your knees, my cock in that hot mouth of yours."

Why yes, thank you very much! Her body seemed to electrify at that suggestion.

She slid her hands down his forearms before he let go so she could get at his pants. Pausing, she angled his arm to see the tattoo on the inside. Something she'd missed because everything else about his body had snagged her attention.

History is written by the victors.

"I like that."

He kissed her shoulder, tracing his fingertips down her shoulder and down her back as she got his pants unzipped and went to her knees to get them and his boxers down and off. She stood again, folding and placing them on the chair with his shirt before turning back to take him in.

"Your back is beautiful," he murmured as she walked to him.

They could talk tattoos after.

She smiled her thanks and went to her knees but he stopped her. "Wait."

Moments later he sat on the other chair in the room and placed a pillow on the floor in front of himself. "It won't be as hard on your knees."

How such a thing could disarm her, she didn't know. But it did and she went with it, adjusting herself to tuck the pillow beneath her knees. It brought her up a little higher as well. High enough to kiss along his flat belly, down over rock hard thighs, behind first one knee and the other. She caressed every part of him she could touch as she did.

But his cock was the main attraction. Meaty and thick and so hard it tapped his belly until she licked up the stalk and then grasped him at the root, angling to better take as much of him as she could.

He groaned when she slid her lips around the head and then down, slowly, breathing through her nose as she did.

He stroked over her hair as she began to suck him off.

"Yes, that's right. Keep my cock wet. Suck it hard. That's how I like it."

So she did it. Because she wanted to please him. Wanted the

hand caressing over her hair to continue that sweet and yet white-hot petting.

She reached down to her pussy to get her fingers nice and wet and then brought them to that place just behind his balls, pressing and then sliding down again to his asshole. He grunted but widened his thighs so she kept on, stroking over the hole and slightly inside as she sucked his cock.

He began to flex and thrust his hips, fucking her mouth as she found his prostate and pressed while she stroked a circle against it. The surface of his cock seemed to harden in response; nearly electric, the energy seemed to hum from him.

"I'm going to come in your mouth, Daisy. And then we'll have a cocktail. Then I'm going to fuck you."

She nodded around a mouthful of his cock and took him deep, wanting to make him feel good, wanting to bring him pleasure in a way no one else could.

It must have worked because he growled, his fingers in her hair tightening as he held her to him, fucking himself into her, and then came.

Chapter 7

He hoped the cocktail would soothe his nerves. God knew he needed something to. Because Daisy Huerta got right inside his defenses and had curled herself around him.

And he didn't have the strength or will to push her out.

The woman in question padded through his kitchen, making him a drink. She'd volunteered, telling him she'd make him something he'd enjoy. And who was he to refuse?

"Where'd you learn how to make drinks?" He considered getting one of his robes for her. Totally naked, in the full light of the room she was even more stunning and clearly comfortable with her state of undress.

She smiled, handing him a glass. "I have a friend who owns a bar. Sometimes he needs extra staffing so I pop in when that happens. And my parents are cocktail-hour people so I just grew up around that. My mother is one of those people who's good at everything. This is her recipe actually. It's a twist on a sidecar."

He sipped and approved. Hearty. Perfect for a cool evening.

"Are you cold? I have robes if you like." He took her hand and she grabbed her glass, following him into the living room.

"I have post-sex warmth still. Unless you'd prefer it."

He barked a laugh and when he sat, she sat at his feet, her head resting against his knee. He sucked in a breath, unable to resist a caress over her hair, dark and so soft. "It's safe to say I'm more than fine with you being naked. I just didn't want you to get a chill."

Turning her head, she looked him up and down. "Thank you. I think you should know that I find shirtless men in worn jeans and bare feet to be one of the sexiest things ever."

That warmed him. "Thank you. So tell me about your ink."

"My dad's family, my grandmother and grandfather, were first-generation Americans. But when I was a kid we went to Mexico a few times every year to visit extended family. Anyway, some of my very first memories were of the colors in my great-aunt's house. Reds and yellows, blues and greens. Bright and vivid. It's part of who I am." She brushed her fingers over the ink on her shoulder and upper arm.

"The woman on your shoulder reminds me of Frida Kahlo."

"It's actually based on a painting my grandmother did." The tattoo was of a dark-haired woman, a flower tucked behind her ear. Her face was made up like a sugar skull. Flowers and other bits and bobs, all Mexican folk art, surrounded her, flowing to her back in a spill of big red roses.

"When it's totally finished, the back will be a side view of a woman, praying hands, flowing hair, with a sugar skull face like the one on my arm."

"It's beautiful work."

"Thank you. The big piece on my back is being done by the brother of a friend. He owns a tattoo shop in Seattle. I'm hoping to have it all done by the end of next year. What about your ink?" As far as she could tell he only had the one on his forearm.

"Sometimes something happens and you were there, but everyone tells it differently and you begin to wonder what the fuck is true anymore. And the version most people think is real is not always the truth, but it doesn't matter."

"The importance is in the lesson?"

He nodded and she wondered what it was he meant. What had happened to him that made him mark himself as a reminder.

"I think," he said, placing his glass on a nearby table, "you should ride my cock."

She grinned. "I think that's a really good idea."

He pulled a condom from his pocket. Thank goodness he had one nearby. She had them in her bag of course, but now she wouldn't have to move to get it.

"Why don't you stand so I can get those off?" She slid her hands up his denim-covered legs.

"Out here?" He looked around.

"Unless you have other ideas."

He looked to the bank of windows.

"Are you worried people will see? Or do you hope they will?"

His pupils swallowed the color in his eyes again as he visibly got himself in check. She couldn't deny loving how it felt to affect him that way.

He stood and she unbuttoned his jeans, pulling them down so he could step from them. But he didn't sit right away. He moved to the fireplace and hit two switches. One turned the overhead lights off and the other turned the fireplace on, sending warm, golden light through the room. He did that for her.

"Your body is amazing." She twisted her nipple bar, noting the way his gaze went to her fingers, noting the way he straightened and headed to her, his face very intent.

"Thank you. Coming from you that's quite a compliment. Does that feel good?" He sat in a different chair, this one a chaise of sorts.

"Yes."

"Is your pussy wet?"

She nodded.

"Good. Come over here."

She smiled and did it, grabbing the condom and ripping it open. Kneeling between his legs, she rolled it over his fully revived cock. He had awesome recovery time, she'd give him that.

Straddling him, she reached back and angled his cock, slowly sinking down.

She had to go slow because he was so fucking thick. He filled her fully as she circled her hips to take him. Bit by bit until he was in all the way and she had to pause to catch her breath.

"This is very, very good." His slow smile made her nipples harden to nearly aching.

It was.

He might have been a very experienced, very skilled man, but she had a few tricks up her sleeve too. Being a dancer meant she was pretty damned flexible and in shape. So she'd show him.

Her hands braced on his upper arms, she began to ride, sliding her pussy down and then back and forth as she undulated, moving her hips rhythmically.

"Christ!" he hissed, watching the way she moved on him.

His cock was deep inside her supertight cunt as she moved. Her head tipped back, her fingers digging into his biceps. Whatever the hell she was doing on him was a miracle. Her inner muscles hugged him, caressing the length of his cock as she surrounded him with all that hot, wet, undulating flesh.

"I took belly dancing for three years. I might be young, but I know a few things."

He laughed. "Thank God for it. Now when you kill me it'll be me going out happy."

She angled her head to look at him, a smile on her lips. "Death by fucking? Whatever would the papers say? I think I'll keep you around. For next time."

Again. Yes, it had to happen again. No doubt about that.

He pulled and tugged her nipples, unable not to look at those piercings. Sexy. He'd seen women with pierced nipples in porn, but not up close. Not while the owner of said tits was riding his cock.

And then he was collaring her. Her throat under his palm, her pulse beating strong.

She gasped, her pussy fluttering around him and he knew she loved it as much as he did. Which allowed him to relax a little and enjoy it, enjoy this moment, with this woman.

"I want your gaze." He said it without having planned to say it. He panicked a moment when she opened her eyes and obeyed. So much intimacy in that, in watching as you fucked someone, seeing every one of their emotions flit over their features.

It meant he gave that to her as well.

Meant he let her see right into his head where she had lodged herself from the first moment he'd seen her.

Her nails dug in to his flesh, reminding him she was there, demanding, pleasing, yes, but needing to be pleased in turn.

He brought his fingers to her mouth and she sucked them in, licking them, getting them wet. He was so damned close. But when he brought those slick fingers to her clit she whimpered and then groaned, her clit hardening under his touch, cunt clutching him nearly to the point of pain. But the best kind of pain.

She sped her movements, clearly getting close as well. She caught her bottom lip between her teeth but when he squeezed her clit gently between his slippery fingers she sucked in air on a cry and began to come. So hard her pussy rippled around him, pushing him right over with her. The both of them coming at once, gazes locked until he let go of her throat and she fell forward, panting for air.

Chapter 8

She walked up toward the house from the yard, having just spent the last nearly twelve hours doing two different jobs. Her muscles ached, but it was a good ache. She had enough for rent and supplies and some left over to add to her savings after that afternoon.

She loved her savings account. Every time she looked at the numbers she was assured that she could continue to do her art, even in a lean time. It was her freedom.

She actually didn't need all the extra jobs by this point. The time was coming, she knew, to consider giving up several jobs. But it was hard to say no when her friends needed her.

That's when she noticed the note on her door and headed up to the big house to see her parents.

"Hey there, cutie pie." Her father gave her a big hug. "These came for you today." He indicated a large box and two dozen red roses. She had a guess as to who they were from.

"Who's sending you flowers? What's in the box?" Her grandmother wandered in and took a sniff of the roses.

Daisy kissed her cheek and handed her a rose. "I just walked in. Let me see." She opened the tiny envelope. Just an *L*. Enough to know her suspicion was right.

"They're from Levi."

"Ah, him. I should have figured. He's a little old for you isn't he?" Her grandmother didn't say it in a judgmental fashion.

"How old is he? Is it serious?" Her father wasn't as enlightened as his mother on such issues, Daisy knew.

"Not serious. We've only been on two dates and had some phone calls. He's a nice man." She evaded the age question, but her father wasn't having it and he repeated his question.

"He's forty." She didn't want to open the box in front of them, but there was no way around it. Both her father and her grandmother stood, waiting.

She peeked and couldn't help a gasp as she pulled the lid off entirely to reveal the contents. A bright red cashmere wrap. Cripes. She picked it up, bringing it to her face. So soft. When she did, she pocketed the card that had been nestled in the wrap, wanting to read it in private. Hoping it said more than *L*.

"Well, he's got good taste." Her grandmother winked at her.

"Hello. Of course he does. He's dating me, isn't he?"

Her father wasn't going to let himself be amused just yet though. "What does this Levi do that he's forty and dating girls?"

"I'm not a girl. He's an attorney." She slid the wrap around her shoulders and sighed. So warm.

"Candace is coming over for dinner. You'll stay?" Her father gave up on nagging, she could tell. But he'd be watching. And that was okay too. He was her dad after all.

Candace was her big sister. She was married and lived a few miles away so they saw her often. But it would be nice to have dinner with her family, even if she was dog tired and only wanted to sleep.

"Definitely. Let me take these back to my place. I'll be up in a few minutes."

In the privacy of her little house, she opened the card.

Next time you won't have to be cold when you're naked. L.

She sighed, she knew totally like a smitten girl, but hell, she *was* a smitten girl. He'd driven her home Monday night and had insisted on walking her not only to the door, but on going inside to be sure no one had broken in. He'd called on Wednesday and texted her the day before. She'd been hoping he'd ask her out again though, and he hadn't. Though the roses and the wrap were certainly evidence he was interested on some level.

But she had no time to get all tied up in knots over him or any man. Or so she told herself as she headed back to the house to have a lovely family dinner.

Levi had tried to ignore it, that growing need he felt every time he thought of her. She'd texted her thanks for the roses and the wrap and he'd nearly called her to ask her to dinner. But he hadn't and now he sat, all by himself in his office at eight on a Friday night like an idiot.

"Why are you here?" Jonah came in and sat.

"Finishing up some stuff. I'm leaving in a few. What's up with you? Where's Carrie?"

"Spending the night at a friend's house." Carrie was Jonah's daughter.

"Want to get dinner?"

"Yes, I do. I just got back from the mediation."

Levi winced. "Long-ass day."

"I need a few drinks before I can process it. I'm brain-dead."

He and Jonah were close. More like best friends than brothers most days, though they had their moments.

So it seemed sort of natural to bring Daisy up once their steaks had arrived. The Metropolitan Grill's large booths relaxed him nearly as much as the scotch in his glass. "So I started seeing someone."

Jonah looked up, interested. "Yeah? Who is she?"

"She's twenty-four." He blurted it out like a shameful secret. But Jonah only laughed.

"Goddamn, Levi. Good for you."

"Her name is Daisy. She's an artist. Mixed-media stuff. Fucking stunning. Smart. Funny."

"And twenty-four. Is it as awesome as I seem to recall?"

He was going to pretend he didn't know what Jonah meant but he was too tired to. "Her body. God. She's a dance instructor too so she's . . . flexible. And she's got a lot of energy. All in all, yes, awesome is a word I'd use."

He wasn't talking out of school. He knew Jonah would keep it all to himself and it wasn't as if he was disrespecting Daisy or anything. But he needed to share or he'd explode.

"Flexible? Is that a nice way to say she's bendy during sex?" Jonah raised his glass.

Levi laughed. "Among other things, yes."

"When do we get to meet her?"

Levi blew out a breath. "Yes, I can just see that family dinner. Hey, Mom and Dad, this is Daisy. She's twenty-four. She has tattoos and pierced nipples. Oh and she's an artist. They'll love it."

Jonah laughed. "Yes, I can see that. So is this like a fling? A midlife crisis? Will you be trading in your BMW for a Porsche? And how did *you* meet this woman?"

"I don't know what it is. Other than new. I've only known her a few weeks. I went to that damned dance class thing. I ended up in the wrong room but she was one of the instructors and well." He shrugged. "I didn't leave right away but I did eventually. And then I bumped into her and learned she was an artist too." He shook his head. "Anyway, again at the grocery store until I gave in and asked her for dinner. Only we ended up at her place and she made dinner for me. We went out again on Monday."

"That's when you found out how bendy she was? And I do love a woman with tattoos and piercings. Sexy."

Levi laughed. "Asshole. She's a nice girl. Christ. Girl." He scrubbed his hands over his face.

Jonah shrugged and took a bite of his steak. "So what? Are you fucking her and making it good for her? Do you respect her?"

Did collaring a woman's throat during sex count?

"I'm not having a midlife crisis. And yes, I respect her. Jonah, you should see her work. She's incredibly talented."

"Has she asked you for help?" Jonah's gaze narrowed.

He shook his head. "No. And she doesn't need it anyway. She donated a piece to me for an auction. She's selling her work. Her grandmother owns a gallery she helps run. She doesn't need me. Not for that."

"Then who cares if she's twenty-four? Unless she talks in baby talk or some shit. 'Cause that's where I have to draw the line."

"What sort of women are you getting involved with that these things come to your mind?"

Jonah'd been married for fifteen years. He had a fifteen-year-old daughter who lived with him. His ex-wife had decided she got married too young, had dumped their kid and their marriage and moved to New York City where she spent Jonah's money and barely paid attention to her old life.

Jonah was a good father. Better than their own. Carrie got great grades. She had friends and worked hard, she even managed to handle Liesl. But he rarely brought any of the women he was with around. Levi knew he kept his relationships extremely casual. He told Levi he had no plans to get serious with anyone, especially not until Carrie had finished school.

"Not the kind who baby talk. Then again, none of them have been twenty-four. I'm totally full of shit to try to lie and say I'd draw the line at baby talk. If I got my hands on some twenty-four-year-old tits, and their owner baby talked, I suspect I'd just pretend not to hear it."

Levi laughed, feeling a lot better. He needed to just call her and ask her out again.

"Thanks, by the way, for getting Cal to write up a new prenuptial agreement. I had lunch with Mal yesterday and handed it over. Thank God I had all the notes you sent along to tell him. I think I got it worded so he didn't think I was judging Gwen. He took it pretty well."

Cal had told Levi the prenup had some things in it that worried him but that it was pretty standard with most of the wording. So they'd had another written up to counter the first.

"He says Gwen will be giving up her career to be his wife and manage his home so she deserved to be paid for that in some way."

Levi blew out a frustrated breath. "We can't do this for him. He has to learn his own lessons about this. I just hope they can get past this stuff. For all the things I find annoying about Gwen, they do seem to love each other."

"She's a featherheaded twat." Jonah sliced his steak to underline the point.

Levi snorted. "Not much different from Kelsey or Joanne."

"Let's hope she is, for Mal's sake."

On his way home, Levi decided to call her. It was eleven, but if she was asleep or god forbid, out on a date, she probably wouldn't answer.

"Hello there, Levi Warner."

He smiled. "I'm in my car, on my way back home. Do you want to have dinner with me tomorrow?"

"I have to work until nine. But I'm free after that."

"Are you busy Sunday?"

"I have a standing date with my friends for dinner on Sunday. Would you like to come? I can promise you what will be one of the best meals you've ever eaten. Mary's supper club has an eight-month wait list now."

"What are you doing right now?"

"Why? You want to sneak on over for some late night action?" He found himself grinning in the dark.

"Tell you what. I have a raspberry honey tart. Well, three-quarters of one. I'm only human. Bring some wine. I'm working now, but I can be finished in an hour or so, if you want to come over. Bring your pajamas."

"I don't sleep in pajamas."

"Well then. Bring your cock." She hung up.

Chapter 9

She should have told him no. That she was busy and he could see her the next day but really, why? She wanted to see him and they were both too old for games.

Candles lit, shades drawn, she took one last look in the mirror and approved. She'd chosen her favorite chemise—she did have a lingerie addiction, she'd be the first to admit. But it hugged her curves with its cool, soft embrace, the deep midnight blue flattered her complexion. She added some lipstick because hello, a hot man was coming for a sex and tart visit. Her hair was loose—he seemed to like it that way—and she opted to go barefoot. She had pretty shoes in abundance, but she liked the way she felt next to him in very little clothing, smaller than he was.

She wasn't a virgin. She'd been in love before, had been in relationships. It wasn't like she didn't know how it worked. This sort of tentative thing slowly smoothing into something else. A relationship. They'd dated and it was moving past just casual dates.

A short period of time, she knew. But this wasn't anything like what she'd had before. This was intense. She thought of him and a thrill ripped through her. He touched her and everything inside went still, everything leaning into him, wanting more.

He was bigger than she was. He made her feel . . . not small and helpless, but protected and taken care of. One part of her was horrified by how it made her so hot when he took control. But another part of her recognized it, embraced it and enjoyed it. She was raised to own her wants and needs. If it made her ashamed, it wasn't something she should do. But this thing between her and Levi wasn't shameful. It was dark and sweet and damn it, it was right and she wanted to see what else lay in store.

Punctual, a knock sounded on her door and she answered it, happier than she wanted to examine, to see him standing there looking so handsome.

"I brought my cock."

She grinned and stepped aside for him to come inside. "Good to know as I plan to use it." Without thinking, she took his coat off, shaking it a little and then hung it in the entry. She liked to do things for him. Liked to take care of him.

"Thank you." He put down the bags he'd been holding and pulled her into a hug. He was warm and real and he smelled like winter.

"You're welcome." She waited, nearly breathless for the kiss she knew was coming.

"I like that you wait." He brushed a kiss over her lips.

She liked it too.

"I don't really want to eat anything right now. No offense to your tart. Unless that was a euphemism for your pussy, in which case I'd like to amend my answer."

Laughing, she threw her arms around his neck, tiptoeing up to kiss him quickly.

"It wasn't. But it can be. The other tart will be just as good with coffee tomorrow morning. My bed isn't as big as yours, but it's comfortable and I'm in it, which should hopefully serve as a draw."

He kissed the tip of her nose. "More than you know."

"Are you cold? I made a pot of tea so the water is still hot if you'd like."

He shook his head, flicking the strap of the chemise off one shoulder and kissing the bare spot, sending a shiver through her.

"Okay then. I'd like you to be naked."

Something happened to her when they got like this. She didn't understand the whole of it, only that he brought something out in her. A desire to serve and comfort.

"You first, beautiful." He pulled the other strap off and the fabric spilled to the floor, leaving her in her panties and nothing else. She'd changed out the bars in her nipples for hoops with beads and he noticed that right off.

He took her breasts in his hands, weighing them, and then he tugged each hoop, flicking the bead and bringing a surprised gasp to her lips. He did things she didn't expect. Things that thrilled her straight to her toes.

He stepped back and she moved a step closer, wanting her hands on him, wanting him to be as naked as she was. He took her hands, clasping at her wrists and again with the shiver. She licked her lips, waiting for whatever he had in mind next.

"You have no idea what it does to me when you submit like that." He said it quietly, as if he wasn't quite sure what it did to him either.

Submit.

Was that it?

He let go of her wrists. "Bring me that bag, the one I left near the door. And be sure the door is locked and your windows are all covered." He smiled and goose bumps broke out. Her pussy was wet and ready, her nipples throbbing, the faint ghost of his touch just moments before still lived on her skin.

The bag was a gym bag of sorts and of course she'd already locked up, though no one would be bugging her at this time of night anyway. Not without a call first.

She brought him the bag and he took it, kissing her quickly.

"I want you to sit over there, on your bed."

She did it, excited at whatever he had planned.

He unzipped the bag, and then looked up at her. "Do you trust me?"

She thought about it. Did she? In the ways that counted, yes. So she nodded.

He pulled out a blindfold. "Good."

When he'd arrived home, he'd stood in his closet, looking at the bag.

He walked out to his car twice only to go back inside. He hadn't used the contents in a few years, but a quick check had told him the rope was still sturdy and free of any burrs, the mask he'd use for a blindfold was still folded, wrapped in a scarf. A scarf he'd bought the last time he used the bag.

Only he never used the scarf, or anything else in the bag. After the last time, he'd come home and put it in the closet and hadn't really thought of using it.

Until Daisy. That hit him as he sucked in a breath.

He'd shoved it from his mind and grabbed the straps and headed out before he could overthink it any more.

She looked at the mask he held and got into a kneeling position. Most likely to get a better look, she was curious that way. But it inflamed him, the way she got into position so automatically.

He walked to her, each step feeling more right than the last. "I'm going to cover your eyes."

She nodded.

When he slid it on and tightened the strap he didn't fail to notice her gasp and then the gooseflesh. He bent to kiss her shoulder and then gave a featherlight touch to her nipple. He wanted something for them and as he pulled out the wrist cuffs, he gave himself permission to look the following week. She needed something hanging from them. Dangly. Sparkly. A little heavy so she'd remember him every time she moved.

The cuffs went back into the bag and his fingertips brushed the rope. Need burst through him with such intensity his heart pounded and he felt light-headed. He pulled the coil out and brushed the end of it against the underside of her breasts, loving the way those lips of hers made an O of surprised pleasure.

"Have you ever been tied up before, Daisy?" He unbuckled his belt, caressing his cock a moment as he did.

"N-no." She licked her lips. "I mean, I think once someone used a necktie on my wrists, but it was a cheap tie and it sort of burned if I pulled against it."

He shook his head, though she couldn't see it. Amateurs.

"For the record," he said as he uncoiled the rope, letting it hit the floor, letting her wonder what he was doing, "all my neckties are silk. And I'm not an amateur. If I want you to burn, you'll know it. But right now what I want is to bind you."

He didn't ask. He just wanted her along with him on the journey.

This fit him so well he would have been terrified if he wasn't staring at a voluptuous, nearly naked woman with a blindfold on, offering herself up for his pleasure. This wasn't a shoe he wanted to wear. Not for a long time. It was something so intimate he'd stopped doing it rather than waste all that raw, naked energy and intimacy on anyone he didn't feel a deep connection to.

He shook his head again to dislodge all that. *Not the time.*

And then he began. "Stand up." He put a hand on her upper arm to help her with balance as her eyes were covered. She was so damned small without her heels on. Small and naked and so feminine it drove him to distraction.

Slowly, relishing every single moment, relishing the scent of the rope, the scent of the lotion she used and the heady, sticky sweet tang of her desire, he began to bind her. Around her shoulders and chest, keeping away from her neck, around her upper arms and then lower. Tight enough to leave a mark. Loose enough that the marks would fade in an hour or so once he untied her. Enough. Enough that he'd see them, remember them until the next time he could touch her.

He guided her back to the bed, her muscles heavy, her breathing slower. "Just tell me to stop if that's what you need." He sat her on the edge, her feet on the floor.

She was deep in, he realized. Her chemicals had flooded her body, leaving her drugged with pleasure. It was a gift and he'd make sure he treated it as such.

He stepped from his pants and approached her again, tapping the head of his cock against her lips.

She opened immediately and he shivered as she took him in.

All she wanted was his cock. She strained against the rope to get more of him, but he controlled everything.

When he pulled back on the ropes, she arched. The scratch was exquisite; it broke over her with bright shards of sensation, keeping her from falling away totally. Without her vision, it was all about how she felt. What she heard. What she smelled and tasted.

He held her by the ropes as she strained harder to suck him deeper. A desperate, needy sound tore from her and he groaned in response.

"Goddamn," he snarled.

She squeezed her thighs together and whimpered at the pulse of pleasure that followed. Not enough. Too much.

And then he stepped back and she growled.

A chuckle in her ear. "Patience."

He helped her stand again and then turned her, leaning her down so her feet were on the floor but her upper body rested against the mattress. She concentrated hard to hear what he was doing. Her skin was super-sensitized. Even the air around her was a caress. But it was the crinkle of a condom wrapper that made her want to burst into tears of happiness.

He nudged her thighs wider and brushed the head of his cock through her pussy.

"So wet."

"Yes!"

He teased around her clit with his cock, pushing her right to the edge and pulling back.

"Why is your cunt so wet, Daisy?"

"You. You make it wet."

"Yes. I'm bringing you your pleasure. It's my responsibility."

The words sent a slice of longing through her belly. To be thought of that way by this man was overwhelming. But fleeting? It was hard to think on it that way when he was like this. This was intimate on a stunning, raw level. The idea that he'd shared this with someone else seemed incomprehensible. But had he?

Enough of that.

All her doubts flew away when he pressed in deep, holding her still with firm hands at her hips before he angled her, using her hips to fuck her cunt back onto his cock.

She struggled for breath, struggled not to fall into the spell he'd been weaving since the first time she laid eyes on him. But it was impossible to hold out against all he presented to her life.

Then he bit her shoulder. Just above the ropes. It was a surprise. Nearly shocking—but when his teeth sank in nearly to the point of pain her entire body flushed with pleasure. Her cunt squeezed around his cock and her clit swelled, sliding against the slick flesh of the hood and her labia.

"More. God, please more."

One-handed, he reached around his cock and found her clit and she sobbed out a joyous breath, rocking her hips to get more friction against his fingertips.

He grunted and then the other hand slapped her ass, shocking a squeal from her. Bright pleasure/pain exploded behind her eyelids. The sound had been as good as the sensation. Until the heat of it spread. And she understood then why someone would want to be spanked.

First, he wanted to. Which was important. His cock slammed home hard over and over. She knew he got off on whatever it was he was doing because he sped up his thrusts, deepening them.

She made him feel that.

She made him gasp and growl and lose his hold on his control.

The victory of it sang through her veins and then orgasm hit so hard she screamed into her mattress.

He pressed in deep, holding her there with a hand at her hip. Inside, she felt the jerk of his cock as he came.

He pulled out. "Be right back." Quickly he got rid of the condom and returned to her, still bent over, still tied up. He blew out a breath. "You're beautiful like this."

She hummed her pleasure, her face turned toward him, the smile on her lips dreamy. He took the blindfold off and she blinked up at him, her eyes glossy. No fear. No judgment. No, she looked at him with acceptance and desire.

That settled into his gut. Acceptance of this darker side of his life was something he told himself he didn't need because it had just been a passing phase in his life. He'd been lying of course, but that smile on her lips and the sweet submission in his eyes only underlined it.

And still.

He untied her, his cock reviving at the sight of the marks in her skin. He kissed them gently, ministering to her as she curled into his side. He wanted to assure himself she was all right. But she was. She rested her head on his biceps, staring up at him as he kissed her forearm where the crisscross of marks was most visible.

"I like the way it looks," she said lazily.

"I do too."

"You still have a shirt on." She frowned and he pulled it off quickly so he could be touching her again.

"You're all right? I didn't hurt you?"

"Sure you did." She shrugged. "In a good way," she amended when he started to speak. "The rope burned a little when I struggled. But not in a bad pain way." She ducked her chin a moment and he tipped it up to see her face better.

"I need you to tell me. If this is going to work, you have to tell me."

"I like that it got you hot when you spanked me. I like the way your breath hitched when you were tying me up."

Heat flashed through him. "I like that too." He kissed her and she sighed into him, her body seeming to melt into his.

"Do you want something to eat or drink?" Her voice had gone sleepy and lazy. It was nearly two. He'd been up almost twenty-four hours and suddenly with her warmth in his arms, he had nothing more he wanted to do than sleep.

"Mmm, no. Close your eyes and sleep. We'll eat and drink in the morning. After I fuck you again."

She smiled against his chest.

Chapter 10

He woke up slow and then jerked quickly to full consciousness. Not his bed. Not his house. Not Kelsey.

She opened her eyes sleepily and smiled. "Hello."

He relaxed. "Morning. Sorry to wake you."

"It's after eleven anyway. I don't normally sleep this late but I have a rare Saturday off. Would you like to go on a walkabout with me today?"

He found himself smiling. "And what's a walkabout then?"

"When I wake up in a good mood on a day off with no plans at all, I just make up the perfect day in my head and then I do it. So, today I was thinking of going over to Seattle to hit SAM. A friend gave me two passes. You can be my plus one. And then, perhaps Top Pot and having too many doughnuts and some hot chocolate. Yes, that sounds appropriate."

It did.

"First things first. We need to stop and get coffee and some pastry. Yes, I know we'll be having doughnuts later. I may amend my choice to something savory if Jules has anything that catches my eye."

She pushed up from bed, naked and gorgeous, and headed toward the bathroom. "Well?"

He took that as an invitation and followed her.

Forty-five minutes later they were standing at the counter of a place in town he'd been wanting to try forever called Tart.

The beautiful blonde lit up when she caught sight of Daisy, coming out from behind the counter to gather her into a hug. "Hello, hot stuff. I'm so happy to see you."

"Heya, gorgeous. We need coffees." She turned back to Levi. "Levi Warner, this is Jules Lamprey. She's the goddess of pastry and this is her place."

Jules gave him a careful looking at as she took his hand to shake. "It's nice to meet you, Levi. Do you want coffee or something fancy like a latte?"

She bustled back behind the counter and pointed to a tray in the case. "Daze, bacon scones made this morning."

"Fuck yeah. I want two, please." She turned to Levi. "One of those is for you. I promise you'll love me for it."

"If it has bacon in it, I generally accept that I'll be pleased with it. I'd like a coffee with room for cream, please."

Jules filled cups for both of them and then bagged up the scones. He tried to pay but Daisy gave him a look that had him rethinking that.

Then Jules snorted and swatted Daisy's hand away. "You work in here so much you've earned freebies forever and ever." She looked to Levi. "Daisy has saved my life behind this counter so many times it's not funny. She's that awesome. Just so you know that."

Daisy blushed. "Hush up. It's what friends do."

Ah, but not all friends. Levi understood that as well as he understood the don't-you-hurt-my-friend look and warning he just received from Jules.

"Where you off to today?"

Daisy poured sugar in her cup and then looked to Levi. "Two sugars, right?"

He nodded, dumbstruck by her once again. A small thing, knowing how much sugar he took. But she knew it. She noticed.

She finished the coffee prep and he took the bags. "We're off to the museum, and then hot chocolate and doughnuts. Maybe a movie if we're feeling especially fancy-free."

"Awesome. I'll see you tomorrow, right?"

"Indeed you will. Thanks for the coffee and scones. Love you." She waved and Jules blew her a kiss on the way out.

He liked to see her around other people. She had an open, easy manner and was clearly well loved by her friends. He'd always cringed away from women who had a lot of people they knew but no actual friends. Daisy seemed to have a smile and a kind word for everyone she recognized and they all seemed to have one in return. It was genuine, not affected.

He drove and she curled into the seat, facing him as she spoke. He normally hated really animated people. But Daisy, as per usual, was different. Her energy recharged him. She was intelligent and creative. Inquisitive. Passionate about the things she believed in so they had a fabulous debate about gas taxes.

He even found a decent parking space near the museum and they walked the few blocks, her hand tucked in his.

She looked at art the way he did, he noted. Her gaze went intent as she took it in and then she sort of went away if she liked the piece.

They spent hours there. He'd never actually spent hours at a museum on a date. Especially not with a woman who loved art as much as he did. She asked questions and took notes. Sometimes she made a quick sketch on a pad she kept tucked in her pocket.

He liked Daisy Huerta. In that *like-her*, like-her sort of way. It was as sweet as it was hot, the way she made him feel. She was remarkably old-fashioned in some ways. At the same time, she was confident in a way he found incredibly attractive. Beauty never hurt and she had it in spades. She had a quick wit and an ability to hear other people's perspectives missing in so many.

They'd come back down to the south lobby and they'd paused and looked at the statues.

"I was here a few weeks ago for a fund-raising gala. I like what they do here," he said as they went down the stairs.

"Me too. My friend, the one who gave me the passes, he has a season thingy so when he gets close to renewing and has any passes left, he gives them to me."

He resolved right then to buy her a membership when he got home.

"I like that you enjoy art. Makes you even sexier. Have you ever taken one of the docent tours? Really amazing." Her eyes lit and he found himself smiling.

"My great-aunt has vision problems, she's clinically blind. They have a program, amazing really. I came with her when she went on a special tour here. Specially trained docents present the art through description and there were some things they could touch to get an idea of brushstroke and all that stuff. Marvelous."

She paused and the light, pale winter light, shone through the windows and over her skin. "I had no idea. What an awesome program. I can't imagine what it would be like not to be able to wake up and see all my art." She turned in a circle. "All this beauty and creation. I'm glad she didn't have to lose it either."

She stood there, her hair held back with a wide, red headband. She wore makeup, but only a small amount. Her sweater hugged that body. It wasn't tight, but it caressed her tits, slid along the nip at her waist and down over the flare of her hips. The pants had wide legs and a pinstripe. The Doc Martens completed the picture. She was so pretty there wasn't anything he could do but dip to kiss her, making himself stop after a heartbeat, or two. Want of her always there roared through him, slammed against his control.

"I'm ready for doughnuts," she said brightly, turning and taking his arm.

"Well then, doughnuts you shall have." He put a hand over the one she'd laid on his arm and led her out, happier than he'd been in a very long time.

It was far too early in the morning the following Wednesday as she stood in Mary's kitchen, dicing onions, trying to figure out how to broach the subject.

"Dude, are you going to tell me or do I have to beat it out of you?" Mary looked up from where she'd been assembling the ingredients for the filling of the pasties she was making for the day's special.

"Have you ever . . . Do you . . . Ah god. So have you ever been tied up? You know, during sex?"

Mary grinned, one of her eyebrows rose slowly to accompany the expression. "Really? Get out of town! I Googled him, you know. Just to be sure he was on the up-and-up. He's ridiculously jump-worthy. And apparently kinky too. Damn."

"He's . . . oh my god, he's unbelievable. Hard and dark sometimes. Ties me up, yep. With rope. Hard enough to leave a mark and I like it. I like it, Mary."

"Good. What would be the purpose of being tied up if you didn't like it? I've never been tied up with rope. I had a guy once who liked to hold my wrists when he fucked me. That was pretty hot. Where can I find a kinky hot lawyer?"

Daisy laughed, letting her tension fall away. Of course Mary would understand. Thank God for friends.

"I really like him, Mary. He's smart and well read. He can have a real conversation about things other than action movies or baseball scores. He never hurts me. Not you know, not other than the way he's supposed to. And he's gentle. I know that sounds weird, but he touches me like I'm precious and fragile. He sent me a cashmere wrap because I was cold at his house. He told me it had to be cashmere because he didn't want anything but something that soft next to my skin."

"Damn, he's good. Jules has met him and I haven't. Why is that, Daisy?" Mary smirked as she pinched the dough at the edges to seal the pasty.

"I invited him to dinner on Sunday but he's going to be busy for a little while. His brother is getting married next weekend I guess and he's got family showing up from all over the country."

"Did he invite you? To the wedding?"

"No. It's fine. It's a family wedding and we haven't been dating that long. He's in it too." And she wasn't so sure she'd fit into his world very well.

"You're nothing like her." Mary shrugged.

"Like who?"

"His wife. No, calm down, his dead wife. She died six years ago. A car accident."

Why hadn't he told her? She supposed they hadn't had the opportunity for that conversation yet. She didn't know a whole lot about his family and she resolved to ask after them the next time they saw each other.

"Well, is that good? That I'm nothing like her?"

"You're you, baby. That makes it good. She was blonde and tall and had big, white, blonde-white-girl teeth, you know what I mean. Like Jules has. Only more a sorority-sister type."

"I imagine, given the position of his family in the region, that's the type of girl all his brothers are going to marry." And where did that leave her anyway? Why did she care? It was just dating. It was more than casual fun, but clearly he wasn't ready for anything more just then or he'd have invited her to the damned wedding she didn't want to go to anyway.

"Makes me happy that you're happy and dating. You work too much. I'm glad you have this guy. You should date more."

"Thanks. He's nice. I enjoy him. He doesn't bug me about working too hard," she teased. "He works as much as I do anyway. Though given the state of his home, clothing and car, he does better at it than I do."

Mary laughed and they kept on working. "Do you have the time later to taste some stuff for me? I've worked out a few menus for Gillian's wedding. She's coming over later tonight but I wanted your opinion first."

"Of course. I'm working at the gallery today. My grandmother called me last night to tell me she was taking a mental health day to do nothing but read in bed." Daisy laughed. "I hope I can live with that much bad-ass attitude when I'm her age. She does not care about silly stuff. If she wants a day off, she takes it."

"Sure. And also, she's getting out of your way. Letting you take the lead at the gallery."

She sucked in a breath. "Yes, most likely." Theirs was a small gallery. It predated some of the zoning rules but it wasn't in a high-traffic area. They didn't get a lot of casual foot traffic and it was time to figure out what the future of the gallery held.

"It's time. She's been training you for this your whole life. Not to run the gallery, but to run your life. All these jobs you do for your friends, you don't need them anymore. You're selling your own work well enough to make your bills just fine."

She had been socking away money for years now. It made her feel safe to have a nest egg. Made her feel like if an opportunity came along she might have the chance to take it. Her savings represented her options.

Her work was selling well enough. But you couldn't always count on regular money coming in. And while she was a free spirit and all that jazz, she also knew she had to take care of her future and have something to fall back on to supplement her art unless or until she had a career that was so financially stellar she could do it full-time without worry.

Daisy cocked her head as it hit her just how well Mary knew her. "You're sort of scary."

"I've known you nearly all your life. I love you. Also, you're not that mysterious."

"Damn. I thought I was getting better at it."

"You are bright colors and star jasmine on a summer evening. That's better. Anyway. We all love you, but you don't need to help Josh out at the dance studio. He can actually get off his butt and find a part-time instructor. All of us have counted on you to fill in as if you don't need a stable schedule and all that. You do."

"I don't need eight jobs, you're right. But I *like* helping you out on catering jobs. It's fun. I get to visit with you and eat yummy things and chat with people. I like helping Jules when she's in a bind."

"Well okay, I get that. And I was going to amend to except when I need you, because I'm selfish. You're my sanity on catering jobs. As a matter of fact, I'd like to talk to you about something. I'm thinking about finding some space to lease here in town."

"Oh my god, finally!" She bounced up and down. Mary had been toying with opening up a restaurant for some time. Daisy knew how monumental it was that she was looking for a space to do it.

"I'm so glad you get it. I'm so glad you didn't try to balance my expectations and all that stuff with a wishy-washy congratulations."

Daisy moved around the big block countertop to hug Mary tight. "I'm thrilled for you. Now tell me what you need because you know I'm in for helping you make this a real deal."

"I need your skills. You know people who run businesses and who are always having parties. You're creative and dynamic. Help me."

"Oh! I totally do. So you're looking for a place to run your catering business so no storefront or front of house for a café? Because, well, I think you should run the supper club from there.

If you have the catering business you don't have to be open for dinner every day."

Mary exhaled. "Yes, exactly. Oh, thank you for being so smart." Mary squeezed her hands. "Yes, I want to have dinner there so I'd need front of house. Doesn't need to be huge. I don't want to get in over my head."

"Or dig into how awesomely special it is that it's not something you can get anytime you want. People like special things."

"I told Ryan you'd be perfect for this job. I know you have the gallery going and I respect that. But around that time, I'd love to have you helping me get all this in place. Whatever time you have." She rattled off a salary that was more than fair and the look on her face dared Daisy to not accept it.

"So you'd need me to find you a place with a big kitchen and enough cold storage and all that jazz for your catering biz and a dining room that'll seat, what, thirty? And then work on some marketing to get you gigs?"

"Yes. Exactly. You're good at all this stuff. I am a disaster at it. Ryan will continue to own part of the business. He and I have agreed to give you the authority you need to find a place and get it set up. And then to hire someone to be my assistant and they can take over the scheduling. I know this isn't a career for you. I just want your brain while we get it set up."

"You got it. Maybe you can have a counter for a few fresh dinner items. Make extras so people can come in and get something for a party that day? Not a lot, you don't want anything going to waste. But it'll be some good word of mouth advertising when people can try you out so easily. Then they'll think of you when they need an event catered. I'll work with Gillian on some graphics."

They continued to plan as one of Mary's part-time helpers came to get the truck loaded and on the road.

Chapter 11

It had sucked not to see her. Nearly ten days since the last time he'd been able to touch her. Even though they didn't live too very far from one another, his life had been filled to nearly exploding with family obligations for Mal and Gwen's wedding.

"I think it's time you stopped moping around and found another wife. Kelsey has been dead for years. You need to move on." His mother said this as she thrust a champagne glass into his hand.

"Mother, this is one of those things that falls under none of your business. With all due respect."

"Levi Warner, don't you talk to me that way. Carrie is smart like her father; thank God she's nothing like her mother but the looks. The best part of that horrid woman if you ask me. But you're second oldest. You need to produce us some heirs. You know I love you all equally, but Mal is clearly under the spell of Gwen's well, her other skills. She's not smart. I worry their children will be pretty and dumb."

He laughed and kissed her cheek. "You should work on speaking your mind. Being so shy isn't a good thing."

She arched a brow. "He's a lovely boy. Got good grades. Never got expelled." She paused long enough that Levi heard, *like you did*, before she continued. "But that wife of his is a twit. She's got decent genes. A good family. That's something. But really, she's not very bright. No, Carrie will take over the firm after you and Jonah are ready, but you need to help him out. I'm beginning to think the twins will never settle down. I know you loved Kelsey, but she's gone. She wouldn't want you pining this way."

Christ, he'd been living the lie so long he nearly believed it the way his mother appeared to. All the things he'd wanted to say for so long pushed at his tongue and he knew it was time to go before he said them. "I have another engagement. Since I won my auction I'm off. Oh, don't fret, I got my picture taken for all the PR. Everyone important saw me."

He wanted to be with Daisy and he was done waiting.

"This isn't over, Levi."

He kissed her cheek again before straightening. "It is, actually. If and when I get married again, it's going to be because I love someone enough to risk exposing them to my crazy family. Right now I have plenty of other things to think about."

"You can't have babies forever, you know. What if you wait until it's too late?"

"Men have babies when they're in their sixties. And there's always adoption." He stood. "I'll see you soon."

"You're living like you're thirty. And you're not. You have a responsibility to yourself and to your family."

He sighed. "I'll see you soon."

And got the hell out of there, dialing her number once he'd reached his car and was on his way back home.

"Are you free?" he asked when she picked up.

"I'm not home right now. But I will be in an hour or so."

"Can you come to me when you're finished? To my place? Stay over."

She paused. "All right. I'll be at your house in about an hour. I have to stop at my place first."

He felt a lot better then.

Daisy had no plans to cut her evening with her friends short, but they were nearly done anyway.

Gillian, Jules, Mary and Daisy all sat on Gillian's back deck drinking hot chocolate and talking about the wedding and everyone else's week and good and bad things.

She'd looked at several places for Mary's place and had found a few that were adequate. And one idea she thought was far better. "I have an idea."

Everyone leaned in. "Can't wait to hear it." Mary winked.

"Mary, I've been looking for a place for you to buy or lease. I've seen a few I think would work." She turned to Jules. "And one I think would be perfect."

"Do tell."

"Tart. Jules's kitchen is huge. She's got plenty of space for cold storage. A place to park the catering van out back. She only uses the space during the day. Noon on weekdays, one on the weekends. You two can share the space. It's central. It has the licensing issue dealt with. She's got enough room to set it for thirty if you set up long tables on supper club nights. She could provide the dessert for your supper club. You could have her sell your self-serve catering stuff. You could share the cost of a counter person to handle any extra business."

"Oh my god. I was just thinking of options to use the space better." Jules's eyes lit. "Mary, I didn't know you wanted to run a restaurant. We could totally make this work."

"Not a restaurant in a big sense. Just dinner three nights a week. What I really want is your kitchen. And you're right, Daze, it's the perfect size. I've cooked in there many times as it happens. If we shared staffing where we could, we could both save some significant money while helping each other's businesses out at the same time."

"Right now you both use as many locally made ingredients as you can in your food. I think you'd be better off combining your work with others in the community. If you get your fruit and vegetables locally, you can note it in the menu for some break in price? I don't know if that's doable, it just came to me as I was working at the gallery yesterday. Oh and by the way, I just thought I'd let you know my piece got chosen for art walk."

There was much celebrating, so much so that Adrian came out to see what was going on and joined the celebration.

"Why didn't you say sooner?" Mary took her hands and squeezed them.

"I only found out right before I left to come over here. Then we were talking about other stuff. I just waited my turn. Everyone is having a great day."

Which was true. Plans for Adrian and Gillian's wedding continued apace. She'd shown them three possible ring designs and they'd loved the second one so much Adrian had called a jeweler right then to make an appointment to have the rings made.

Mary had landed a big catering job and she and Jules had decided to share the building Tart was in. A lot of great news for the people she loved most. And now she was going to see Levi for the first time in ten long days.

"I can't wait!" Jules raised her mug of chocolate and everyone followed suit. "To Delicious."

"Delicious!" everyone echoed.

She stopped at her place and grabbed a change of clothing and her toiletries bag. She liked his house well enough. Loved the view most certainly. But it was so neat and serene. It made her want to muss things up. His bed though was very nice, especially with him in it.

She did two quick braids and touched up her lipstick before leaving. He liked things that way. With that in mind she also changed into a skirt she knew he'd like as well.

And then she went to him.

She went to him, all the while knowing how much she'd come to need him in the last weeks. Knowing she wasn't being mysterious at all, about her need for him. She couldn't have even if she'd tried.

When he opened his door it was while holding the sculpture she'd donated to the auction.

"I thought today was the auction." She came in and kissed him before taking off her coat and hanging it in the hall closet and dropping her bag nearby.

"It was. I bought it. I've been planning to buy it since the first moment I saw it. I put a stack of your cards on the table where it sat for the bidding and every single one is gone."

Warmed, she smiled. "Really? Thank you. You didn't have to buy it. Unless, oh god, were you the only bidder? Wait, don't tell me. I don't want to know."

Smiling, he put the piece down on a nearby shelf. "I'd planned to put it in my bedroom and I still might. But I'm trying it out here too. I think it's going to look pretty there in the morning." She walked to the spot and liked her barbed rose there just fine.

"That was my very first thought when I saw it at your studio. I had to have it."

She liked him just then, far, far more than was wise. There was nothing else she could do but like him far, far too much than was wise.

It filled her with joy to be there with him. To stand and look at her artwork right there, in his home. It felt staggeringly intimate and she had to swallow back a knot of emotion.

He pulled her to him and she went, sucking in a breath when they touched and all she could see or feel was him. Greed rose up from her gut. Greed to have him and not share. To be the only one in this part of his life.

"I'm wildly flattered."

"Part of your allure is how talented you are. Part of my reasoning was purely business, I can't lie. You're going to have a healthy career ahead of you. Snapping up a piece I love is wonderful. Snapping up a piece I love that will be worth ten to fifteen times more than what I pay for it now makes it even better."

She drew a shuddering breath as he dipped his head to breathe in at the place where her neck met her shoulder. His teeth abraded the tender skin there.

One of his hands slid down her back to her ass and squeezed, hauling her closer and then spinning her, backing her against the doorway. The breath left her as her adrenaline spiked and then she found that place where everything went soft and slow, so torturously good that she'd begun to recall these moments with him when she masturbated. This was better than any fantasy or remembrance, though. This intense swell of energy and chemistry between them swept her away and she held on, letting him take over.

Every place he touched as he kissed her, her back pressed to the cool wood at her back, seemed to make her skin come alive. Sensation pulsed through her as he opened her shirt and popped the catch on her bra in mere moments.

Nearly rough at first, as if he couldn't stop himself from rushing to touch her, his fingers first made featherlight touches of her nipples. Slowly, he drew her deeper, the heat of him dizzying, the little flicks of pleasure as his touch grew bolder, the light touches turning into tugs of her nipples until her breath caught.

Her knees went weak as she held on, as he dropped to his own, kneeling before her.

He shoved her skirt up and hummed in pleasure when he saw her panties. He liked the sheer ones so those had been what she chose. She slid her fingers through his hair as he kissed the tops of her thighs, above the stockings she wore. His perfectly manicured beard had gone scruffy and he looked entirely disreputable. Like a pirate in a suit.

The beard tickled her skin as he rolled the top of the left stocking down, kissing all the skin he bared.

This big, elegant male with the big, broad shoulders knelt at her feet and kissed her tenderly and she had to close her eyes a moment as he snagged the sides of her panties and drew them down her legs.

He nibbled his way back up her thighs, his palms skimming her skin and then he twisted his wrists and slid her open with his thumbs, baring her clit to his gaze.

"You have the loveliest pussy." He took a lick, swirling his tongue around her clit.

He gripped her upper thighs and held her still as he nuzzled her clit gently with his lips. And then his tongue lapped, licked, flicked, drove her to the edge and backed off. Each time he drove her up again, the pleasure grew sharper. His grip on her hips tightened, pressing her back and tipping her as he flattened his tongue against her clit over and over until she splintered apart, her fingers tangled in his hair as he continued past the point where the first orgasm had ended and into a second one, so hard she had to let go of his hair and grab his shoulders to keep standing.

He kissed the inside of each thigh, pulled up her stockings and stood, tucking her panties into his pocket. Two steps back and he'd grabbed her overnight bag and was standing at her side again like he hadn't just blown her in his front entry against a doorway.

"Now, hello. Come and have a drink with me and tell me what you've been up to over the last ten days." He tucked her arm in his and walked her upstairs.

"I can sadly confess I've not had any such fine welcomes at all during the last ten days."

His bedroom had an outer sitting room that she'd quickly decided was her favorite place in his house. The view was incredible, the big trees to one side, the water to the other. There was a fireplace and a bar, an overstuffed couch, a television and good speakers from the house system.

"I love this room." She let go of his arm and moved to make him a drink. "Laphroaig?" She removed her shirt and bra before she went to the bar.

He'd already changed his clothes and so he settled on the couch and watched her, pleased that she'd taken her shirt off, baring her breasts to his gaze like he preferred. "Yes, thank you."

She brought it over and placed it at his right hand and dropped to the floor with a happy sigh, sipping from her glass as she looked at the fire. Her head rested against his knee, his fingers automatically seeking the softness of her hair.

They'd spoken on the phone and had texted quite a bit over the last week and a half, but it hadn't been as good as touching her, having the weight of her leaning against him.

"I was about to tell you that I was not the only bidder on your piece. In fact, there was even a bidding war between me and two other people. I did of course win gracefully."

She laughed. "I'm sure."

"I gave them both your information and card."

"Thank you. Truly."

"It was my pleasure." And it had been. Even without this other thing between them, he'd have been promoting her work to the other collectors he knew. "What else did you do?"

"I quit three jobs and got one more." She told him about her job with Mary and the idea she'd had to combine Jules's and Mary's businesses in the same place.

"You've got a great mind for business on top of a great amount of artistic talent. You look better than ninety-nine percent of the population both clothed and naked. Really I've yet to see something you're not good at."

She scrambled around to kneel between his legs. "So says the man who is perfect at everything."

"Not everything."

"Oh yes? What is that then?"

He paused, on the verge of sharing. Instead, he put his tumbler down and took hold of the end of each of her braids and pulled her close to kiss those lips.

She allowed it, but they both knew he was ducking the subject.

"What was your favorite part of the week?" he asked as he broke the kiss.

"Other than this part?" She smiled. "Arch, the red piece with the woman you said you wanted?"

He nodded, hoping like hell she hadn't sold it because he'd meant every word when he said he wanted to buy it.

"I told you I had other plans. I entered it into the art walk selection process and they called me today. A few hours ago actually. They chose me."

He stood and swept her up into his embrace, genuinely pleased for her. "Wonderful news. This calls for a celebration."

"This *is* a celebration, silly." She smiled, her face tipped up to his, her arms around his shoulders.

It was a simple thing. Affectionate. Given without any expectation of a return. It felled him. It made him happy. It had been a long time. Probably since the earliest of days with Kelsey when what they'd had was still good. Before he'd finally opened his eyes and everything had fallen apart. Too long to have gone without a woman making him feel this way.

"I like you in my life."

Her smile widened and she kissed him. "I like it too."

Cupping her cheeks in his hands, he kissed her. "On your

knees." After he got rid of his jeans, he dropped a pillow there and she tucked it beneath her knees. He brushed his cock against her lips and she opened immediately, licking around the head and crown, keeping him very wet.

He took a braid in each hand and pulled her forward on his cock that way. She rewarded him with a low moan, the kind she made when he did something that made her hot.

"Unless I say otherwise, even when you're not cuffed, I want your hands clasped at your back when my cock is in your mouth and you're on your knees."

She did it without hesitation as he continued to pull her forward by her braids before she slid back slowly. Her breasts swayed as she did this.

"And I want your eyes."

She dragged her lids up slowly, her gaze slowly clearing and focusing on his.

He was getting close. He needed to pull back now. But the sweetness of her mouth on him was so hard to resist.

"You're irresistible. Ten days without you is no fun."

He hadn't meant to say it but once he had, once he saw the way her eyes lit, he was glad he had.

"Okay, okay. Enough. I want to be in you. But first . . ." She pulled off his cock and looked up at him, watching, waiting.

He drew her into the bedroom and unzipped the bag, bringing out the crop and slicing it through the air to hear that sound. Her eyes widened.

"I bought this last week. Just been waiting to use it on you. Hands on the bed. Bend at the waist."

She didn't know what to expect. All she knew is that her knees trembled with excitement. And when the first strike came, preceded by the *whick* of the crop as it split the air on its way to her ass, she wasn't expecting it to hurt. But it *totally* did.

Right before she was about to turn and say no, thank you, nice experiment but I don't desire more of that, the sting soothed into a slow spread of heat. His cock at her hip was hard and so hot it burned through the thin material of her skirt.

He liked it. Which made her like it if for no other reason.

Again. And this time it hurt less, though the vibration of it seemed to echo through her body. Each strike came in a different place on her ass and thighs and she sort of lost track of everything but her hands against the cool material of his bedding and the near rhythmic sound of the crop cutting through the air before it struck.

He put the crop down nearby and paused to take in the glory of her ass and thighs. In their time together he knew her skin marked easily, so there was a network of welts from the crop. Nothing she'd feel an hour from now. The marks, so apparent right then, would disappear soon enough. He bent to blow over the sting and her skin pebbled.

He caressed up her legs and she made a soft, sweet sound and that need snapped back into place, straightening his spine as he stood.

Gently, he pushed her thighs wider and found her wet. So fucking wet. He rolled the condom on and pressed into her slowly, trying to let her adjust around him, trying to catch his breath before he came three seconds after he got inside.

She was hot around his cock, tight and perfect. The skin of her ass and thighs radiated heat against his body as he stood behind her. But when he pulled back on her braids she stirred, coming up from sub space, taking a deep breath and looking back at him over her shoulder.

It was right then, he realized, that his thing with Daisy tumbled past *becoming serious* into something else entirely. She fit him in ways he hadn't let himself really feel, but now it was unavoidable.

Orgasm filled his veins, rushing through him as he fucked into her deep and hard. He kept it walled back, needing more, needing to be in her as long as he could be.

Her back was beautiful. The tattoo glistened with her sweat as he pulled her back to meet his thrusts over and over. The flare of her hips incited him, her skin so soft as he held on. But she wasn't fragile; she was strong and willful and the way she gave herself to him was a gift. A gift he should have turned down, but couldn't.

Her body was a lure, yes, but it was who she was, all the parts of her, body and soul that felled him so utterly.

"Make yourself come again."

She shifted her weight to one hand and reached back with the other. She fluttered and squeezed him as her fingertips met her clit. And then moments later she sucked in a surprised breath as she came all around him.

And it was more than he could withstand and he followed her, headlong, letting climax take him as he snarled her name.

Chapter 12

He sat back and took her in. Candlelight suited her features. She wore the earrings he'd given her earlier in the evening with a dress he'd picked out for her. That was something new, something he hadn't done before.

But when she showed up wearing something she knew he'd like, or wearing something he'd told her to wear, it got to him in ways he couldn't have begun to articulate.

He'd begun to leave notes telling her which panties to wear, or what blouse. Even if he wouldn't see her that day, he knew she'd obey. And that got to him.

"I can't believe I've never eaten here before." She paused to sip her cocktail.

"I come here often. It's not very far from our Seattle office so my older brother and I end up here for dinner at least once a week or so. Business lunches are good here as well."

"It's very old-school steakhouse in here. I love these big booths."

He liked them too. He had her all to his self this way, as they were tucked out of sight unless someone was seated across the way from their booth or in that general area.

She'd done something with her hair, victory rolls she'd called them, and together with the dress and her makeup, she looked like she'd stepped out of a vintage photograph. But with a modern edge.

"Which brother is this?"

"Jonah, he's the oldest."

She smiled. "Are you two close?"

"Yes. There's only a year between us. So we competed a lot."

She laughed. "I bet. If he's like you, I can only imagine all the taciturn competition. Two alpha males with big giant brains locked in friendly combat. Which sounds like the plot of a book I'd totally read. I'd like to meet him."

He took her hand and kissed the palm. She didn't take him too seriously outside the bedroom. He liked that. Submission in sex was one thing. But he didn't want a submissive woman in any other way. She poked fun at him and still managed to make him feel like a superhero.

"We should get the rest of this to go."

Her smile changed, deepened, dripped with sensuality and it sent a shiver over him.

"Levi. Hey."

He tore his gaze from her, that filthy fantasy about what he planned to do to her once they got back home dashed with the cold water of reality as he took in the sight of his brother and his new wife.

Mal looked back and forth between Levi and Daisy, one brow raised. Gwen, on the other hand, stared at Daisy, who sent Levi a look that told him he'd better handle it or she would.

"Mal. When did you get back?" He and Gwen had gone to Hawaii for a week after the wedding. "You look nice and sun-tanned."

"Just this afternoon." He turned a genuine smile in Daisy's

direction and held his hand out. "I'm Malachi Warner. Levi's youngest brother."

"Daisy Huerta. Nice to meet you." She looked around him after they'd finished shaking hands. "Congratulations to you both. Levi tells me you're newlyweds."

Gwen frowned and glared.

"Stop talking about us as if you know us," she snapped at Daisy before she rounded on Levi. "Who is this?"

"You need to lower your voice and remember your manners," Levi said, attempting not to lose his temper. "This is my date. She told you her name. Rein it in."

"Rein what in? Are you her dad or her boyfriend? What sort of example are you setting anyway? You're a Warner! You don't take your young little bed friends to dinner in a nice restaurant where anyone can see you. It makes us all look bad."

Daisy jerked back. "Excuse me?"

Gwen turned her gaze to Daisy. "Look, he's not the marrying type, so if you're thinking he'll be a nice shiny cash machine, you're incorrect."

Daisy's demeanor chilled to icy cold. Her face implacable, her back ramrod straight. She looked like a fucking queen right then. "You're not only rude, you're so off base it says far more about me than you. Though your fascination with your brother-in-law's affairs is quite interesting. Is that why *you* got married? Because I was raised to take care of myself."

Before this devolved any further, he shot a look to Mal. "You need to get this moving elsewhere. Your wife is out of line."

Mal put his arm around his wife's waist and attempted to steer her away.

"This is an old, established family. You're not their kind. Look at his choice in wives, why don't you?"

Daisy scooted to stand and Levi did as well, quickly inserting himself between them, his back to Gwen. "Let's go."

"Stop acting like you're going to prevent me from punching her in the face. I'm not the one who needs to chill out." She looked around Levi's body. "If by their kind it means I need to be a bigoted bitch, I'm grateful for it." She grabbed her bag and shoved Levi out of the way, storming from the room.

"We'll talk about this later," he told his brother while tossing down some money. "You're an ugly bitch sometimes, Gwen."

He rushed out to find her crossing the street already. He ran to catch up and she gave him a look that would have sent a lesser man running the other way.

"I apologize. She's rude and wrong." He took her arms in his hands and held her, wanting to say this where she could see his face. "She's wrong, Daisy."

"My god, what the hell?" She kept walking, eating the pavement in long strides even in her sky-high heels. "Is this some sort of time warp back to a movie set in the fifties? I'm not your kind? And what does that mean? Mexican girls needn't apply to have your precious white babies? Hm? Oh, I get it, her assumption is that because I'm brown that I must be fucking you to trick you into marrying me so I can have your money?"

All of that was most likely exactly what Gwen had been thinking. But it wasn't what *he* thought, damn it.

"What does it matter? I don't believe it. Where are you going?"

"To catch the ferry home. I'm done with this evening."

He caught her again. "Why? I've said I don't think the way she does. She's not my wife, she's Mal's wife. I'll deal with them both another time. I'm sorry you were attacked and offended. But why punish me for someone else's ignorance?"

"Speaking of wives, how is it that we've been together for nearly two months and I have to hear about this wife of yours from everyone but you?"

"I don't have any plans to do this on a public sidewalk. If you want to talk about all this, let's do it in private. My car is at the ferry dock. Let's catch the ferry and talk about it when we get back."

"Whatever." She turned and kept walking.

And voila, she was 100 percent, magnificent, pissed-off woman. He stood there stunned for long moments and then hurried to catch up.

"That's our first whatever. What's the present for that?"

Her brows flew up and he knew he'd missed the joke mark by a mile with the present comment.

"I don't need your presents! I'm not with you for presents."

The ferry had a line of cars, but luckily the walk on lane was empty and so no one was around to watch him realize it had been a long time since he'd dealt with a pissed-off woman who wasn't his mother or someone else he just ignored. How this woman felt was important.

"Do you think this is news to me?" He guided her to a pair of seats at the back of the ferry, near the windows. "I'm trying to lighten the conversation up. Just teasing. Why let a person like Gwen ruin our night?"

"It's not about her. Not entirely. You duck the subject when it comes up. You hold back with me."

"Just because I don't want to fight in public like a television cop show doesn't mean I hold back. There's a time and place for this stuff."

She looked out the windows, her body shifting away from his.

"We were having a good time before that mess happened. I already told you I don't agree with a single thing she said. I'll be talking to my brother tomorrow about this."

"You make me irrational," she muttered. "I'm not irrational. But you make me irrational."

He tried not to smile. "I don't make you irrational."

"Fuck off."

He couldn't help it; that made him laugh.

Then his phone rang and when he looked he noted his mother's number and sighed, putting it back in his pocket.

"Are you cold?" He took his overcoat off and draped it over her shoulders.

She wanted to cry.

It was stupid to be mad, she knew. But she was mad anyway. Because of his stupid sister-in-law and his stupid past he never wanted to tell her. Up until that moment, she'd been awash with her feelings for him.

She'd gone and fallen in love with Levi Warner and then that horrid woman went and ruined it all.

Because she couldn't pretend anymore. Couldn't pretend she didn't want to meet his family because he wanted her to. No more pretending that he wasn't avoiding the subject.

Oh, she understood that he didn't want to do this in public. She didn't either. He made her irrational plain and simple. She needed to talk to her friends about it, to work it through.

But the big alpha male at her back wasn't going to let her walk away with all this unsettled between them.

She didn't say anything else as they made their way toward Bainbridge. She texted Mary, but knew he could see over her shoulder.

I just finally met some of Levi's family.

Mary replied nearly instantly. Oh yeah, how was it?

One of them was nice. His wife was a vicious bitch who seemed quite alarmed by a young Mexican clearly whoring herself to get Levi's money and family power.

He growled behind her. "You know that's bullshit."

"Then stop reading my texts."

Oh no, she did not! Do you need me to bail you out of jail?

She laughed. Thank goodness for Mary.

He put his chin on her shoulder.

I'll call you later to tell you the whole story.

At least tell me he defended you. If not, you need to kick him to the curb.

He made a sound and she was torn between shrugging him off her shoulder and turning around to reassure him.

He did. Sort of.

"Not sort of. You know that."

"Why are you reading over my shoulder if you get pissy about what I'm saying?"

"My life used to be simple."

"And now you have a twenty-four-year-old in your bed. Women come with complications, Levi. We don't just animate the moment you decide to notice us."

"I never said any such thing."

Sort of?

He's reading over my shoulder now. She made all this shrill noise about how I wasn't their kind and all that shit. He told her she was wrong. He said it multiple times. She brought up the wife. She doesn't think I'm like her either.

The sick realization that they were going to have to argue when they got in private made her stomach roil. Clearly there were things, she realized as she held back from saying it all, that she had been feeling and burying.

He helped her up and she allowed him to lead her to where his car was parked.

"Her name was Kelsey. We were both young. I'd known her practically from childhood. Her mother and mine were friends. We dated and it seemed natural to marry her. To get started on life as an adult. I was just a little older than you now when we got married."

She said nothing as he drove to her place.

"She drank. We all did of course. But she liked it more than I did. It got worse over the years until I would wake up and wonder what the fuck I was doing with my life. She said she wanted kids, but with her drinking, I doubted it could happen. I didn't think she could give it up for nine months. Her health was on the decline as well. She passed out every night. Started drinking at noon and never stopped until she lost consciousness."

He pulled into her driveway and followed her into the house. She hung his coat and toed out of her shoes. Bending to untie his boots because it was what she did.

"You're nothing like her." He caressed her cheek as she straightened. "You're smart and strong. Compassionate and giving. You're inherently grounded in who and what you are. She never had that sort of confidence."

They moved to her bed and she curled up, readying to listen to the rest. "I wanted a divorce. Nearly ten years we'd been together. My parents urged me to stay and try to work it out. My mother reminded me what it would cost if I moved first." He shrugged one shoulder and she really hated his mother.

"Why would your mother say such a thing? You should want your children to be happy."

"She's old school. One simply doesn't walk away from a marriage. Not without trying to make it right. And in her own way, she was correct about the scandal it could have caused and the price of it. I mean, Jonah, my older brother, went through an ugly, very public split with his wife just last year. She took off, leaving him and their daughter behind. It was a big topic of gossip for months. My mother is averse to such things. To her, a reputation is part of what you own and build. Kelsey came from a good family. To my mother, these things are integral."

Which is why Gwen was so horrified by Daisy's very presence, she wagered. Their kind meant affluent and most likely white.

He smiled at her but there was sadness at the edges. "So I asked Kelsey to get into therapy."

He took her hand, latching his fingers with hers. She wanted to soothe and pet. Wanted to rage about his mother and her self-ishness. But she made herself listen because that's what he needed.

"It didn't last very long. It wasn't even a month before she started missing therapist appointments. I tried to talk to her about rehab, but she dropped her best bombshell yet; she was pregnant."

Oh, this got worse and worse. She squeezed his hand.

"But as I said, we weren't having sex so it wasn't mine. A friend does family law and I went to him that next day to get things in motion to file for divorce. Prenup or not, I had to be free of her. I did urge her to quit drinking for the baby's sake, but she ignored that. Two nights later, she drove the wrong way up an off-ramp on the viaduct and hit a car head-on. She was killed instantly as was the baby she was carrying.

"And then it wasn't about the shitty excuse for a human being I'd married. Overnight everyone just pretended she was a saint. Pretended she hadn't been sleeping with so many other men she didn't know who the father was. Pretended she hadn't been totally able to kill the person she ran into, though thank God she didn't. Overnight she was the love of my life and everyone expected me to play along. And I guess I did."

"Hence the tattoo." She understood him so much better now. Understood those words on his arm were his way of making sure he never forgot the truth he lived even when everyone else wanted him to.

He nodded.

"I'm so sorry. I'm sorry that instead of supporting you, all you got was grief."

"I'm sorry you had to hear about it from someone else. I should have told you myself."

"Yes, you should have. But I understand why you didn't."

"I apologize for what you had to deal with tonight. Not everyone in my family thinks like that."

"But some do."

He shifted uncomfortably. "Yes. Some do. But as time passes, less and less."

There was more she should have said. But all she wanted to do was be with him. It made her weak, but it was true either way. So she snuggled into his body and he held her with a sigh of his own as he kissed her temple.

She didn't believe he thought the same way his sister-in-law did.

He said he was sorry for what happened and she believed that totally. He'd never disrespected her.

So she let it go because she was being irrational and silly and they could talk about the other stuff at another time when she wasn't tired and on the verge of tears.

Chapter 13

"So that's the story." She finished up the saga of the stupid fight she'd had with Levi two weeks before. She'd told Mary, but hadn't filled in all the others so Jules pounced on her right as they'd begun tying their aprons. "We patched things up, but there's some unspoken stuff between us."

Daisy made sure everything on the tray she was getting ready to carry out looked pretty before she shifted it to rest on her arm.

"I don't like it. This bitch needs to be punched. How dare she call you names? She doesn't even know you." Jules glared at her a moment.

"She doesn't. And it's not like I've been at family events for her to get to know me. So there's that."

"There is that." Jules agreed. "And also, this unspoken stuff. Baby, you know that's not a good thing, right?"

"I can't go into that right now. Let's get this stuff out there. Then we can complain about my boyfriend and his dumb family when we get back."

She cruised through the party, an event she'd actually helped land for Mary. The woman throwing the event was a friend of a friend and when she'd bumped into Daisy at a party in Seattle a month before, the topic of catering and parties had come up. Turns out, her parents were getting ready to celebrate their fortieth wedding anniversary.

When she'd broached the subject with Mary, Mary had said, "Weddings, anniversaries, birthdays, that's all catering bread and butter. You better bet your ass I'm thrilled to do this job."

She passed around tray after tray of gorgeous food as she visited with the guests. Not inappropriately of course, but people did like to chitchat here and there at a happy event.

The evening sped by and she was glad tomorrow morning wasn't a gallery day. She'd have time to work on a new piece she'd been mulling over for the last few months.

She even had a coffee date with a gallery owner who'd picked up her card at that auction Levi had given them out at. He was interested in talking to Daisy about a possible show in the early fall with two other up-and-coming local artists.

It was nearing midnight when they'd finally finished cleaning up and getting all the gear packed back into the catering truck. She headed home and discovered Levi had left a few messages for her on her cell.

He had court first thing in the morning so she'd return his call when she woke up.

And then she paced. A lot.

She got dressed again and went for a drive to see if the light was on in Gillian's office. Mary was out cold, but Gillian often worked late a few nights a week.

The light was on and she tiptoed up to peek carefully. She didn't want to barge in on Gillian and Adrian getting hot and heavy. Though it wouldn't be a chore to see Adrian Brown naked and giving the business to someone. Mmm!

Feeling a little better, she nearly left before tapping, but did it anyway. Gillian started and looked up from her work. When she recognized Daisy her face lit and she motioned her to the front door.

"You could have called." Gillian opened the door to admit her.

"I didn't want to wake anyone."

Gillian hugged her. "Miles is off with Adrian for some Brown male fest thing. He's got the rest of this week off from school."

"Well, considering how pretty those males are, that's not a bad place to be."

"You know, I met you first when you weren't even ten yet. I've known you a long time. We've both done a lot of growing up over the years." Gillian took her hand and they went to sit on the couch. "You're the most well-adjusted, emotionally centered twenty-four-year-old I've ever met. But you're upset. I've been meaning to ask you and I haven't because life keeps getting in the way. But you're always there for me. Tell me."

So she poured it all out.

When Gillian laughed at the end, it was rueful. "I'm so sorry I've been so caught up in all this wedding, renovation and life stuff that I've neglected to see how upset you are."

"Don't apologize for having a life. I love that you're so busy and happy with all this stuff. Seeing you with Adrian gives me hope. You know? He makes me happy, Gillian. Not Adrian, though he's nice to look at. Levi." She buried her face in her hands. "I'm in love with him. And I shouldn't have allowed it because we *are* from two different worlds."

"Oh, sweetheart, so what? I'm going to marry a rock star. Me." She took a deep breath. "Different isn't always bad. You'll keep him on his toes. I imagine a man like him is used to people just sort of following whatever he says. You won't do that."

She laughed, unable to help herself. "Not in most things, no. The thing is . . ." She blushed and blushed. "When it comes to sex stuff I do. Obey him and stuff. It's so hot and it feels right and I know people will think it's weird and maybe it is. But I like it and he likes it and so whatever."

It was Gillian's turn to blush.

"I'm sorry for embarrassing you." Daisy was perilously close to a giggle.

Gillian laughed then. "Don't be sorry. We've been friends a long time. You didn't embarrass me. You said you liked it, he likes it too so that's really all there is to it. You're both adults. I'm glad you're happy with your sex life. And I'm thrilled to hear you're in love." She smiled at Daisy, squeezing her hands. "But I don't like that you're feeling off balance and that maybe he's hiding you from his family. I don't want you feeling as if you're not good enough. That makes me quite cross with your Levi."

"The thing is, I know I'm good enough. And you know, we go out in public so it's not like he's hiding me really. He actually"— she paused to find the right words—"he makes me feel beautiful. Special. I'm just. God. I'm being irrational. I hate that."

"Of all the people I know, the last word I'd use to describe you is irrational. Sometimes when we love someone else it makes us see things differently. Sometimes we second-guess what we know is true and sometimes we're right. I think you should talk to him about it."

This is why she came to Gillian and Daisy said so.

Gillian grinned at her. "Come on. You're staying over. Let's watch something scary, eat nachos and have margaritas."

"Oh, that sounds so good. I don't have to be up until after ten."

Levi walked into his parents' front entry and narrowed his gaze when he heard Gwen's voice. He hadn't spoken with her in person yet about the scene she'd made two weeks before at the Met.

Mal saw him first and steered him out of the drawing room and into the hall. "I'm sorry for the other week. She'd had a few drinks."

Which only made him angrier. "Yeah, been there, done that. I'm not really fond of drunks."

"Hey! That's my wife. She was out of line, but she did it because she cares."

"Keep her away from me unless you want me addressing my concerns to her in person."

"She's concerned for our position in the community."

"Over what? My having a steak with a friend in a public place? Or is it that my friend isn't white? We were raised better than this. Don't feed me your bullshit, Mal. *You* might be content to listen to your wife, but I'm not."

"It has nothing to do with her race."

"Really? Because from where I'm standing a different story is being told."

"What on earth is going on out here?" Their mother came out, looking back and forth between her sons.

"Nothing I can't handle. When's dinner?"

She narrowed her gaze and Jonah stepped in, saving him. "Time to eat." He inserted himself in between their mother and Levi and led the way, holding his arm out for their mother.

He kept himself away from Gwen, not trusting his tongue. The unfairness, the ugliness of her behavior burned in Levi's gut. Daisy was one of the finest people he knew. Giving to a fault.

A person like Gwen had no business judging her.

His mother kept giving him the eye all through dinner until she finally got around to it. "So guess who I saw yesterday?"

"Liesl." His father gave her the eye, which she ignored, and Levi's stomach tightened, just waiting for whatever was next.

"Jenny Martrek. She says hello of course. And Dyan, her daughter? The one your age, Levi, I'm sure you remember her. Anyway, she's moving back here to Seattle. I told Jenny you'd be happy to reacquaint her with the area. I gave her your card and invited them all to dinner Sunday."

"I'm busy on Sunday, actually. I'm sure Dyan has plenty of people to squire her around town when she moves back." He ate and kept his gaze down, not wanting to tangle with his mother but he would if she pushed it.

A man could only be pushed so far.

He blinked and cocked his head, but yes, that was indeed Daisy sitting at a nearby table with another man.

Her face was animated as she talked with her hands. The man, all Levi could see was the back of his head, nodded and leaned toward her.

Levi sat and waited for her to notice him, but she didn't. Finally he got up to go to the bathroom, which happened to take him past their table.

She looked up at him and then smiled. "Levi, I wasn't expecting to see you."

He started to say he bet, but then he turned and realized her lunch date was Mark Schneider, the owner of a gallery on the Eastside.

She stood and he kissed both cheeks and clasped her hands. "I don't want to interrupt. I'm meeting one of my brothers for lunch in just a few minutes. Good to see you, Mark."

He walked off, feeling better and also a little like a jerk for thinking she was out at lunch with someone else for romantic reasons. He realized he felt greedy for her. He liked it better when all that animated beauty was aimed at him.

And all he had was lunch with Jonah.

When he returned to his table she was still chatting with Mark and not looking his way. Of course, he told himself, she didn't look at him because this was business for her. He saw her portfolio leaning on the table leg and made a note to ask her all about the meeting when he saw her next.

When they both got up to leave about twenty minutes later, his brother finally asked, "What the fuck are you so distracted by?"

She walked past, still engaged in conversation but she sent Levi a quick smile and a wave.

"That's her, right?" Jonah stared. "Christ, you weren't kidding. Why are you acting like you barely know her?"

"I'm not acting like I barely know her. She was having some sort of business lunch with Mark. I told you, she's an artist. He must be considering giving her a show."

"She's gorgeous."

Levi smiled. "Yes."

"What's the story then? Clearly your face tells me this is more than a casual fuck. And the way you nearly threw down with Gwen underlines that too."

"I like her, I told you that. But she's too young and too . . . everything. We enjoy each other." He shrugged.

"You're a moron. Too everything? What? Pretty?"

"Tattooed. Artsy."

"So you buy Gwen's line about her not being our kind?"

He clenched his jaw. "No. That's not it. It's not her race. It's not her class, though Gwen being a racist bitch wouldn't imagine that Daisy's father and sister are dentists and her grandmother is a successful painter."

"So then what? She's an artist, a damned good one from what I can tell. She's beautiful. Her body is holy-shit wow. She's intelligent and funny you tell me. She clearly enjoys your company enough to overlook your horrid sister-in-law. You're not going to take it another step because she's got ink and makes art? Because you collect art, Levi. You love art. Tell me how this is not a perfect match?"

He wiped his mouth and tossed his napkin down, his appetite gone. "Shut up."

"You're forty years old. How long are you going to flit around with dumb women who you don't care about? Is that your life-style now?"

"Is that *your* lifestyle?"

"My lifestyle is a private one. I also have a teenager I'm doing my best to raise into a real human being. Don't you think she deserves to see her uncles with women who aren't Gwen or her own bitch of a mother?"

"Oh, so it's my job to do that?"

"Yes. Kelsey was a mistake. You think you're the first person who had a shitty marriage? This woman is the first I've seen you show a real interest in since you brought Kelsey home."

"I don't want to have this conversation with you."

"I know you don't. And you know why. Because you're being a punk and a coward and making excuses about it."

"I haven't punched you in the face in a while. It might be time."

"If you think you can do it, go on ahead."

"Um . . . is there anything else I can bring you?" The server looked back and forth between them nervously.

"An espresso please. Don't worry, I won't make him bleed all over these lovely hardwoods." Jonah smiled at her charmingly and Levi rolled his eyes.

Chapter 14

When Levi came over she was on her front lawn building a snow-man with Miles, Adrian and Gillian's fourteen-year-old son.

She waved a mittened hand and ducked the snowball Miles had lobbed while her attention was elsewhere.

He smiled at her and her heart lifted as it always did when she saw him. "Hello there. I hope you're not going to stand out in the snow in those shoes."

Miles wrapped a scarf around the snowman's neck.

"Hogwarts snowman?" Levi grinned.

"Do you really think a snowman on my lawn would be Slytherin? Puhleeze. Levi, this is Miles, Miles, this is Levi."

Miles looked to Daisy carefully before he smiled at Levi. Sweet boy, that one.

"I would have worn my snowman-making shoes if I'd known this was on the day's menu." Levi reached out and pulled her hat lower to cover her ears.

"Miles is hanging out with me until his dad gets back."

"Mum made him because he drives back and forth between our

house here and his old place in West Seattle." Miles did that one shoulder shrug his father was so good at and it made Daisy grin.

"I'm going to run home and grab a pair of boots suitable for snowman making. I'll be back shortly." He ducked to kiss her and it made her happy.

"So who is that guy?" Miles worked on the second snowman as he spoke. It had dumped an uncharacteristic amount of snow two days before and it was cold enough to stick around, though thankfully the roads were clear.

"That's my boyfriend."

"He's all right. Got a nice car."

"He totally does have a nice car. You can't hear anything when you're inside it."

"Dad says the kind of car a dude drives says something about him. I say yeah, it says how much money he has."

Daisy laughed and kept packing snow. "He's a lawyer so I guess he's got a few pennies to spare on a nice car." She had a Mini Cooper, which got her where she needed to go and was totally cute too. But Levi's big, dark, luxury-on-wheels BMW was another league of vehicle.

"I'm saving now. Only two more years until I get to drive."

Daisy loved how despite the fact that Adrian was a rock star, they were raising Miles to be down-to-earth and work for what he wanted.

They talked about cars until Levi returned dressed far more appropriately for the weather. She had to pause and look at him a few times because he looked so gorgeous. Boots and jeans, a fisherman's sweater and a watch cap pulled down over his ears. She wanted to lick him from head to toe.

Levi talked to Miles about school and his studies and Miles's shyness began to wear off as he got used to Levi. It was lovely. And normal. It made her happy.

When Adrian came back to pick Miles up he gave Levi a long

look. She figured Gillian had told him at least a little, though she knew Gillian wouldn't have spilled any secrets, even to Adrian.

"Adrian Brown, Levi Warner."

Adrian held his hand out and shook Levi's as the two men gave each other the look as she and Miles watched. She had no doubt Levi recognized Adrian. One had to be a hermit who never got online or turned a radio on to not recognize the voice or face. Adrian was a musician. A very popular one. It was still odd, getting used to having him as a friend. She'd come around a corner and he'd be standing there and she had one of those ohmigod-Adrian-Brown-is-standing-right-there moments. And when his family and all Gillian's friends got together it was even worse because his sister was a rock star too. They were down-to-earth people, but it was still sort of cool.

"Gotta hit the road, kid. Your mum's expecting us." He looked to Daisy. "Appreciate your hanging out with Miles today."

She looked to Levi. "Gillian has the flu so we decided to give her a few hours' quiet this morning."

"Next stop is Mary's. She's been making soup today." Adrian put a hand on his son's shoulder. "It's good to get in with these women, Levi. One of them is an amazing cook. Another one is an amazing pastry chef. This one here is an incredible artist as well as a great friend." He winked at Daisy who blushed.

Levi took her hand and squeezed. "Good to know."

And they were off, leaving her alone with Levi so he pulled her into a hug and kissed her before heading back inside.

"How about some hot chocolate? Or tea maybe?"

"Tea would be really good."

She bustled around, taking his coat and hat, laying the hat and gloves near the fireplace to dry. "Sit, I'll start it now."

"So tell me about your meeting on Wednesday. With Mark."

"He offered me a spot in a three-artist show he's doing at his gallery in the fall." She grinned, still thrilled about it.

He stood and moved to her, pulling her into a hug and her feet left the ground as he spun. "Congratulations. That's wonderful news." He kissed her soundly and put her down.

"I have several pieces already done for it. He's going to come out to the studio in a month or two. He knows your mother, said she was an avid collector. Is that where you got it from?"

He got that look, the one he got whenever she mentioned his family, and it pissed her off. Was she his girlfriend or not? Why did he seem so freaked about her meeting them? Or even knowing about them? Unless they were all like his sister-in-law he swore wasn't like his family.

"Things are beginning to really take off for you. I'm thrilled." No mention of his mother.

"Will you be there? At the opening?" She shouldn't have asked, but then she got mad at herself for thinking that. Why shouldn't she? She'd ask any other man she was dating and in love with.

He hesitated and she realized they were actually going to have to talk about it. Like right then.

"So, your brother, the one you had lunch with the other day. Is that Jonah? The oldest?"

She busied herself with tea prep.

"Yes, of course I'll be at your show. That's first. And yes, that was Jonah." He shouldn't have hesitated. She heard it and things were uncomfortable now when they'd been nice and easy up to that point.

This little house was a comfort to him. A place he could go and relax and just be. She gave him that. But with this unsaid stuff between them it was less so.

"It would have been nice to have met him. Jonah, I mean."

"Well you were at a business meeting. I didn't want to interrupt."

She turned and he hated the way he felt.

"Okay. So when is it that I do get to meet your family?"

"You met Mal."

One of her brows shot up. "By accident. And it went sooo well."

"Seems to me that's a good reason for you not to meet them. Why are you so curious about them anyway?"

"Because they're part of your life. I want to know you, I want to know your family." Her face fell and he felt like an asshole.

"You do know me. I'm here with you now."

"I've invited you to dinner at my family's house twice now and you've been busy. I ask about your family and you look like you swallowed a bug. I get it. I just want to know if you're always going to be busy."

"What do you mean?"

Was he going to make her say it?

"Never mind. You should go home. I'll see you later this week."

"No. Say it. There's too much unsaid so far. What do you mean?"

"I mean, Levi, is this something real? This thing we have? Because it feels real to me. And I can't bear the idea of having you run interference between me and your family because you don't feel the same."

"Of course it's real."

"So then why can't I meet your family? Why are you so hesitant to meet mine? If we're real and in a relationship, why do I feel like you're hiding me?"

He pushed to stand. "I don't hide you."

"Really? All right then, I'll be ready for you to pick me up tomorrow."

"For what?"

"For your family dinner."

"You wouldn't even have a good time. Hell, Daisy, *I* don't even have a good time and they're my family."

"Do they know about me?"

He scrubbed his hands over his face. "Jonah does. Obviously Mal does."

"My parents know about you. My friends know about you. Do your friends know about me?"

"What's brought all this on? We're here together. Clearly I want to be here. I'm not seeing anyone else, nor do I want to. I'm a forty-year-old man; I don't fill my parents in on my romantic life like that."

"You're so full of shit." She shook her head. "You see your family weekly. You have lunch with your brother, who you told me is like your best friend."

"And he knows about you."

She bit her lip. She never gave ultimatums. Ever. They were silly. She didn't want to say or do anything to drive Levi from her life. She liked him in it. Hell, she loved him in it.

But she really just didn't think she could bear it if she stayed with him and he continued to hide her like a dirty secret.

"You make me feel special, Levi." She walked to her kitchen sink to look outside.

"Because you are special."

She closed her eyes a moment.

"When you touch me, so gentle even when you're firm. Even when you're using a crop on me—you touch me like I'm precious. No one has ever touched me like that."

He moved to her, putting his arms around her, his front to her back.

"How can you doubt you're special to me?" He kissed her neck. "If you know how I feel every time I touch you?"

"Because it's all a lie if you don't treat me that way all the time."

Once she said it aloud, she knew it was true.

"What is it you want from me? We've only been together a few months. Are you expecting marriage this early on?"

She spun, pulling herself from his embrace. "Don't. You're disrespecting us both to play that game. I'm not asking for you to marry me. I'm asking you to own what we have in public. I'm asking to be a part of the life you have when you're not off work or here at home on the island. You have this whole other life you seem totally determined not to let me be part of."

"I've been with you in public many times. In fact that's when you met Mal."

"I don't think that example helps you."

"What is this? Just say what you want."

"I want you to be with me. Openly. I want to be part of your life. I don't want to feel like your filthy secret."

"What we do in the bedroom is no one's business."

She sought patience, counting to ten before she spoke again. "I didn't say I wanted you to tie me up and whip me in the middle of Pioneer Square. Don't try to play lawyer ball with me. I'm young, but I'm not stupid. I get it, I get that you have this important family and all. I get that you have traditions to live up to and I respect that. It's a good thing. But why can't I be part of that? Are you ashamed of me?"

"How can you say that?"

"When you seem to go out of your way to avoid bringing me around your family and friends. That's how I can say that. Is it that I'm young? Or inked? Not blonde and perfect with big horse teeth like that dumbass your brother married?"

He laughed and she wanted to join him. But she didn't. Her heart was breaking because the way he avoided the subject, even when they were fighting about it and on the verge of something awful, made her sick inside.

"Have you looked in the mirror lately? That you'd ever compare yourself to a woman like Gwen and find yourself less attractive is mind-boggling. You're stunning. You're individual and vibrant and you own what you have. There's no comparison."

She smiled and reached up to brush his hair off his forehead before she turned to pour the tea.

"So what is it then? Tell me."

"It's nothing. You're making stuff up."

"Oh my god! Levi Warner, you owe me some honesty. I'm being honest with you right now. I'm telling you how I feel. I'm exposing my fears and worries. I expect some damned truth. Anything less is a charade and I don't want to *play* love with you. I love you. I love you enough to demand that you show me some truth."

He paused. "You can't love me. Not yet."

"Oh really? Tell me what it is. Why you won't introduce me to your family then."

"We don't bring dates to Sunday dinner. We bring fiancées and wives. That's how it works. You're not any of those yet. Over time you'll be invited to things. But it's early."

She stared at him. "Is it my age or my skin tone?"

He threw his hands up. "Christ, Daisy. I know Gwen was a raging bitch, but this isn't the forties. It's not your race. But you're young. She's going to think you're a passing fancy. Being with one of us comes with all sorts of stuff. I'm actually saving you from it."

"So you hiding me from them is for my own good?"

"You could be a lawyer with all this fast-talking."

"You just don't like it that I don't buy your crap. Look, I'm not going to live in a closet. I'm not going to be your Bainbridge Island girlfriend. I'm not going to pretend not to know you when I see you in public. Or have you get a panicky look on your face if I bump into you and you might have to introduce me to someone. I'm with you. Or I'm not with you. But I'm never anyone's secret."

"Is this an ultimatum?" His eyes narrowed and she wanted to cry so much.

"I guess it is. I don't like them. I've never given one before. But I can't see any other way to live with myself if I don't ask for what I need and walk away if I can't get it."

"I'm glad I got to know you, Daisy. But I don't do ultimatums. I'm a big boy and I don't need a boss."

He stepped back and she felt so very empty and sad.

"All right. I can't make you stay. I can love you and let you go. I do hope you have a lovely life."

And she stood there and watched him grab his coat, hat and gloves and walk out her door.

Then she let the tears come.

Chapter 15

Mary walked in without knocking to find her huddled in her bed, watching *Steel Magnolias* with a big box of tissues and the nearly empty Ben & Jerry's pint clutched in her hand.

"Oh my god. I've never seen you eat ice cream for a man before. And *Steel Magnolias*? I'm crying already." Mary shook her head. "I brought carbs. But you are getting out of bed and we'll go to Jules's place. Gillian will meet us there with a fistful of non-weepers to watch. And then we're going out."

"I am not company ready. Or going-out ready, for that matter."

Mary stomped over, ripped the blankets off and glared. "This has gone on long enough, Daze. We gave you a week. You're done. He's not worth this. Snap out of it."

Cold now, she rolled from bed and shuffled to her room to find something to wear.

"Shower first," Mary called out.

A very good idea given her current state of messy tears and clogged-up nose.

When they arrived at Jules's Gillian was already there. "You look like shit." Jules hugged her tight. "You must really dig this guy to be this upset. I'm sorry. Gillian and I are thinking of heading into Seattle to kick his balls."

Daisy laughed for the first time in a week.

"I'll get over it. Right now I don't know how, but I know I will."

Gillian took her hands. "There's our girl. Adrian says he knows a ton of hot single dudes if you want to be fixed up."

"I found her with a nearly empty carton of Chunky Monkey. She was watching *Steel Magnolias.*" Mary shook her head. "That totally calls for some ball kicking."

They all nodded and she felt better. "It'll hurt awhile, right? And then it will hurt less every day and then I'll be over it."

"Exactly. Now, I say we skip this movie stuff and we all go shopping and then to dinner and drinks." Gillian kissed Daisy's cheek. "He's a total idiot to not love you right back. A right prat."

So she allowed them to dress her up. She did her hair, a braid wrapped at her crown and put on makeup for the first time in a week.

"You look fabulous." Mary hugged her and they were all off for a day out.

"Mind telling me just exactly why you're being such a grumpy asshole?" Jonah asked him in an undertone as they milled around a cocktail party he allowed his mother to fix him up for.

"I'm not being a grumpy asshole."

Jonah rolled his eyes. "Not that Carrie doesn't appreciate all the girly-type presents you've sent over the last week, but maybe you should tell me why you're not giving presents to Daisy and why you're here with Dyan when you clearly don't have a single romantic or sexual tingle for her."

"She's a beautiful woman; why wouldn't I be here with her?"

"Um, because you have a girlfriend already."

"We broke up."

"I figured that out when you showed up to this event with Dyan and not Daisy. What'd you do?"

"Why do you assume I did it?"

His brother snorted. "I don't question gravity either. It just is."

"She wanted more than I could give." He shrugged.

Dyan made her way back over, sliding her arm through his. But it wasn't the way Daisy did it. When Daisy did it, she only saw him, let him lead and fit him perfectly. This woman wanted everyone in the room to see she was with him. She wanted everyone else to see him, though she didn't necessarily see him at all.

Jonah made small talk but when he caught sight of his date, his daughter who looked lovely and sweet as her grandfather escorted her through the crowd, Jonah put his glass on a passing tray and said his good-byes.

Dyan spoke and he nodded, only halfway hearing what she was saying. He hadn't laughed once the entire evening. Daisy would have not only made him laugh, but she'd have made a few friends here. Dyan waited for people to come to them.

And he was sure his mother approved.

"I'm sorry, Dyan, but I'm not feeling very well. Can we say our good-byes and I'll take you home?"

"You could stay over if you like. You can rest of course."

The memory of Daisy telling him she didn't fuck on the first date hit him with so much force he physically longed for her.

He'd move on. He had to of course. But he didn't fuck on the first date and he was done fucking anyone he didn't care about.

"I appreciate your very fine offer, but I'm afraid I'd be horrible company."

She shrugged. "My mother is here, I can get a ride home from her. Give me a call this week and let me know how you're feeling."

She kissed his cheek. She'd been aiming for his lips but he turned his head.

And he went home.

Two weeks passed and it hadn't stopped hurting. Daisy thought the whole concept was utter balls. She wasn't supposed to be thinking of him all the time anymore.

She was oh-so-lucky enough to see a picture of him in the paper at some swanky affair. In a tux no less. Christ, how much was she supposed to take anyway?

Still, she shoved it all into her work. May as well use it, her grandmother had said. So she'd been working every night past midnight and had completed two new pieces.

"That's some dark shit right there." Mary looked the largest over. A painting in dark blues and purples.

"I'm bruised. It sort of fits," she mumbled as she held two different frame pieces up against it. "This one I think I want to put in the show. I sent Mark a picture of it and he's excited. At least there's something."

"I'm heading over to Tart. Come with me. Jules will be there and she and I both love your ideas."

"All right." She cleaned up and headed out.

"Thank God for you guys. I'd be wallowing in a pint of ice cream right now if I didn't have you."

Jules put a mug of tea in front of her. "Have some tea. He doesn't deserve your ice cream tears, baby."

"He totally doesn't."

"So you know what I was thinking?" Jules sat across from them, Mary on the end of the little table. Tart was closed for the night so they had the place to themselves.

"Do tell."

"If this place is going to be Mary's home base as well as mine and there'll be people in here in the evenings as well as the daytime, I need to spiff it up. Adult it up, I guess. So, I think we need art." Jules looked at Daisy. "And you're my connection."

"You want me to see what I can find? I can see if local artists want to have stuff up here? It can be on display for a certain period of time or until it gets sold. Good idea."

"No! I want *your* art on the walls. Look, I know the gallery is far off the beaten path. I get a lot of foot traffic so why not set up part of Tart as your gallery? Hell, I've got five times your current space."

"So this place could be Delicious central?" Mary grinned. "I love that."

"Tart makes a decent profit. But if we combined the space we would all benefit. If I can wrest some of those art people who sit and slug back coffee up the street, my business will improve and you'll have customers in here looking at your stuff."

"We decided to do a minimal lunch like you suggested." Mary perked up. "Something super easy and limited, we don't need a full menu. But if we start small with some bites and have them finish with tarts or pastry? And seduce them with your art? Unstoppable. And I think we should continue to call this place Tart. She thought we should change it."

"Oh don't! Tart is a fabulous name. It's fun and sexy and flirty."

They grinned and continued to plan and for the first time in two weeks her chest didn't hurt.

He didn't want to get up. So he didn't, calling in sick and trying to go back to sleep. Which of course was interrupted by his brother pulling the bedding off him an hour later and shaking him, hard.

"What the fuck are you doing?" He tried to grab the blankets back but Jonah had pulled them totally from the bed.

"This is the third time you've called in sick since you and Daisy broke up. So you're just going to let *everything* go to shit? Really?"

"You burst into my house to wake me up and yell at me? Fuck off, Jonah. Go home. It's none of your business if I want to take a personal day. I have enough of them."

"Your work is suffering. Your writing is shit. Your attitude is shit. Your house is a pit and for what? A woman?"

"Go. Home."

"No. What's your damage, Levi? Fix this thing with her. You're a miserable prick without her."

"She's a twenty-four-year-old pinup, Lindy-Hopping artist with tattoos. Oh and she's built like a brick shit house. I can totally see her at fund-raisers with Mother at her side. Do you know who her best friend is engaged to?"

"Do tell." Jonah tossed himself in a nearby chair.

"Adrian Brown. Adrian Brown's teenage son builds snowmen in her yard. Her friends are as funky as she is."

"So what? I mean, I like Adrian Brown's music. Why is her knowing him a bad thing? Did she fuck him?"

"What? No, he's engaged to Daisy's friend. Daisy wouldn't ever do that. I just mean she knows rock stars. On top of everything else, she knows rock stars."

"Okay another thing in her favor. Does she have a drinking problem? Does she bang the neighbors while you're at work? Because that's what you had before. Though she looked pretty on your arm at parties. Is that all you want? So Daisy's not that. You *had* a sad, mixed-up girl who drank because she had no idea who she was otherwise. And that worked out well, yes?"

"Yes and I knew her at twenty-four! Only I was twenty-six."

"And she was a young twenty-four. Kelsey was spoiled. Petty. Fluffy. She didn't think about anything difficult or sad and she treated you like shit." Jonah straightened his cuffs. "You're missing the point and I can't tell if it's deliberate or not. This Daisy of yours is *not* a young twenty-four. She's got an emerging career with her art. She runs a gallery with her grandmother. By the way I own three of her grandmother's paintings so again, knowing her has perks, right? You said she works with her friends and does marketing too?"

"Why won't you go away?"

"Manners. Anyway, so to cap, she's a beautiful, intelligent, ambitious, successful, sexy woman. And you broke up with her why?"

Levi put the pillow over his head.

"You should just tell me. You can never hold out longer than I can. Forty years you've been my brother so you know this is fact. So tell me and once we've figured out a way through it, I'll take you to breakfast."

The only person who could ever hold out against their mother was Jonah. He was the most stubborn individual Levi had ever known.

"She wanted more than I could give. It wasn't about her. She's not a bad person."

"That won't even get you a cup of coffee." Jonah studied his watch a moment. "If you can't be honest with yourself, then you're wrong."

"I already told you. She won't fit in my world. She said she felt like I was hiding her and I guess I probably was. It's shitty, but it's true anyway."

"Are you kidding me? You? The guy who got expelled from school three times because he had issues with authority? You? The guy who shamed Park and Howe into finally naming more women partners? You can't possibly really be worried that your hot young girlfriend won't fit in at some stupid charity mixer. If you do, first I'm going to punch you in the balls. Then I'm going to punch you in the face for being a stupid bastard. That old-school crap Mother does isn't a barrier to your seeing Daisy. You're making stuff up to keep her away."

Levi watched his brother, who stared right back, not taking any excuses.

"You're textbook. You love this woman. She gets to you. And as long as she goes along you're fine. But she pushes back and you realize how deep you're in with her and you let that be your excuse to keep her away."

He sucked in a breath.

"It's not the tattoos, though yes, we both know Mother will swallow her tongue. But no one else who matters is going to think twice. Other than to think it's hot. Which I do, by the way. You're not a classist asshole. This two different worlds thing is a shtick. An excuse. You keep saying that and hating all the women in our circle you never have to fall in love again. Or risk yourself.

"That's what this is. You're scared because the last time you did this dance, you ended up with a dead wife everyone pretends was a saint. Love can break your fucking heart. I get it, right? I have to look in my daughter's face every day and see parts of the woman who ripped me up. But what's life if you shut yourself off to anyone who makes you *feel*? I can tell you the Levi before, when Daisy was in his life, was far preferable to this one. So get your ass up and get ready to grovel."

"You act like it's easy."

"Easier than being alone. That's your choice. She's your future. Don't fuck it up because you're afraid. If you weren't afraid, it wouldn't be a very bold choice would it?"

Daisy balanced on the ladder as she drilled the hardware into the wall at Tart. Once they'd made the choice to operate the space together, things had come along quickly.

Probably because she thought about Levi less if she was very busy.

"You're going to get dust all over those pants."

She halted, turning slowly to find Levi standing in the doorway. All the love she pretended not to feel anymore rushed up, nearly choking her. Why the hell did he come here? There were other places to get coffee and something sweet.

Her chest hurt and she gripped the drill so tight she was afraid she'd break it.

"Do you have a few minutes?"

"For what?" She was afraid to say more. Afraid she'd cry.

Gillian walked in, talking and laughing with Jules, who halted and gave a serious-menace-face to Levi. "*You.*"

He held his hands up in surrender. "I'm here to talk to Daisy."

Daisy climbed down and Gillian took her aside. "You don't have to. We can shoo him away."

"No. I have to." She put the drill back in the case and the case in the utility closet. While back there she took a moment to get her breath and to smooth a hand over her hair and reapply her lipstick.

Damn, she was glad she'd had an appointment before she came to Tart so she was dressed up and had makeup on. Levi needed to see just what he was missing. Ass.

"Do you have a coat? I thought a walk would be nice."

He had really good manners. She'd forgotten that. No, no, she hadn't. She didn't get close enough to let him help her get her coat on and she again was glad for that earlier appointment because she had her cute gloves and shoes on too.

"I'll be back in a bit."

Jules gave Levi the eye for long moments before she leaned in to kiss Daisy's cheek. "No matter what, you are special. You are awesome. If he can't see it, there will be others who will."

"Love you guys," she said quietly before turning to the door and going out while he held it open for her.

"You look beautiful." He shoved his hands in his pockets as they walked. It wasn't a cold day, but a brisk breeze had kicked up, sending her hair all over the place.

"What do you want, Levi?"

"I wanted to see you again."

"Why?"

"You're tough once you really get mad."

She stopped, really, truly mad. "You broke my heart, Levi. That's not me being tough, that's me trying to hold my shit together so I won't cry." Her bottom lip started to wobble and she had to look heavenward and blink fast before she actually did it.

"You tear me apart. I swore I'd never give anyone that power over me again. But I never counted on you." He said it quietly. Vehement. "All that stuff you said was true. I was hiding you. Sort of. Not for the reasons you think."

There was enough traffic up and down the sidewalk that they had to continually move out of the way. "My car is there." He pointed. "We can sit out of the wind and talk."

She chewed her lip as she considered it.

"Please?" He held his hand out but she didn't take it. She did nod and cross with him, pausing as he opened her door. It smelled of him so strongly she nearly burst into tears. She didn't want to hope. He could be there to talk to her about any number of things.

She took her gloves off and laid them carefully in her lap as he got in.

He got in and they sat there, silent for several moments. "I'm sorry."

She looked to him. "For what?"

"For breaking your heart. For making you cry." Anguish washed over his features and she had to wrestle back her need to touch him, to comfort.

"You were right. Like I said. I let myself think Gwen was right. But she isn't. It's not that you and I are from two different worlds.

Though we are. It's that I didn't want to imagine a world without you in it. And that freaked me out. You matter to me in a way I promised myself I'd never allow again. Only it's different in that I never felt this sort of intensity before. Not with anyone. Which made me feel like an asshole. After all I was married to Kelsey, shouldn't I have felt like if I didn't see her or hear her voice, I'd simply waste away?"

"You feel that way about me?"

"That's what I'm saying. You matter to me, Daisy. You matter to me and I matter to you. You took care of me and never let me get away with stupid stuff. You were my safe place to be and I shit all over that."

She wrinkled her nose. "Ew."

He smiled. "Can I touch you?"

She shook her head. "No. Why are you telling me this?"

"This is groveling. Am I doing it wrong?"

She tried not to be amused but it was impossible. "I don't like groveling because it means you've done something bad enough to need to grovel."

"I told my parents I was bringing a guest to dinner on Sunday. I hope you don't mind. I want you to meet them. I'm telling you this because I love you. I love you and I want to be with you. I hate that I hurt you because I was dumb."

"You were scared."

He nodded, heartened by the way she'd shifted herself in the seat to face him instead of looking down at the gloves she kept rearranging so carefully.

"I don't want to hide you. I want to show you off." He'd told her he loved her, damn it. Didn't she have anything to say to that?

She was so beautiful there. So real after he'd done nothing but dream of her for the last two weeks. She smelled good, looked good. Her lips were shiny red but it still hurt his heart when her bottom lip had trembled as she'd fought back tears a few minutes earlier.

"What if I've moved on?"

He frowned. "Have you? I told you I loved you. Don't you have a response?"

"I told you I loved you two weeks ago, mister. Your response was walking out my door and going out on dates with tall, thin blondes."

He cringed.

"Yes, exactly. I *saw* the pictures in the paper."

"Nothing happened. Not with any of them. I didn't even hold hands with any of them. None of them was you. I love you, Daisy Huerta. And so I refuse to accept you've moved on. Because I know you love me too. Give me another chance, Daisy. I promise to make you glad of it for the rest of your life. I'll fuck up again. I'm a dude, this is part of the package. But I won't betray your trust. I won't hide you. I respect you and damn it, come on. Love me again."

"I never stopped."

He didn't ask to touch her this time, he simply reached out and took her, brought her into his arms and held on tight as she buried her face in his neck. "If you ever do something like this again I will let my friends loose on you. You have no idea the pain I saved you from."

He smiled. "That's so true in so many ways."

Chapter 16

"I can't believe you never play on the Wii. What's the point of having it if you don't use it?"

She stood in panties and a tiny shirt, her hips circling again and again as she did some sort of Hula-Hoop thing on the screen.

"Goddamn, I'm a lucky man."

She looked back over her shoulder at where he lounged on the couch in his sitting room, watching a half-naked woman pretend to Hula-Hoop.

Her smile told him she knew exactly what she was doing.

They'd gone to dinner at his parents and mostly had left unscathed. Gwen didn't get anywhere near them. His brothers were charmed fairly immediately, as was his mother of all people.

Levi hadn't expected that at all. But Daisy had started a conversation with her about art and it had gone from there. By the end of the night his mother had advanced to the double cheek kiss and a hand squeeze.

Daisy had been sweetly insufferable ever since they'd arrived back at his place.

"You should come over here."

Her mouth tripped up into a smile. "Should I? But you'll try to touch me in my no-no place if I do."

He burst out laughing. "I will definitely do that, yes. But I promise you'll like it."

"I haven't heard that one in a very long time. Does it work for you?" she asked, settling herself in his lap, straddling him.

"Looks like it does."

"You're incorrigible."

"I am. It's a wonder I got into college at all. I was expelled three times from two different schools. My mother had to scare a lot of people to get me back in."

She grinned. "She's totally scary. I sort of like her. On the other hand, Gwen is a dingus. I don't like her. Mal is adorable; what he sees in her I don't know."

"I have an idea, let's speak of them no more. You should fuck me instead."

"Okay."

She put her arms behind her back and waited, sending him off into a fantasy for several vivid seconds.

His hands shook as he balled them into fists for a bit until he wrestled his control back into place.

He stood and she wrapped herself around him as he walked them into the bedroom and tossed her on the bed.

She laughed, her hair a tumble around her face as she got to her knees, pulled off the T-shirt and put her hands back into position.

He opened the box he bought only a few days before they'd broken up. A box for all the things he used and wanted to use on her, with her, to her.

She shivered as he slid the cuffs into place on her wrists and tightened them. He breathed out slowly, kissing up her back to her shoulder where he bit and she made that soft sound of hers.

He was so hard he had to count things and recount the rules

of adverse possession just to keep from coming. It had been too long. Longer than he'd ever wanted to be away from her again.

The mask dangled from his fingers as he moved around so she could see it. Her lips parted and her pupils swallowed the color in her eyes. He leaned in to nip her bottom lip, tugging it between his teeth and then securing the mask over her eyes.

She loved when he used the mask. The dark soothed her, opened her senses in every other way. Each touch of her skin, each kiss he laid over her shoulders, every breath against her body was an underlined, exclamation-pointed declaration of what he felt.

"You're the most beautiful thing I've ever seen."

She breathed in deep, moved by his declaration.

"I missed you so much I can't even tell you."

"You should try."

He kissed her smile. "Jonah came to my house and rousted me from bed and yelled at me for not coming after you. I didn't even punch him because I knew he was right and I needed him to push me."

She frowned. "I slept like shit for two weeks. I'd wake up every morning and remember you weren't going to be next to me and I'd be mad all over again."

"Show me how much you missed me."

He'd been gently brushing her temples with his thumbs and those hands slid into her hair and yanked, exposing the line of her throat to him. Shivers worked through her as she fell, softly and slowly into that warm place where all she felt was him.

He growled as he scraped his teeth over her neck and she jumped with a cry when he bent and bit her nipple, tugging hard enough for her to see stars. Enough that when he licked over the sting every part of her tingled.

"When my hands are on you, when you're here exactly how I want you—*because* that's how I want you—I feel invincible." Covetous hands slid all over her body, igniting her senses, making her need him so much she ached with it. "I don't know why you do it—give yourself to me the way you do. But I'm glad you do."

"Because you deserve it. Because you cherish me and make me feel beautiful. When you didn't anymore it was like a punch to the face. I never want that again."

He kissed her lips, sweet and full of contrition and she took everything he gave. Giving back, giving everything.

There was a tug on one nipple and the ring and then a weight. The process repeated and then he did something so that the cool metal of what had to be a chain with weights, pulled her nipples until they throbbed.

"I've been looking for the perfect chain and weights since the first time I saw the piercings in your nipples. How does it feel?"

It took a moment for her to find her words. "G-good. Really, really good."

He rolled her to her side and then onto her belly, pulling her panties off. The rustle behind her told her he was taking off the rest of his clothes so she pulled her knee up, knowing how much he loved to fuck her that way.

He kissed up from her ankle to each cheek of her ass before slapping it until she went a little numb. And then he spread her open and teased her clit with the head of his cock until she squirmed and got close enough to beg.

"Yes, that's what I needed to hear."

And then he pushed in, his cock filling her, his weight on her, pressing her throbbing nipples into the cool bedding, the heat of his skin actually cool against her ass where he'd spanked it.

He adjusted her hips, angling her so her ass was tipped up, and he rested her pubic bone on his knees as he fucked her in quick, shallow digs.

He looked down at her ass. At the pinked, high, tight cheeks. He watched his cock disappear into her cunt over and over again, only to pull out, dark and wet with her honey.

Her wrists were bound with wide, black leather cuffs, lined of course, because he didn't want her to be in pain. Not unless he planned it.

Something about the way she looked with her eyes covered in the mask never ceased to move him. When she slept and used a mask because his place was so bright in the mornings, he'd lay awake for an hour or so, just planning on what he was going to do to her when she woke up.

The mere sight of her inflamed his senses. He leaned down as he fucked her to breathe in the scent of her skin. The change in his balance took him deeper, tilted her ass higher.

She stuttered a breath as he reached around and found her clit, sliding a fingertip back and forth over it very, very slowly.

"Oh god."

He smiled though she couldn't see. "Do you like that?"

"Yes. Yes. Yes."

"Good. I want you to come all around my cock. Can you do that for me?"

She nodded and he dug his fingertips into her hip while he increased his thrusts. Harder. Deeper. And kept his pace on her clit. Slow and steady.

It went on between them for some time, a slow, insanely good buildup to climax. She squirmed and tried to hurry him along but he kept his pace.

"When it happens, when I let it happen, it'll be good. Be patient, beautiful."

She gave a frustrated sort of sniff of indignation and it made him laugh. He kissed her shoulder. "I missed that snotty little sniff you do. Saucy. Makes me think later on tonight after I've rested a bit that you might need to be tossed over my knee so I can use the paddle."

"Oh!" She tightened around him and began to come, turning her face into the bedding to yell out.

Too late to hold himself back, he let it go, pressing deep and hard and coming with such intensity he tingled from head to toe as he kept climaxing as her cunt squeezed him to near blindness.

He took off the cuffs before he left to get rid of the condom. She still lay there where he left her moments before so he got back in bed and turned her over, taking off the blindfold and kissing her wrists where he'd had her bound.

"Hello there."

He kissed her hard. "Hello there and welcome back."

"Let's do that again soon." She stretched and loved the way his gaze followed the way her breasts moved.

"I like this, by the way." She slid her hands up her belly and cupped her breasts, knowing he liked it, liking it just as much. There was so much energy between them she swam through it and let it wash over her.

"You left one of your shirts at my house. I slept in it every night for the first week. Then I put it in the trash and then I pulled it out of the trash. But then I had to wash it because hello, trash. And it didn't smell like you anymore."

He kissed her softly. "I'd come down and stand in front of the rose, just watching the light, remembering the day when I brought it home and you were here. Christ, I missed you like crazy."

She hugged him, relieved. "Good. I missed you too. I wish I could have gone on dates and put it in the paper for you to see. Hmpf. Yes, yes, I believe that you didn't touch any of them. Which is good for you, because if I had doubted that I would have kicked you in the dick. A few dozen times. You're taking me to all those things from now on. All these women need to get the picture that you are off the market."

He hugged her again. "I love it when you're vicious."

"No, you don't. My vicious streak is what made me want to punch you in your pretty face. But you like it when I'm jealous."

"Distinction duly noted."

"I love you, Levi."

"Thank God for it because I love you too."

Her laugh was back in his house again. Her scent on his sheets. Her crap on his bathroom counter and her stuff in the drawers in his armoire.

She lived in him and he had no plans to ever let that change.

It didn't matter that she was younger than he was. All that mattered was that she loved him and he loved her. The rest they could work out as time passed. She'd keep him in line. Decorate their house and fill it with music and love. And one day with children.

They had time, he realized. Time to be in love and be engaged. Time for her art and his job, time for weddings and honeymoons and nesting. She was his, forever. As deeply as he was hers.

Made the groveling worth it.